A TIME OF NINES

FEATURING A HERO YOU'LL COME TO LOVE. OR HATE. (IT'LL BE A LITTLE STEAMY, TOO).

LISSY PORTER

Previously published as The Innkeeper.

Cover design by HSBookCovers

Chapter Headings by WhimsyanaBookGraphic

ISBN: 978-1-917374-87-3 (Ingram paperback)

ISBN: 978-1-917374-96-5 (Amazon paperback)

ISBN: 978-1-917374-98-9 (ebook)

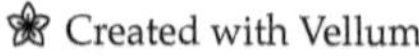 Created with Vellum

CONTENTS

PART ONE

ONE

A BEGINNING

Chapter 1

THERE WAS SILENCE.

And then there wasn't.

A swirl of snow and hail, a blizzard of ice and sleet fell on the deserted wintry spot where before there'd been nothing but endless white. A silence rang out deeper than quiet, as complete as nothingness.

'Bollocks,' the voice boomed preternaturally loud as the revolving snowstorm of ice disappeared as quickly as it had arrived, depositing in its wake the most ridiculous of sights. A naked man, struggling for balance and sinking knee deep in the snowy landscape. In his wake, a more natural whiteout continued to blow, making it hard to focus on his quivering shape.

'Bollocks,' echoed once more, the voice strong and thunderous, although there was no one to hear it.

'Bollocks,' resounded again, accompanied by a jiggling from foot to foot that should have been impossible in the thigh-high snow yet which he accomplished easily all the same. His feet, already turning blue in the cold, reached almost to shoulder height as he tried to save them from the perils of frostbite.

'A bloody blizzard,' he managed to shout, his anger and rage causing spittle to fly from his mouth where it immediately froze, landing on his exposed chest with an icy tinkle of broken glass.

'Bollocks, bollocks, bloody bollocks,' he gasped, rage adding intensity to a voice that he'd never heard before.

'Boooooooollllllloooooocccccckkkkkksssss.'

TWO

AN ENDING

Chapter 2

THE CACKLE of laughter set Mann's perfectly white teeth on edge, as he turned to glare at the person it had emanated from. He wasn't surprised to discover it came from the sour-faced woman who'd arrived that day. He didn't know where she'd come from, or even why she was here, or how she could afford a room in his well-appointed inn, and quite frankly, he'd be pleased when she damn well left.

Mann had known she'd be trouble when he'd first laid eyes on her, but the cause of her hawking amusement was beyond him.

As such he was astonished to feel her grey eyes on him, mocking as she gurgled and gesticulated at him. Mann didn't know the woman other than the occasional passing word or request that he do something for her. Why would she be laughing at him now and in such an unpleasant way?

Surprised, his head swiveled behind him, just to make sure he was the object of her amusement. Convinced he was, stood as he was in front of the inn's back wall with nothing behind him but his shelves of almost priceless spirits, Mann returned her gaze levelly. His eyes were hard and his expression nonplus. He'd long learned the best way to deal with out-of-control drunks like her.

Still, it annoyed him. What the hell was up with the old bag?

Mann considered her. She was reasonably well-dressed, and certainly, she'd been handing out enough copper coins during the last few days for him not to be unduly worried by her. They were of a low denomination, but they were still a high enough denomination, just, to pay her way.

She was no-looker; her appearance resembled that of an old boot, once well-made but now very well-worn and down at heel.

Mann wracked his brain but didn't recognise her other than the glimpses of the last few days. But, and he'd learnt this over his long years of experience, it was no good attempting an altercation with someone such as this, in her current condition. Mann held his tongue, but still, she gurgled at him with delight. The noise was harsh, abrasive, and he gritted his teeth against a knee-jerk reaction that would see her jettisoned from the inn.

'You don't know me,' the woman gasped, sucking in breaths through her old and tired teeth, as Mann shook his head in disgust at her actions. She'd had too much to drink. Or perhaps she'd inhaled too much of the good old spice being pedalled in the corner of the room by an enterprising young woman, convinced Mann didn't know what she was up to. Mann rolled his eyes at that thought. Nothing happened in his inn, and never had, that he didn't know about.

Mann tolerated the young woman's presence, both because he admired her outrageous audacity and also because he liked to imbibe himself, on occasion. It was always worth having a ready contact for when he needed it.

'But I know you,' the cackling woman continued, and this

brought him up short. Mann had met few people over the eons who'd known him intimately, but no one like this. Never.

'How do you know me?' Mann asked neutrally, seeing if she really did know him or if she was just letting the spice fill her mind with its promises of illusions.

'You really don't know me?' the disbelief clear in her voice, between amusement filled grunts and groans and her high-pitched cackles. 'It really worked?' she quizzed, her delight coming under control at the same time her expression intensi-fied with incredulity.

'Truly, you don't know me?' the woman asked once more, her tone a little more normal now, her breathing regular as Mann shook his head at her words. Something in his move-ment, innocuous as it was, set her off again, and once more she gasped and chortled, maliciousness washing from her. Mann didn't understand any of this but held his ground.

Mann had had more than enough experience of neutral-ising difficult patrons.

Mann made to turn away, convinced he should be anywhere but here, but a claw-edged hand abruptly grabbed his arm and he only just managed to turn around once more without viciously snatching his arm away from her contact.

Mann didn't want her to touch him, not with her shrivelled, ancient hand, its long nails yellowed with age.

Before he could do more than shrug her off, another voice joined what he thought had been a private conversation.

'Leave off,' a younger man drawled, drawing Mann's atten-tion from where he'd been hiding in a darkened corner of the inn. Mann hadn't served the meddler, but he held a jug of ale in one hand, a cup in the other he was slowly filling with the contents from the jug. He'd clearly been inside the inn since the early morning. The stranger wore a dark hood over his face, and there was little to differentiate him from his murky surroundings. All Mann caught was a flash of bright, white teeth when the man spoke, and nothing else.

The voice was light, airy, and Mann mused that the contrast between the two other participants in the conversation couldn't be greater.

'Feck off you cock,' the older woman spat toward the younger man, and immediately four regular inn goers who'd been sharing a table with the man who'd spoken, stood and lifted their ale from the table before moving away to the far corner. Mann only wished he could do the same.

'We keep it clean and polite in this establishment,' Mann tried to admonish only for the woman to chuckle and start laughing again.

The younger man, moving further back into the uninhabited shadows, gave an eloquent shrug, visible even through the gloom and under his thick, fur-lined cloak.

'You can keep it anything you want,' the younger voice trilled, 'it won't mean shit when the midnight hour strikes.'

It sounded like a threat, and yet Mann couldn't help thinking he'd never seen anyone who looked quite so benign or a warning offered in such a pleasant tone.

Mann had seen bar fights before, too many to count, although he'd never lost a single one of them, but this didn't look like developing into one.

'What won't mean shit?' Mann asked, drawn to ask the question even though he wanted to ignore the two strange characters. If possible he'd evict them from his inn and out into the stark blizzard howling around every corner, dumping feet and feet of snow wherever it could find space to do so.

When Mann had glanced outside the inn door earlier, he'd wondered where more snow could possibly be deposited. He'd also begun to fear for his roof. He winced every time he heard a creaking groan coming from the rafters high above his head.

Already Mann had made the decision that tomorrow, no

matter the weather, he'd have to make the perilous climb onto the slanted roof. He's clear away the clumping snow before the roof collapsed under the massive weight of yet another snowfall.

'Any of this,' the youth said expansively, his arm snaking from inside his cloak to take in the interior of the inn. Mann noticed the stranger's sleeve gleamed a little in the light from the fire and the lamps. Whoever this man was, he had money enough to dress impeccably well, even within this remote inn, far from the markets and fairs where such fine cloth as his sleeve were made from could be exchanged for coins or barter of equally precious fabrics. Such wealth rarely made it so far North. The extra tariffs made it prohibitively expensive.

'What? The inn?' Mann asked, trying to determine whether it was a threat or just the bantering of two people deep in their cups.

'All of this,' the youth tried again, but the old woman screeched in denial.

'You don't know that, young sprout?' she chortled merrily to herself, and Mann found himself watching them both, his head going from side to side as though he watched a game of chance and not a conversation between two apparent strangers. He genuinely had no idea who would say what next.

'I know,' the youth trilled decisively, and now the old woman stepped toward him, anger in those steps that reverberated thanks to the inn's thick wooden floors and stout wooden walls. Mann was suddenly aware of a silence filling his home, and it angered him. It was the end of the year, the end of the millennia no less, and this wasn't what he'd planned for the occasion. Far from it in fact. He pondered on who had let these two into his inn. He knew he hadn't, and wished they'd damn well leave. Immediately, no matter the baying storm outside.

'You can't know anything,' the woman stomped, her hands

resting either side of the ale jug on the youth's table, as she menaced him. 'I know what's about to happen,' she stated, trying to infuse her voice with the disdain of earlier but failing, as her voice wavered with a question at its end. For all her laughter, it seemed she was far less confident than she'd first appeared.

'You know nothing, and you never have,' the youth sighed, anger crossing his unlined face. She roughly shoved back his all-encompassing hood to reveal thick silver hair threading its way down his shoulders and putting paid to the idea of youth his light voice and unlined face had initially given Mann.

The silver-haired man sat back on his wooden chair, crossing his arms and trying to stay away from the spitting face of the woman, as he winced and curled his body away from her.

'I've been around long enough, thank you, young sprout,' she hissed, and Mann struggled to understand what they were discussing. It sounded very much like an argument that had been on-going for a lot longer than the last few moments, and yet he'd thought they were strangers. They appeared as strangers. The attitude toward the other lacked either the amiability or the intense displeasure that arose from knowing someone for any significant length of time. Instead the silver-haired man exhibited only disdain to the older woman's angry words.

'You've been around just as long as me, and I know you comprehend nothing. You never have. Neither does Mann here, is it?' The question was directed at him, but there was no pause for an answer.

'Mann got his wish. You didn't get yours, and I doubt you ever will.'

Now the woman's face scrunched into an ugly glare, rage seeming to cascade from her like flames through kindling. She flared almost as brightly as flint on tinder and Mann flinched away from her, desperate, suddenly, not to be caught in the wake of her wrathfulness. At the same time, Mann tried to decide if he'd been introduced to them or if they just knew his name because they'd been in his inn and everyone knew who he was. Everyone in the settlement knew his name. In fact, people from much further afield knew the name of the innkeeper of Slutet, people from places he'd never visited, and never would.

'He only got his wish because he's a None,' the woman further hissed, jerking her head toward Mann, and something like ridicule crossed the youthful face of the ancient silver-haired man.

'He got his wish because he's a Nine, you daft old coot. No one bothers with a None. I thought you knew that by now.' The silver stranger's voice had lost its softness to be replaced with a steely resolve, and very evident contempt.

'They wouldn't have allowed a Nine to do what he did,' the woman gobbled, as though desperate to convince herself, her body shaking with each word she spoke as though to reinforce it.

'They'd allow a Nine to do anything they wanted. They've nothing to gain from this ever ending. Why not give the daft sod what he wanted?'

They were both watching him now, and Mann found his mind prickling with unease. They spoke about him as though they knew him and yet he knew he'd never met them before. Ever. And they talked as though old adversaries, ancient adversaries. The fact they seemed to know more about him than he did was also unnerving. Despite everything he knew to the contrary, they still claimed to know him.

'No,' the woman howled, the sound so screechy it set the hairs on the back of Mann's neck on end. Annoyed Mann rubbed his neck with his weathered hand, cracked from the intense cold outside, and red from the constant work of pouring ale and washing mugs and looked at them both again. He needed to remember to coat his hands in scented fat to stop them disintegrating further.

'Yes,' the ancient youth responded, his voice weakening now he'd said what needed to be said. There was finality in his voice that Mann took to be acceptance. 'Once more it will all begin,' the silver-haired man muttered softly, and now the woman's shriek was so terrifying Mann was sure he heard one of the thick spirit bottles crack and the subsequent trickle of liquid off the back shelf.

'As soon as the sand timer turns to the middle of the night, there'll be a reckoning, as there should be, and everything will begin once more. You know that. I know that. The only poor bugger who doesn't know that is stood in front of us with his mouth wide open, listening to his finest spirit drain away into the wooden floorboards.'

Mann shut his mouth abruptly, wishing he didn't feel the urge to retrieve his expensive bottle of spirits rather than complain about being called a 'poor bugger'. It seemed the silver-haired youth did know something about him. But what was a bit of fluid, if what these two hinted at was really true?

'What will begin?' Mann was finally forced to ask. He refrained from asking what a Nine or a None was. Why did he need to know, after all?

'The new age,' the youth muttered ominously, but Mann was nodding. He knew about that. For the last twenty or so years, it was all anyone had spoken about.

'The new millennia doesn't mean a new age,' Mann tried, his voice reasonable as it had been whenever his clientele had become a bit rowdy in the past discussing the passing of the millennium.

'You don't know what it means?' the woman squawked again, and he scowled in irritation. Mann was sure all the bottles of spirits were slowly leaking now from cracks caused by her shrieking. Far better to use barrels and jugs to store his expensive stock, Mann thought to himself, resorting to his usual innkeeper priorities in the wake of the strange events unfolding before him. Forget the fact it might disturb the taste a bit, as Helbe had once cautioned him. It would save him a bloody fortune.

'And how do you know what it means?' Mann prodded, trying to stay focused on the conversation, but she pursed her lips, sliding onto a seat next to the silver-haired youth as though they now shared a secret and weren't about to divulge its meaning to Mann.

The silver-haired youth's face curdled in disgust at the rancid older woman, and he tried to move away from her, but his mouth didn't open to answer the question. He simply watched Mann with apathy, when he was settled as far away from the woman as he could get while remaining at the same table.

'If it was about to happen,' the youthful silver-haired man finally said, turning to face the older woman as though Mann hadn't spoken, 'then we'd all be here.' He spoke calmly, no trace of the older woman's bitterness on his face. Whatever it was they conversed about, it seemed he was reconciled to it in a way she wasn't.

'What do you mean?' she shrieked once more, trying to turn her back on Mann, as though the conversation had suddenly become private. Mann bit back a smirk of amusement at the strange characters. 'Of course we're all here,' the woman insisted, but the silver-haired man just raised his eyebrows at her, disbelieving her words.

'There are three of us. We need all of us. You know that?' he provoked, and she shook her head with delight.

'But everyone's here. Really, you hadn't noticed them?' This time something like interest flickered across the, until now, remarkably impassive face of the man.

'Where, there's no one I recognise?'

'I suggest you look a little more closely,' she muttered, a chortle of delight forming on her lips with the anticipation of him agreeing with her assertions now she'd shown the lie to his assertion.

As though pleased to have something to do, other than sitting by the woman, the silver-haired youth stood suddenly, and took stock of his surroundings.

He was a tall man, almost painfully thin. Although he swirled his cloak around him as though to disguise himself, Mann still noticed the extremely long limbs, and the large hands as they wrapped the cloak tight to his body. Mann wondered how the stranger could scrunch himself into such a small chair without discomfort. Surely his thighs must have been too high to rest under the table top.

Mann followed the stranger's line of sight, but saw nothing other than people he either knew, and had known for many long years, or travellers, seeking shelter from the raging winter storm outside. There were a few characters determined to see in the new millennium at Slutet.

No one looked like the two unlikely acquaintances. Mann had been studying them as they spoke, and he'd decided, although it was difficult to imagine two people looking more different from each other, that they shared a 'look' about them, not one of desperation, but rather of both determination and understanding.

They knew something Mann didn't know, that was most obvious, but it also appeared they knew a lot more than anyone else within the inn as well. In fact, more than anyone he'd ever met.

Mann wracked his long memory. There was something familiar about them, and the knowledge ached inside his head. A memory that didn't want to be remembered. He had many of them and rarely paid them much heed. This, though, was different.

A decision made, the silver-haired youth strolled to the right of the bar, his long legs making the movement lightning fast. A group of regular patrons were huddled there. They'd been watching events unfold with wary eyes, but quickly convinced that Mann had everything under control, they'd returned to their card game and their drinks. They weren't even aware of the scrutiny they were under as they bickered and argued over their game. The cards before them exchanged hands at some speed, and then slowed as one or other considered the next move, the next gamble, from the piles of coins before them.

Mann knew they'd been planning this game for half of the year. They'd been discussing the size of the stakes for most of that time, and even he wasn't sure what they'd finally agreed upon. He could see they all had huge piles of copper coins in front of them. Some even had more treasured items, precious stones gleamed from the glossy expanse of the highly polished table, or small pots of herbs and the even more sought after, spice, in front of them. The stakes appeared entirely acceptable, just enough to give an edge to the game, but not enough to impoverish any of them. Mann had been firm on that point.

Mann had envisaged they'd gamble and play cards all night and long into the new millennium without any care or thought for the doomsayers amongst the general population. He'd hoped to join them, and there was an empty seat for him, but he doubted now he'd get the chance to game. Not with these two strange characters within his inn.

Mann sighed, thinking of his own stack of coins waiting for him in his locked chest. The days were long gone when he needed to 'ask' for his coins, or in fact, for anything. He was a well-appointed man, in a small community, where he'd managed to remain for almost all of his long life, occasionally disappearing for a year or two before some 'nephew' or other came along to take over his business. He'd been content. Until now. Not for the first time, he wished the two daft bastards would disappear and leave him with his contented patrons.

Mann was distracted from his thoughts by the intent expression on the face of the youth when he looked at Sal. Sal had been coming to his inn for nigh on fifty years. Why would the old man be of any interest to the silver-haired man? As Mann pondered the question, the stranger moved on, seemingly dismissing Sal from his thoughts.

Now the silver-haired man turned his attention to a solitary woman sat before the fire. She was of middle years, and Mann had been amusing himself with thoughts of making a better acquaintance with her, if he could manage it without Halla noticing.

She was a traveller, but she'd decided to stay in the inn for the last seven days, as the mid-winter storm had raged and rolled against the sturdy wooden construction and barred doors.

Mann had never met her before, and although she raised her eyes from her examination of some gems in front of her, the ancient youth barely registered her mild interest before he moved on again. She too reminded Mann of someone he'd known, long ago, but then, most people did.

The next group were a rag-tag selection of young men. There were three of them altogether, ranging in height from really quite small, to almost as tall as Mann himself. They'd only arrived that day, covered in snow and freezing cold, but with huge grins on their faces to have made it to the most desolate place possible for the mid-winter night. Mann had overheard them talking about some of the more rampant rumours concerning what would happen when the millennium turned over, smirking to himself to hear the belief and fear in their voices.

The young men had decided well over three years ago to venture north in the hope of avoiding whatever plague or catastrophe was about to be inflicted on the general population as the new millennium began.

Mann thought them fools but admired them all the same. Not content with the empty words of reassurance from family and friends, and even from the higher authorities, they'd decided to take action. Mann couldn't fault them for their firm commitment to staying alive when the new millennium started, not that he thought they had anything to fear. The worrying rumours were little but that.

Well, Mann hadn't feared. Now he wasn't so sure, not based on what the mad old woman and the silver-haired young man had been talking about.

Here the youth stopped and really examined the men, lingering on their faces, and also, Mann noticed, on any visible skin showing at cuffs, necks and faces. Which wasn't much, even with the fires raging away, the storm outside was violent and routinely seemed to suck much of the heat from his inn. Most still wore their cloaks even though the fires raged at the centre of the inn.

Mann was just relieved that he had supplies enough to last near enough a decade in his cellar and stables, and in his more private store. Mann wouldn't freeze to death, and neither would his patrons while they remained inside the inn. Although the cost might increase. Mann never guaranteed his prices. Especially not when a storm struck. There was always room for a fresh negotiation.

One of the three men was uninterested in the silver-haired youth, but two of them, the smallest and the tallest, met his gaze openly and without fear. Perhaps, just perhaps, these men had met the silver-haired youth before, but if they had, they gave no other sign. Not like the older woman, who cackled with delight and shouted, 'I told you as much,' as the silver-haired man continued to survey the occupants of the inn.

By now some of the small parties had become aware of the inspection they were under, and some were openly hostile while others called out disparaging remarks, telling the man to go back to his 'woman' friend and stop seeking out someone more salubrious.

Mann held his amusement in check for as long as it took the silver-haired youth to turn his gaze onto Halla. Returning to the main room in the inn from whatever errand she'd been running within the complex of patron rooms upstairs, Halla immediately noticed the silver-haired young man and fixed him with a saucy stare, a look of amusement on her face as she became aware of Mann's scrutiny.

Mann cursed quietly. Damn the woman. How she could still arouse such fierce jealousy in him after all this time never failed to amaze him, especially when he'd only just been considering a little dalliance with another himself?

'Good evening traveller,' Halla trilled, her voice low and husky, and Mann growled once more, as the silver-haired youth became aware of his study. He turned and offered Mann a puzzled glance before turning away from Halla with barely a glance.

Halla used it as an opportunity to saunter over to Mann. She'd been making her demands well known all day about her expectations of the evening to come, and they'd not involved him playing games and cards with his friends until the 'morning' came. Now, though, Halla seemed distracted by the silver-haired youth.

'I didn't see him come in?' she commented, her breath warm and inviting in his ear as she stood on tip-toes to reach him.

'Then who served him, because I bloody didn't? Or the old hag?' Mann asked, nodding toward the older woman. She was lasciviously slugging down the youth's ale with a relish that should never be seen in a public place, or so Mann decided with a grimace of distaste.

'Nope, neither of them. Didn't you? I know the woman has a room, but he's new?'

Now Halla mentioned it, Mann realised she was correct.

Mann looked around the inn. The room was full, almost to bursting. The silver-haired youth would need to sleep on the floor if he planned on spending the night, as he surely must, with the weather so fierce outside.

'How did they get drinks then?' Mann continued to muse, and Halla laughed.

'You know Sal will serve anyone when you're not around. I imagine he did. Sal probably thought he was helping. He's a bit strange though,' she muttered, sliding past Mann suggestively as she went to check the contents of the cook pots over the twin fires. Mann watched her go, his mind far from where she wanted it to be that evening, and he knew she'd be disappointed if he should ever tell her. Thoughts of a warm bed, and a warmer woman, were banished to the extremities in the face of this mystery.

Who the hell were these two strangers?

Mann continued to watch the silver-haired youth as he turned and examined everyone within the inn. Some, his eyes lingered over, and others, he barely glanced at. Mann tried to determine what the silver-haired youth was looking for, but other than prying eyes over exposed skin, it seemed to always be something different that either caught his attention or didn't.

Belatedly, Mann realised his own neck was exposed, his shirt button undone lower than usual. He rushed to cover the traces of the strange marks covering and stretching over his tall body. Each year on this evening, a new mark appeared. They were a constant reminder of his strange longevity, appearing with fixed regularity time and time again. He'd long stopped trying to count them. There were simply too many, and his scattering of chest hair at his neckline was simply not thick enough to mask them all.

Still, he smoothed his plain brown shirt straight, aware the action would cover most of the marks. Then he rearranged his white apron around his waist, as though to cover the action.

He'd dressed carefully that day, keen to look his part for the new millennium. Highly polished black boots covered his large feet, and half way up his calf, they met his best trousers, fashioned from green velvet and cut just tight enough to show his fine legs to their best advantage. Not that he thought they were good, but enough people had commented throughout the ages for him to pay particular attention to them. On his upper body, he wore a silk brown shirt, perhaps not the most suitable for the Hvite Lands, and the job of innkeeper, but one he felt comfortable in all the same.

His hair was thick and iron grey, despite his age, curling around his ears. He preferred to be clean shaven and only that had day spent some time scraping all the previous weeks growth from his upper lip, cheeks and neck. His hair had been the same colour for so long, he almost wished it would turn the white of old age.

But what was it this the youth was looking for? Mann tugged his rolled sleeves down. It was rare that anyone ever asked him about his unusual marks, they'd all known him far too long for there to be even the hint of a mystery about him, even though he preferred to keep them covered. But the silver-haired youth and the old woman, had they noticed them and was it that which had set them off on whatever mad escapade they were currently taking part in?

Eventually, the silver-haired youth returned to the older woman. She was watching him avidly, but any interest he'd had seemed to evaporate.

'You're wrong. There are no more than six of us here, and that's including him,' he nodded in Mann's direction. Mann felt a razor sharp-shock of surprise down his back. They were counting him in their number? But what number and why?

'There's time yet,' the old woman cackled again. 'They'll come. I have their word. Four of the Nine are here, and three of the None, when you include Mann.'

A desultory smirk crossed the youth's face.

'You have that the wrong way round. I told you. You're the None, I'm a Nine, and so is Mann. I suggest you try and count a little better.'

'Blane, you've always been a fool. We all know who's who, and no longer will we Nine,' and she stressed the word, taking in the expanse of the inn without pointing to anyone in particular, 'listen to your lies, and accept that we're the None. We know who we are. It's about time you accepted the truth as well. It would get all this over and done with much sooner.'

'Think what you want, Jenna, but we're the Nine, well, Mann and I are, and the rest of you poor souls are just the None. And it will not happen tonight. The Nine will not come. They know, and they've known since the second year this wasn't the correct cycle. Time will roll around once more, as it has done before, and you must accept it. Not that there's anything you can do about it.' The silver-haired youth spoke with passion, for the first time an emotion other than disdain or mild interest riding over his youthful-looking face, mobile after being straight for so long.

Mann truly wanted to ask what all the nonsense about Nine's or None's was, but at that moment, a stray gust of wind ruffled the long silver hair trailing down Blane's back, and Mann caught sight of similar markings to his own snaking down the exposed neck. Was Blane right in what he said? Were he and Mann similar? Had Blane also lived nearly a millennia? The thought confounded Mann. He'd long known he was alone. To realise he might not have been was a dizzying realisation.

But Mann had no time to consider the possibilities for the old woman was hawking and gasping once more, her fingers pointing at the new arrival who'd forced their way into the warm inn without so much as a please or thank-you. Behind, Mann caught sight of Sal struggling to seal the door tightly, his stocky body forcing the sturdy door closed, from where it opened inwards. Always inwards. A precaution against falling snow blocking the doorway and preventing anyone from leaving after each snowstorm.

Unable to tell whether a man or a woman had walked into their midst, Mann still strode to welcome the new appearance, Sal still struggling to seal the door tightly closed. The new arrival was swathed from head to toe in a thick white cloak, perhaps the fur of the rare white bear, more myth than reality in the Hvite Lands, and Mann immediately knew this person was wealthy beyond measure. Mann was unsure what they'd think of his humble inn at the end of the known world.

As Mann opened his mouth to speak, a hand came up to rest on his chest, while the other hand silenced him with a cold finger on his warm lips. Quietened, Mann merely stood and watched as long gloves were rolled from slim fingers. The deep hood of the cloak was finally pushed back to reveal bright golden eyes, reflecting the firelight of the fires and lamps, and a smiling face set inside the brightest blonde hair he'd ever seen.

But before he could enjoy the spectacle, Mann groaned. This woman was no stranger to him. In fact, he knew her rather too well.

'Branwen,' Mann croaked, his voice strangled and immediately on edge. Branwen grinned at him as she flung her cloak from her shoulders and dumped it unceremoniously in his arms, with a kiss on his cheek and a swirl of the icy cold about her.

'Hello darling,' she purred, and immediately he was transported back in time to many centuries before. Mann knew this woman. He'd thought her long dead. Certainly, she'd never alluded to her long life for the short time they'd been avid lovers, before she'd just disappeared, never to be seen again.

She squealed with delight on seeing Blane and crashed into his arms. Blane looked anything but pleased to see the much shorter woman, but as with Mann, she blithely ignored his annoyance and settled beside him at the table he was sharing with the older woman. Only then did a grimace touch the golden face.

'Oh,' Branwen moaned, 'I'd forgotten you'd be here,' Branwen grimaced at the older woman and shuffled closer to Blane, as though for protection.

'I don't see everyone,' Branwen whined. Mann, discarding her cloak in an untidy heap near the door, having absent-mindedly given Sal the help he needed in closing and sealing it, strode over toward her. Mann bent his head low and growled into her ear, inhaling her intoxicating fragrance at the same time.

'Branwen, what the hell are you doing here? And how is it even possible?' Mann could feel his head spinning wildly with the possibilities.

'You always were so self-centred,' Branwen admonished, as though they spoke of small matters and not half a year of loving that had ended with her abrupt departure. She turned her golden eyes to face him.

'Why didn't you tell me?' Mann demanded, as Branwen ran her finger down his face, cupping his chin as she'd once done when she'd wanted to win him over.

'You weren't ready to hear what I had to say. It looks suspiciously like you still aren't. How bloody disappointing?'

Branwen pouted, turning to wink at Blane, as though this was all a great game she was pleased to be included in.

'I knew it wasn't worth the journey, but well, it's always such fun to see what he'll think of next. Mann, the only Nine to never have accepted his fate.' Blane, as Mann now knew the silver-haired youth was called, almost sounded disappointed.

'Why did you leave?' Mann demanded from Branwen, as her molten eyes flashed back to him.

'You thought we were in love, but you only ever love yourself, and quite frankly, I was bored of you. Even with all the time in the world, a girl needs to have some fun. Why did you choose to live here, in the arse of beyond, all your long damn life? There's so much else to see.' And then Branwen smirked. 'So many men and women to 'do' as well.'

Mann thought back to their time together, and then over the years of his life. Was he truly 'boring?' Was he genuinely only concerned with himself? Certainly, Mann had been troubled with keeping his secrets for all that time. It seemed Branwen had been, and also hadn't been.

'Why are you here you screeching bitch?' Branwen suddenly spoke with malice dripping from her usually pleasant voice, angling her conversation toward the older woman who'd been watching their exchange in disbelief.

'You've met before?' the old woman croaked, and Mann hoped her high-pitched squeaks and squawks had robbed her of her voice for the time being.

'Yes, why? Haven't you?' Branwen sneered. 'Did you think you'd worked it all out this time? Dear Jenna, you've always believed you had far more skill than you truly do.' Branwen's voice dripped with derision. Once more Mann listened to them. It was evident they all knew each other, and very well as well.

'Look, little bitch girl with your golden locks and simpering smile, I worked it all out long ago, and as you can see, we're all here. The Nine are nearly all here,' she once more indicated the entire inn with her outstretched arms ending in claw edges, 'and when the rest of the useless None arrive, it will all be over, and we'll be free of this age.'

Branwen's laughter warbled delightfully at the words, and immediately Jenna leaned toward her, with a threatening pose.

'Jenna, you think you're a Nine? That's a new one. Where've you spent your time? Clearly learning to delude yourself into thinking you're something that you're not. And no, the rest of the Nine, the real Nine, aren't coming. I sent word to them all years ago to say there was no point. Everyone else is holed up where they hope to begin.'

Anger flashed through Jenna's eyes, but then she hooted once more.

'They will come. I told them to, when I visited them.'

Now Branwen's eyes flashed with the fire of molten lava, and she reached across the table to grab Jenna's neck roughly. The old woman squealed in surprise, and Mann felt it best to block the view of those nosy patrons who had, finally, been distracted by this strange tableau playing out in their usual drinking establishment.

'If you've put their lives in danger, I'll kill you myself as soon as the new era rolls around and then at least I'll get some peace from you, you damn bitch.'

Jenna was sucking in deep breaths and trying to twist free when Blane placed his own cautionary hand over Branwen's.

'Let the old hag go,' Blane reproved. 'It would be good to see everyone again, even if there's no need for it.' Blane's voice was once more laced with boredom and Branwen released Jenna too fast, so the older woman, gasping for breath, slumped and fell to the floor, banging her head on the thick wooden table on the way down, losing consciousness in the process.

'Thank goodness for that, silence at last,' Blane growled,

and Mann found himself unsure what to do for the best, as he looked from the collapsed form to the grinning Branwen. Mann had never experienced such violence from Branwen before.

'Just leave her, dearie,' Branwen trilled. 'And get me a drink. I'm damn thirsty after all that time on the road. I hope my poor horse will be well cared for in your stables.'

'You brought a horse out, in this weather?' Mann raged, finding some solace in such a normal concern. No one rode when it was this bitterly cold. Most barely ventured more than a few footfalls from their home. The cold attacked everyone who opened their mouth or breathed too deeply through their nose, literally freezing the air as it tried to enter their body.

'The beast is fine. I ensured it was well warmed, fed and cossetted each night. She's a beautiful beastie. A shame she'll be gone come the morning.' Branwen ended her words with an elongated sigh.

Mann didn't understand why, and he thought he probably didn't want to. They all seemed to know a great deal more about 'something' compared to him. Instead, Mann busied himself at his bar, finding and then decanting the deep red spirit she'd always favoured, flavoured with some exotic spice from the deep-south. It was poured from a bottle thick with dust, under which a blue glow could just about be detected.

Mann had never met another person who liked the flavouring. Why the hell he'd kept this for over five hundred years he honestly didn't know.

With a swirl into a small goblet, the smell of the drink pulled him back half a millennia and by the time he passed Branwen the drink, Mann could feel all of his anger at her abrupt departure filling his large frame. Yet he wasn't about to ask. Not again.

Absentmindedly he kicked the prone frame of Jenna. He was tempted to leave her where she lay but decided against it.

Wrinkling his nose, and taking a sharp breath so he needn't inhale again, he lifted her. He was surprised by her weight when she was such a slight woman, but carried her to the only spare seats in the inn. It was before the fire where it tended to get too hot for anyone to sit comfortably. Sleep was apparently a different matter entirely.

As Mann laid her down, one of the men sauntered over to him. He'd been sitting in the group of three, playing games of chance, and Mann had harboured the belief he knew Jenna. Mann now had it confirmed.

'Daft old boot,' the man muttered, disdainfully lifting her hair from across her face and looking at her intently. 'She's dragged me here, and now she's three sheets to the wind. I should have bloody stayed in the South.' The man was hard to age, but his complexion reflected a lifetime spent in warmer climates, even without his mass of thick black curls and piercing yellow eyes. He seemed to be a piece of volcanic rock, shot through with the deepest gold.

Mann thought he'd walk away then, but he didn't.

'This is all your damn fault, you know. You and your bloody high ideals of what it means to be a Nine. Yours, because you're so bored with the same millennium time and time again. If only you'd kept your memory, this might have been the last time I had to endure this shit.'

'What are your plans for next time? Are you going to ask to be killed as soon as you get there so the rest of us have to endure a millennium knowing it's all a fruitless, bloody waste of time?' There was anger in the voice, and an intensity Mann could understand. This man might well be incited to violence on the smallest of reasons. He sounded like someone at the end of his tether.

'Who are you?' Mann asked, instead, and the other man rolled his yellow eyes but kept his anger in place.

'Bloody hell,' he mouthed, 'you really don't remember

anything, do you? I'm Jan. You're Blair. Introductions have been made, so be happy with that, you bastard.' The words weren't so much infused with anger as with resignation.

'I don't know what any of you are talking about,' Mann tried, but Jan had wandered off, as though happy he'd seen enough, and there was nothing else he could do about any of it.

Mann turned to view all those in the inn. Some he knew, many he didn't, and others he'd known for only the length of time they'd been one of his patrons. Yet several watched him avidly, and a few just ignored him. Branwen and Blane were talking animatedly, Blane showing far more interest in what Branwen had to say than he had in Jenna's words.

It was clear they knew each other well, and shared each other's secrets.

Jan was another matter entirely. He'd returned to his friends, if that's what they were, and was now pouting into his ale. One of his friends, the smaller of the men, was watching him carefully, as though worried about what he'd do next, while the other man, his eyes crossed with too much ale, was gazing lustfully at Branwen.

Angered, Mann walked toward the three of them, and as he passed the table, he dislodged the drunk fool so his arm shot out from beneath his head, where it had been resting, and knocked on the table. Another one out cold, Mann thought with pleasure. If only he could knock them all out, and have this lunacy over until the morning when he'd be able to think with a clearer head.

'Bugger off, Mann,' Jan muttered at his action, but he made no attempt to reciprocate, and so Mann picked up the empty jug of ale from the table behind the three and returned to his bar. He banged the bar hatch down and allowed himself a long moment of solitude, confident no one would disturb him or come into his space. No one was allowed behind his bar. No one. Unless they happened to be a member of his staff.

Moodily Mann turned to replace the glass container filled with Branwen's tipple of choice to its place on the shelf, but he felt a hand on his shoulder and turned to see her mocking face.

'There's no need to be irritated,' Branwen muttered, allowing her hand to fall away from Mann's shoulder when he ineffectually shrugged it away. 'This is what you wanted. This is what you made happen. None of us is to blame, and really, neither are you. It's just the way of the Nine.'

Mann squinted at her, trying to determine if she was sincere or if she was playing games with him. Her elaborate sigh convinced him, as nothing else could have done, she spoke the truth.

'We've all been here before. All of the Nine have sought you out over the last millennium; only Blane was strong enough not to come before now. He's known all along there'd be no convincing you, and no changing anything. You knew as well, when you made your little bargain.'

'The problem we have now is if you don't accept what we've told you, it's all going to start all over again. There's no tomorrow unless the new age can begin and that's not going to happen, not this time. You need to accept you're a Nine and do it quickly, and then when tomorrow does come, or rather the repeat of a thousand years ago, we can all work toward bringing this age to an end and starting a new one. You need to remember everything.' She ended with an exasperated exhalation.

Branwen's words were so sincere Mann couldn't doubt them and yet none of what she said made any sense to him.

'Tomorrow will come,' Mann stated, 'I have no effect on it.'

She smiled, a slow thing that spread across her face and highlighted all the dips and grooves he'd once loved so fiercely, but the pity in her golden eyes brought him up short from luxuriating in her being close to him once more.

'You have an effect, I have an effect, as do all the Nine, and for some bloody reason, as do all the None. We are what starts a new age, and right now, we've failed, and we failed the moment you asked to forget everything you knew, and start your life afresh. A fat lot of use it's done you. Still, you can try again. As normal.'

Branwen reached for the bottle he'd not yet returned to the shelf and poured a very full goblet of the stuff. The sweet smell made him want to gag.

'Why did you keep this?' Branwen asked, her voice persuasive, holding the bottle before him despite the sheen of dust, broken only by his fingerprints.

'I thought you'd come back,' was Mann's honest reply, and she nodded. 'Tane said you'd return when you were bored.' He offered the last with a shrug of his shoulders, as though the hurts of her leaving him could be dismissed so easily. 'And then, when time went by, and I assumed you were dead, I just couldn't bring myself to remove the trace of you from my inn.'

'You always were a bloody idiot,' Branwen teased, her tongue running over her lips, reminding him of the time they'd spent as lovers. 'For five hundred years?' she quizzed, eyebrows raised in mockery.

'Explain all this to me,' Mann asked, and she nodded as though she would and drank deeply from her glass goblet.

'I can't,' she shocked him by replying. 'You have to know it yourself. I shouldn't even have said what I have, but I'm fed up of this age. I want to move on. I want technological advances. I want to live a life that's a little more luxurious and a little easier than this one. I've had enough of famine and plague and war, and, and outside toilets,' she added with a sarcastic laugh at herself.

Branwen's words were heartfelt as she met his eyes,

frankly. He'd forgotten their unusual shade of gold. She'd always been a beautiful, strange little creature.

'You don't have the marks?' Mann demanded, and she nodded.

'I don't need them. I know who I am and I know how damn long I've lived. They're a little reminder for you. One that clearly hasn't worked.'

Branwen's words sort of made sense, and yet they also didn't.

'You've lived before?' Mann asked, and she nodded, as though forgetting her assertion she couldn't tell him anything.

'I'm one of the Nine, I've lived many lives and all of them beyond a reasonable length of time. Don't get me wrong. Like you I've made bad decisions, sometimes I've died before I should, and sometimes I haven't. There's a futility to us we can't always stomach.'

'I understand, unlike the others, exactly why you did what you did. I've never judged you, dearie. I just wanted to bed you, and that was fun, while it lasted. But I couldn't stay forever and watch you squander what you are. For that's what you've done. Hopefully, next time around, if we can set this right, there'll be a different ending, and we can be together, as we should be, for all that time.'

'Next time around?' Mann asked, just to be sure, and as she poured more of her favourite drink into her goblet, she nodded. Mann resisted the urge to clean the dusty bottle. It seemed wrong, to see such age beneath her delicate hand.

'We're caught in a loop, have been for a long time. Only we can pull the world into the next age, and we're all selfish idiots, too concerned with our own needs and wants to give a shit about the rest of humanity. You snapped, lost your temper and demanded an end to it all. It doesn't look like it worked out too well for you, but, well, you seem calmer than you have done for many an eon.'

'How do you know all this?' Mann thought to ask. Events had spiralled wildly out of control during the evening. He felt himself being sucked into something he'd never heard of before but which made a hideous, logical sense to him, finally, after all these years.

'We remember,' she sighed dramatically. 'Everything.'

'But I don't?' Mann pressed, just to be sure.

'You did, but you asked for a boon, and your boon was to forget, to lose your path, to try and start all over again and see if a new age could begin without your involvement, or rather without knowingly doing whatever it is you're supposed to do. You were wrong.'

'Well, what is it that you do? For a thousand years? And what is it that I should have done?'

Branwen laughed now, her short hair falling over her face as she thrust her head back, laughter spilling from her with warm, spirit-filled breath. Mann felt a stab of desire in his gut at the smell of her, but he tried to stay focused on his questions.

'I can't tell you that. None of us can ever speak to the other about our actions to one of the other Nine.'

'Don't you think that might help matters?' Mann asked, confusion rippling his face as he considered the stupidity of her words.

'So, I've ensured the new age doesn't begin, and yet you don't know what I should have been doing, other than running my inn, which I've been doing, and you won't tell me what you've been doing either. Sounds like a load of bollocks,' Mann added. At his disparaging tone, Branwen's head snapped back up, and she fixed him with an appalled expression.

'You've always been difficult to keep on track. You question too much and accept too little without proof and explanations. Why have you never been able to just do what needed to be done?'

There was a thread of anger in Branwen's voice, and yet also genuine interest.

'I don't know what you're talking about,' Mann tried to say, but she shrugged eloquently at him.

'It doesn't seem to matter whether you know what I'm talking about or not. Whatever you do is wrong, or at least, it seems to be wrong. Not, and I'll admit this freely because it has been discussed, that the others seem to know what you should do to make it right, or even if it is your interactions that cause the problems. For all we know, it might be the None 'cocking' everything up, as you so eloquently put it.'

'Well what are the None?' Mann asked, turning to look at the still prone figure of Jenna, snoring noisily before the fireplace.

She shrugged again.

'A pain in the arse,' Branwen muttered, and then shook herself all over, as though a dog shedding water. 'I shouldn't say that. It's not their fault they're as wrapped up in this as we are, and as to what they do, I've no idea either. They've no purpose, as far as I can tell, other than getting in the way and turning up in the most awkward of places. Like here. I'm unsure how Jenna managed to convince them all to come. She's delusional, I'm convinced of it.'

'So the None are all here?' Mann questioned, but she shook her head.

'Not yet, but there's time.'

Mann scowled into the recesses of his inn, as though they'd make themselves known to him. Just who the hell were they all?

'But only three of the Nine.'

'Yep, just the three of us.'

'And will they come?' Mann looked toward his door, unsure if he wanted it to open or not.

'Possibly. I told them not to, but we're a curious bunch.

They might want to watch what happens this time, so they remember, for the future. Tell me,' Branwen said, changing the conversation abruptly, 'because you never have, how did all this begin?' She turned to indicate the inn with her free hand, and he felt a smirk touch his face.

It had been a very long time since he'd considered how everything had begun, a very long time. Although he'd taken the time and the effort to ensure no one even guessed at his longevity, those first few days had long faded to almost a myth. But Mann smiled once more, and then he shivered. Bollocks, he'd been cold back then. And that brought a whole new series of questions to his lips.

'I'll tell you, in time, but first, you tell me something. What can you do? I never guessed you could do anything out of the ordinary, but I'm assuming it's all to do with our being Nines or Nones or whatever the hell you think I am.'

Now her eyes blazed smelted gold, and Mann didn't know if it was anger coursing through her, or frustration.

'Rules, dearie' Branwen trilled, trying to make light of his question, but he sensed something else.

'What can I do?' Mann probed, and now she turned away on the bar stool, as though afraid to meet his eyes.

'You know, don't you?' Mann grilled, but Branwen remained stubbornly silent.

'What about your damn rules?' Mann growled, but still Branwen looked away from him. Mann thought back to their time together. Half a millennia faded away before his eyes, and he could see her, as she'd appeared back then. In all honesty little had changed about her. She looked almost identical, a curse of his own long life as well, and yet. Well, Jenna was an old woman, Blane, a silver-haired youth. Had they all been stuck like this for a millennium? Would they be stuck like this if, as Branwen said, the new age didn't begin and this millennia simply restarted once more? Was age even an issue?

'I know enough,' Branwen sighed dramatically, glaring at him angrily as she turned to face him. 'But I must keep your secret, and you must keep mine because I'm sure you know it, even if you think you don't.'

Mann remained silent. She'd just revealed more in that sentence than in many of her others, both confirming his special abilities were part of being a Nine, and also that she had them as well. Mann imagined all of the so-called 'Nine' did. Mann wondered if the 'None' did. Here was something he, at last, could understand. None of the talk of the ending of this age, or the beginning of a new age, meant a great deal to him. But his strange ability and the unfortunate consequences of it were of great interest to him.

Mann only wished the damn bitch had spoken to him about it five hundred years ago. Maybe then he'd have been less circumspect in using his abilities.

As Mann thought that, he happened to actually look at the goblet in her hand, filled with the last sips of her favourite spirit, and he allowed a smile to form on his strained lips. Mann had forgotten, but now he remembered the little glass. It had taken a very long time, but Branwen was in for a surprise. Or so Mann hoped, and it would go some way to proving what she was trying to tell him was correct.

'I'd drink that quick if I were you,' Mann cautioned, and immediately Branwen placed the goblet on the scarred wooden surface of the bar and rolled her eyes.

'Get me a wooden mug, quickly. I don't want to lose my drink,' she instructed, immediately understanding his amusement, and showing she truly did understand his special abilities.

Mann was already reaching for a wooden mug and watched with amusement as she poured her precious spirit into it. And not a moment too soon. With a shriek of surprise, for all he'd warned her, the goblet disappeared before their eyes.

A long moment passed and then Branwen looked at him, long and hard, her eyes seeming to harden as she did so. No longer a liquid glaze of gold, but instead a bastard-shaped mass of solid yellow, hard and unyielding.

Mann considered her eyes might just be a clue to her 'special' ability. Belatedly he looked toward Blane. His eyes reflected silver, but for the time being he had no interest in their conversation, and in fact looked as though he were about to fall asleep, his head resting on his upturned hand, his elbow on the side of the table.

'I really wish you'd learned a bit more about your ability before you used it,' Branwen complained, and Mann offered an apologetic shrug, before truly considering his strange beginning. At the same time, Mann thought he heard a strange noise, a shriek and then a thud, coming from far below his feet in the depths of his cellar, and he allowed a small smile to touch his face. At last.

'It was a bloody emergency,' Mann growled, a grimace on his face, in memory of that time. It had been a predicament he was lucky to have survived. He could have died out there, especially in the position he'd been left in.

'Then tell me about it,' Branwen prodded once more, and this time he allowed himself to consider events of a millennium ago. It seemed like only yesterday, and he had no problem recalling precisely what had happened to him.

PART TWO

THREE

A MILLENIA AGO

Chapter 3

THERE WAS SILENCE.

And then there wasn't.

A swirl of snow and hail, a blizzard of ice and sleet fell on the deserted wintry spot where before there'd been nothing but white. A silence rang out deeper than quiet, as complete as nothingness.

'Bollocks,' the voice boomed preternaturally loud as the revolving snowstorm of ice disappeared as quickly as it had arrived depositing in its wake the most ridiculous of sights. A naked man, struggling for balance, and sinking thigh deep in the snowy landscape. In his wake, a more natural whiteout continued to blow, making it hard to focus on his quivering shape.

'Bollocks,' echoed once more, the voice strong and thunderous, although there was no one to hear it, and it masked another noise, a thud. The sound swallowed by the snow and unheard by the naked man.

To look at him closely would have been to discover nothing other than a normal human. He was merely a man; a muscular one, but at the moment his pride and joy had shrivelled to nothing, more withered than swinging from side to side as he shivered in the snow.

'Bollocks,' sounded again, accompanied by a jiggling from foot to foot that should have been impossible in the thigh-high snow yet which he accomplished easily all the same. His feet, already turning blue in the cold, reached almost to shoulder height as he tried to save them from the perils of frostbite.

'A bloody blizzard,' he managed to shout, his anger and rage causing spittle to fly from his mouth where it immediately froze, landing on his exposed chest with an icy tinkle of broken glass.

Furiously the man looked around, seeing nothing but snow and the ink of deepest night all around him. He squinted, scrunching his eyes against the implied glare from the white landscape, but it afforded him no new vision.

'Some clothes would be nice,' he shouted more to himself than any other, for who was there to hear? At his words, he felt something, a prickle of a memory, and an icy shard of 'something' in his mind. He tried again.

'Clothes,' he shouted, feeling foolish but doing it all the same. He was in desperate circumstances after all. This time he felt nothing but his glacial limbs, his hands under his armpits, still dancing from leg to leg in the r high, powdery snow.

'Clothes, please,' he tried, cracking a smile in his desperation. Still, nothing happened.

'Bollocks,' he shouted once more, his breath hitching in fear and rage.

Then a lazy grin spread across his face as something flared within him. With a jaunty smile, he finally stood still and thought a moment longer.

'I would like some clothes to keep me alive in these freezing conditions.' As he said the words, he felt it, a strange 'sound' reached his ears, as though someone screamed out in surprise or annoyance, but he was more concerned with the burn of heat enveloping his tall body.

Furs encased his long arms, a hat sat upon his head, and his legs were suddenly sheeted in thick leather, cured to keep the damp of chill from his skin. His hands, deeply speckled red only a moment ago, were now warming inside a pair of sealskin gloves, the trace of someone else's fingers, he thought, still embedded in the material of the ambient warmth he found there.

Still, he waited, the heat working its way up his body, and then he sighed loudly with annoyance.

'I would like some boots to keep me alive in these freezing conditions,' he bowed mockingly, and yet the sound rang in his ears, and he looked down the length of snow he stood within to find leather boots, lined with fur, reaching up to his high knees. He winced slightly as he lifted his left leg to try and take a step. Really? Had he needed to specify they fit him?

'I would like some boots to keep me alive in these freezing conditions, and I would like them to fit my feet,' his words were clipped with amusement as he heard the sound of them echoing in his head and a strange half scream of outrage as new boots encased his wide feet and the uncomfortable ones just disappeared. He listened, waiting to hear the opposite of the initial cry that had preceded their arrival but there was nothing.

He bowed once more, still mocking, but also grateful.

'My thanks,' he called, his loud voice echoing in the quiet of oblivion. He heaved his right leg up higher than his shoulders and attempted to dig himself out of the snow hole he now occupied, using his leg as a lever and forcing his upper body forward, over it, hoping his left leg would naturally follow suit.

'Bollocks,' he groaned as sweat streaked his face, his clothing making him almost too warm after the deep chill of his nakedness, and bulky to boost. Maybe he should have done this first before demanding to be clothed.

With far too much effort, he hauled his body above the snow line and quickly spread himself out flat across as much of the surface as possible. He didn't wish to sink so deeply again.

'Bollocks,' he panted, his fierce breath echoing in his chest, surrounding him in a foggy cloud of his own making, as his nose hovered just above the snow. He closed his eyes. He needed time to think and decide what to do next, but he had no time as he felt the deep snow shifting beneath his unexpected, and unwanted weight.

'I would like some skis to stop me from falling into the snowy drifts,' his words were breathless, his exertion depriving his voice of its clarity.

Still, his request worked.

In no time at all, he heard the strange sound, akin to an angry screech, and felt heaviness descend on his legs.

'Bollocks,' he managed to holler in rage, the weight of his new equipment threatening to overbalance him back into the hole he'd just laboured to extract himself from.

He dug his elbows into the fine surface of the snow and heaved upright, swinging his suddenly heavy feet to either side of his body, while shuffling away from the hole. He needed to stand upright and not fall down any chasms in the snow. His face glistened momentarily with sweat before freezing in icy streaks, his warm tears quickly icing and threatening to seal his eyes and still he worked.

He had only himself to rely on as he tried to balance on the sliding mountain of snow.

'Bollocks,' he kept repeating, over and over as he worked, as though the words would give him the power he needed to lift from the ground. And eventually, they did. He tottered, upright, his arms wind-milling furiously as he tried to keep his balance.

The skis on his feet were heavy timbered things, made from some sort of blackened wood, the bottom surface slippery and well oiled. His legs and feet fought for purchase as they slithered backwards and forward, his arms circling and his face a rictus of rage.

'Bollocks,' he grasped, reaching for empty air and finding it, unsurprisingly, empty.

Yet, somehow, he managed to cartwheel himself into a reasonable approximation of upright. As he stood, he strained to keep his legs in just the right position to stop them from slithering either forward or backwards, gaining himself a precious moment to catch his breath, and breathe out deeply.

As he did so, an enormous plume of cloud shadowed his face. His heat forced its way into the frigid air, before pausing briefly to fight with the icy tendrils of cold snaking across the landscape. Quickly it lost its fight, succumbing to the overwhelming chill. It turned to tiny glacial particles tinkering softly to the ground around his blackened skis.

For just a moment it was impossible to see the expression on the man's face, and when it emerged from the cloud bank, it was resolute with determination.

'Bollocks,' he shouted once more, as though it might be the only word he knew and understood, despite his previous demands. Then his head began to peer through the inky night, looking first one way and then another, nose scrunched as though he scented the air like a hound on the hunt. His eyesight surely saw little but the black of night, and the white of endless ice and snow that appeared in snatched images through the haze of the continuing blizzard.

A war played across the man's face as soon as he'd ascertained there was no help to be had from either his nose or his eyes, and then his lips broke once more into an ironic grin.

'I would like to know which way to go to warmth and safety,' and yet there was no answering rush of sound or even an idea of an answer to his question, and his eyes flashed with defiance.

'Bollocks,' he muttered, bending down to ensure his feet were well attached to their skis. He checked ties and catches and then, almost satisfied with what he found he asked for one more thing.

'I would like a lamp to allow me to see as I try and find my way to warmth and safety.' The sarcasm of his tone was as heavy as the black of night. Immediately a cut-off cry reached his ears, and a thump presaged the arrival of something hitting the ground. He groaned.

'I can't believe I have to ask for these things to come to my hand,' he grumbled, straining to reach down to where he thought the object had landed. He didn't know what he expected, but it wasn't the chill of ice-cold metal, felt even through his thick gloves, almost colder than the howling wind. Neither was it the long tube stretching further than the distance from his elbow to his hand.

He shook the object, roughly, surprised to hear the clunk of something inside, as his fingers quested over the smooth surface of the tube, only to hitch on a catch that quested inwards under his touch forcing a harsh beam of yellow light to illuminate the ground by his feet.

'What the hell?' he mouthed, allowing his fingers to depress the catch again, and his world to return to one of cold and darkness.

A grin spread across his face as he repeated the action of pressing the clasp and a cruel beam of light sheeted its way far into the distance. It illuminated no change in his environment. Whatever he'd been expecting, it wasn't this answer to his request, and yet it was efficient in its design and purpose, for all that he had no idea how it worked without the help of flame and pitch.

'Which way should I bloody go, though?' he whispered,

unaware that the thought was made aloud, as he shone the torch into the near distance, looking for anything that might give him an indication of which way to go. He sniffed again, hoping for a trace of wood smoke or decay but nothing reached him other than the clean, dry smell of wind and cold, a smell only possible when there was an uninterrupted passage of wind over a huge expanse of snow and ice.

He peered all around him once more all the same but found nothing to entice him either one way or the other.

'Bollocks,' as ever was produced from his mouth, and then he just started moving, his right leg sliding forward, his left leg following suit, almost as though they'd known all along which direction the man above them would take.

He wobbled uncertainly for long moments, his left leg overextending itself as he fought for balance, his right one coming up a little short, and then he found his rhythm. He almost flew through the air, too fast for the falling snow to actually land on him, as the illumination from the torch allowed a flickering image of unending snow to flash before him.

And yet on he drove, first one leg and then the next. His right hand held the torch, his left held out a little at waist height to aid his balance and his breath, made solid, flowed behind him as he sped through the too-brief clouds of heat he created.

His face, on closer inspection, was creased in concentration, the smooth movement he was managing much harder to accomplish than it looked as he was bathed in the afterglow of his torch.

The silence of the falling snow deadened all sound, not even his rasping breath reaching as far as the edge of the circle of light he glided through. Behind him, he left nothing but the tracks of his skis and a faint disturbance in the soft snow where his expelled breath had frozen and fallen in little icy drops of rain leaving a pattern similar to water flicked from fingertips on a sandy beach. Not that he knew what a beach was.

Anyone out hunting in the frozen landscape would have quaked to know what sort of beast left such tracks, but it was no beast, merely a man, or rather, a manifestation that wore the clothes of a man (well, now it did) and came armed with little more than a foul mouth and formidable strength.

And on 'Mann' sped, the sound of his skis reaching his ears, the heat of his impassioned breath forming a clear line or two around his mouth to keep the frost and snow at bay. On and on, to who knew where? Certainly 'Mann' had no idea and neither did he concern himself with the thought too much. Not now he was warm and had his skis.

Time passed. He had no idea of how much, and on he went. He knew the tang of thirst on his ice dry tongue, and the rumble of hunger from his stomach, but he pushed them aside for as long as he could. Eventually, as the darkness stretched even further away with no sight of anyone but himself, he allowed himself to pause.

Muscles burned with the exertion of his skiing. His skin prickled with icy sweat but it was his thirst and hunger forcing him to ask once more for the things he needed.

Still, he smiled condescendingly, his face a rigour of sweat and cold, and he swept a mocking bow before he spoke.

'I would like some food to fill my empty belly, and some drink to warm my throat and drive the ache of cold from my mouth. And,' he added almost too quickly, 'I would like them to arrive in a container so I don't spill or drop the items.'

He thought he was covering all eventualities as he heard the same old strange half screech and a whistle in the air. Hopefully, he placed his hands in front of him, in what he believed was a fair approximation of where the desired items might arrive.

Mann squinted into the darkness, keen not to be caught

unawares, only for dampness to spread across his foot and a strange heat across his forehead. He looked down first, as fluid trickled down his forehead and onto his nose, dripping onto the container he'd inadvertently kicked and spilt the contents from. He sniffed, and the spices of something delicious assaulted his nostrils. He snatched for the lump on his forehead, his gloved hand coming away with warmth nestled in its centre.

He turned whatever it was from side to side, first one way, and then the other, but he had no idea of what he'd been gifted to eat. The lump glowed brown in the darkness, and with a shrug, convinced his request shouldn't harm him; he lifted it to his mouth and took a huge bite. No hesitation would assist him as his stomach desperately growled.

The substance allowed an explosion of taste to judder through his body. Licking his lips again and again, he scrubbed the chilling juices from his forehead with his gloved hand and considered what he should do now.

He was hungry and tired and seemed to have done little in all his time skiing across the barren landscape. No light had pierced the gloom, and still, there had been no trace of any anything! He was alone, and he was tired, and there seemed nothing more to do than ask for some shelter to keep himself warm and sheltered while he tried to sleep.

He chewed on reflectively, considering how best to phrase his requests. But first, a more pressing demand presented itself as he chewed and swallowed.

'I would like a drink to arrive in my hand and in a suitable container.' He grimaced as he heard the same half screech and odd pop and held out his spare hand to welcome whatever was coming. He tried to wait with a loose grip, ready to grab if the need should arise, and not with a clenched fist as he had an idea it would result in yet more spilt fluid.

He wasn't disappointed in his belief.

He felt hot fluid cascade down his chill face, dripping down his neck and back, mingling with the sweat of his exertions so he felt sticky as well as sweaty.

He sighed deeply, licking his lips to taste whatever it was he'd been sent.

Sweetness and warmth temporarily blossomed on his parched tongue as he growled for more. A sharp tinkle behind him, and he turned to see the remains of the vessel that must have contained his drink. A see-through substance lay on the white snow, in the tracks left by his skis, only the spill of the light from his torch reflecting deeply in the cracks and crevices, giving a sense of its previous shape.

Mann almost bent to pick up the pieces, to see if he could lick more of the sweetness from them, but snatched back his gloved hand at the last moment. A memory tugging in his mind predicting pain and blood if caught a sharpened edge.

He shrugged as he straightened his long body. He still needed to drink. But how to accomplish it?

The food had been much easier to arrange, but then it had no need of a receptacle to keep it in to stop it spilling and draining away to nothingness in the layers of snow before he could consume it.

Mann took some time to consider his words before he spoke once more.

'I would like a sealed container of drink to arrive before me, and to come with both the means to open it and a vessel to decant its contents into so I might drink it.'

He winced as he spoke, sure somehow his words would be misinterpreted again and half-amused, when his raging thirst allowed him to be, by the thought of what might actually arrive this time.

Again the strange sound and screech of outrage, followed by a thud of something heavy hitting the snow before him. He gasped in surprise as a massive wooden barrel wobbled precariously on its rimmed metal bottom before settling to rest on the snow. He winced then, knowing exactly what would happen next and neither was he disappointed.

The base of the barrel was too small to try and spread its weight evenly over the snowy, powder-like surface. With quiet satisfaction, Mann watched the massive barrel, its wooden straits held tight by three bands of blackened iron, sink slowly before him. The barrel opener and sturdy iron tankard disappeared beneath the snow he precariously balanced upon.

Once more Mann sighed, the irony of the situation bringing a curve to his dry lips. It appeared he was capable of demanding almost anything he wanted and yet if he couldn't access it when it arrived, or stop it from spilling, there seemed little to no point in having whatever ability he currently had.

But, he was still thirsty, and he needed to drink. He thought once more. Whatever this ability was, it was a tricky thing. He seemed unlikely to get what he wanted unless he was very specific in his request.

'I would like a small container of drink that I can hold in my hand and pour easily, with a vessel to drink it from,' he felt the strange ring in the air, and he growled angrily. 'I haven't bloody finished yet.' The ringing sound diminished and he fancied he heard a shriek of rage and then disbelief, as though the item had disappeared and then magically reappeared before someone. 'I would like it to arrive in my hand so it doesn't spill, or get lost in the snow.'

This time there was a slight pause, as though waiting to make sure he was finished with his demands. He grinned. He didn't understand any of this, but couldn't deny the humour in the situation.

When the ringing sound once more echoed in the air, a cry of despair greeting the noise, he half closed his eyes and held his hands out before him. He could only hope this time, the drink he received was accessible.

Something cold slid across his outstretched hand. He stifled a cry of shock as he looked down. His right hand held a green container, with something stuck to its side, while his left held a delicate vessel made from what appeared to red ice flashing under the gaze of the torch placed on his ski before making his request.

There was also another item in his left hand, made from some sort of shiny silver and he wondered what it was for, before he looked at the container he held and noticed the intricate seal to the top, where a piece of shiny paper, just visible, was held in place by a thread of string wrapped tightly around it. He could just glimpse the bottom of something almost touching the fluid inside the bottle as well.

It looked as though he had everything he wanted, apart from the fact the drink wasn't warm, and yet he still needed to work out how to open the container. He held it upwards in his right hand, feeling the comforting swish of the fluid inside moving from one side to another without leaking. He licked his parched lips. He could almost taste the fluid but knew he was a long way from actually being able to drink it.

Beneath him, his legs began to ache. He was tempted to sit down but knew he couldn't take the risk. Not after what had just happened to the barrel and so he strove to distract his tired body by working out how to get into the bottle.

First, he pulled his gloves from both of his hands and held them between his knees, where the red drinking vessel already nestled. He placed the silver contraption onto his skis, fearing its sharp edges would pierce his trousers if he put it between his knees. He was already wary of the red glass, worrying the fragile thing would break from his touch, or look. He was also concerned the cold would shatter it.

He pulled at the thread holding the silver wrapper over the top of the bottle, and managed to work it lose, even though his fingers were already numb from the cold and difficult to control. Then he picked up the strange silver contraption and wondered how it related to the piece of wood stuck into the top of the bottle.

Turning both the bottle and the silver item from side to side, he shook his head in frustration. Why was this all so complicated? Why could he not just get what he wanted and what he needed?

Bending at the waist, he placed the bottle onto his right ski and manipulated the silver tool in his hand. Mann thought he could almost see how it was supposed to work, the long thin protuberance with a thin band of metal circling up its length was clearly intended to grab hold of the piece of wood, to enable him to pull it from the bottle.

What he couldn't decipher was how to even get it in the piece of wood in the first place. He couldn't imagine he just pushed it in, thinking that if he did so, the portion of wood would be pushed down into the fluid, making it impossible for him to drink any of it.

Mann stared, and he stared, touching one part and then another, finally thinking to turn the element on the top of the tool. As he did so, he shrieked in delight as the long thin protuberance circled down from its cage.

Delighted with his find, he bent to pick the green bottle up only to realise he'd made a fatal mistake. In putting the bottle down, he'd exposed it to the freezing chill and he now held in his hand a bottle filled with frozen liquid. Even if he managed to get the top off the bottle, he doubted that any of the fluid would actually come out.

He growled again, his thirst driving him onwards even though he wanted nothing more than to give up. He could sit here in the snow and let it take him as it had the barrel now nestling at the bottom of such a deep snowy hole, he could barely see the top of it when he flashed his torch down it.

Not wanting to, but understanding that after spending so

much time trying to resolve this problem, he was unprepared to be presented with a new one, he quickly slid the frozen bottle under his clothes. The instant chill burned his chest as it settled against him. He gritted his teeth, appreciating this was the only source of heat he had to return the frozen substance to its fluidic state. He shuffled his chest about, ensuring the bottle was wedged around his waist, in the band securing his trousers and keeping them up.

Once more, Mann licked his cold lips and released his gloves from his knees so he could protect them from the chill as well. Momentarily he forgot about the fine red glass and groaned when he felt it fall.

Luckily, or not, so he thought as he bent to retrieve it, it landed with a soft plunk into the snow and nestled there. Quickly he bent to recover it before wondering why he'd bothered. To thaw the drink he needed to ski on, and he certainly couldn't do that while he was holding the delicate object in his hand.

But he was reluctant to let it go. Raising it to his lips, he imagined what it would be like to drink from such a delicate container, the rim barely wide enough that it touched his nose when he tipped it backwards, as though to sample the last little bit of fluid inside it.

Mann might well look stupid, but he thought the idea of drinking from it was a good one. So, teeth gritted, he did what he should perhaps have done a long time ago.

'Please, can I have a bag or sack to sling across my shoulders to hold my possessions in? It must be waterproof and lightweight,' again there was a brief hesitation, as though ensuring he'd finished speaking, before Mann heard the strange sound and saw a soft weight settle before him.

He bent to catch it, feeling its softness and lack of weight and wondering at it.

It seemed to be made of deepest black and had many

catches and pockets all over it. He didn't take the time to work out what they all were, instead nestling the red glass and the strange silver tool inside it, and then scratching his head as he looked at the tangle of straps on the bag.

He imagined they were to enable him to slip his arms through the bag and hold it tight to his back. The straps looked too small to be of much use. After the confusion of the silver tool, he appreciated the working of such a simple device was likely to be far more difficult than he thought.

Resolved to his predicament, he managed to thread one of his massive arms through the two straps and shunted the bag so it almost rested on his left shoulder. It was uncomfortable but meant he now had his hands free to hold the torch and keep his balance at the same time.

Against his chest, he could still feel the tingle of the bottle, and he shivered at the thought of it against his skin and the burn he knew would mar it.

Enough. He needed to get even warmer to melt the fluid and finally drink it.

Mann stretched out one leg, anxious to avoid the slowly refilling hole caused by the massive barrel, and then he was flying once more over the relatively even surface of the snow-covered area.

His breath came in quick gasps as he forced himself onward. Every time he breathed in, the shock of his intense thirst struck him, and Mann wondered why he couldn't work out the correct words to just get a drink when he'd managed so well with his clothes and his skis. What was it that made getting a drink so problematic? Mann allowed himself to muse over the possibilities, anything to distract his mind from his current problems.

He had no idea how much he needed to do to thaw the fluid, knowing only to stop when his thirst became too great a thing to ignore.

When he stopped, he bent double at his knees, catching his breath, before threading the bottle from beneath his clothes. With his gloves still on, he could feel the heat of the bottle, but however much further he'd skied on, it wasn't enough to have completely restored the fluid inside the bottle to its natural state. Chunks still rattled against the bottle, although there was also a comforting sloshing sound to accompany it.

Mann hoped he'd done enough. Loosening the bag from his shoulder, he quickly pulled the silver tool from inside, his fingers brushing over the red glass, but left it where it was. He pulled his gloves from his hands and hastened to affix the tool to the bottle in the way he thought it worked.

Carefully, he wound the thin protuberance into the wood at the top of the bottle, feeling it bite into the wood, and then, unsure what to do next, he attempted to reverse his actions, holding the tool close to the bottle.

He felt sweat beading down his face as he tried to work the wood loose, unsure if he was even using the tool correctly. He was aware he needed to do something before his thirst beat him, and the fluid froze once more.

Slowly, he felt the wood begin to move, and with mounting excitement he moved his hands in small, economical movements, crowing with delight when the wooden stopper finally came loose with a dull thwack. Mann grinned, reaching for the bag to replace the silver tool, wooden stopper and retrieve his glass, allowing himself to sniff the contents of the bottle as he did so.

He grimaced at the sour smell, hoping it would taste better when it was finally in his mouth. His hand closed on the small red glass, and he pulled it free from the confines of the bag and gleefully poured the defrosted liquid into it.

Mann took a massive gulp, almost emptying the fluid in the glass in just one swallow. As it hit the back of his throat, he gasped and almost gagged. Whatever he'd been sent was bloody disgusting.

Mann swallowed convulsively, trying to convince his body it wanted to retain the fluid. He grimaced once more, trying to dispel the need to heave and expel whatever it was he'd been sent to drink.

All this effort and then it was bloody repulsive.

Mann held the bottle up so his torch played over the contents. He grimaced again. There was some sort of writing there, but he had no idea what it said. Instead, he sniffed the bottle once more, wincing as the acrid stench wafted up his frozen nostrils. Now he really did need to retch.

But there was nothing for it. He'd gone to a lot of effort to get his drink, and he wasn't prepared to play the guessing game again. Discarding the small red glass back to his tangled backpack, he lifted the bottle to his mouth, attaching his lips to the glassy surface even though the action was making him want to heave already. He paused, and then tipped the bottle further and further back, allowing the abrasive tasting fluid to cascade down his throat with as little effort as possible.

He made it almost to the bottom of the bottle before he felt his stomach begin to roll as it attempted to reject the disgusting stuff. Abruptly, he bent over, trying desperately not to suffer the indignity of tasting the vile drink on the way back up, as well as down.

Mann clamped his mouth shut against the bitter swill in his mouth, and the burp rising from his throat. He would keep the drink inside him. He needed it as he continued his journey to who knows where.

When he was finally able to stand, he took great delight in pouring the dregs of the bottle onto the snow. He was surprised to hear the liquid sizzle and turn the snow a shade so dark it looked like day-old blood. He even took the time to jiggle the frozen elements through the narrow neck, so disgusted with it all.

Mann shuddered to think what was happening inside his stomach now he'd drunk the same stuff. He couldn't deny he felt much better with the desperate thirst driven from his mouth.

Mann licked his lips as he tugged his gloves back on, fearful of waiting any longer. His lips were cold and salty with sweat and also tart from the drink he'd been given. He belched. An ugly, loud sound in the still air and was forced to wipe his gloved hand across his mouth to clear away a thin layer of drool.

He might feel better in and of himself, but his stomach was a riot of agony. He knew that the disgusting burp would merely be the first of many.

He reached down to return the torch to his backpack. He could see well enough now to ski in the light from the snow, and the brightening horizon.

He wrinkled his nose as he did so. Where was he going? And why was he going anywhere? Shouldn't he just ask for whatever he wanted and stay here, forever, or for however long this strange existence lasted?

But no. The image of the sinking barrel still haunted his memory, and Mann knew he needed to at least find some sort of safer footing before he began to contemplate what he'd ask for next. Right now, his needs were little and few. He just needed to find a way off the snow, or find somewhere where the snow was more stable. He was sure it couldn't continue like this for much longer. Surely?

Resolved, he set out once more, amused to find his skiing skills so much improved in the brief time he'd been using them. If he glanced behind, which he didn't do for fear of falling over, he knew there'd be a reasonably even double groove in the snow marking his passage. Oh, and the small spill of drink, but other than that, he seemed to be alone in a strange land of snow. Of all the places he could have manifested he determined this was the worst of them all.

In little to no time, his muscles were burning. He could feel the twin pinch of thirst and hunger gnawing at his stomach and throat. Yet, his landscape hadn't changed. What was this? A place of only snow and half-light?

Mann also thought he detected a faint whiff of something in the still air. What it was, he couldn't name, but it was at least a change. He trained his skis to head toward where he thought the smell emanated from. As he did so Mann saw the first thing in the environment that was nothing to do with him.

Nestled half in, and half out of the snow he saw a small speckle of what could only be blood. He was sure nothing else could glow that blackly and darkly. He bent to examine the stuff more closely, wondering where it had come from. Looking all around, he scouted for some sort of prey beast, or even a predator, but found nothing. In his eagerness to see precisely what it was, he leaned forward on his skis. He realised too late he was close to overbalancing. In a panic he stuck his arms out to either side and barely managed to stop himself sliding into the small hole caused by the strange speckle.

'Bollocks,' he shouted, his words taking on the glassy feel of long drawn out echoes as he hung, suspended by his arms, and little else.

'Bollocks,' he gasped once more, trying to force his way fully upright even though his left arm was entangled in the twisted straps of his backpack.

He could feel himself wobbling. A vision of the heavy barrel unhelpfully shot through his mind. He wouldn't endure the same fate for himself.

Mann heaved, and pushed. Eventually, perspiration once more pooling down his face, he stood upright and slid his twisted skis backwards so he could put some distance between himself and the strange speckles.

'Bollocks,' he wheezed, happy there was now more than enough room between where he stood and the small hole. He would have preferred to know exactly what he'd been looking at and why it was there but wasn't prepared to risk falling in again.

With a last look behind him, and in front of him, he snaked his skis forward and pushed off, into the slowly reducing blackness of night and over the smooth surface of the powdery snow. He'd not be stopping again, or so he vowed, until he reached firmer ground.

FOUR

Chapter 4

TIME PASSED, how much he had no idea of knowing, other than every part of his body ached and twanged with each and every slide forward he took over the snowy surface.

Mann didn't so much object to the pain, at least it made him realise he was alive in the otherwise dead landscape, but it was slowing him down. That was annoying him.

His stomach grumbled loudly, its complaints far too easy to hear over the rasp of his breath and the swish of his skis. But as of yet, he'd found nowhere to stop. The surface merely consisted of deeply compressed snow, its surface powdery white, but if he even threatened to stop, he could feel himself beginning to sink deeply.

Mann wished he could sigh with annoyance, but even that would have hurt his constricted chest. Breathing in the frozen air was a painful experience.

He trudged on through the long and lonely inkiness. He somehow felt sure the sun should have risen by now and had long since decided there was no sun here. There was only the black of night, and then a fainter grey on the distant horizon, but never any actual sun. His light, or torch, or whatever the metal tube was, provided the only illumination. Even the moon and stars were shy, hidden behind a sweeping mask of cloud scudding in the stiff breeze, occasionally threatening to overbalance him.

And on Mann flew, or rather, stumbled.

He could feel a time would arrive, far sooner than he might like when he'd be unable to stand upright any more. Yet he pushed himself onwards, trying to ignore the pressing need for food and sleep and more liquid. His mind was awash with what he could ask for when the need became too great and how he'd phrase it. Yet he also knew, when the time came, he wouldn't receive quite what he was expecting.

Slowly Mann became aware of a strange smell.

At first, he thought he imagined it. Until now he'd smelt nothing but the tang of air frozen clean, so pure it hurt to ingest it, and the blood he'd discovered. As soon as he was cognizant of the pungent aroma in his nostrils, he wondered how he hadn't noticed it sooner. It was all-pervading, so dense it almost had a taste to it.

Abruptly Mann stopped, stuck his tongue out and tasted the air. It was a poor decision. Immediately, his tongue froze any moisture in his parched mouth, becoming solid. He coughed, his tongue retracting into his mouth so he almost bit his tongue in his haste. Mann's throat spasmed. He thought he might vomit, only then he started to drool, liquid appearing from nowhere.

He sniffed appreciatively, and slowly began to walk his skis forward, his nose high in the air. Instinctively he followed the smell. In the chill air, the scent seemed to visibly hang in the air, twisting its way across the landscape. It was brighter than a lamp, always almost in reach, but still far away.

It gave Mann a new sense of purpose. He once more lost track of time as he followed the twisting tracks of the smell.

Nothing else changed, not for a long, long time until unexpectedly, 'something' began to take shape in front of him.

Still only able to see what was visible in the narrow beam of his light, nevertheless he could 'sense' a weight in front of him, an expanse of 'something.' He could hear other noises now, to accompany the smell he'd been chasing for so long. And then Mann ground to a stop. His mouth hanging open in shock, he looked at the vista in front of him.

The smell he'd first noticed was strong here, the scent of an enticing 'something' mixed with other, headier smells. There was light and sound, and without him even noticing, the snowy expanse slowly ran out. He slid to an ungainly stop. Before him, he could see a huge structure.

Rising so suddenly out of the landscape, Mann's mouth opened in shock. What was this? A forest? Perhaps not. Indeed, as he skied toward the enclosure, hand out before him, he was amazed as a gap opened under his hand. He entered an entirely new world, where there was light and sound. And a distinct lack of snow and wind.

Still with his skis on, Mann moved forward, hampered by the lack of thick snow. His eyes were fastened on what had appeared before him. A building of some sort, its planking brown and black, interlaced with snow, its roof, mainly green, but again, hidden under dirty grey snow, and from the roof, the smell that had driven him here.

'Hello stranger,' the voice was melodic. It came from the building itself. Confused Mann allowed his eyes to travel its length, before forcing a smile to his lips.

'Hello,' he offered to the buxom figure before him. The hood of a cloak covered the face. He could see little but curious eyes and full lips. Glancing behind him, Mann saw he'd entered some sort of enclosure. Even now, the gap he'd come through had disappeared. He didn't take the time to consider whether he should have come inside or not.

'Well, are you coming within?' the figure queried. Mann moved to step forward, forgetting in his eagerness he had skis on his feet and the snow was no longer deep enough for them. In slow motion, Mann felt himself tumble to the ground. His right leg tried to move as though he wore no skis, forcing him to overbalance. His left leg followed with both skis still attached to his feet.

Mann heard a strange sound as he hit the snow-cleared ground, filled with muddy puddles and another new smell for him. When he looked up, the figure on the top step was laughing, a hand over the mouth as though to prevent the sound escaping.

'I'm sorry,' the voice called. 'I can't come and help you, I have the wrong shoes on.' The words seemed to make perfect sense to the person, but to Mann, they merely added to his confusion. Still, he nodded and tried to untangle himself from skis, arms and legs all alone.

It took much longer than he thought it would. Once or twice he was sure he heard an exaggerated sigh. He ignored the noise until he could straighten up, and walk with just his boots, his skis in hand. Moving without the skis felt strange. It took him time to stop sliding his legs forward, and merely move one foot in front of the other, using his knees, instead of his thighs to power the motion.

'I thought you were going to take all day,' drifted down to him. Mann tried to grin around his frustration, but felt the intention come off a bit more leering than he'd have liked when he caught the amused eye of the person again.

'Come on. Let's get you warmed up and see who you are and what you've come to trade.'

Again, the words made sense to the person uttering them, but Mann had no clue what they meant. Unsteadily, Mann stumped up three short wooden steps, the noise of his footsteps too loud for ears grown used to nothing but the swish of skis and the rasp of his breath.

And that was nothing compared to when the figure opened a heavy wooden door and beckoned him within. Firstly, Mann was assaulted by heat so intense sweat beaded his upper lip before he'd even stepped fully inside the room. The smell guiding him here hung heavily in the air. His eyes were drawn to two huge blazing fires at the centre of the room. Smoke glided through the roof, making sense of what he'd seen from outside.

Again, a small huff of annoyance sounded. Mann realised he was standing in the open doorway, preventing it from shutting. Stumbling to get out of the way, he once more lost his balance, tripping over his new, shorter feet, bereft of skis, landing heavily on the closing door at his back. It sealed itself with a great screech and five pairs of dull eyes turned his way.

Mann struggled upright, looking down at his feet as opposed to at the mild curiosity on the faces of those who confronted him. Instinctively, Mann thought coming inside had perhaps not been the wisest of ideas.

'Welcome stranger,' a deeper voice called. He faced a tall man, his visage sheeted in so much facial hair, only a small nose and tiny brown eyes peeked through the mane covering it.

'It's not really the season for travelling, but you're welcome all the same. Come, take a seat by the fires, warm yourself. We'll sort out some hot food for you.' The man, an appraising look in his small, beady eyes, walked behind Mann, his hands going to Mann's shoulders. It was with alarm Mann realised he was trying to take his cloak from his back. *Should he let him,* Mann panicked, before quickly understanding no one else in the room wore a cloak. He was sweating profusely.

Awkwardly, Mann tried to remove his backpack, skis and cloak all at the same time. Once more, he failed to complete any of the tasks easily, tangling his arms with all of his equipment. Mann felt his face flush with heat and embarrassment.

'Take your time, fella,' the man said to him, the faint trace of interest starting to merge with annoyance in his voice. 'There's plenty of time,' the man offered, 'it's not as though the world's about to end.'

'Apologies,' Mann spoke. He hadn't known if the words would come when he opened his mouth to voice them. He was pleased he knew how to communicate with the stranger.

'Brrr,' the innkeeper said, hefting the bulk of Mann's cloak in both hands. The innkeeper spoke to cover his surprise at its great weight as it dragged both of his arms low. 'You carry the chill of a long trip about you. Quick, warm yourself, as I said.' Again, the innkeeper pointed Mann toward the fire.

Free from his cloak, backpack and skis, Mann felt suddenly lighter, and taking his time, walked carefully to where another had made room for him by one of the blazing hearths. Mann wasn't blind to the curiosity he saw in everyone's eyes, and certainly not to the hopeful edge in the innkeeper's voice. He chose to ignore it all. For now. Mann needed his own questions answering before he was prepared to answer anyone else's.

'My thanks,' Mann muttered to the other members of the small group as they shuffled and resettled themselves, hugging the welcome warmth from the twin fireplaces. Mann strove not to look too fascinated in anything while at the same time trying to determine exactly what was going on here, and how it all worked.

While the party around the fire made up the vast majority of people inside the long wooden room, there were other tables with patrons sitting around them. They all drank from wooden tankards, filled with the scent of something that made Mann lick his lips with anticipation, but he wasn't stupid.

Mann also understood the piles of shining objects next to tankards and wooden bowls, containing food from the cauldron bubbling over the second fire, were part of an agreement. It clearly existed between the men and women who chose to drink and eat here, and the man who'd taken his cloak, checking its weight for any sign of wealth.

Mann's stomach rumbled loudly. The man next to him looked at him in sympathy.

'It's a hard path to travel at this time of the season,' offering what he thought was a genuine smile on his lips. But Mann knew better. This was just another attempt to extract information from him.

'Aye, it is,' was his terse reply. But the man, his brown eyes merging into his brown eyebrows, long shaggy fringe and deep overflowing moustache, hadn't finished yet.

'I arrived a few days ago. But the storm hasn't let up since then. How did you make it through?'

Still considering how to procure some form of exchange for the food and drink he so desperately wanted to consume, Mann simply waved his head and his hands, shrugging his shoulders.

'Luck,' was all he offered. The innkeeper had returned to him, an expectant look on his face. Mann still had nothing to offer in trade for his warming arse and to ease his rumbling stomach.

'Good sir,' the innkeeper smirked expectantly, as Mann simply glared in return. Whatever response the innkeeper had been expecting, it wasn't that. He hovered, for a moment too long before walking away again without a backward glance.

Mann turned to the others in the room. In one corner a group of no more than four were playing some sort of game and proudly displaying their wealth before them. Small piles of dull metal sat, puddled in leaking fluid from their wooden tankards.

Mann licked his lips. He knew what he needed to do.

'I would like some coins to pay for a meal, a drink and

some other necessities?' He thought the words, rather than spoke them out loud, and hoped it would have the same effect. His growling stomach was attracting the attention of more and more people, as was his failure to order or offer the innkeeper coin in exchange for his thawing frame.

Mann winced as he heard the telltale noise of his request being carried out. He opened his eyes wide as one of the men at the gaming table yelled angrily. This was a little different from the usual screech. Yet Mann felt the weight of coins settle, quite comfortably, in the palm of his open hand, held out of sight below his right leg. He was congratulating himself on finally accomplishing something easily with only a few words, when he felt a thick, meaty hand on his shoulder.

'Thief,' the word was spat into his surprised face by the man from the gambling table. Mann had no time to even consider what the word meant before he felt his body being roughed up as the man grabbed him and forced him to his feet.

Instantly the innkeeper appeared, concern and worry on his face.

'Really Robert, how can he be a thief? The man's not moved an inch since he arrived. You need to keep better track of your own coins.'

The innkeeper had, or so Mann thought, bravely stepped between the quivering wreck of outrage and him. Even now, he was attempting to shove the man back toward his companions. The three other card players were jeering and calling to his accuser, none of the words particularly pleasant. Mann winced once more in sympathy, hefting the welcoming weight in his hand.

Were they the other man's coins? Is that where everything he'd so far asked for had come from? Was he little more than a? What was the word the man had used, thief?

Mann could feel his heart beating a little too fast. He knew a brief moment of fear. It was different from the way he'd felt when he'd first realised the nature of the predicament out on the snow. Out there, he'd been alone. Here, Mann was surrounded by people, who even now were giving him strange looks. The innkeeper moved Robert aside, and returned him to his table. Robert was quaking with outrage, his eyes never far from Mann's face. In a swift movement, he was reinstalled on his chair, with a newly filled tankard, and the innkeeper was patting him on the shoulder and whispering in his ear.

Mann allowed himself to relax, and palm the small pile of coins into his pocket. He couldn't use them here. Not now. He'd have to hide them or find a way of returning them to the man he seemed to have unintentionally stolen them from.

Yet, he still needed coins. The realisation he might be stealing from another was unsettling, but he had no choice.

'I would like some coins to pay for a meal, a drink and some other necessities, and can they not come from inside this room, and can they appear in my left pocket?' Mann hastily amended in his mind, hoping this time he'd get what he needed. Already the innkeeper was turning back toward him, Robert placated and seemingly calm, his attention having finally returned to whatever game his friends were encouraging him to play.

Once more Mann heard the strange noise, a half screech of outrage and then the heavy and satisfying feel of more coins in his left pocket. Mann slipped his hand inside, hoping to decipher what they were before the innkeeper appeared, but he was too slow. The man was before him before he could examine his treasure.

'Good sir,' the man was trembling with an apology. 'I'm afraid Robert is a regular customer, although he often loses track of his own winnings. I can't apologise enough for his behaviour. You're lucky it didn't end with violence, it often does. I hazard a guess he took one look at you and thought better of it.' Apology given, the innkeeper began his 'sell' in earnest.

'Now, what can I get for you today. A meal, ale? Board for the night, or perhaps an introduction to the game of chance, although I wouldn't recommend it at the moment.' The innkeeper's voice had gained in confidence as he continued speaking. It wavered again as he eyed up the gaming table.

'Meal and ale, good sir,' Mann responded, reaching for and hoping the coin he offered was of sufficient value. Too much and he'd arouse suspicion, too little, and he'd be insulted. For some reason, Mann understood this game better than the game of chance the four men were bawdily playing in the corner.

From nowhere four women appeared and now perched on each of the four laps. Neither of the women was what Mann considered attractive, and nor were they young. He swallowed back his revulsion. He doubted the women actually belonged to the men. No doubt, their services had been paid for, just as the innkeeper's were.

The innkeeper was all smiles at the order. He walked away happily, not even glancing at the coin Mann had offered at his request for food as he did so. Mann could only assume the innkeeper was pleased with weight of the coin and happy to accept it in exchange for his services.

Mann tried to settle himself, while at the same time considering what he thought he'd learned. Was he genuinely stealing another man's coin, another man's clothes? Or was it just all a strange coincidence?

The fear he was a thief stirred strange emotions in him. He wasn't sure whether he cared or not.

He'd needed to survive in the snow and the storm. He'd required those things he was given. But did he need coins now? Did he need to keep stealing?

Moodily Mann stared into the fire without truly seeing it and was surprised when a bowl of food materialised before him. He turned, expecting to see the innkeeper, but instead was met by the interested green eyes of the woman who'd first invited him into the inn.

'It's good,' she offered, placing the wooden bowl and a small loaf of bread on the table. 'Eat it before it gets cold.' She turned away from him abruptly, something like recognition on her face, which Mann dismissed as her eyes washed over the four women sat on the laps of the game of chancers. He saw her shoulder droop as she shook her head at them. Maybe she didn't approve of their profession.

Or so he convinced himself. Hungrily, he tore a piece from the bread and dipped it into the bowl. The smell of the cooked food made his stomach growl ever more loudly, and he was keen to sate it. Sliding the bread into his mouth, he grumbled his appreciation as he watched the woman saunter away.

Mann wondered what her name was, as he continued to tear bread, dipping it in his stew and wolfing it down. Only as he neared the bottom of the bowl did he use his fingers to pick up the succulent pieces of meat. As Mann bit into the first piece, juices rolled down his chin. He moved his hand quickly to catch them before they dribbled down his front.

With delight, Mann leaned back in his chair, chewing as he did so, and finally looking around the room once more. He'd been too engrossed in his feeding frenzy to pay any attention to anyone else. Now he watched the gamers with narrowed eyes. The movements of the three men who'd not accosted him were furtive. He watched in surprise as the pile of coins before the fourth stealthily grew higher and higher, even though their game didn't proceed at such a pace.

Ah, Mann thought, he hadn't stolen the man's coins. No, his fellow chancers had stolen from him and were now trying to make good on their discovered theft. Mann considered whether they did this every time they played. Certainly, the fourth player seemed to have had so much to drink his eyes were splayed all over the place. The woman on his lap had to keep shifting her weight on him just to keep him awake.

Mann held a smile in place. She seemed content. She had good right to be. He doubted her workload would be more than ensuring Robert made it to his bed and stayed there all night. Not so for the other three women. The men they sat astride were groping and fondling them with evident delight. No doubt they'd enjoy themselves throughout the evening, the men that was, not the women.

Mann felt a tightening at his waist and looked down in surprise. He could see his cock straining against the material of his trousers. The knowledge shocked him. He'd thought he pitied the men and the women, but now he considered making eye contact with the woman who'd be sleeping alone that night. He was sure he could keep her warm if the other couldn't.

More amused than angry with himself, he turned away from his musing to meet the eyes of the woman he'd first met outside. She seemed able to read his mind, and turned away from him, angrily, his empty bowl in her hands, for all they shook with rage.

Mann tried to meet her eyes, but she was gone too quickly, and instead, he concentrated on convincing his manhood to be less obvious.

It was the innkeeper who brought him his next plate of food.

'She's a feisty bitch,' the innkeeper grunted under his breath, sliding the large piece of well-charred meat before him. 'She tried to serve you the blackened end, but I said a man who paid so well needed the best part of the reindeer. She screamed at me, but you got it all the same.'

Mann turned to meet the innkeeper's gaze, and he offered a shrug of apology.

'Be careful, my friend,' the innkeeper offered in his imitation of a whisper. 'She'll find subtle ways of punishing you for your interest in the whores. She's no respect for them. None at all, even though they're the reason most men come here. Oh, and the fact that we're the only inn in Slutet, the most northerly settlement of them all. There's nothing beyond Slutet but the glacier.' The innkeeper's voice was lined with irony at his comment.

'My thanks for your warning,' Mann replied. 'I think a bed for the night would be appreciated,' he continued. The innkeeper nodded as though expecting the words.

'I'll ensure there's a room ready for you, but I'll not give you the key yet. She'll find out otherwise and reward you in some way. Better to ask me just before you retire. She'll not want to soil all the rooms just to piss you off. Otherwise, she'll be left with putting them back to rights, and I'll have surly patrons all damn night complaining.'

The innkeeper meandered away, his hands absentmindedly reaching for empty tankards as he went. He took orders from those who still wanted to drink, as Mann turned his attention back to his meal, and away from the gamers and their whores. Mann considered moving position so they no longer entered his eye line, but his arse was warm by the fire. In all honesty, he owed the green-eyed woman nothing. So what if she disapproved of his interest? He couldn't help his body's requirements.

The meat he chewed was well cooked and well spiced. He tried not to think about the fact it was the green-eyed woman who'd prepared his meal. If she produced food this well, it was clear why the innkeeper put up with her tetchy behaviour regarding the whores.

Mann's eyes, keen to find something else to fasten on other than the women, scanned the room, coasting over other people eating, drinking or just staring morosely into the twin burning fires. Then he met a pair of eyes as curious about him as he was about them.

The eyes were shadowed, barely visible under a layer of straggly hair, but all the same, he could tell he was being watched. The intent behind the gaze appeared benign, but he had no way of knowing if that was wishful thinking on his part or the truth.

Intrigued Mann met and held the gaze, and so did the other person. It was an uncomfortable moment. He felt, in that look, that the shadowed eyes learned much more about him than he did about them. It unsettled him.

Turning away from the inquisitive gaze, Mann glared into the fire. His meal was forgotten about before him. His previously empty stomach was filled to capacity. Mann finally turned his thoughts to where and when he was, and more importantly, where he'd come from.

Mann sincerely doubted any of the other occupants of the inn had just manifested, naked, in the middle of nowhere. He suspected none of them were as lacking in information as to who they were, as he was.

He considered himself. He apparently had some basic skills, besides his ability to 'steal' or gain what he needed just by asking for it. He could speak, understand the other people in the room, and go along with some of their customs. He understood the requirement to eat, drink, piss, probably take his pleasure, and that coins would open previously closed doors to him. But anything else? He had no idea. Where had he come from? And why the hell had he been abandoned, naked, in the middle of a freezing landscape?

Had he been supposed to die there? Was it some sort of punishment? That no one here recognised him, allowed some confidence that at least they didn't know who he was. Provided he could get by without making too much of a spectacle of himself, he might be able to find some answers. But how?

For now, he needed to blend in. Mann shook his head in frustration, as he did so meeting those curious eyes again. Immediately, he glanced away, back toward the gamers and the whores. He felt his arousal once more as he noticed the man who'd accused him of theft was all but somnolent. His whore was looking around the room with interest for her next client. Could it be him?

He thought of the green-eyed woman, whose name he'd yet to learn. He felt his passion flare. He looked for her, his head turning a slow arc of the room, but before he could find her, the weight of another settled on his lap. Eager fingers brushed across his manhood, causing him to shiver with excitement.

She smelt of ale and the stale indoors. For a moment, her musk was too powerful for him to contemplate pursuing the matter. Then her warm breath snaked down his neck, and he shivered with delight once more.

Whatever had happened to him, it had brought him here. It was clear he had desires and wants that needed to be resolved.

Mann allowed her to sit on him, and then spread herself over him in much the same way she'd mounted the gamer who'd been the victim of his friend's jokes. Then he caught the eye of the innkeeper. The man looked neither pleased nor displeased but dangled a key for him to see.

Mann jumped to his feet, the woman sliding from his lap in surprise at the sudden movement. Then she laughed, a soft throaty noise that further excited him, as she tracked his movements.

'Been a while, has it?' she purred. He led her to the innkeeper. The innkeeper whispered something to the woman, his eyes never leaving Mann's face. She guided him away, toward the back of the large room, and then up a short flight of stairs. All the time she swayed close to him so he could see her partly exposed cleavage clearly. With each tilt of her ample hips, she brushed against his increasing desire.

Mann knew by the time they made it to wherever they were going, he'd barely be able to contain himself. Her hands slipped lower, inside his trouser pocket, and she once more growled with pleasure, mock or genuine he had no way of knowing, until she pulled one of his purloined coins from within and gave it a quick bite. The quick movement revealed to him the coin was silver, and not the bronze he'd seen on the gaming table.

'My, my,' she whispered, her face close to his again, leading him down a small corridor lined with a selection of closed and open doorways. So intent on following her, Mann barely glanced through the open doors other than to see they all contained a reasonably large bed, heaped high with furs. Some of the rooms had small fires or braziers in them, but most were dark, without even the light from a candle to reveal the shadowy recesses.

When his woman pulled up short before one of the closed doors, Mann took advantage of her distraction with the key to snake his arms around her and finally take hold of her plentiful breasts. Now it was his turn to groan with delight, as she circled her hips. His breath was becoming too rapid as he caressed her neck beneath her mop of greying hair, while she fumbled with the lock.

For a split moment he thought he was having the same effect on her as she was on him, but then she turned toward him, her face showing neither the flush of passion he felt nor the breathlessness he was fighting.

'Calm down, big man,' she exhaled into his face, but her hands on his belt buckle were making that just about impossible. 'You don't want to spend it all in one go now, do you.'

Her words sobered him more than a bucket of cold water. He felt his passion die away just as quickly as it had appeared.

For a long moment, Mann considered what he was doing. He had no feeling as to whether it was right or wrong, after all, the woman would be well paid for her time and efforts, but his mind returned to the green-eyed woman. He'd much rather take her to his bed, but right now, he didn't have the time or the inclination to make the correct advances.

Mann had urges, and he was going to sate them, as soon as possible.

'Come on, woman,' Mann grumbled and the door opened before them. He allowed her to lead him inside. His excitement had returned, if not his need to rush. Now he was curious to see whether she had any skill or not. And whether he did.

Walking freely into the room, he took the time to examine the bed for any surprises from the green-eyed woman. The innkeeper might not have been able to keep his room number a secret from her. He found nothing. As Mann turned around, he was presented with the naked body of the woman who'd been driving him to distraction with her gyrating and her presence. He reached for her. She came, half-eagerly.

————

'My, my,' she whispered once he'd taken his pleasure. Mann grinned. They'd barely spoken to each other, despite their intimate knowledge of each other's body. It didn't seem to bother her or him. 'Well, I'm glad old Robert didn't want me tonight. This has been much more … enjoyable.' She enticed him to begin once more, and he grinned. Why on earth not!

And so the night continued, with neither seeming to tire or grow bored of the endless movement. Only the low burning of the candle gave any indication of how long they'd been entangled with each other. Only when darkness lit the room, did Mann appreciate that not only had the candle gone out, so too had the low burning brazier attempting to warm the room.

The woman he bedded refused to let him leave her side, and so they carried on, creating their own heat, and working from prior experience of how to bring each to climax. He giggled, and she laughed, a low sound that throbbed in her throat and made him harden all over again.

And then a knock at the door tore at his attention. Ignoring the persistent knocking, Mann continued, moaning and rocking, the woman's upper body pink from her exertions. Even when the door flung open, he gave it no thought.

The sheets and blankets that had initially covered the bed had long been discarded, lying on the floor in a tangled mess. This meant the green-eyed woman, fury on her face, saw everything as she stamped inside the room.

Mann met her angry gaze, but nothing could stop him. He was compelled to complete his coupling. So he drove on, uncaring that she watched, taking in every movement.

Neither did he notice when others joined her at the open door. Only as he finished, for what must have been the twentieth time, did he even think to look back. What he saw on her face surprised him.

A desire, a need, a want was evident on her face. She was flushed, her green-eyes hectic. He could detect longing. She too licked her lips, unabashed now at being discovered watching. Behind her, he saw the three other whores.

They all wore envious gazes, as the men they'd spent the evening with watched on with evident interest, for all that they were too damned drunk to stand properly, let alone maintain the sort of attention they'd need to accomplish what he had.

Into the sudden silence, broken only by his panting and that of the fourth whore, he heard a low whistle of appreciation from the innkeeper, a slightly frantic look on his face and a bulge in his own trousers.

'I never knew you made that sort of noise?' the innkeeper offered, with a half-embarrassed shrug. The woman beneath him grinned before panting. 'Get away with you,' to her three sisters in fake passion. 'He's paid for the night, and I mean to give him the damn night. You'll have to negotiate with him later on, when I'm done with him.'

The younger of the women, or so she looked, dark hair cascading down her back, grinned.

'You bet I'm next on his list. You can't keep all that to yourself,' she taunted, steering her client from the room by his belt.

'It's me you want next, fine man. Me,' she called, a delicate smile on her reasonably pretty face. The man she was with looked outraged. All heard their conversation as they made their way to their own room.

'You better hurry up, you brute. There's a real man for me there,' she said, a wooden door slamming shut on an outraged denial.

'Is there a reason you're all still here,' his woman asked.

'I think it was just the noise,' the innkeeper muttered, his eyes roaming over the fourth whore's body as though for the first time ever. He looked quizzical as he tugged at his own trousers.

'We'll try and keep it down,' the woman muttered. 'Now, if you don't mind,' she said, but one of her whore friends was shaking her head.

'Can't we watch,' she asked, her hands caressing her own breasts as she spoke, but his woman shook her head.

'See to your own man. It won't take you long. Look.' She pointed her head toward the others evident desire, a cackle on her lips.

'I told you, you wanted me,' she teased the man, her breasts starting to sway in time to her gentle rocking. The man swallowed heavily, perhaps embarrassed at being caught in such a position, taking the hand of the whore who wanted to watch, and leading her away. Again, as Mann felt his face flush with passion, he heard a conversation ending with a shut wooden door.

Now the innkeeper remained, with the green-eyed woman, one of the whores and her man. And still, Mann and his own woman pleasured each other, as though they were alone.

'Ah, um, I think we should leave,' the innkeeper suggested softly, desire in his voice, as he reached for the hand of the green-eyed woman, only to have it snatched away. Ah, thought Mann, the two were a couple. He supposed that made sense.

Still, Mann met her green eyes. She was furious, and filled with desire. At that moment, despite the enticements going on to his lower body by the skilled woman he rode, he'd happily have left her, and begun the process all over again, if only to fill those jade eyes with the same surprise when she reached her pleasure.

She gazed at him, watching his face, not his body sway forward and backwards and then she stamped from the room, pushing past the other couple as she went. The other whore, clearly thinking to watch as her compatriot had wanted to, had turned her own man toward her and was working hard to elicit a response from his limp body. She twisted and turned, rubbed and cajoled, and then turned her back on him as she continued to watch Mann and his woman. Her mouth was open, her lips flushed bright, but her eyes gave away her absolute desire.

Mann smiled at her, a promise on his face, but his woman shooed her hand at the three remaining individuals and claimed Mann's full attention.

Only later did Mann realise that in those instants someone had replaced the candle and also rebuilt the brazier, for he and his woman had not moved from their bed. In fact, he'd barely moved from inside her. His entire body fizzled with the passion of their constant coupling. He could have gone on all night, but eventually, she sighed, and rolled away from him, unhappiness on her face.

'I need to sleep,' she growled. 'Just let me sleep, and then we'll carry on in the morning. Don't leave, just stay where you are,' she said sleepily, rolling herself within a white fur. Mann watched her, the candlelight making shadows of her face and he thought her almost pretty until deep rasping snores burst from her chest. And then he did feel his ardour dampen, but only for a moment.

He tried to lie on his back, to sleep as she did, but in his mind, he could see the appraising eyes of the three women, and also the green-eyed woman, and his passion stirred once more.

'Why not,' he thought to himself. Reaching for his tunic, but nothing else, he stepped from the bed, and padded softly to the wooden door. It opened with a slight squeak. He stared at the bed, hoping he hadn't woken her, and then felt a warm hand on his arm, as he was pulled through the doorway.

The first of the whores to speak was there. She was naked, and in the dim light from the candle she held, he could see she had less weight to her frame and her breasts were tighter. He grinned at her. She met his grin with delight in her own eyes.

'If you're as good as you look, I might have to pay you,' she joked, stepping close to his body so he could feel the slight chill of her skin against his warmer body. She giggled, excited by the feel of him against her, and then she pulled his head down to her full lips and kissed him.

She kissed differently to the other woman, her mouth fully open all of the time so Mann breathed her in. Desire exploded and he rumbled low in his chest, as she jumped against him, encircling her legs around his back so he slipped inside with no effort at all.

He stood firmly, his body acting outside of his control, as he fondled and caressed and she rubbed her hands up and down his back. She gasped and moaned, and neither cared that they stood, butt naked, in the middle of the hall of the inn, or that the other woman slept on inside the closed door.

The gasps of the younger whore became louder, more frantic, and with a shudder, it was all over.

'Come on take me to my room,' she whispered into his ear, when she could breathe against the explosion of her delight. She turned her head to guide him.

'Isn't that man in there?' Mann thought to ask, but she shook her head.

'No, he's in his own room. I have my own. Come on, hurry. I want to do that again.' She bit his ear as she talked. Already he knew he was ready for yet more.

'My, my, you really are as good as you look,' she whimpered, frantic red staining her neck and her breasts, as Mann considered their next position. He'd enjoyed the first whore, but this one, well, she seemed to offer him all sorts of new experiments to try, and he was keen to try. Everything.

Only an outraged screech and the simultaneous banging of the door distracted him. He looked into the wrathful face of the first woman. He offered what he hoped was a smile of welcome, but she didn't even glance at him.

'You filthy bitch,' she hollered, grabbing for, and catching the long hair of the woman Mann was currently enjoying. 'He's still mine,' she screamed, yanking on the hair. Mann's new woman went flying, long legs all over the place as she fought for balance.

He stood abruptly, looking into the incoherent faces of two women denied their treats.

'I'm sure we can sort this out,' Mann tried to mollify, but the women were beside themselves with thwarted passion. The first women, the one with the larger breasts, reached for him, keen to grab him and take him back to his room. But the second was quicker. Before he could do anything, he felt a soft mouth over his ripening passion and saw bright eyes shining up at him.

The first woman screamed again, pulling the other woman's hair so the second released her grip on him, and then, Mann seemingly forgotten about, for all he was ready for one of them, preceded to tussle, naked on the floor. Mann watched with amusement, his pleasure building at the sight, only for another to appear in the doorway. He'd thought it might be the innkeeper, but instead, he met the eyes of another of the whores.

'Leave the bitches to it,' she offered, a nightgown sliding over one shoulder. 'My bed's warm and empty this evening.' Mann looked between the squabbling duo and the other women and wisely shook his head.

'Perhaps enough for one night,' he offered, an abashed smile on his face, and he walked past all three women and returned to the dishevelled room the innkeeper had provided for him. Still naked, he drank deeply from a jug of cold water, and then washed quickly with a cloth and a small bowl of water left on top of the brazier for just such a purpose.

Feeling refreshed, he tugged his trousers back on. It would, he considered, be best if he was found next in the main room of the inn, hopefully, surrounded by others, so the warring three-some might leave him alone.

A pity, Mann shrugged, gazing back at the ruffled sheets from the bed lying on the floor. He'd rather been enjoying himself. He had the sense, he might often enjoy himself in such a way. Perhaps, then, that was why he'd been abandoned, naked, in the middle of a bloody blizzard.

FIVE

Chapter 5

SURPRISINGLY, Mann wasn't alone in the main hall of the inn. As he descended the stairs, the green eyes of the woman who'd first welcomed him to the inn watched his every-step.

'Are they fighting?' she asked, nodding toward the source of the noise.

'Unfortunately,' Mann confirmed. She nodded, as though reassured, as she wiped clean mugs behind the bar.

'Did you just come here to cause bloody trouble?' she asked, laughing as she spoke. He wondered if she'd intentionally made a pun. 'I didn't know the reputations of the innkeeper's whores reached outside Slutet.'

'Slutet? Is that the name of this settlement?' Mann asked, a smile on own face at the knowledge. Now, he remembered the innkeeper had also told him the same.

'Yes and so the answer to my question is clearly not. You didn't know where you were?' she queried, concern knotting her eyebrows. It made her jade eyes shine even brighter in the light from the two fireplaces and the line of candles she'd lit on the front of the bar.

'I got lost,' Mann quickly offered, cursing for speaking without thinking.

'So you got lost, and didn't come for the whores?' she qualified, eyes flashing with fury. 'What did you come for?' she taunted.

'To find myself,' Mann tried, shrugging his shoulders. He watched her work behind the long running wooden bar.

The passion was slowly draining from his body, making him feel sluggish and sleepy. Yet there was something about this woman making him wish he'd not been caught with his cock in not one, but two other women.

'What sort of shit answer is that?' she goaded, filling a mug with something from a jug and handing it to him. He sniffed it suspiciously and gulped the clear water down. It was sharp and clean.

'From the ice,' she offered when he raised his eyes in appreciation. 'It always tastes the best from the glacier.'

Ah, Mann thought to himself, had he come here from the glacier? Was the glacier the source of the settlement's wealth and attraction?

'My thanks,' Mann offered, wincing at the screams and thunks still coming from upstairs. The green-eyed woman looked up, as though she could see through the wooden floorboards and shook her head.

'Daft women,' she muttered. 'The others will be loving this. Up and out of their bed twice in one night. More excitement than they've had for the last decade.'

She spoke angrily, her actions short and sharp. Mann reached over and stayed her hand. Or rather, he would have done, but she shook him from her, a wrinkled nose showing displeasure at his familiarity.

'I don't know where you've been,' she grumbled, stepping back.

Mann didn't offer, 'neither do I', but he thought it all the same.

'I didn't come for the whores,' Mann tried to mollify. She shook her head, and looked up once more. Around the top of the stairs, Mann could see flashes of bare skin, and flickers of clothing.

'He'll be bad-tempered tomorrow,' she muttered. Mann knew she meant the innkeeper.

'Your husband?' he asked, and she nodded, unhappily.

'Yes, an old man for me. A randy one as well. He likes his whores, that's why they're here.'

'Must be difficult for you.' Mann said, but she shook her head.

'Keeps him away from me. He's not very skilled, and it's over quickly. I'd rather not.' She spoke sadly. He nodded once more as though he understood what she was saying, although he didn't.

'I can't have children,' she turned to him, fury on her face, daring him to say anything. He swallowed abruptly, and then choked, having to cough heavily before he could speak again.

'Children?' was all he managed. She nodded sharply.

'Yes, you know, little people, born when people have sex, if they're lucky. The woman... oh it doesn't matter,' she ended. He understood what she meant. It seemed he'd known all along but hadn't appreciated what she was telling him.

'As such, I'd just rather not,' she said. He groaned once more, a faint worry playing through his head. He'd just had a lot of sex, with two different women whose names he didn't even know. He hoped he hadn't just created any children of his own.

'There'll be no one to leave this place to,' she said, indicating the inn with a shrug of his shoulders.

'There's time yet,' Mann tried to console. She swished him

with her length of cloth for drying the mugs, as she once more looked up.

'Bloody hell,' she muttered, and Mann turned to follow her gaze.

The innkeeper, wearing only his underclothes, roused as he was from his bed by the squabbling women, was coming down the stairs. He had one hand on each of the women, as he tried to keep them apart. With each step, he raised his legs high to cover the part of himself that had popped out of his underclothes in the fight.

Mann laughed softly before his eyes were drawn to the naked women.

The green-eyed woman huffed behind him. She reached for something behind the bar, before striding out and flinging one each at the women, and standing before the innkeeper so he could sort himself out.

Both women wore outraged expressions; hand-marks clear to see on the body of the other, as well as a few bleeding scratches, pulsing in the light from the banked fires.

The first women, her belly overhanging the top of her legs, tried to offer him what he assumed she thought was an enticing smile. But blood dripped from lips he'd happily found another use for earlier. Even the younger woman had lost her allure as half her blonde hair was clutched in the hand of the other.

Mann swallowed down his slight revulsion. He watched the innkeeper, or rather, his green-eyed wife. She'd flung small pieces of cloth at the two whores. They both endeavoured to cover themselves with the skimpy stuff, while the innkeeper kept hold of one of them, and the green-eyed woman the other.

The innkeeper, now contained once more inside his underclothes, offered Mann a wry smirk of apology. He sat between the two women on the seats closest to the twin fireplaces. Mann felt a moment of remorse. Surely this was his fault?

'I'd like an explanation,' the innkeeper asked, not of Mann, but of the two women. Others had been woken by the commotion. Dome trundled down the stairs while low moans of complaint could be heard from those who remained in their beds.

'She, she, stole him, and he was mine, for the night. See, he gave me this?' Somehow, despite it all, the first whore still had his coin in her hand. It flashed briefly into view.

'Well, yes, that does seem to have been ample recompense for the night,' the innkeeper agreed. The other woman was shaking her head.

'I found him, and I asked for no coin, just a little ride,' she giggled. She touched her head gingerly, trying to determine the extent of the damage done to her hair.

'You gave yourself to him for free?' the innkeeper asked, eyebrows high in censure, but she nodded.

'Oh yes, I wanted me some of that,' she spoke with a growl of appreciation for their brief time together. Mann was driven to raise his mug of water to her in gratitude. Their coupling had been too brief. He wished he'd had her first.

'You never give yourself to me for free,' the innkeeper growled. The woman leered toward him, her tight breasts on his arm.

'But I do give myself to you,' she cautioned, her voice husky, as the green-eyed woman rolled her eyes at her obvious ploy.

'Well yes, I suppose you do. I suppose that if there was no coin exchanged, then no harm was done,' the innkeeper smiled, just about stopping himself from reaching out to stroke her breast as the other woman grumbled unhappily.

'He was mine,' she tried once more.

'But he left,' the other jibbed. The innkeeper, eyeing the two almost naked women, nodded his head.

'It's done, enough. Off to your rooms. We'll speak no more

of this. Go on.' As the younger woman stood, he squeezed her bottom. She winked at him, an invitation in her eyes, that was quickly understood.

Mann watched, unsurprised as the innkeeper followed her up the stairs, the older woman forgotten about. The jade-eyed woman watched the innkeeper go, her eyes free from jealousy and filled with detachment, as she escorted the older woman away.

Mann turned back to the bar. An eventful evening all round.

He thought about returning to his room then but quickly reconsidered. Finally, he felt sated, and also not very tired. But he was curious. Where had his need and desire come from? He rested on the side of the bar, pulling a stool beneath him, considering his activities of the night, and on what had happened before that.

Where had he come from? Why did he have a pocketful of coins he'd done nothing to earn? And why was he such a randy bastard?

'Well that's sorted then,' the green-eyed woman said matter-of-factly when she returned. Her face, for the first time, was surprisingly free of judgment, both at the whores and at him. 'A drink?' she queried, as though nothing had happened, and he nodded.

'That would be nice,' Mann agreed, watching her as she pulled a jug from the shelf behind her, and placed two fresh mugs on the bar. She removed a stopper from the pitcher. A fragrant aroma filled the space between them. He sniffed and smiled.

'From the South,' she offered. 'It smells of the heat and the sun.'

Mann nodded, as though understanding what that was. He reached for his mug. But a warm hand on his own stopped him. Her gaze was sharper now.

'It's expensive. You should appreciate it as opposed to just guzzle it down.'

He nodded, his eyebrows high in surprise at her words, they sounded censorious.

She reached out for her mug, having released his hands. She closed her eyes to smell the fragrance of spice and heat. Only then did she take the smallest of sips, and as she did, her body juddered.

'You try,' she said. Mann did, mirroring her actions.

The act of actually swallowing the mixture set off all sorts of strange sensations in his mouth, down his throat, in his belly, and this surprised him, in his lower body. He stumbled and reached for a wooden stool to fall onto. But she was behind him, her expression far from amused.

'It deadens the desire,' she mumbled, something like embarrassment on her face. 'Well, it does in those who have too much of it. In others, well in others, it brings it on.' A rare smile touched her face, as he rested his suddenly too heavy head on his hands, watching her.

This was much more than just a friendly drink.

'You use this a lot?' Mann slurred. She smiled, really smiled, her teeth shining whitely in the candlelight.

'I use it on my husband a lot. He thinks it's just a nice drink.'

'Ah,' Mann slurred once more.

'The whores as well,' she added, a sharp look on her face, quickly replacing her genuine smile. 'In fact, everyone. I just wish the stuff was a little less expensive,' he watched her, horrified by what she was saying. But then she smirked again, coming to stand beside him, suggestively close. He groaned as his eyes strayed down the front of her blouse.

'I see that look in your eyes,' she grumbled, reaching for his cock, and grabbing it tightly, pinching it so his eyes started to tear from the pain as well as from the sharp drink.

'You should know. I'm no bitch to be mounted, like the other whores. My husband knows that. I've made sure of it. And while you're here, you'll remember it as well. Now finish your drink and get back to your bloody room and sleep. When you wake, you'll be deemed a man in my eyes, as opposed to a bastard.'

Mann growled, low in his throat, but reached for the mug and swallowed it all down, despite his wishes to the contrary.

'Off you go,' she shooed with her hands, pure anger on her face. Still he followed her instructions without so much as an argument. He couldn't even wonder about what she'd done to him or why she seemed to hate him quite as much as she did.

SIX

Chapter 6

MANN WOKE WITH A THUMPING HEADACHE, and a growl of outrage, as the shutters in his rooms were roughly thrown open, allowing a weak light to flood the room.

He grumbled, his hand over his eyes, but there was no way getting away from it. The jade-eyed woman looked at him unflinchingly.

'Feeling better?' she asked, wrinkling her nose at the feisty smell of sex hanging in the room. She bending over to pull back his sheets and examine his manhood as though it belonged to her.

'You certainly look better,' she quipped, her sharp eyes missing nothing as they wracked over his naked body, taking in the bite and cut marks as she went.

'They'll heal. Now, do you have the means to pay for another night or are you leaving us today?'

Mann rubbed his head, while his eyes adjusted to the faint light. He gazed at the woman he'd found enticing the day before. She looked sharp and haunted in the natural light, but still, he couldn't deny his stir of desire for her.

'Another day, if you'd be so kind,' he spoke, licking his dry lips as he sat upright.

'The coin?' she said, standing over him with her hand held out.

Frantically he looked around, unsure where his clothing had been left. Disdainfully, she bent and handed him his trousers, and he rifled through the pockets, almost gratefully. He allowed the sheet to fall away from him as he did so, after all, she'd seen all he had already. He watched with amusement as her breathing quickened at his evident interest. So, she wasn't all deadened, he thought wryly, pleased when his fingers closed over the same amount of coins he'd handed out the day before.

Mann placed them in her hands, feeling the dampness of her desire there, and she snatched them away from him.

'Another day, nothing more,' she barked, as though reminding her, not him. 'Make your plans today. Tomorrow you'll be leaving.'

With that, she turned and left. Despite what she said, he couldn't help admiring her swaying backside.

When he was dressed, Mann made his way back downstairs. He thought it quite early, for there were few about, only the innkeeper and his green-eyed wife, and they weren't speaking to each other. Instead, they moved around one another in silence, the only smiles for Mann. He smirked. She was a hard-woman, it was clear to see. But maybe she needed to be with a husband whose eyes constantly strayed to the more welcoming embrace of his four whores. It was no life for a good woman, or so Mann thought.

Once he'd eaten, and still spoken to no one, he made his way toward the entrance he'd used the night before. He fully expected some sort of snide remark from the green-eyed woman, surprised when one wasn't forthcoming.

Mann stumbled into his purloined cloak and opened the

door. It creaked loudly at his touch. He winced, but still, no one spoke to ask him his business.

Watery sunlight filtered through low hanging grey clouds. He breathed deeply of the dampness and the clean scent of the snow, and stumbled down the three steps onto the cleared walkway.

Slutet was a tiny place. He could tell from the small number of shop-fronts flung open, despite the cold, and the handful of people walking up and down those shop-fronts. Pulling his cloak tighter, he walked first one way, and then the other, eyes keen but unsure what they searched for.

Shop-fronts offered goods he didn't want: mugs and pots, baked loaves of bread and spices, warm clothes and boots. He shrugged. He didn't need any of these things. He turned, the weak sun illuminating the gateway he must have staggered through in the dark the night before. It was built of wood so dark as to be almost black and reflected wetly.

As Mann approached the gateway, curiosity finally finding something to interest him, he was stopped by two gate wardens, lightly armoured, but with murder in their eyes.

'Who the hell are you?' the older called, a thickset man with a full beard and moustache. Little could be seen of him but his small, black eyes, hooded by bushy eyebrows.

'Mann,' he retorted, surprised to be asked.

'Who let you in?' the younger said, a skinny lad who was evidently his son, or nephew, but definitely related in some way.

'I... I don't know. It was bloody dark, the gate was open.'

'The gates are never open unless we open them,' the older man said, a furrow between his eyebrows.

'Well I didn't just bloody materialise, did I?' Mann said, a smirk at the truth of what he'd said.

'Well, now, I suppose not. Did you shut the bloody gate last night?' the older man asked the younger. The youth nodded vigorously.

'Of course I did. You watched me do it. And it was shut this morning. It's always bloody shut. No one comes to the arse-end of beyond unless they're mad,' the youth continued. Mann was inclined to agree. There was nothing in Slutet, apart from an inn, with four whores, and a rampant innkeeper.

The gate was above head height, and he could see tantalising glimpses of what lay beyond, provided he stepped far enough back. Mann was hoping to catch sight of his ski prints, to determine where he'd come from.

'Where did you spend the night?' the older guard asked.

'In the inn,' Mann replied, annoyed by the constant questioning.

'Ah, the lovely Onna must have enjoyed you,' the lad said, his eyes shining with admiration. Mann suddenly realised he knew no-one's names.

'Maybe. I'm not very good with names.'

'Oh, she'd have told you if it was her. She's the innkeeper woman. Lucky old git.'

'Then yes, Onna took my money and let me spend the night, and tonight as well.'

'Why did you come to Slutet?' the older man pressed.

'I just wanted to see it,' Mann shrugged. 'Can I go out there?' he asked, indicating what lay beyond.

'What, into the Hvite Lands? There's bugger all there. What do you think you're going to see? There's nothing but white and ice as far as the bloody eye can see, which isn't very far at this time of the year. You're too late for the lights,' he continued, and Mann nodded as though he understood.

'I just fancy seeing, you know, the white expanse,' Mann tried to joke, but still the two seemed far from keen to let him pass.

'Don't want to have to come and find you if you get bloody

lost. Not like the sun will be around for long today. Been black as night forever, but now the millennium has started it should get a bit lighter, for a bit at least.'

Still, Mann nodded, as though he understood what they were talking about, but really he could feel his feet starting to itch. What was it about people in this place telling him what to do?

'Well, how about I just step beyond you, and stay within your line of sight, and then you'll know I'm not getting lost?' Mann spoke to beguile, but stubborn lines were forming on the faces of the two men. He feared he might never step foot outside Slutet again.

'Ah, go on with you then,' the older guard finally relented. 'We see it every damn day. It's lost its appeal, there's no denying it. Arse-hole of beyond, this place. You're lucky you get to leave. I've lived here all my damn life. Too bloody cold, no matter the season, and no one ever comes here, so it's not as though you get to meet too many new people.'

As he rumbled along, the older guard was opening the large wooden gate and it screeched loudly. Then he waved him through with a grand gesture.

'Stay where we can see you,' he cautioned, bowing elaborately, and Mann grinned. He had no intention of getting lost in the Hvite Lands. Mann knew, from his own experiences, just how bleak, lonely and devoid of life the place was.

He breathed deeply once free of the stink of Slutet, allowing his nostrils to fill with the bitingly cold wind blown in from the North. Bollocks, it was damn cold. He shivered and crouched into his cloak, ensuring his mouth and nose were covered against the penetrating cold.

Mann looked at the ground, hoping to see some sign of his passing the night before, but there was nothing, no matter where he looked. He stopped, turned and waved to the two guards. They watched his idle meanderings with all the interest of men who do the same thing each and every day, where nothing ever changes, and even this caused some excitement.

They waved back to him. He grinned behind his cloak.

This was a strange place. Mann only wished he knew why he was there.

He walked out into the expanse of the endless white, ensuring he never lost sight of the stark black wooden walls or the smell of smoke that occasionally caught at his nose, even though the wind was like a sharp whip.

The guards were right. There really was nothing to see. Nothing at all.

Mann sighed. He'd been drawn to the gates, to the thought of escape from inside Slutet and the angry glare of the jade-eyed woman, but what had he really done that was so wrong? He'd paid for his whore, admittedly, he didn't understand where the money had come from, and he'd paid for his bed and his food and drink as well.

Maybe Onna, as he now knew she was called, just didn't appreciate strangers in the inn. A strange thing for an innkeeper's wife, but possible all the same. Or maybe she was jealous. If her husband never satisfied her, perhaps she searched for someone who would.

Bored, and almost as cold as when he'd been naked yesterday, he turned to make his way back toward Slutet. Mann needed to consider what he'd do the next day. How would he leave this place? Onna had made it clear he couldn't stay. He was sure the small settlement would only boast one inn. Would there be a means of travelling south? Longingly he looked in that direction. What would the South hold for him?

The drink Onna had foisted on him might not have had the most pleasant effects on him, but the smells it contained had spoken to him of another world, one where the primary colour wasn't white, or black, and the wind didn't whip and freeze him.

'See everything you wanted to see?' the younger guard quipped when Mann came back into view. The two men had apparently taken it in turns to watch him, and the gate both. The older guard was huddled around a blazing brazier inside a small wooden hut, attached to the gates. It looked comfortable and cosy, apart from the open doorway. Although. Well, Mann noticed it faced into the settlement, not away from it. Even with the door open, it worked well to shield its two residents from the blasting wind.

'Yep. Not much out there, is there?'

'Not much at all. There's a sled from the South once a week in the summer, more like once a month at this time of year, but they bring idle bastards like you to stare at us and wonder why we live here.'

'And why is that?' Mann asked, not at all offended by the bitter tinge to the younger guards voice.

'Who the hell knows,' he muttered, a smirk on his face for the civil question and Mann nodded.

'What do you do, when you're not here?' Mann asked, genuinely curious.

'Spend our nights in the inn, with the whores.'

'Only come payday,' the older laughed. Mann grinned at their knowing stares.

'Oh, and we play games of chance as well, and....' But the older guard nudged the younger as though he spoke about something he shouldn't. Mann smiled and started to walk away. Instinctively he understood the good-natured banter was over.

He waved as he walked away, a thank you as well as a dismissal. Everywhere he looked he saw only small homes, and even smaller businesses, all hemmed in by walls of deepest black wood.

Mann sighed, his adventuring for the day done, and ambled back to the inn. He didn't fancy facing Onna, but the wind was brisk, the scent of snow in the air, and he shivered. It would be better to be inside and whipped by a sharp tongue, than outside by a stringent, snow-filled wind.

Stomping up the three steps, he pushed on the wooden door and heard it screech in outrage, the black wood quivering. A wave of heat assaulted him, as he fought the door. The accusing eyes he'd expected to see were instantly aroused by the noisome arrival.

Forcing the door shut, Mann took the time to compose his face, and then turned toward Onna, shrugging from his cloak as he did so. The warm smile of welcome quickly slid from the face of the green-eyed woman as she realised who was returning. He smiled at her, unable to stop the taunt.

Turning from him, Onna left the bar area, circling toward the stairs. He watched her go, as did the innkeeper. The man beckoned him over. Mann heeded the instruction.

'A feisty woman who knows her own mind,' he said, neither an apology nor an explanation, as Mann accepted a mug of ale, and sipped it, savouring the woody taste. He raised his mug in thanks as the innkeeper, his jowls wobbling from side to side, rubbed the scarred surface clean of muddy looking bubbles.

'Not easy to keep happy,' the innkeeper bemoaned. Mann grunted what he hoped was an acceptable response.

'Still, it's not often a woman like that staggers in off the ice looking for a home and a husband.'

Mann started at the admission, his heartbeat racing. His eyes flickered to the staircase, at the top of which Onna watched him. It was as though she'd expected her husband to speak as he did.

'When, when was this?' Mann gulped, as though the answer was of no importance.

The innkeeper laughed at the memory. 'A while ago, I assure you. I was young and handsome then. A catch, some would say. Not like now.' The innkeeper patted his over-hanging belly in explanation. Mann tried to force a smile through his suddenly tight lips.

'She's a beautiful woman,' Mann stated.

'She is. Certainly, every other man in the settlement thinks so. But the passage of time has been unkind to me. I fear, my body has demands she simply will not meet any more.'

Mann nodded again, as though he understood, but his mind was racing. He glanced back up the stairs, but Onna was gone.

'The sled comes in tomorrow,' the innkeeper continued conversationally, as though he'd not just admitted to his rampant wishes. 'That's why she says you can stay. The sled will come and take you away. I wouldn't miss it if I were you. When she sets her mind to something, she never changes it. Believe me, I know.' The innkeeper spoke ruefully.

Mann nodded once more, pleased to know he could leave Slutet.

'I should be going anyway,' Mann offered, slinking to a seat closer to the flames with his drink and his thoughts. The innkeeper nodded, pleased with accomplishing something, and turned back to his tasks.

Mann watched him work as he let his mind wonder. So much he didn't know, and so many questions, but he knew, without even asking them, that there was no one here to answer them for him. Apart from perhaps Onna. Her story sounded far too familiar to his own to be mere coincidence.

That night, as he tried to eat his meal, think about his next move, and avoid Onna's blistering stare, the women from the night before accosted Mann. The first woman he'd shared his passion with watched him with hurt eyes, while the second, a huge bruise covering much of the right side of her face, tried to smile enticingly at him, only to groan in pain and bring her hand up to cover the green and purple bruising.

Mann offered them nothing but a smile, not prepared to endure another night guided only by the desire thrumming through his body.

Yet the inn was quiet that night, Mann quickly realising the locals were avoiding Onna and her deep anger. No doubt, the entire settlement had heard about the altercation the night before. The thought made him smile. He was unsurprised when, as the fire burnt low, the third and fourth women came to him.

They smiled seductively, the younger of the two allowing her dress to show off shoulders that glowed enticingly white in the glow from the twin fires and the candles. Without waiting for an introduction, she sat beside Mann and reached out to run her hand along his jawline, her fingers lingering over his lips. The other woman, a little older, but not by much, took advantage of Mann's inattention to slide her hand across his lap, hunting for him beneath the privacy of the table.

He smiled at the two women, his head swimming from the ale he'd consumed, fighting his growing desire.

'It would be unfair if we didn't see what you were made of,' the older said, her lips polished with maroon rouge that showed fine, straight, white teeth behind them. Mann tried to focus on her mouth, and not the actions of her hand, while she bent so far forward he could see the gentle curve of well-rounded breasts, heated to the same colour as her lips.

'Crame and Tolly told us how good you were. There'll be no cost,' the third breathed into his face. The heavy spice she'd imbibed before coming to him, fogged from her mouth and blurred his vision. He could feel his breath coming in more and more ragged burst. Then he met the furious gaze of Onna, and instead of sobering him, it angered him. What did she know? What right did she have to circumscribe his actions? Mann winked at her, spilling the drink she placed on his table with clumsy hands as he rose to retire to his room, the two women following him with laughter and giggles, uncaring of Onna.

Mann nodded as he passed her, so close he was sure she felt his arousal. Fury lit her jade eyes. He found it only excited him more. Mann wished he could add her to the little harem following him from the now deserted main room of the inn.

SEVEN

MANN SMILED with delight at the revelations of the night before. He doubted the sight of the two naked women would leave him anytime soon.

Mann stretched, and groaned, and tumbled from the bed to a loud knocking on the door.

'The sled will be leaving shortly,' the burly innkeeper bellowed. Mann raised his voice to thank him.

Looking around the room, the first bed he thought he'd ever slept in, he picked up his few possessions. Which consisted of the bag containing the glass, the bottle, his gloves and the lamp. He reminded himself he'd also need his skis. Mann patted his trouser pockets, keen to see if his money remained. He was pleased to feel the metallic clunk of pieces hitting one another.

Snaking his hand inside, Mann pulled out the various shapes and sizes of the coins. He'd not had the opportunity to properly examine them yet, and he was surprised to discover coins showing different imprints, weighing surprisingly different amounts.

Mann squinted in the dull gloom of the room and hefted

the coins back into his backpack. He thought they'd be safer there. But then he had a thought, and a slow smile spread across his face.

'I would like some more coins, enough to last me for ten days.' As Mann spoke he heard the familiar strangled cry, and then a huge crash of wood hitting wood filled his senses. He turned, surprised, not to find a small pile of gleaming and battered coins, but rather a luxurious box, made of varnished black wood, shimmering in the room.

Mann stepped closer, his foot catching in the tangled remains of the sheets from the night before. When Mann steadied himself, a gust of wind alerted him he was no longer alone.

He turned, meeting the disinterested gaze of the innkeeper.

'Come on, let's be having you,' the man beckoned, and Mann nodded. He palmed the surprisingly heavy box into his backpack, mindful of not breaking the delicate glass.

'I'm coming,' Mann muttered, annoyed at the interruption, as he secured his treasure and strode from the room.

At the doorway, the innkeeper stopped him.

'The women, they weren't free. I know they said they were, but you owe for their services.' The innkeeper spoke with puffed up importance, his face flashing angrily red, while Mann shook his head.

'They came to me, not vice versa. They said there was no cost, and I've nothing more for them. The good lady took everything from me, apart from the cost of my sled. Sorry, but you're shit out of luck with that little trick.'

'Then you owe for the room, and the food,' the innkeeper tried again, but Mann shook his head.

'Speak to your good wife about that. I've a sled to catch.'

With that Mann forced his way past the bulk of the innkeeper, his own temper rising. He clattered noisily down the stairs. Onna was standing behind the bar, counting piles of coins. While she opened her mouth to speak, Mann swept out of the doorway, grabbing his skis, from the exit, as he went. He'd had enough of the supposed hospitality of the inn and was keen to be away. Whatever Onna wanted to say, he wasn't interested.

With the creak of the wooden door and the thud of his boots on the three steps down into the street, he strained his neck to seek out the sled and was unsurprised to find it ready and waiting by the closed gate. The two guards from the day before were engrossed in a conversation with the sled owner, their laughter filling the street with the welcoming sound.

Disgruntled, Mann strode to the sled, noting the animals that pulled it, not horses but some other beasts with long antlers. They stood in two rows, three deep. Amongst them, a hound could be seen sniffing, its short black and white snout, standing out amongst the strong brown legs of the animals. Another hound sat in the sled, perhaps older than the other one. It sniffed the air, as though distrustful, and when Mann came closer, he noticed the animal had milky-white eyes.

'Good day,' he called. All three turned to face him. He'd been expecting the sledder to be a man, but was unsurprised to meet keen grey eyes, and the pointed stare of a young woman, covered from head to foot in furs and leathers. She looked animal-like, almost a spitting image of her two dogs, who now sniffed him as though prey.

Mann bent down to run his hand along their backs.

'Don't,' barked out. He jumped and stood, the eyes of the woman cautioning him.

'They're not pets to be pampered,' she grumbled, indicating where he could place himself on the almost empty sled.

It was built of the same black wood that seemed to predominate in the settlement. However, the runners were made of long cream coloured bone, and Mann shivered to think of the size of the beast they'd come from. The sled rested heavily on the ground almost devoid of snow. Mann clambered aboard, and settled himself, and his skis, which he slid into the near empty compartment to the rear.

'Not really worth coming,' the woman grumbled to the two guards, only for a commotion up the one roadway to cause the angry glint of her eyes to lighten. A sly smirk tugged on the part of her face exposed to the bright daylight.

'Or perhaps not,' she muttered, reaching out her gloved hand to demand payment from Mann. At the same time, she watched the struggling figure, pushing a barrow filled with an assortment of sacks and barrels toward her.

Mann had no idea of the cost of the sled and began by forcing five different coins onto her outstretched hands, only for her to shake her head, her other hand indicating more and more. Only when ten coins shone in her palm, did she snatch it closed and move on to her more lucrative cargo.

'You're the talk of Slutet,' the younger of the gate wardens leaned over to say to him. He'd clearly cut himself shaving. A fine ink of red marred his chin, as both he and Mann watched the negotiations between the sled owner and the man, who puffed through cheeks turning pink from the cold. It seemed, in his haste, he'd forgotten his cloak and every so often, as he bartered, he shivered, gesturing to his load of supplies.

'Well, it's a good job I'm leaving then,' Mann grumbled, but the man shook his head.

'Not at all. The details of your antics will be missed. Two last night again, or so we heard. Tell me, who's the best. I want to know for next time.'

Mann shook his head in annoyance at the question, but then reconsidered. There was one he'd enjoyed more than the others. What harm if he shared the information.

'Black hair, straight teeth, red lips. She's the most experienced, and the keenest of the four. Don't tell her that, though. The others won't be happy. Here, for your enjoyment,' Mann said, determined to amuse himself at Onna's expense again, as he pressed five coins into the man's hand.

Mann winked as he did so. The young man, turning to ensure no one had seen him, quickly pocketed the coins, a bark of delight issuing from his mouth.

'Safe trip,' he offered, slapping Mann on the back. Then he meandered to the back of the sled, where negotiations seemed to be coming to an end.

The sled owner's hound, the one with milky eyes, sniffed at him one more time, and content, curled on the floor at his feet and was soon softly snoring. Mann laughed. At last, a creature that almost seemed to approve of him.

It had been a long night, and the thought of mirroring those actions, almost had him closing his eyes, only for a heavy bundle to land in his lap. His eyes fluttered open in shock. He met the amused stare of the sled owner.

'Wrap up warm, it's bloody windy out there today.'

'My, my thanks,' Mann stuttered, the softness of the thick furs under his fingers reminding him a bit too forcefully of the night before. Laughter bubbled from the lips of the sled owner, as she noticed. He grinned unashamedly.

'I think the cold might drive those thoughts from your mind, but if not, well, there's just the two of us, and it can be a long and lonely journey. I might see what all the fuss is about.'

She laughed and turned back to the task of ensuring all was safely stowed, before mounting the sled and settling herself at the reins. Her eyebrows high in surprise at the dog curled up asleep beneath his feet, she offered nothing more, other than a loud 'hah,' as she lifted the long whips while the gates swung inwards.

'Safe journey,' the two gate wardens called. Mann raised his arm in farewell, but then they were flying, literally, across the white expanse, he'd walked the day before. The stinging wind, and the speed of the animals as they powered the sled, caused white particles to fly into Mann's eyes. The sled-owner handed him something and mimed putting it over his head. He did so, and the strange glass-fronted goggles kept the wind and the snow from his eyes.

'My thanks,' Mann shouted. She shook her head, indicating her ears with one hand. The wind was a cruel beast, roaring around the sled. Mann settled back to watch the journey. It was clear conversation was impossible.

For a long time, Mann was lulled by the motion. He dosed, his eyes opening and closing every so often at the bumpy mode of travel. The sledder, he really wished he'd asked her name, never turned away from guiding her animals over the deceptively smooth looking-surface. Eventually, and to Mann's surprise, she hauled hard on the reins and brought the sled to a stop. He looked at her in surprise. She smiled, her eyes mischievous behind the mask she wore. He felt a stirring below, but she merely handed him a metal contraption and indicated he should attach it to a long wooden pole behind his head.

Mann did as he was asked, toying with the metal chain and winding it tight enough around the four available hooks, that the metal box, with a few glass doors, hung tightly clasped to the wood.

Aware of eyes on him, Mann turned, and almost bumped noses with the woman. She grinned again. He thought she was going to kiss him, only for her to thrust a burning brand into his face. It was then that he understood.

The metal contraption was a lamp of some sort. Feeling foolish, and not a little aroused by the close touch of the sled woman, he fiddled with one of the glass doors, opening a catch that allowed him to extend the brand inside the metal. The flame caught quickly on the long wick. He slammed the glass door tight against the wintry blast of air.

Instantly, a powerful ray of light reached out from the

lamp, driving back shadows Mann hadn't even noticed snaking closer and closer to the sled. He shook his head in amazement. The light was powerful beyond imagining. He reached out to touch it, only to snatch his hand back as warmth sheeted up his arm.

He turned, expecting to find the woman still beside him, but she'd hopped from the sled. With her sighted dog in watchful attendance, she was attaching a similar looking metal lamp to the front of the sled.

Mann had wondered what the stray pole was for, wedged somehow between the lead animals, but it was apparent it was to allow them to see where they were going.

'Bloody short days,' he heard muttered as she returned to her position in the sled. Bathed in the glow of the two lamps, she once more encouraged her animals to move off. They did so, a little slower, but assured all the same, as Mann settled back to watch, considering how the two lamps managed to protect their illumination as far as they did.

Time passed, as the night grew ever darker around the sled. He shivered when the wind whipped itself back into a tempest. Only then did the sledder speak again. Her words were far from reassuring.

'Bollocks,' she muttered. Mann glanced around him, surprised by the worry lacing her words.

'Wha?' was all he managed, his throat clogged from lack of use. He coughed. 'What?' he asked once more. She pointed behind the sled. He squinted into the pitch of night, unsure what he was being shown, and then he understood.

The sky, black for so long, now swirled and undulated, the edges of something huge panting at their heels.

'I thought the storms were passed,' she groaned again, bringing her animals to a halt, busy about the sled.

'What?' Mann asked again, feeling stupid as he watched her frantic actions.

'We can't outrun it,' she shouted, fear in the harsh words. 'Here, help me.'

Unceremoniously, a heavy canvas was thrust into his hands. Still, he looked at her hopelessly.

'We need to cover the sled,' she explained, enunciating each word over the suddenly screeching wind. He nodded, finally understanding, as she fumbled for the edge of the canvas. Quickly she grabbed a rope Mann hadn't seen before and threaded the hooped, metal catches through the canvas. Instantly he saw what she was doing and began to spool out the canvas into her willing hands.

Around them the wind had reached a near deafening whine. The canvas already tied down fought against its confinement, billowing uncontrollably. Mann strained to keep hold of the remaining canvas, as the sledder worked quickly and frantically. He was concerned about the animals at the front of the sled, as the weight of canvas in his arm evaporated, and they were still exposed to the shattering wind.

But as Mann tried to retain his footing on the slick surface, the storm trying to force him to the floor, she motioned for him to get inside the canvas. She drew it tightly above the make-shift roof, her two dogs already hunkered down in the small space. They watched her with all the loyalty and love of someone who relied wholly on one another. After she threaded the final piece of the rope through an ingenious contraption that clamped it in place as a fail-safe against the knotted rope, she turned to her dogs and ran her hands over both heads.

They settled immediately at her touch, but she wasn't finished yet. Taking something from her pocket, she popped it into her mouth and puffed her cheeks. Mann watched her in consternation, unsure what she hoped to achieve. She took hold of the reins of the animals pulling the sled and let them go.

Mann's mouth opened in shock. Had she just abandoned

them to the whim of the storm? Had she just let the animals free to roam through the violent blizzard?

She turned to him then, and of all things, winked. She blew once more on the strange lump of wood she'd put in her mouth. At her action, Mann watched the reins slip through the gap between the flapping canvas and the top of the sled. He closed his eyes, in disgust. It seemed his competent and experienced sledder had released the animals.

When he opened his eyes again, laughing eyes greeted him, her head shaking at his worry. He became aware of movement around the sled. Unsure what was happening, but too curious for his own good, he shuffled his way toward one of the few gaps between the canvas cover and the wooden frame and peered outside.

Mann was assaulted by the ferocious wind at first, his eyes tearing as he tried to stare outside. He sensed something out there, moving against the force of the storm. Irritated, he looked away, raising his still gloved hand to clear his eyes, and then he looked once more. Only then he understood.

He had no idea how, or why, but the animals that powered the sled had all moved from their original positions, at the instigation of whatever the wooden object was the sledder had in her mouth. Now they lay, nose to tail, around the sled, hunkered down beside the runners, so little of them showed, just the brief outline of a black antler against the paler black of the wooden sled.

Mann nodded then. He forced the canvas tight, and joined the two dogs and the sledder on the floor. They were lying down, furs piled around them, and one of the lamps, the other extinguished, cast a pale glow illuminating the confined space of the sled.

His sledder had her eyes closed, each hand resting on one of the dog's heads. Mann tried to follow her example. Clearly, and despite his worries, this was something that happened often enough she was well prepared for it, and seemed unconcerned, even though the sled rocked alarmingly from side to side with each and every violent gust.

As Mann settled himself beside her, he felt a gentle pat on his arm and turned to see amused eyes watching him. Conversation was impossible because of the shriek of the wind. He nodded, hopefully with thanks, and lay back down, his eyes closing and opening with every buffet of the sled and every screech of wind.

Mann swallowed thickly. It had been bad enough when he'd been alone on the ice. This was better and worse. He wasn't alone and was clearly with someone used to the storms, but the force of the wind was far more ferocious than when he'd first manifested.

Mann sighed, squeezing his eyes tightly shut as he tried to still his erratically beating heart, and think of anything but the peril of his predicament. He almost wished he'd stayed in Slutet and felt the wrath of Onna's heated glares. At least he'd have been away from the full brunt of the storm.

Yet, he wasn't alone for long. A slither of a warm hand over his face, and his eyes shot open. The laughing face of his sledder met his own, but still, they couldn't speak. The intensity of the storm was truly something to behold.

Somehow she'd manoeuvred herself so she lay beside him, her two dogs to top and bottom of their entwined bodies, the partially sighted one close to Mann. Had he fallen asleep for he certainly hadn't felt her move, and he should have done?

She paused, a question in her eyes, and then she leaned down, her lips caressing his own.

Surprised, it took him all of a heartbeat to reciprocate her actions. Her lips were unexpectedly pliant, gentle even. For some reason, he'd expected them to be harder, because of exposure to the snow and the cold.

A tugging began at his clothing, soft at first, and then

more insistent, and fire burnt inside him. He'd only just managed to forget his passions from the inn in Slutet. The sledder had only to touch him, and they were once more dominant.

Without even pausing to consider the peril of an icy coupling on his straining manhood, he pushed aside the hand and worked himself free. A rumble of amusement vibrated through the sledder's throat, detected as they kissed, tongues entwined, barely pausing to breathe.

The storm receded from his consciousness, the cold as well, as the sledder finally broke away from him, and wriggled around in the confined space of the sled so her lower body was naked.

The shuttered light cast a rich glow over her naked form, as his own trousers slithered down his long limbs, before tangling in his boots. The sledder merely shook her head and settled herself over him. Mann eyed her speculatively. In this light, she was an attractive proposition. In this situation, she was also his only proposition, and yet, his body couldn't deny he desired her.

Fierce eyes met his, glowing yellow in the sparse light. The dog, closest to their heads, eyed him with milky eyes, hot dog breath mingling with his own, and a tension to the dog that Mann didn't appreciate.

But the sledder only laughed, ruffling the animal's ears until it subsided, and then turning her attention back to Mann, an arched eyebrow showing her question.

He reached for her, his hand tracing limbs warmed from their passion, not the outside air. Soft hands wound their way beneath the clothing on his chest, and then lips touched his again. A veritable explosion of passion swamped him as she slid herself over his urgent need. Then they were rocking together, the movements merging with those of the strong winds so Mann had no idea if they powered the rocking motion themselves, or if they worked in concert with the storm.

He little cared.

Mouth filled with the tongue of the sledder, buried deep inside her, he heard her gasps and moans of pleasure, as he held her in place, never once letting go, never once letting himself go, until she sagged over him, her breath little better than a pant, her eyes closed almost in exhausted sleep.

Only then did she slide from her place above him, pulling furs to surround their naked lower bodies, the dogs, by now, sound asleep.

A lull in the gust and she leaned against his ears, her eyes a little open.

'They didn't lie about your qualities,' she offered, a light lilt to her tired voice. Then she sprawled against him, her breath silky on his face, as the storm penetrated his consciousness once more. Was this to be his life? Mann thought, a smirk on his face. He bloody hoped it was. This he could certainly enjoy.

EIGHT

MOVEMENT DISTURBED him from a fractious sleep. Able to blank out the storm when his body was otherwise engaged, as soon as he'd been left alone, his partner sleeping at his side, Mann had nothing to focus on but the billowing canvas, accompanied by short, sharp tugs. He'd convinced the cover was in danger of imminently blowing away.

Uncomfortable in the confined space, cold after his exertions, and with no easy means of returning his trousers to their usual position, Mann had lain awake for too long. He'd considered that perhaps a life of debauchery and sex wherever and whenever, was not quite as enticing as he'd thought when warmed from the glow of spent passion.

Now, rocking and the sudden silence from outside forced an annoyed groan from his mouth.

'Well bloody move,' was the equally aggrieved response. Mann's eyes shot open, and he stared into the alert eyes of the sledder.

'Come on, the storm's moved on for now. I want to be away from here before the bloody thing returns.'

No words, or sweet promises, or even mention of the night

before, as Mann, freed from the constraints of her body tight against his, finally managed to drag his trousers over his cold bottom.

Mann considered a joke, a request for a kiss, but she was busy about her work. With a final shriek of outrage, their canvas roof slid free, exposing Mann to an abrupt drop in temperature. He glimpsed the soft blue of a sky that knows it's been harsh on those beneath it, and perhaps wants to apologise.

Standing, on unsteady feet, Mann saw the sledder's reindeer were all returning to their usual positions, as she worked quickly to try and roll the canvas tight. It was nigh on impossible. The canvas was frozen hard in some places, billowing freely only over the section warmed all night by the breaths of the two of them, and the two dogs as well.

Arms battered against the board-like hardness of the canvas, as Mann watched, faintly amused, by the sheer determination of the sledder. He waited, hoping she'd ask for help, unsurprised when instead of turning to him, she called on her dogs. He laughed then, as both animals settled themselves, offering the gush of their urine as a counter for the cold. Wrinkling his nose at the acidic smell, he couldn't deny the sense in the action.

With a waft of acid, the canvas finally folded, and the sledder busied herself with stowing it away. Mann watched her actions. They seemed casual and yet also jerky. A small smile touched his lips. Was she embarrassed by last night? He hoped not. After all, a bit of distraction during a rogue storm wasn't to be frowned upon.

But Mann wisely held his tongue, as he stretched out his cramped body, and took in the view. Any tracks from yesterday had been long ago obliterated, and he had no idea which way was which. Scratching his nose, he turned a slow circle, peering, eyes watering in the stark white of a new day.

'The reindeers will know,' last night's voice offered, softer than he might have expected, so perhaps not embarrassed after all.

'Good, because I sodding don't.' Mann spoke with a trace of amusement, happy to mirror the mood of his companion. 'It looks clear,' he mused, 'why the worry about another storm?'

'They never come alone,' she laughed, her back to him, and for a moment he considered their nighttime activities. It would be nice to repeat them, but perhaps not now. His belly rumbled, almost as loudly as last night's fierce storm, and she laughed.

'Come on, you're not the only one. Hopefully, we'll arrive by noon.'

Settling himself inside the sled, the fully sighted dog ejected out to run alongside the reindeer for a while, Mann shivered beneath his fur. He pulled his hood down over as much of his face as possible, while still being able to see.

'What will you do when we arrive?' she asked, as the sled resumed its forward momentum.

'Eat,' Mann complained, rubbing his aching belly. She laughed, a sound that rang loudly over the crisp surface.

'And then?' she pressed, but he shrugged.

'I really just needed to get out of Slutet. What happens from here on in will be down to chance and happenstance.'

'Genuinely, you have no great plan? What were you even doing in Slutet at this time of the year, in the first place?'

'A traveller,' Mann answered enigmatically, considering if there might be any truth to his words.

'Then you could travel with me for a while,' she suggested, an arched eyebrow giving him the once over so intense he felt as though he were naked and not swaddled in mountains of furs.

'I'd not be averse to such a proposition,' Mann admitted, a

smile playing around his lips, his mind dwelling on last night's activities.

'I might have a job for you, as well, if you've a mind to it.'

'A job?' Mann asked.

'Yes, I might need a big strong oaf like you to help me.'

'Well, I'll let you know,' Mann laughed. 'I might find something better to fill my time, when I actually see this place.'

A sudden fury replaced her joking countenance. Mann realised he'd misread the situation, only for her to surprise him.

'If that's where I actually take you?' was her quick retort, and now he laughed, the rumble of amusement covering that of his belly, and echoing through the empty landscape.

'Why, where else might you be heading?' Mann asked, playing along to pass the time as the reindeer gained speed.

'Ah well, I can't tell you that, it wouldn't be a surprise would it?' Now she laughed freely, and Mann allowed himself to consider the possibility he could be content with just one woman. After all, she'd proven most adroit last night. If she could accomplish all she had, in their cramped confines, what could she do when there was more room to be found?

'But no, I plan to take you to Bosetting, as I said,' the timbre of her voice changed as she spoke. 'There's someone I've been trying to avoid, hence, my dash to Slutet. But a strong man like you might just put the little tit off and leave me in peace.'

'An admirer?' Mann asked, but she shook her head.

'No, a little tit. With ideas above his status.'

That gave him pause for thought.

'A business associate?' he attempted. 'Trying to shoulder in on your route to Slutet?'

'Something like that,' she complained.

'The other storm?' Mann asked, pointing to where a haze was starting to appear on the distant horizon, a mass of boiling grey clouds, seemingly laden with fresh snowfall. *Does it do nothing but snow here?* Mann pondered.

'Well, some might call Bosetting that,' she laughed. Mann peered intently. The swirling clouds seemed to only be that, but then, as they came ever closer, he realised they were artificial.

'Smoke, you fool,' the sledder laughed. 'Surely you saw it over Slutet when you went there?'

'No, I arrived in the dark,' Mann explained, hoping his lack of knowledge wouldn't force too many questions from her.

'The dark? You were lucky you found the place,' she joked, but Mann remained silent. She had no idea how lucky he'd been to stumble into Slutet. It could all have ended quite horribly, had he not found shelter.

'We'll head for the East Gate. The food stalls will be doing a thriving business by now.'

As if in agreement, his belly growled once more, as the sled ground to a halt in front of the black gate.

'Bloody idiots,' she complained, the gate still barred against their entry. 'This should have been open by now.'

'Hey, come on, let me in. It's Freg.' Her voice was shrill but seemed to carry in the silent air, as Mann realised he finally knew what her name was. The second, blind dog took the opportunity to jump from the sled. Together, the animals ran toward the gateway and began barking raucously, as though this wasn't an unusual occurrence.

'Why do something yourself, when others will do it for you?' Freg smirked.

Yet, the dogs were doing no better than Freg in getting the gate opened. After a few long moments of frantic barking, no progress had been made.

'Bloody hell,' Freg grumbled, jumping from the side of the sled. 'Daft bastards will have drunk themselves insensible.' She spoke with mild irritation. Mann deduced she probably knew the gate wardens rather well, no doubt because of her trade with Slutet. He couldn't imagine many others made use of the east-facing gateway. It offered little, as far as he could tell, but an opening onto the Hvite Lands, and there was sod-all there.

The crunch of Freg's snowshoes over the freshly fallen snow meant Mann could have closed his eyes and still known exactly what path she'd taken. But he watched her, all the same, enjoying the way her body moved beneath her cloak. Anyone who could still arouse such sentiments in him when enveloped in such a shapeless piece of cloth was worth his attention.

Her dogs barked raucously, the noise the only thing to be heard without the howl of the wind. Freg made use of her fists to hammer on the black, wooden gateway. As with so much else Mann had seen, the gate was fashioned of the blackened wood, shimmering in the reflection of the snow and the blue light of the day. Long icicles hung down from the reinforced top of the gate, perhaps a walkway or some such, above them. Both sides of the gate clearly opened wide, for they were patterned with strengthening planks of wood running side to side where they joined together.

Mann eyed the pattern of wooden planks carefully. Surely it would be too easy to climb over the gate? In fact, if the buggers inside couldn't be roused, he thought it would be easier to do so than try and find another entrance. Mann glanced behind. Already, far in the distance, he could see the real swirl of heavy clouds. The second storm Freg had spoken of would be upon them soon enough.

Abruptly, the gate juddered, before slowly opening, inwards. The dogs immediately rushed through the small gap. Freg immediately turned to return to the sled. She was shaking her head, but Mann found his eyes distracted by the view opening before him.

He could see no hands that worked the gate, no doubt

hidden behind it, but he could see what lay inside the gates. Slowly, a small piece at a time, the settlement came into view.

Unlike when he'd stumbled into Slutet, beneath a cloak of night, he could immediately detect which buildings were dwellings, and which, businesses. His stomach rumbled once more, as Freg threw herself into the sled.

'Lazy gits,' she grumbled, raising the reins so the reindeer knew to go on. Mann braced himself for the sharp movement, and then they were moving slowly forward once more.

'I'm bloody starving,' he muttered, as enticing aromas reached them as they passed between the gates. Only now did Mann see the gate wardens, and he chuckled softly. Neither figure seemed to be able to stand without the support of the gate. Even now, they swayed unsteadily as they both worked one of the gates independently. They could close the gate without opening it all the way, but neither seemed to have the strength to do so.

'Shut them, you damn fools,' Freg bellowed. Unintelligible replies reached Mann's ears. He winced. He doubted the words were kind.

'Right,' Freg announced, jumping down once more, her reindeer stalling just inside the slowly closing gate. 'Food. I'm starving.'

She strode out, not waiting to see if Mann followed her, but he did, as did her two dogs. They were circling her legs excitedly, just about managing not to trip her, in their excitement. Mann found the streets cleared of snow, with braziers warming the air outside each storefront. Not that many people were around. Mann realised it was probably still early on a winter's day. Most would still be sheltering under their furs and covers.

The enticing smell of fresh-baked bread flooded the air, and Freg made her way straight to the bakers.

As Mann struggled to catch up to her, having failed to remove his snowshoes, which were worse than useless on the cleared street way, the baker greeted Freg amicably. They began bartering. Mann paused then, considering. He had his coins. They'd been good enough within the inn. He hoped they were here as well.

Under the pretense of bending to untie his snowshoes, he reached deep into his pocket, fingering some coins he'd moved from his bag to his pocket for easier access. He hoped he didn't pull out anything that would raise eyebrows. A loaf of bread was likely to cost far less than bed and board. And the whores he'd enjoyed.

Freg waited for him at the baker's, her dogs sitting patiently as she offered them small portions of whatever she'd purchased. Only when Mann drew closer did he realise the baker offered far more than just bread. Indeed, the beguiling smell engulfing the entire street seemed to come from the stall. It's shutters were flung wide so Mann could see the baker's boy at work, moving cooked and uncooked bread from oven to cooling racks.

'Best damn pasty you'll ever have,' Freg announced, thrusting what Mann took to be her own open pasty into his face. The inside of the bright yellow crust tempted with chunky meat and sliced vegetables. It was one of these that Freg was sharing with her animals.

'Two,' Mann said, holding up his fingers without realising he did so.

'A cold night on the way here?' the baker chuckled; perhaps used to finding his earliest customer was Freg.

'Freezing, and another one coming,' Freg announced ominously, as the baker shook his head.

'Bloody weather,' the baker complained. 'It's interrupting the supplies from the South. I might have to start limiting you to one pasty,' the tall man chortled, his moustaches coated in a thin sprinkling of flour, mirroring the icicles hanging over the black gateway.

While the baker bantered with Freg, Mann and he were haggling over the cost. Mann knew a moment of concern as he passed the dulled coin over, hoping it was the right one. But the baker pocketed it with barely a glance. It was apparently good currency.

Mann took hold of the two pasties tied in a small piece of linen, and quickly wrenched one free. With a moan of delight that would have surely excited the women he'd so recently known quite intimately, Mann bit deeply into the pasty, allowing the juices to fill his mouth, despite being too hot to truly taste.

'Good,' Freg asked laughter lines on her ruddy red face.

'Excellent,' Mann agreed, to the delight of the baker, who turned to his baker's boy.

'Bring the scraps,' he bellowed, and the young lad, almost buried beneath clothes that dwarfed him, came shuffling outside with two wooden bowls, and a bucket of scraps. He divided what he had between the two circling dogs. They waited patiently for their food, although whines burst from their mouths until Freg made a sharp hand gesture, and the two dogs launched themselves at the bowls.

Mann would have laughed, but he was trying to shovel the second pasty into his mouth and felt less civilised than the hungry dogs.

'What's the matter with those two?' Freg pointed toward the gateway. Mann's gaze swept around, taking in the sight of the two gate wardens. They staggered together, the one holding up the other, trying to return to the small wooden building that was clearly theirs to shelter within when they were on duty.

'Been up all night. No one could see anything in the storm so the other two lads couldn't relieve them. Of course, they didn't take the opportunity to sleep, but rather to drink themselves stupid. I heard you banging. I' have woken them for you, but the damn boy can't be left alone with the baking. He muddles the bread and the pasties every damn morning.'

A faint sniff emanated from beneath the mass of clothing. Mann felt a moment of pity for the lad. Not that the baker spoke with any real malice. Instead, he sounded resigned to it all. No doubt the two were related, probably father and son, and the father merely despaired of the boy ever taking over the running of the shop.

'Jemp's been looking for you,' the baker added conversationally. Even Mann was aware of a sudden chill in the conversation. He turned his attention to Freg, mouth stuffed with pasty. Any good humour on Freg's face had been replaced with fury. Mann decided Jemp wasn't someone Freg wished to speak to.

'Did you tell him I'd gone to Slutet?' she demanded, but the baker shook his head.

'I told him nothing, but I imagine he determined the truth for himself when he couldn't find you. It's not as though you might have gone anywhere else.'

'No, I suppose not. I wish he'd leave me alone. I've told him enough times.'

This didn't sound like a romantic relationship under discussion. Mann deduced Jemp might be part of the job Freg wanted his help with.

'And you, stranger, where have you come from? I don't think I've ever seen you here before. I have an amazing memory for names and faces.'

'Ah,' Mann began, trying to think of some sort of excuse but Freg chuckled, dispelling the sudden tension.

'He's just been 'exploring.' Spent a few days in Slutet. Got himself in trouble with Onna and decided to make himself scarce.'

The baker's face reflected sympathy.

'It would take a much braver man than me to take on Onna.

Her reputation travels further than anyone else's in Slutet.' Mann laughed along with Freg and the baker, relaxing no Freg had averted uncomfortable questions. The boy hurried to return to his tasks when the smell of slightly burnt bread wafted through the air.

Mann realised he'd really need to decide on some sort of story to account for how he came to be in Slutet. Briefly, he considered just telling the truth. It might be enough to shut people up because it was so preposterous. Or it might make them distrust him.

Either way, perhaps he should try and put his glib tongue to better uses than of late.

'What did you do?' the baker asked. Here Mann felt on firmer ground and opened his mouth to speak, but Freg beat him to it.

'He upset all the whores with his bedroom skills. They were fighting over him.' The baker's boy, returning with a tray of pastries, looked at Mann with round eyes, while the baker looked embarrassed.

'Well, yes, yes, those women. They do have their uses.'

Freg chuckled again, while the baker's boy tried not to peer at Mann. The scrutiny was unwelcome. Mann puffed his chest out and adopted a manly pose all the same. Perhaps the boy had never had a woman.

'The trick is to leave them wanting more,' Mann said, a wink for the baker's boy, whose mouth dropped open in shock.

'Yes, well, perhaps not for the boy,' the baker bluffed.

'I think I'll take another two of these,' Mann said, restoring some propriety to the conversation. 'Nothing like being stuck in a storm to make a man hungry.'

While they haggled once more, Freg's dogs slunk their way back to the reindeer and sled, and Freg seemed keen to be gone as well.

'Come again in the morning,' the baker called to Mann as he too made his way back to the sled.

Mann waved his arm, neither in agreement or dissent.

By now, the gate wardens had stumbled back inside their hut. More and more shutters were being thrown wide open along the street. Mann licked his lips as he passed a stall offering dainty pastries, and another with hunks of meat on display.

A few characters were making their way along the cleared street, while others reloaded the braziers that had burned out from barrows filled with charcoal and black logs. They called greetings, one to another. Mann watched everyone out of the corner of his eye, his focus on Freg.

Getting away from Slutet had been his only concern, so far. Now the baker had made him realise he had no plan. He had nothing to his name, other than some coins that had appeared from nowhere. Oh, and some skis. Not a great deal for a man. Not out here, in the bleak landscape.

'Who's this Jemp?' Mann asked, clutching his two pasties to his chest, to eat later, although he craved them now.

'A total pain,' Freg grouched. Mann detected an undercurrent but asked nothing further.

'What's this job you might have for me?'

'Come with me now, if you're interested. If not, the inn's down that street there,' Freg pointed down the street that apparently ran through the centre of the settlement, and on, toward where, no doubt, the western gateway stood.

'I'll come with you,' Mann announced. She nodded, as though expecting the answer.

'Good, jump on then. We've a way to go yet.'

Mann did as asked, surprised. He'd expected Freg to live close to the gateway she'd use most often to venture to Slutet, but clearly not.

The dogs chose to run to either side, leaving more room in the sled for Mann, but he too quickly leapt down from its side. Here, with the street cleared of almost all snow, apart from that which had fallen during the night, the sled faltered time and again. The reindeer were being forced backward more often than forward as they tried to drive the sled to their destination.

Man walked forward, to the head of the lead animals, noting how they sweated freely with their endeavours. He glanced at Freg. She was shaking her head in annoyance.

'Why not leave it here?' Mann called to her. She shook her head, the curious eyes of those about their own business watching the exchange. Her lips pursed, and Mann let the matter drop immediately. There was no point wasting his breath. Instead, he ventured to the front of the sled once more, eyeing the way forward speculatively.

The snow on the right-hand side snaked further out into the street than that on the left. The wind must have been blowing from the right-hand side during the night.

'Steer to the right,' he called. Freg's huff of annoyance was clearly audible, but she did so all the same.

'Better to have the use of the runners on one side, at least,' Mann called back to her, coaxing the animals onwards. While it was only half a solution to the problem, it did seem to work. Mann ran ahead with the reindeer just behind him.

He closed his ears to the angry cries of those outraged by the fleeing sled, instead chuckling whenever he heard Freg shout an apology even he could tell was little meant.

Now he turned his eyes to the settlement around him. It was certainly far bigger than Slutet. He looked at wooden boards above shutters, and those that swung over wooden doors with interest. There was apparently a great deal of business to be done.

The smell of the inn reached his nostrils long before he saw it. He eyed it critically. Almost twice as wide as the inn in Slutet, it had little of the same charm, hunkering out into the street, as though a foul beast waiting to engulf all who tried to pass. He could feel eyes on him as he ran but declined to meet them.

He had no one to answer to here.

Eventually, Freg called an order to him. Mann swung into a small side street where snow still clung to every surface from last night's storm. No one had bothered to clear it away.

Abruptly, the sled stopped before two large wooden gates. He leaned his hands on his knees, slightly bent forward, his breath catching in the back of his throat.

'Bloody fool,' Freg muttered as she walked to the gateway. She pulled something from her pocket and used it to manipulate the contraption in the middle of the gate.

With a screech of protest, the twin gates opened inwards. Mann whistled at what he saw. The dwelling nestled behind the gates was long and narrow, reflecting blackly as all the buildings did. But it was the yard that truly impressed him. It seemed even bigger than the one at the inn in Slutet. There were two smaller buildings he decided must be where the reindeer sheltered. They looked to be built of wood as well-seasoned as the hall, but, if possible, maintained to an even higher standard.

Recognising the smells of home, the reindeer and their sled followed Freg inside while Mann turned to pull the gates closed behind them. As he did a small figure darted inside, stumping Mann.

'Been to Slutet, have you?' a whining voice filled Mann's ears. He turned away from his task in surprise. Had that noise come from the small figure?

'Bloody hell Jemp, I've just returned. Will you sod off? I've got stuff to do.'

'But you said we'd talk about my proposition when we last met. I've been waiting.'

Mann restrained an amused chuckle at the dancing face of Jemp. It was clear he was much besotted with Freg, but Freg couldn't stand him. Not that Mann was surprised. Jemp reached barely above his waist, with long straggling hair, pulled back beneath a thick fur hat. It only served to accentuate his beady eyes and too-pointed chin. He wasn't a fine specimen of a man, not for someone like Freg, who seemed to have enjoyed her tryst with Mann.

'I had a last moment opportunity for trade in Slutet, and so I took it. I brought back Mann as well, so the trip was profitable.' Only now did Jemp even seem to notice Mann and the small man jumped in surprise, suspicion quickly covering his face.

Mann opened his mouth to say hello, only for Jemp to give yet another small squeal, as though recognising Mann. The suspicion quickly turned to fury on the smaller man's face.

'You,' he screeched, pointing a long thin finger at Mann. 'Bloody you,' he waggled his finger as he backed away from Freg, toward the gateway, and as far away from Mann as it was possible to be.

'You,' Jemp said, one final time, before yanking on the gate Mann had only just closed. The wooden structure refused to open, despite Jemp's best intentions. He refused to turn around, making his attempts at escape futile.

Mann chuckled softly, while Jemp glared angrily, before Mann reached around the smaller figure, to push the gate inward. Now it opened, and Jemp, without turning his back on Mann, made good his escape. As Mann pulled the gateway closed once more, securing the catches and latches, Freg started to chortle.

'Well, I didn't think you'd get rid of him quite that quickly. You have my thanks all the same.'

'Was that the job you wanted me to do?' Mann asked, perplexed, and even more so when Freg nodded.

'Yes, I needed someone to scare off the bloody idiot. He's been harassing me for the last few months. He wants to form a partnership with me. I, obviously, don't want to form one with him.'

'A partnership doing what?' Mann asked, walking closer so he could help remove the harness and head halters from the reindeer, who then made their way into their respective stables without further guidance.

'Sledding and trading.'

'Right?' he still wasn't sure why she sounded so outraged.

'He has no money, no reindeer and no damn sled. He thinks to woo me with his striking looks. He came from nowhere, during the summer, and he's been stalking me ever since. It's a bloody joke.'

'So, he has nothing to offer you, at all?'

'No, he just wants to travel to Slutet, for free. Damn bastard.'

The information amused Mann. 'Does he desire the charms of Onna?' he laughed loudly at his own joke, but Freg was too exasperated to join him.

'I thought if you stay around for a few days, a week or two at most, he'd get frustrated and leave.'

'Has he said as much?' Mann questioned. The thought of having something to do for a few weeks wasn't unpleasant, but he wasn't sure he wanted to stay forever. Not when there seemed to be so much more to explore.

'I, I've been asking around. Trying to find out what I can about him. All I know is he's a persistent bugger until he either gets his own way or gets bloody bored and leaves. I was hoping to speed up his leaving.'

'Well, I'll consider it,' Mann replied, following Freg into one of the stables, with his hands filled with harnesses from the reindeer. She worked quickly, hanging the equipment onto pegs that made little sense to Mann, but clearly a great deal to Freg.

'Well, there's no pressure. You seemed like you could do with a roof over your head, for free, for a few weeks. It's not like the Passen will be open further south, so it's either here, or back to Slutet.'

Mann shrugged.

'You make a good point. But is there really no other settlement between here and Passen? It seems a long expanse of open land.'

'Open land, piled high with snow for three-quarters of each year, and no easy access to amenities. It's not many peoples idea of a thriving venture.'

'How big is this place?'

'There are about a thousand people here, I believe. Not that I go around counting them, but the tax collector likes to ensure we know our tally when he ventures north.'

'Tax collector?' Mann thought he should know what that meant but didn't. 'What gets taxed?'

'Where have you come from?' Freg asked with incredulity. 'The tax collector taxes everything. Depends what he can think up next, and what he can get away with. Anything from how many people to how many barrels of ale we have, both entering, and then leaving Slutet. Sometimes it's even the amount of wood brought here, or how much we send south. Anything and everything all depending on who his master is.'

Mann considered her words, as he once more followed her around the stables, checking on the reindeer, and ensuring they had food and water aplenty. Only then, when she was happy, did she make her way toward the low building, Mann assumed was her home.

Pushing open the doorway, having used yet another key on a chucky mechanism, Mann shivered at the rush of cold air around his feet.

'It's always so bloody cold when I get back,' Freg complained, striking a flint to light a candle, and making her way toward duplicate fires. Mann was surprised. He'd assumed a twin-hearth was just for the inn in Slutet. But evidently not.

It might have been cold, but Mann felt residual warmth over one of the fires and looked quizzically at Freg.

'Someone comes in, when I'm away, to set a fire each day. If we'd made it back yesterday, then the house would have been toasty. Sadly, being delayed has ruined my plans.'

Again, she talked while working, stacking logs and kindling in the one fireplace and then holding a flame to the small shavings. Orange flared in the centre of the construction. Freg turned to do the same to the other fireplace. Mann stood, holding his hands out and hoping for warmth, as the flames built and leapt from kindling to kindling, before snatching at a more substantial log.

He heard a similar snapping of twigs and kindling from behind him. Soon Freg had both fires blazing and was pulling her cloak from around her shoulders, and leaving it to dry on a peg hanging over the flames. Mann took in the dwelling. It seemed reasonably luxurious, rich furs hanging over a huge bed, with a well-stocked wooden cupboard into which Freg delved, time and time again, as she brought forth two wooden mugs, into which she poured heated water, and also some dried leaves.

'Here, this will thaw you out,' she offered, Mann inhaling deeply of the sweet smell, as the mug warmed his hands.

'I'll prepare food for later,' Freg muttered, throwing all sorts of interesting items into a small cooking pot. Mann didn't know what half of them were, but was content to sit and watch her. He was surprised she didn't have a servant to keep the house for her.

'You live here alone?' he couldn't stop himself from asking.

'Yep, just me and my reindeer. And it's going to stay that way. Bloody Jemp.' Mann was starting to understand Jemp's pursuit of her. She was clearly a wealthy woman, with a profitable business. No doubt she was an attractive proposition, not counting her beauty.

Yet there was an edge to her voice. Mann doubted she'd always been alone. Perhaps it had once been a family home, or maybe not? He certainly wasn't concerned enough to ask the question.

'Do you sled south then, as well as north.'

'It depends on the Passen, and whether I can get through or not. The snow can be bad. No point going south if the sled's not going to be able to travel over land devoid of snow, and no point going if there's no way through the passes. Mostly, I content myself with Slutet.'

'Why not employ a servant?' Mann asked, but she was already shaking her head.

'There's only me. I'm either here, or I'm not. The person who lights my fire is all I can tolerate when I'm not here. I like to be alone. Nothing wrong with that.'

Mann held his tongue. This home was affluent; old even, well maintained and extravagant. Few people would have two huge fireplaces. Few people would have the coin to fuel it with seasoned logs. Few would light both of them if there were only one or two people in the house.

'I have a comfortable existence, I know that,' Freg mused. 'I'm not in any great rush to change that.'

Mann held his tongue. There were secrets there. Ones he didn't need to question, although he couldn't deny there was some curiosity to know Freg better. His thoughts drifted to last night's activities, as he eyed the large bed.

Silence engulfed the room. Mann felt his eyes closing as he leaned back in the wooden chair he'd found, feet resting on the side of the fireplace, his boots discarded beneath the chair.

'If you want to bathe, you use the larger cauldron to warm the water,' Freg spoke with her back to him, her voice seeming to come from far away. The prospect of a warm bath excited him, but he was too sleepy, and couldn't be bothered to move.

Indeed, when he woke from his sleep, the room was filled with the twin aromas of cooking food and soapy water. Blearily he peered around, seeking out Freg, and his eyes settled on her still body, encased within the large wooden half barrel used for bathing.

Mann chuckled softly. Now would the perfect time to make her re-acquaintance, but he hesitated. They'd shared a brief coupling in the middle of a storm. Being alone with her within her home was different. And yet, she'd invited him. He'd not come unsolicited.

Coughing as he came to his feet, alerting her to his wakefulness, he sauntered to her side. Freg's eyes didn't open, although she was evidently aware of his presence, for her posture tensed.

Mann examined her critically. Her flesh was a pale white, almost blue, and her hair, before now always held in place under a fur hat, was a dark twist ending just before it reached the floor of the dwelling.

As though resting on the water, Mann could make out her breasts, her skin warmer where it was touched by the heated water. A sudden passion stirred him. For all he'd actually seen little of her the night before, it was evident she was a striking woman. He reflected on his luck at finding her.

'I doubt there's room for two,' she complained, her eyes still closed. 'But you're welcome to try, all the same. Grab yourself a linen first. Otherwise, you'll drip all over the floor when you're done.'

Mann grunted, looking around for the offered towel, and quickly grabbed one from the open wooden chest close by. As Freg had done, he stretched the linen out before one of the hearths and quickly divested himself of his clothing.

Freg had offered to share much with him, and he wasn't about to stint in repaying what he could.

NINE

THE FOLLOWING DAY, Freg dispatched him to the wine-merchant, a scrunched piece of vellum in his hands and instructions on where to go.

She was busy with her reindeer, while her eyes sparkled with some unspoken mirth. Mann went begrudgingly. The storm Freg had worried about had returned in full force in the night. The wind had clattered against one of the doors, or perhaps the gate, forcing it to bang all night long. The noise had driven Mann to distraction, but he'd refused to put on all of his clothes and seek out the disturbance, not when he was so warm and comfortable in Freg's bed.

He regretted that choice now, trudging down streets that hadn't yet been cleared of snow, fighting to stay awake. More people were walking the streets, and he watched them with mild interest, coupled with annoyance, whenever they wobbled into his path, slipping on the lingering snow and icy patches.

Hunched inside his cloak, his hood covering most of his face, he felt very much like an outsider. The stares of the inhabitants of this place knew him for what he was. A fraud. Or so it felt.

Freg's instructions were succinct and easy to follow. He soon found himself outside a neat wooden doorway, crisscrossed with small wooden signs that seemed to depict something, although he couldn't quite work out what. Above his head, a wooden sign blew softly in the more gentle wind, this one easier to decipher. A wooden barrel indicated the occupant was a purveyor of beer or ale, no doubt wine and spirits as well.

Yet the door was closed, and he hesitated. What was the custom? Should he knock or just enter? Luckily the door was pulled inward, a woman of medium height appraising him instantly.

'Ah, be welcome,' she said, her hand gesturing that he should enter.

'I see you have the list from Onna,' with dexterous fingers she plucked the vellum from his fist, and quickly scanned it. As she did so, Mann walked into the room, stifling laughter. The place was fashioned to resemble an inn, complete with bar and shelves lined with bottles and jugs holding who knew what. A number of high stalls lined the bar, and he perched on one of them without being invited to sit.

'I'm Helbe,' the woman finally introduced herself, a warm hand shaking his own. 'Master vinier.'

'I'm Mann. Master of little,' he replied, appraising the woman before him. She was young, surely too young to have such a reputation. But it was evident she was comfortable with who she was, and her position in society. Mann supposed she might have inherited the business but wasn't convinced.

Helbe's skin carried far warmer tones than Freg's. Mann doubted she was a native of the Northern lands. Far more likely she'd brought her trade with her, from the deep south.'

'I see Onna demands her usual, boring collection of wines

and spirits, with just enough to make the shelves appear as though she's a connoisseur, should it be needed. But she's not. Mostly she just needs wines and the odd spirit. But you, in you I detect someone who likes something a little different.'

Mann smiled at her captivating charms, wishing he could indulge in a little dalliance here, but knowing it was a foolish endeavour. He was to stay with Freg for the time being. He imagined that jumping into bed with the first woman he met, wouldn't go down at all well. He'd learned that in Slutet. And quite simply, he was enjoying Freg's lure and her well-appointed home too much to risk losing it.

Still, perhaps it would be acceptable to dalliance.

Only then did Mann realise they weren't alone in the room. Another figure, sat, hunched over the bar, a fine stemmed glass goblet before him, being twirled between long fingers, and ever in danger of tumbling.

Mann didn't need to see more to know it was Jemp before him. Perhaps that was why Helbe had been so pleased to see him. Maybe Jemp pestered all the women who were business-women in Bosetting.

'Come, I can't let you go without trying something special, from my homeland.'

As Helbe spoke, she carefully laid down the vellum list, weighted a corner of it below a stone jug, and began running her hands along the top shelf of her delicacies, stopping and resting over certain labels and then moving on until she found what she sought.

Jemp seemed not to notice what was happening. For that, Mann was relieved. He didn't wish another confrontation with the other man. Not when it seemed he'd managed to excite hatred in him because of his friendship with Freg.

'Here it is,' Helbe announced with triumph. She held in her hands a bottle blackened by age, or contents, running her hand over a small label Mann couldn't decipher, the meaning of the curling letters eluding him.

'But, I must get the right vessel for you to drink from.' Now she bent low behind her bar, Mann admiring the curve of her hips at the same time.

'Hah, here's the little blighter.' Helbe held a dusty ceramic cup aloft and removed the lid from the blackened container. A pungent aroma immediately permeated the room, much to Helbe's delight.

'If I didn't have business to do today, I'd happily join you in sampling this, but no. I must retain my wits.'

Helbe poured the smallest amount of fluid into the cup, really just enough to cover the bottom, as Mann discovered when he swirled it around as he grasped the offered cup. His nose wrinkled, as Helbe chuckled.

'Trust me,' she offered. Mann, not entirely sure that he did, knocked the entire concoction back in one swallow. He grimaced, the taste a blend of exotic herbs and spices he'd never encountered before. For a long moment, his vision blurred, before clearing. Laughter rippled from his mouth. The after-taste was far more preferable to the actual taste.

'What is it?' Mann asked, but Helbe shook her head, holding a finger to her lips.

'A master vinier must have some secrets.'

Mann thought it an odd thing to say.

'How then can you make any money if no one knows what the drink you serve is called?'

'Ah, well this is only for personal use. I couldn't allow just anyone to have it.'

For a long moment, Mann considered the logic of the response. Then Jemp turned his way.

Mann felt consumed by the peering black eyes of the man. Mann was perplexed he'd not realised the man's eyes were all black when they'd met yesterday. Surely something as strange as that would have stuck in his mind.

'I knew she'd send you,' Jemp began, malice in his voice. 'Helbe agreed to help me, just a little. Now, Mann, or whatever you're calling yourself these days, I suggest you tell me what your plans are now. I must know.'

Man's head felt foggy, his thoughts unclear. Yet he wasn't fool enough to actually answer Jemp's questions. Instead, he asked his own.

'You make it sound as though we've met before, but I don't know you. And I would remember someone like you.'

Jemp's face flushed with fury. His eyes looked behind Mann's to meet Helbe's.

'It doesn't work on everyone, I warned you.' Helbe's voice sounded bored, rather than intrigued. Mann fumbled to make sense of what was happening.

'Why don't you tell me your intentions toward Freg?' he asked. Jemp's response surprised him.

'Freg is a means to an end, nothing more. It's you I'm interested in. No one else.'

'Me?' Mann didn't quite understand why Jemp would have been harassing Freg if he were the real object of his intentions. How would Jemp have known where he was if Mann hadn't?

'Yes, you, Mann, if that *is* your name. Always you. Now tell me everything I need to know.' Only Mann was already on his feet, moving toward the exit.

'I think I'll depart now. Make sure you have everything ready for when Freg next heads north.'

'And when will that be?' Helbe asked, with only mild interest. Mann wasn't sure of the interplay between Jemp and her. He didn't think Jemp was anything more than a means to some small excitement for Helbe, in what might have been a somewhat mundane existence.

'Ten days,' he didn't like to give the information before

Jemp, not suspecting his motives as he did, but neither could he withhold the information.

'Then please tell Sledder Freg everything will be ready, as requested. Good day.' As she finished speaking, Helbe made her way to the door and held it wide for him to exit. As she did so, he felt a tug on his hand, and something was thrust inside it, under cover of his cloak.

Stepping into the limp daylight, Mann marched quickly away, back the way he'd just come. He was keen to be away from Jemp and his strange eyes. He was perplexed by what Helbe might have given him to drink, and what the intention behind it could have been.

Mann had been content to play the fool a little, enjoy himself with Freg, while she wanted him, but now he felt uneasy. Jemp seemed to know more about him than he knew himself. That wasn't a comfortable feeling.

He was beginning to agree with Freg about Jemp.

Sliding his way through the double gates into Freg's compound, Mann finally stopped his fast pace and reached for whatever he clasped in his hand.

What he pulled forth offered no answers, none at all, for in his hand, he held a small golden or copper amulet, he wasn't too sure which. Either way, the twisting, ceaseless shape intrigued him. Cast so small as to only just be visible to the naked eye, the looping amulet wound its way inside and outside of itself, but there was no visible join. Truly, it was an endless amulet, without beginning or end.

But why Helbe had given it to him, he had no idea.

He doubted Freg would know either, and so he pocketed the amulet, his fingers caressing the cold metal before letting it drop from his fingers, and banishing it from his thoughts.

Jemp, however, had other ideas. It seemed although he'd made himself scarce when first visiting Freg and finding Mann there he wasn't to be distracted from his intentions.

Later that night, when the reindeer were once more tended to, and drifting to sleep in their stables, a resounding knock on the far gateway set the two dogs to barking. Grumbling, Freg stood from her place beside the fire.

She'd been scrutinising some pieces of vellum. Mann had declined to ask her what they were, content to watch her at work as he dosed in the delicious heat between the twin fires, feet up on the warm bricks.

'Bloody Jemp,' instant fury descended over Freg's ruddy cheeks, at the noise. 'Only he comes banging at this time of the day.'

Snatching her cloak, and forcing feet into boots, Freg wrenched the door open, allowing a blast of cold air to wash over Mann. She disappeared into the pitch of night, while he shivered and cursed Jemp violently.

Mann considered what best to do. Freg wanted him to hang around to get rid of Jemp, but Jemp seemed to have other ideas on his mind. Whatever the discussion had been about earlier that day, Mann was even more perplexed by Jemp's motivations toward Freg and himself.

What was it that the wholly black-eyed man was after, if not Freg?

Before Mann could make a decision, the door banged open once more, letting in another slice of the night, and revealing Freg, with Jemp and her dogs trailing in her wake.

'He wants you,' she complained loudly, discarding her cloak and boots, and turning an accusing stare his way. 'Something to do with the vinier's earlier.'

Mann didn't appreciate Freg's tone, or Jemp's intrusion and stood to greet the uninvited guest. As Freg had failed to offer any refreshment to Jemp, Mann followed her example. Mann made his way to where Jemp stood, dripping cold water onto the wooden floorboards from the snow shower falling outside with a soft shush.

'What about the vinier's?' Mann demanded to know. It had been a strange conversation, and not one he hoped to ever repeat. The drink he'd been given had been intended to force him to answer questions he didn't know the answer to.

'You didn't answer my questions,' the smaller man screeched, his voice racking up a few octaves as he spoke. 'I asked you, and you left.'

'That's because I've no idea what you're talking about. I don't know you.'

'You don't know me?' Jemp sounded perplexed. 'You sure about that, Mann? You've always been a little tricksie with your elusive answers.'

Mann was about to answer, with an angry denial, but then he realised what Jemp was saying.

'So you do know me?' Mann asked. Perhaps here might be the answer to his own questions about why he'd ended up, naked, in a blizzard, just about as far from habitation as it was possible to be.

'Obviously,' Jemp retorted. His dark eyes were unreadable. Mann could tell a great deal from the man's stance. It spoke of a hatred between the two. Why, Mann couldn't say.

'Then you tell me how we know each other, and I'll consider your request.'

For a moment, Mann thought Jemp would do just that, but instead, a howl of rage burst from his mouth.

'Fine, play your bloody stupid games. As usual. I'll find out what I need to either with or without you. Just bloody sod off, Mann.'

As he spoke, Jemp flung the doorway open once more, leaving it flapping in the wind. Mann had to rush to close it before even more snow piled up on the wooden floorboards inside the door.

'He won't be able to get out,' Freg complained. 'At the gates. You'll have to go and help him.'

'Bloody bollocks,' Mann muttered, shrugging into his own boots, and flinging his cloak around his shoulders.

'Stupid prick,' he mouthed, opening the door once more, and stepping into the yard.

The snow that fell was fat and gentle, only the wind stirring it to flurries in the corners of the yard. Above his head, Mann could make out the texture of smoke floating into the air against the deep black of night, as he made his way to the gateway despite the lack of light.

At the gate, Jemp was arguing with himself, while he tried to open the bolts and locks without success.

'Wait, I'll do it for you,' Mann bellowed, entirely out of sorts with everything. Jemp was proving to be as much of an aggravation, as he apparently had been for Freg.

'Why do you always have to be so difficult, Blair, or whatever you're calling yourself now? Mann, is it? Not very bloody original. You know you always cock everything up.'

Still clueless as to Jemp's complaints, Mann swung the gate open and waited for Jemp to leave. But the smaller man hesitated, as though trying to think of a new tack to extract what he wanted to know from Mann.

'Don't you want to know, why I need to know?'

Mann couldn't care less, thinking only of returning to the warm interior, but, for Jemp's sake, he asked the question.

'Why do you need to know 'everything?''

'Now, that's the correct question. I've much to accomplish if we're to succeed, and I need your help to do that.'

Mann couldn't help himself. He laughed at the ridiculous response, while Jemp glowered, furrowed brows visible even in the poor light.

'I don't know anything you need to know.'

'Yes you do, you always do.'

'Jemp, I can't help you. I'm sorry. I think you must be confusing me with someone else.'

Jemp stamped his foot in petulance but held his tongue for the count of a few breaths.

'There'll be a reckoning,' Jemp complained. 'And it's always your bloody fault.'

With that, Jemp slid through the gateway and trudged down the street back to wherever he lived.

Mann watched him quickly disappear out of sight before turning, and closing the gate once more.

Jemp's persistence interested Mann. Why would he think Mann knew anything about 'everything?'

———

The following day, Mann hefted the weight of his coins, refusing to contemplate where they'd come from. They were his, and that was all that mattered.

But, were they something to do with Jemp, or was Jemp another matter entirely?

Freg has asked him Jemp's intentions after he'd returned back inside the previous night. He'd been entirely truthful, and genuinely mystified. As was Freg. She'd hid her frustration Mann seemed to be encouraging Jemp, more than she ever had, poorly, and this was why Mann now considered his next steps.

Freg wanted him to remove Jemp from her view, but if Jemp persisted in seeking him out, the only way he could do so, was to distance himself from Freg. The thought wasn't entirely without merit. Freg wasn't quite as easy to live with as he might have hoped. She was demanding on his time and could be petulant when he didn't understand her tedious instructions. Even their time in bed together could no longer make up for the difficulties of sharing the same living space with someone.

But, and this was why he hefted his coins, how long could

he afford to live in another inn for?

Ideally, Mann wanted to head south, but Freg had made it clear the Passen would still be blocked by snow. Effectively he was stuck, but it didn't mean he had to be stuck with Freg. Should he risk 'asking' for more coins to smooth his time within the settlement, or should he just stay with Freg? He liked the heft of his coins in the wooden box and was loath to deplete it further without good cause.

'You look troubled?' Jemp's voice was an irritant at his elbow, as Mann sat within the only inn the settlement could boast, considering his options.

'No, just a bit too much of this fine beverage,' Mann affected a slur to his words, but Jemp seemed unconvinced.

'It never bothered you before. I can't see why it would now.' As he spoke, Jemp had a beaker that steamed slightly placed before him on the bar. Mann couldn't tell whether it was a warm brew, or rather a concoction of other spirits and spices, constructed in such a way they let off steam.

Mildly interested, he watched Jemp sniff the beaker and then swig deeply from it.

'You seem to crop up wherever I go,' Mann said the words without irritation. Perhaps a simple conversation with Jemp would answer some of his questions.

'Like shit on a shovel,' Jemp barked, his black eyes swirling menacingly, perhaps in response to his strange drink.

'Great,' Mann muttered. He'd wanted some peace and quiet, but also to draw Jemp away from Freg while he considered what to do for the best. That his ploy had worked didn't improve his mood.

'What do you want me for?'

'I want to know when Freg's going to Slutet again. We must go with her.'

Mann chuckled at the persistence but shook his head.

'I'm never going back there. Onna wouldn't welcome me.'

'It's not Onna who needs to welcome you,' Jemp complained.

'All the same, I want to go south, not north.'

Now it was Jemp's turn to laugh at Mann, and laugh so hard he snorted black liquid out of his wide nostrils.

'South, you really must be quite delusional. There's no south for you. Not now.'

This, at least, did interest Mann. He watched Jemp writhe about on his wooden stool, his face creased with laughter that accentuated the swirling black of his eyes.

'You know you're bloody irritating, don't you?' Mann muttered without malice, but it made Jemp chortle all the more.

'Mann, this is where you live. Here, nowhere else. It's North or bust. Until all is accomplished, as it must be. Then there might be a change, but I've no idea.'

Again Jemp alluded to events he seemed to assume Mann knew all about. Mann had grown tired of explaining his ignorance. He sighed heavily, feeling the heft of the coins in his pocket as he considered how long he might be stuck in the inn, if the Passen, as Jemp seemed to be implying, were impassable.

More coins would definitely help him. Perhaps later that night, when Freg slept, he'd say the words, and hope for many and high-value coins to join those he already claimed as his own.

'How many do you have?' Jemp asked. Mann, assuming he spoke about his coins, looked surprised.

'Is that the sort of question you ask, just like that? I thought it rude to do so?'

Jemp's face turned quizzical, unsure.

'What do you think I'm asking?'

'What are you asking?' Mann refused to answer directly.

'How many you have? You know, like Helbe showed you?'

Puzzled understanding flickered over Mann's face.

'I have the one.'

Whatever answer Jemp had been expecting, it certainly wasn't that. It was evident in his shocked expression and open mouth.

'Ah, well, that might explain a great deal then,' Jemp conceded slowly, his eyes raking Mann with renewed intensity.

'Well, I'm glad it explains something for you,' Mann huffed, turning back to contemplate his coins under cover of his cloak.

'It might be I've misjudged you somewhat,' Jemp offered, the hint of a conciliatory smile on his lips.

Even more perplexed, Mann felt his temper begin to build at the ludicrous conversation taking place. He knew nothing about himself before the day he'd appeared in the blizzard. He was tired of Jemp's bizarre questions and assumptions.

'You know what, Jemp, I would like it if you disappeared, just went, just like that,' yet as Mann continued to speak his words, heated in annoyance at the beginning, they faded away to almost nothing. Slowing as his sentence continued, his mind continuing the words he'd wanted to say, his eyes blinked, and then blinked again, gazing around in disbelief.

Before him, Jemp's beaker filled with whatever strange brew he'd been imbibing, continued to froth steam, yet, there was no sign of Jemp. None at all.

Where had the tricksie man buggered off to now?

Only then Mann replayed the words he'd just said in frustration, and realisation slowly dawned.

Abruptly Mann stood, knocking over his own tankard, as the stool he'd been settled on fell onto the wooden floorboards of the inn. Mann looked and looked around the inn, even going so far as to peer under the empty tables, and between the twin hearths, but it was evident what had happened.

With his heart beating too fast, Mann met the startled eyes of the innkeeper.

Trying to joke, Mann spoke.

'I hope he paid for that drink before he ran off, like, like that,' the innkeeper's eyes immediately flickered to Jemp's beaker, and then back to Mann's.

'He did yes, not like him to leave it half-cocked like that,' the innkeeper mused, as Mann swallowed down his fear at what he'd done, relieved the innkeeper hadn't witnessed the conversation.

Trying to recover his wit, Mann ambled back over to the bar.

'Give me something strong, and tasty,' he asked, unsure what all the drinks were called.

For a moment the innkeeper appraised Mann, but, Mann had made it known he had the coin to pay for his drink. So the innkeeper reached to his highest shelf and brought down a bottle so coated in dust it looked brown from the outside.

'Try this. Drink it quick though. The taste is pretty disgusting. It's all about the after effects.'

And Mann did just as he'd been told, knocking back the drink that fizzed and gurgled on the way down, almost making him gag.

'Five coins,' the innkeeper demanded a smile of satisfaction at a job well done on his face.

Mann gagged at the cost of the rancid drink, but as the tension left his body as soon as he'd swallowed, he decided it was probably worth it after all.

He'd made Jemp disappear.

What else could careless words cause to happen, he thought, as he handed over the five coins, his mind slowly numbing, as he made his way back to Freg's.

TEN

TWO MONTHS LATER

TWO MONTHS LATER, and not in the middle of a blizzard, Mann found himself back in Slutet, with Freg as his companion.

Since Jemp's disappearance, and Mann still worried about it, she'd been a much happier companion. Mann had become used to following the ebb and flow of her life. Although he wasn't thrilled to be back in Slutet, Freg had merely smiled and told him not to worry.

Only now, as he surveyed the building before him did he understand why she'd been teasing him. There was no need for Mann to go anywhere near the inn, or Onna, for Freg was even wealthier than he'd thought.

'This is yours?' he asked her again, as the reindeer settled in their stables, somewhat smaller than her main home, but comfortable enough all the same.

'Yes, it's more convenient,' she confirmed, laughter lines wrinkling her wind-redden face.

'For me as well,' Mann agreed, tending the reindeer as he spoke, as had become their custom.

He'd not thought to enjoy spending time with just one

woman, not after his experiences in Slutet last time. But he found there was just as much pleasure to be had in exploring the same woman, time and time again. Now that Jemp was gone, of course, and Freg was more content.

'You could have told me,' Mann complained.

'What and spoil the silence you've been wrapped up in ever since you knew we were coming to Slutet. For a man, you rarely shut up most of the time. It was nice to be able to think my own thoughts for once.'

He laughed as Freg teased him.

'I think you're talking about yourself, not me.'

'I think you know who I'm really talking about,' was her quick reply. Mann subsided into silence.

She was right. He'd been concerned about returning to Slutet. His silence had also made him think of Jemp and his disappearance.

Since that fateful day, he'd been careful not to utter, or even think the words that had caused the problem. His pile of coins had slowly decreased, but he'd made no attempt to rebuild it, other than by the payments Freg had given him for his help with her delivery jobs.

But money was becoming a concern. He didn't earn enough to cover the rich food and spirits he'd become used to consuming, and he was loath to stop. He would, he was beginning to understand, have to do something about his finances, and sooner rather than later.

'I'm going to the inn tomorrow,' Freg commented, still laughing. 'There's no obligation for you to come. You can stay here and fret some more.'

Mann growled at her tone but held his tongue. He wasn't sure why he was avoiding Onna quite as forcefully as he was. Had she really been that awful toward him, or was it that he wanted to avoid the women he'd lavished his favours on?

After all, the inn would be a perfect place to take a gamble.

'I'll come with you,' Mann eventually muttered. After all, Freg knew all about him. She'd known before they'd even met, and begun their relationship.

'Then I shall enjoy your blushes,' she smirked, as she sidled past him and into the smaller dwelling. He remained, running his hand over the animals' legs, as she'd taught him, to ensure they weren't injured after their journey.

The animals were docile at his touch, aware he'd never injure them. Indeed, of all who shared Freg's home, it was only her one dog that remained wary of him. He resented Mann sharing Freg's bed, and spent much of the night trying to force him out of the bed they all seemed to share.

He hadn't succeeded yet, but unlike the reindeer, he'd learnt nothing and was bloody persistent.

As Mann turned to walk into the house, he heard their nips and barks and wished he could make them disappear as well before he banished the thought. Carefully he listened to make sure the dogs still fussed around their mistress, and only then did he yank open the door and march inside.

Just to be sure, he sought out the dogs with his eyes, before removing his boots.

Freg had asked him about Jemp, and other people had grilled Freg about his abrupt disappearance. Mann had been forced to speak in general terms, pleased the innkeeper hadn't witnessed or understood what had happened. But it had been difficult to devise a convincing story on the spot. No one had seen Jemp leave for the south, and it was impossible he'd gone north when Freg was the only sledder who ever went that way. And storms had blown almost daily for the last two months, delaying Freg's return to Slutet.

In the end, Mann had been forced to purchase a seat on the first sled south, and pretend to be Jemp himself, a feat almost impossible to accomplish. Some way out of Bosetting, he'd fallen from the sled, leaving behind nothing but a lumpy collection of clothing, and the hope no one would ever work out what he'd done.

Since then he'd stayed close to Freg's side, talking about absolutely anything provided it stopped her asking about Jemp. At some point, he hoped she'd stop. Surely it would come soon?

Every time Jemp came up in conversation, Mann considered afresh what had truly happened to him. It was impossible he'd simply ceased to exist, but that meant that he was somewhere. But where?

Mann still hadn't managed to work out where his money and the other objects had come from. He felt he should make an effort. If only to understand where Jemp was. Was it even possible he might just reappear in front of him when he was least expecting it?

Perhaps returning to the inn in Slutet would make it easier for him to think more clearly. After all, it was back where it had all begun. Almost.

And if not, it would remind him of the pleasures of the flesh there. All in all, it seemed to him it was better to return to the inn than avoid it.

If it stopped Freg teasing him, it was all to the good as well.

After another night of arguing with Freg's dogs for room on the bed, Mann helped Freg harness the reindeer for the short journey to the inn. The weather had been too fierce to come north for the entire two months since he'd left the last time. So the supplies the sled now carried were bound to be much needed.

Perhaps that would make his appearance more welcoming than otherwise.

But then again, maybe it wouldn't.

As Freg settled her reindeer outside the inn, the innkeeper appeared, a massive smile on his face.

'Ah, Freg. You're a wonder,' he began, before his eyes settled on Mann.

'Ah,' he began, looking frantically over his shoulder back into the inn. Whatever he saw there, lent speed to his downward descent as he rushed to Mann's side.

'You would do well not to make a nuisance of yourself.' Mann watched him, a wry smirk on his face.

'And good day to you as well,' Mann grumbled softly.

'Does she know?' the innkeeper asked, and now Mann laughed.

'Of course she bloody does. I'm not a fool.'

As Mann laughed at the exasperated look on the innkeeper's face, Onna made an appearance. Whatever pleasantries she'd been about to exchange with Freg, they dried up as soon as she caught sight of Mann.

Onna's lips pursed. A sudden fury crossed her face, green eyes flashing with rage.

'Stay away from the women,' she admonished, striding to see what Freg had for her to upload.

'I don't need the women,' Mann offered, but his words were ignored. Feeling aggrieved, he stood and watched the innkeeper, Onna and Freg argue back and forth about what it had been possible to bring this trip, and what it hadn't. There was only one soft cry of disappointment. Mann bitterly resented the effort he'd put into organising the sled so Freg could fit even more inside it than usual. He wished he'd saved himself the bother of trying to win over Onna with his attention to her needs.

Moodily, Mann kicked the snow into small piles with his boots, before stamping on them so the snow merged once more with that lying on the ground.

Perhaps he should have stayed in Freg's home rather than visiting the inn. To make matters worse, news of his arrival had clearly reached the ears of the four women he'd encountered that first night. Now they bickered amongst themselves as they tried to reacquaint themselves with him, from the three steps leading into the inn.

They weren't dressed to be outside, and his eyes bulged as he finally saw the women in the daylight. They weren't unattractive, any of them, and he could see why they ran a successful business from the inn, but neither did they have the power to excite him, not as Freg now did. Indeed, his manhood hung limp and cold against his body, spent from his exertions with Freg when they'd first woken in the grey of a new day.

Mann strode to the far side of sled, content to hide behind the reindeer. As he did so, he jingled the coins in his pocket. Should he risk his request for more? Or was it just not worth it?

He heard the jangle of coins swapping hands between Freg and the innkeeper, and the sound filled him with a pang of hunger. He enjoyed having money, and he wanted more of it, no matter the risk.

For two months now he'd been arguing with himself. If he merely asked for inanimate objects, surely he could do no harm? Surely. And yet his conscience had been pricked by what had happened to Jemp. He feared to utter the request, just in case it did prove to be terminal.

But Mann hungered for more coin and the sure knowledge he'd not go empty-handed again.

'Come, we'll eat together,' Freg's voice at his elbow jarred him from his thoughts.

'What?' he said, not having heard her words.

'Come, we've been invited to eat so they can decide on their next order. Onna will be civil with you, provided you leave the whores alone.'

Mann considered the request, weighing it up as he tilted his head from side to side. In the end, he followed Freg inside, quickly removing his cloak in the thick heat of the room. He's taken the reindeer and the almost empty sled to the stables, at the rear of the inn.

Onna was ushering the women away as she walked to the fireplaces. Mann ducked down, pretending to remove his boots until he was sure they were all gone back to whatever tasks they contented themselves with when there were no clients to entertain.

Sitting beside Freg, he listened with half an ear to the conversation between Grans, as he now knew the innkeeper was called, Onna and Freg. He really wasn't interested in their discussion about quantities and prices, but neither did he wish to appear rude. Instead, his eyes shot, time and time again, to the pile of coins on the bar top, no doubt placed there by Onna in anticipation of settling her account with Freg or some other supplier.

Mann coveted those coins, and yet he didn't want to ask for them. Rather he wanted other coins, and more of them, and the need to try his strange ability tugged at his already shaky resolve.

No matter what had happened to Jemp, Mann couldn't help thinking his talent was there to be used, not ignored.

Well-oiled with ale by Grans, Mann sunk further into a stupor where all he could think about was coin. As the day drew on, and more and more people entered the inn, forcing Onna to leave her conversation with Freg to tend to their needs, Mann focused more and more exclusively on the pile of coins. So much so, without truly appreciating what he was doing, he whispered the words again.

'I would like some coins to settle my bar bills.' Mann was shocked at the words, but the telltale ring of a bell echoed in his ear, followed by an outraged shriek. Suddenly coins were cascading through his fingers, and tumbling to the wooden floor at his feet.

Freg turned to glare at him from her seat, Onna as well,

from her place beside the bar, something like disgust on her face, which Mann tried to ignore. He dropped to his knees to hastily scoop up his coins. Under cover of the table, he hazarded a glance at Onna's pile of coins, relieved they were still there. These then were nothing to do with Onna.

Hastily retrieving the cascade, Mann stuffed them inside his pocket, and resumed his seat, as though nothing had happened. Freg was watching him with wry amusement, while Onna's cold eyes chilled him. Warning him. Did she know? Did she realise what Mann was capable of doing? Surely not?

Pretending what had happened was anything other than unusual, Mann turned to survey the inn. It was reasonably sparsely populated, few travellers, for no one was travelling north but Freg, so those who remained had been in Slutet for two months now. Mann saw nothing but boredom and frustration on those faces. It was clear, from the jerky movements from one of the men, he was keen to speak to Freg, no doubt about when she'd be returning to the civilised south.

Mann sympathised with him. He'd lasted barely a handful of days in Slutet He couldn't imagine how anyone could have survived for two long months. No doubt, the bill for the inn had slowly decreased over time, after all the inn had been missing any number of the niceties that added to the cost of staying there. Still, the continuing storms would have cost the man a great deal of coin.

For a moment Mann considered the other individual was almost as desperate for coin as he had been.

Onna remained engrossed in conversation with Freg when she was able to return to their table. Mann, taking pity on the fidgeting character two tables away, stood and made his way toward him.

'Do you mind if I join you?' he asked, and the other figure shook his head.

'My name's Mann,' he offered. 'Companion to Freg. Is it her you wish to speak with?'

Nodding vigorously, the man spoke.

'My name's Slinst. I'm desperate to leave here, and someone must remind me, should I ever consider coming to Slutet again, there's nothing but sorry whores and poor ale to comfort a man throughout the worst winter he's ever encountered. I've set aside enough coin to return to the south, and I'd pay more, if only I could leave here, now.'

Mann chuckled softly in sympathy. Indeed he could understand such desperation.

'I think a day or two before we return. No more than that. I'll let her know t you wish passage on the sled.'

'And you? Will you be returning with her?' There was an unsettling flicker of heightened interest from Slinst Mann didn't appreciate. Immediately, he felt a prickle of unease.

'Yes, we're business partners.'

'Then you've struck a good deal since your arrival in Slutet.' It was a statement, not a question. Mann declined to comment.

'You left behind all sorts of problems. Onna and the innkeeper are barely on speaking terms, and I believe your antics are to blame.' Mann found the statement strange. How could it be his fault what happened between Onna and the innkeeper?

'I was only here for a handful of days,' Mann argued, sure he didn't remember meeting Slinst. But Slinst was shaking his head, his eyes filled with hatred.

'Whatever you did, has made my stay here intolerable. Arguments all day, and silence all night. The inn of Slutet is no longer worthy to hold the title of the most luxurious and accommodating inn in the whole of the north.'

Mann laughed at what he took to be Slinst's exaggeration.

'I'm sure it can't be anything to do with me. Onna and her

husband were here long before my arrival. Any problems will have been brewing for a long time.'

'That's not what the whores say. They blame you, and so does Onna.'

'Then that's their prerogative, but I can assure you, I paid for my time with the whores, and then left. I did nothing else.'

Slinst shook his head, denying Mann's words.

'I won't be the only one on the sled when it leaves. I can assure you.'

Before Mann could ask for more information, Onna stood once more, some duty calling to her, and walked away from Freg, who now looked for Mann. She gestured to him to return to her side, and so he made his apologies and stood.

Slinst reached out and grabbed his arms.

'Don't forget, I asked for room on the sled first.'

Irritably, Mann shook the limp hand from his sleeve, grimacing at the damp touch.

'What was all that about?' Freg asked.

'He wants out of here. The sooner, the better.'

'Onna as well,' Freg confirmed, much to Mann's disbelief.

'Slinst said as much, laying the blame at my feet. Is she leaving Slutet?'

'Yes, she and her husband are not on the best terms. I'm sure she'll return in a few months.'

Yet the news unsettled Mann. Was it truly his fault? Had the innkeeper perhaps taken up with the whore he preferred and discarded his wife?

'She owns the inn. She'll come back,' Freg announced confidently, while Mann held his tongue.

'When do we leave?' he asked instead, not sure he really wished to travel back with the wrathful Onna.

'The day after tomorrow.' Freg allowed. 'Another day of rest for the reindeer.'

'And Onna is aware I'll be with you?' he asked, just for clarification, and a shadow crossed Freg's face.

'Well,' she said slowly, and Mann closed his eyes. He could well imagine what he was about to be asked to do, and in all honesty, he could hardly complain. Onna and Freg had been trading partners for far longer than he had known either of them.

'So I'm to be banished to Slutet so she can find her own freedom?'

'It'll only be for as long as it takes me to get there and back. I'll come straight back for you.' There was a protest in Freg's voice at his evident anger. Mann cautioned himself to calm.

'Can I stay at your house?' he clarified. He didn't really want to be in the inn with all its temptations.

'Of course you can. Why, did you think I'd make you stay here? I don't think Onna would approve of that.'

'Then I'll happily do as you ask, provided you take Onna and Slinst far from here. I'm already fed up of their evident disapproval of me.'

Freg ran her hand along his arm, as though in apology, but held her tongue.

'Well, let's at least have a decent drink?' he moaned, signalling to Grans

The man waddled over to him, took their order and turned away, before pausing.

'I would thank you,' he finally said, peering at Mann. 'You showed me I should be with the woman I love, not the woman I married.'

Apparently content, the innkeeper moved away. Mann watched him, his eyebrows almost reaching into his hairline in surprise.

Now Freg laughed in earnest, while Mann shrugged his shoulders. There was just no way of accounting for every eventuality.

———

When Freg left two mornings later, Mann found himself bored and restless. The reindeer were gone; firewood was stacked and ready for another two months of storms. There was plenty of food in store for him, so he didn't even need to visit the small market street. But the disappearance of Jemp, now he had the time to think about it again, plagued him.

What else had he done in his short time since the blizzard? Were there others he'd inconvenienced, or even worse? Annoyed with his own company, Mann stood and made for the inn. Somehow, despite his words to Freg, he'd known much of his time would be spent there. It called to him in a way he'd never experienced before, the coins he had in his pocket, weighing him down. Better to spend them, or gamble them, or whatever he could do with them.

Halfway to the inn, he paused mid-step, confused he'd not considered the option before. Why didn't he just try and reverse Jemp's disappearance, call him back to his side? Tossing a coin from one hand to the other, Mann considered how he'd phrase the request.

'I would like to return the coin,' he finally whispered, feeling strange for speaking out loud, walking down the snowy side street. When nothing happened, he couldn't decide if he was pleased or not, pushing open the door of the inn in irritation. Above his head, the inn's sign fluttered softly in a gentle breeze, almost threatening to land on his head.

Two sets of eyes immediately greeted his, a slightly guilty look on the face of Grans, perhaps worried his wife had unexpectedly returned, while the whore wore a look of deep satisfaction.

'Good day,' Mann offered, a smirk for Grans, and another to the woman who nestled at his side. She was the second of the women from his first night in Slutet, and the one the innkeeper had clearly preferred to his wife.

'Didn't expect to see you today,' Grans tried to retort, colour rising on his face.

Mann just shrugged and took a seat beside one of the fires.

'A drink, I think, and perhaps a game of chance, when you have other customers.' For now, the inn was all but deserted. Mann thought he should have dallied in the street a little more, trying out a different way of getting rid of his coin.

'Well, I've few enough guests, now they've all gone with Freg. But, I could join you. Just a few small wagers.'

Mann liked the thought of that and readily agreed. Occupying his mind with something other than Jemp would be good.

Ferreting in his pocket, Mann pulled out a number of smaller denominations, those suitable for any game of chance. As he did so, he caught an expression on the woman's face alerting him all wasn't quite what it appeared. A look of pure greed passed over her face. Mann was pleased he'd not placed anything of a higher denomination on the table.

'Plenty more where that came from?' the innkeeper queries, settling himself opposite Mann, a pack of playing cards already occupying the table.

'A bit more where that came from,' Mann agreed, watching the woman lick her lips, and tighten her grip on the innkeeper's arm. What was all this about?

'Onna has gone to raise the capital to buy my share of the inn,' Grans chatted away, placing the cards one on top of the other as he dealt to the three of them. Mann was yet to see the coin of either of his two players, but smiled widely all the same, as though he were at ease, and not deeply suspicious of their intentions.

If they were trying to play him, they were in for a rude

surprise. And if they weren't, they were probably still in for a rude surprise.

To begin with, the game went as any other Mann had played in the last few weeks. A few gains, a few losses. The size of the pile of coins growing and decreasing for every player. No other came into the inn, and the conversation was of little consequence. Yet Mann could feel he was being played. What was it Grans was after? What was it the whore wanted? He still didn't know if she was Crame or Tolly, somehow remembering the names uttered to him the morning after by another of the women.

Eventually, Mann tired of the game and stood to leave.

'Return tomorrow,' Grans queries, his pile of coins starting to teeter, for he'd been the most successful of the three

'As you wish,' Mann replied. He'd drunk and eaten well, but now he was tired. Stepping outside into the gentle wind, and dark night, he turned for a final time to glance at the two people he'd spent much of the day with. They were whispering frantically to each other, as if unaware he hadn't left.

What was it that they were up to?

The next day passed very much the same as the previous one. Mann found the games of skill and chance just interesting enough to keep him playing, whereas that day the whore, who he now knew was Crame, made all the gains. And so the days passed, one from another, with barely any difference to them. Not that he was idle while he played. He'd decided Grans and his new woman were up to something devious and it involved him. But with nothing else to do until Freg returned, he was prepared to play the long game and bide his time.

Only on the fifth day, when the inn was still devoid of all but himself, Grans and Crame, did anything change, for that was the day he won. His own pile of coins grew ever higher and ever wider. He smiled at his luck, feeling his confidence grow.

The following day, the coins on the table, were of a higher denomination, their sides highly polished. Mann's reservations grew as he mirrored the collection of coins. What were they trying to do?

Again, his own pile of coins grew and grew. It was Grans who became bored with losing, his temper rising for each and every loss. At his side, Crame kept patting his arm in consolation. Mann could tell Grans was only growing more infuriated at his inability to win.

'Enough for today,' Mann announced, not wishing to endure the hostile atmosphere any more.

'Yes, enough for today. But tomorrow, well tomorrow come prepared to gamble on your most priceless possessions.' Mann found the words confusing. He had no priceless possessions, none at all, and yet Grans was boisterous in his demands.

When Mann returned the following day, unable to stop himself, he was surprised to find not a pile of coins on the table, but rather a tightly rolled piece of vellum.

'What's that?' Mann asked, pointing to the out of place object.

'My most prized possession,' the innkeeper retorted carefully. 'And have you bought your own items?'

Mann had nothing but coins to his own name, but all the same, he buried deep within his bulging pocket and brought out the very coin he'd tried to restore to its owner, but which had stubbornly refused to move.

'Ah ha,' Crame chortled. 'I told you he had one.'

Mann looked from the coin to her delighted face, unsure what it was he possessed. He'd never shown the coins to any other, but somehow he'd appreciated that the larger coin, polished to a high sheen, was too valuable for casual day-to-day transactions. He'd kept it well hidden, or so he thought.

Mann wished he knew what it was, but Grans reaction was enough for him to realise it was exceedingly valuable.

'With that, all our little problems will be resolved,' the innkeeper said, his voice high with relief. 'Now, let's play, and this time, for real stakes.'

Mann nodded. 'But what is that?' he asked, the innkeeper fixing him with a perplexed expression.

'The deeds to the inn, of course. Or rather, my half of the deeds to the inn.'

'What?' Mann spoke in shock. 'You would gamble the inn away?'

'I would yes because I'll win and that shiny bauble you have will ensure I can buy the other half of the inn from bloody Onna. The bitch. She might think she can claim the inn as her own, but I'll have it for myself, when you lose.'

Grans had kept a pleasant tone to his voice throughout nearly all of their previous games. Mann was beginning to appreciate it had all be a ploy, as he'd thought, but it was too late to renege on the promise of his coin.

'As you wish, but if you lose, I'll take your deed and throw you out,' Mann countered, both trying to put the man off, and also assure him he'd take the prize as his own, if he should win.

'And I'll take your rare coin,' Grans retorted his colour high, his resolve easy to hear in his harsh tone. 'And beggar you.'

Holding his tongue, Mann watched the cards being divided between them, unsurprised when the hand he held was poor. He thought they'd been manipulating the cards. Now he was sure of it. But he, of course, had a skill they knew nothing about.

He'd not deployed it in previous games, preferring to rely on his skill, or lack of, when playing for small stakes.

Now Mann was content to play along, and see what happened. His coin wasn't as valuable to him as it was to Grans, and all of a sudden, the thought of the inn being his own was a delightful one. He'd enjoyed sledding with Freg, but, as was evident from his time spent inside the inn in the last week, it was here he truly felt at home. If Grans was right, and he won half of the deeds to the inn, he could happily use the coin to buy out Onna and keep the inn for himself.

The thought cheered him as nothing else had since Jemp's disappearance.

Perhaps, after all, this was what he was supposed to be doing.

Still, there was also a pile of smaller coins to wager, and the games went slowly, more and more of the coins falling to Grans. Mann was happy for him to have smaller coins. Finally appreciating how they'd suckered him into the high stakes game over the last few days, he wasn't above doing the same now.

Let Grans have all the coins on the table before him, bar the one he wanted. Only then, when Mann brought the coin into play, and Grans his deed, would Mann truly be concerned about losing, and consider using his special skill.

Eventually, the stakes were so high Grans pushed the deed onto the table. As Mann pushed his seemingly priceless coin next to the rolled vellum, he kept his face devoid of expression. Without even trying, he had a hand of cards that was impossible to beat. There was no way Grans could win the hand, none at all. The knowledge made his heart beat faster. What would Onna say to him when she returned and found him in possession of the inn? Would she be pleased to be rid of her husband? Surprised at Mann's wealth or shocked she'd been beaten to her prize?

With bemused eyes and a wide grin on his face, Grans laid his own cards on the table, a squeal of delight coming from Crame's mouth. By now, the other three women had also joined the show. Their eyes reflected the belief they thought

Grans had won. Indeed Crame bent down and kissed the innkeeper even before Mann could reveal his own hand.

'Steady yourself,' Mann said, and two pairs of angry eyes looked his way.

'Nothing but a Reign can beat that,' Crame trilled. 'And no one ever gets a Reign,' she gurgled, but Mann was shaking his head.

'Don't they. Then I'd introduce you to my royal family.' As he laid his cards flat on the table, Grans eyes flashed wide open in shock. He stood abruptly, his chair crashing to the wooden floor.

'You cheating bastard,' Grans yelled, the warm colour draining from his face, but Mann shook his head.

'Not at all. If anyone's been cheating, it's been you. I have these cards because I played the game to win them.'

'No, you didn't,' Crame's voice was high pitched with anger, her face, Mann thought, the same shade of red as when she was aroused. Not the most pleasant of thoughts.

'I've seen what you can do. You're like a conjurer or something. You've conjured these cards. Look, see.' She was rifling through the discarded cards as she spoke. Mann wondered what she was doing.

'There'll be two of each of those cards, and there shouldn't be. There should be only one of each Reign.' Her voice lost its edge as she neared the last card, her expression perplexed as well as angry, at not finding what she'd been expecting, looking around as though more cards would just materialise before her.

'Hey, how did you do that?' Crame croaked, her finger jabbing into Mann's shoulder. 'You can't have had those cards. It's not possible. Nobody ever gets a Reign.' She repeated the words as though they would prove Mann didn't truly hold a Reign in his hands.

Still standing, the innkeeper was watching Mann with the same amount of fury and confusion.

Only then Crame turned on him.

'You bloody fool. Did you deal these cards to him? Those were the ones you were supposed to keep a hold on.'

'I didn't. I swear on this inn,' the innkeeper's voice wobbled as he spoke, so fierce was his denial.

'You don't even own this bloody inn any more,' she screeched, while Mann quietly sat back and listened. He was concerned by Crame's mention of his abilities, but more, he was enjoying the altercation between the two. He smirked wryly. That would teach them to try and take advantage of him.

'Indeed you don't,' Mann agreed. 'But you can remain here, until Freg returns, and then you can leave.'

'I, I'm not leaving Slutet,' the innkeeper complained. 'I've lived here all my life. This is my father's inn.'

'It was your father's inn, yes,' said Mann. 'But now half of it is mine.'

'Onna won't go into business with you,' Grans screeched, but Mann merely laughed.

'Onna will have no choice.'

'Onna bloody hates you,' Crame screamed, as the door opened, and the woman herself walked into the main room of the inn, Freg behind her.

'I don't hate anyone,' Onna stated flatly, stamping snow from her boots.

'Well you will,' Crame screeched. 'When you hear Mann has cheated at cards and your stupid husband has wagered his half of the inn.'

Whatever Onna was expecting to hear, it clearly wasn't that. Yet Mann admired her calm acceptance of what she was being told. Behind her, Freg watched Mann with quirked eyebrows.

'A week. I left you for a week. What have you been doing?'

'Playing cards,' Mann replied, feeling it really wasn't his fault.

'Well, perhaps a partnership with Mann will be more successful than the one with you,' Onna eventually replied, settling herself next to the other hearth, as far from Mann as it was possible to be.

Freg went to sit beside her. Mann wished he could join her, but the glowering shapes of Grans and Crame hemmed him in.

'And a partnership it will be,' Mann agreed. 'Or, if you want, I could buy your half share, and you too could leave Slutet.'

Onna's mouth dropped open in surprise.

'But the inn is my home.'

'It's mine as well,' Grans whined.

'It was,' Mann and Onna said at the same time, causing Freg to laugh at the two enemies working together.

'Partners already,' she commented sourly. Mann had no idea what her true feelings were about this unexpected development.

'And as Freg has returned, you can arrange passage back to the south as soon as she's leaving.'

'I've only just got back,' Freg complained, but Mann was sure she was enjoying the angry scene she'd walked into.

'But I've nothing to start a new business, to even pay for my passage south,' Grans complained.

'You should have thought of that before gambling your life's savings away,' Onna chided, but her tone was harsh. Mann was assured no matter her antipathy toward him, this changed situation was very much to her liking.

'I can pay for your passage south,' Onna offered, only for Crame to howl.

'I'm not leaving Slutet. I've lived here all my life. You'll bloody go alone,' at Grans, a not unpleasant smirk on her face.

Now Onna stood and chuckled again.

'Oh how quickly she discards you when she realises you've no money to your name.'

'Shut up Onna,' Grans whined, but Mann could hear the fear in his voice.

'I suggest we give the matter some careful thought, away from each other,' Freg's words were well received by the other members of the party. Mann stood quickly, waiting for the path to be cleared for him.

'I'll return tomorrow,' Mann announced. 'We can discuss the future then.'

With that, he gathered Freg into his arms, and with a wink for Onna, which she looked shocked at, turned to leave the inn. Mann was sure by the time he returned, there would be a new proposition on the table. In all honesty, did he really need an inn? All the same, Mann reversed and grabbed the rolled deed before he left. The innkeeper made a hasty snatch for it, but he was too late. Mann had it, and he strolled from the bar clutching it tightly in his hand.

Outside, the sled was bulging with supplies. Freg glared at him.

'It needs unloading,' she complained.

'Then I'll unload it into the stables. I don't want to speak with those two, rather three, again today. They can argue amongst themselves and present me with a solution.'

'Will you really take the inn?' Freg asked when they were inside the shelter of the large stables. Her voice gave no indication as to how she felt about it.

'I won it. The bloody fool shouldn't have been trying to steal my coin from me.'

'What coin?' Freg asked, an edge to her voice.

'The high value one. The one that everyone wants.'

'Ah that one,' her words concerned him, just for a moment,

until he turned and saw her grinning wildly at him. Did everyone know about the bloody coin apart from him?

Freg stepped closer to him.

'I missed you,' she said, her arms going around his neck. 'It feels strange to say that when all I ever hear about you is terrible things.' She finished her sentence with a kiss. Mann rumbled low in his throat, his passion rising immediately.

'Ah, I see you missed me as well. Perhaps we should hurry home and unload tomorrow.'

'Perhaps we should just pull the door shut, and make ourselves comfortable over there.' As he spoke, Mann was working his way along Freg's jawline with his mouth, trying to reclaim her lips. She pushed him away, perhaps to see if he were joking, but then she giggled again.

'Why not. It's not like those three are ever going to stop arguing.' Freg allowed herself to be kissed, while moving around the sled, to the open doorway, pulling it shut behind her. Mann went where she did, but he never broke contact with her, and neither did he restrain himself, rather working quickly to undo her many layers of warm clothing.

As the doors finally swung shut, he felt a nudge on his backside, and turning in surprise, he eyed one of the reindeer with amusement. It seemed the animal had also missed him, for it nipped his hand, and then his arse, and then, while Freg giggled, shoved him so hard they tumbled inside the sled, where they'd first shared each other's bodies.

'Here is fine,' Mann complained, while Freg laughed once more. Then, there was only silence, the heating exhalations of passion, the soft sound of skin on skin, and the occasional huff of annoyance from one of the reindeer.

———

Later that night, lying beside Freg, his arm around her, she turned to him.

'Passen is open, you can get to the south now.'

'Okay,' was his only reply, his thoughts on the inn and what would genuinely happen with Grans, Onna and Crame.

'I thought you were going to head south?' Freg quizzed him. He laughed at her ambiguous tone.

'I thought I might, but now I'm not so sure.'

'Well I have to go south, I have a cargo to take. Will you be staying in Slutet or coming with me?' There was an edge to her voice Mann heard but didn't understand.

'I believe I'll go wherever you go. I don't want to miss you again.' He laughed as he spoke, kissing her forehead, but Freg's body tightened in his arms.

'Is that not the right answer?' he quizzed, unsure what he'd done wrong.

'No, no, it's the right answer. I think,' Freg spoke as though unsure. Mann held his tongue, before changing the subject.

'What does Onna mean to do with the inn?'

'She came to try and reconcile with Grans. She has no means of buying him out.'

'Ah, then everyone there is unhappy.'

'Will you really take the inn from him?' she asked again, talk of the south forgotten about.

'I won it. Why shouldn't I?'

'Well,' but Freg hesitated. He hoped she'd realised it wasn't his fault if Grans had acted the fool and lost all he had.'

'No, you're right. We could run it together,' she offered, with a sly smirk. 'You could have the inn, and I could bring in your supplies.'

The proposition was an attractive one. Apart from one problem.

'But what of Onna?'

'Well, you can just make her disappear like you did Jemp.'

Her words were flippant, but now Mann froze, fearing to breathe.

Freg turned, laughter on her face, that dropped away at whatever expression he had on his face.

'What?' she said. 'I was teasing you. Bloody bollocks, Mann. You look like death. What is it?' He breathed then and tried to laugh, all at the same time, ending up choking on his own tongue.

'Nothing, nothing,' Mann said, but she was right. In a way. He'd make Jemp disappear, could he not do the same to Grans and Onna? But did he really want to?

'I'll return with you, and then we'll go south, and then I'll have time to consider what to do about the inn. It's half mine, after all. But I'll be fair,' Mann smiled at his choice of words. 'I'll give them the rest of the summer season to work out an arrangement whereby they can repurchase it from me. If not, then Grans will be a man without a home, coin or wife come the snows.'

The solution was a neat one for him, and he slept, content, with Freg by his side.

———

A month later, as they neared Passen, Mann was still smiling over his good fortune. Onna and Grans had been relieved at his decision. He was pleased to be away from the bickering couple.

Before him, the south seemed to be arranged as some sort of picture or painting. While, if he glanced behind him, he could see nothing but a snowy landscape, in front of him he could see new colours appearing over the horizon as the reindeer travelled ever closer.

Freg had warned him the journey might be difficult. The reindeer were creatures of the Hvite Lands. They would struggle when trackways actually appeared instead of snow, and they'd have to remove the runners from the sled and replace them with a set of six wooden wheels that took up a great deal of room in the rear of the sled. For now, this side of the snowy pass, the reindeer all thrived, the two dogs as well, but Mann could tell it wouldn't be much longer until they had to make the necessary changes.

Then, their journey would slow down.

Loosening the tight catch on his cloak, Mann breathed shallowly. The smell of growth and greenery was reaching them, even on the wrong side of the passes, and it was making him feel nauseous.

'What's the matter?' Freg demanded to know when his hands dropped from the reins and landed in his lap, his head lolling to one side. Quickly, she took control of the sled, her eyes looking at him and on the reindeer at the same time.

'I can't breathe,' Mann heaved, his hands beginning to tingle. 'Feels bloody weird,' he tried to joke, but his eyes were fluttering closed. He couldn't hold his head upright.

'Mann, Mann,' Freg called, 'what's the matter with you?' Mann was vaguely aware of the sled coming to a stop, and of chill hands on his even colder face.

'Don't know,' he gasped. 'Feel strange.'

Freg watched him carefully, holding the reins with one hand.

'Have you eaten something?' Freg asked, patting him, as he felt his eyelids flutter. Panic was making his heartbeat too fast. He could barely hear her words over the sound of his heart, pounding erratically in his ears.

'No,' he mouthed, but no sound came from his mouth.

'Mann,' Freg's voice was rich with urgency, but it also faded as he lay there until he could hear nothing.

When he finally regained his senses, he found himself lying

on the floor of the sled, Freg above him, her eyes watching him critically.

'Oh, hello,' she said. 'Just what I thought. You were trying to get out of a bit of manual labour.'

Mann gazed at her, perplexed, as he struggled to sit upright. He wasn't sure what he expected to find but regained the seat to see the sled heading back toward Bosetting, the view before him giving their direction away, snow instead of greenery. He looked at her in shock.

'I thought we were going south?'

'We've been south. You've been insensible the entire time. I've delivered the order and picked up the new supplies, and we've just come through Passen, and you've regained your senses.'

'But I couldn't breathe,' Mann argued, wondering how much time had elapsed.

'Yes, but you were breathing, or at least, your heart was still beating. It was all bizarre, but with a bit of trial and error, I realised I could still make it to the south, while you slept, or whatever it was that you were doing.'

'So, you carried on to the south, even though I was passed out cold?' He couldn't deny he was outraged and hurt by her actions.

'There was profit to be made, and I made it. Anyway. You're fine. Stop fussing like a baby.'

'But what was all that about?' Mann asked, trying to keep the fury from his voice.

'You're just a work-shy bastard,' Freg laughed, but he could hear a slight tremor in her voice. He appreciated she wasn't finding it quite as easy to be heartless as she was implying.

'I don't know what was wrong with you. But it all seems okay now we're back through Passen and in the Hvite Lands.'

Mann looked all around him, the sun only just starting to lower in the sky. Then he glared behind him at the passes.

'Turn the reindeer around. Head back the way you've just come.'

'Why?' Freg asked, doing it all the same.

'I'm just curious,' Mann said, trying to make sense of what had happened to him. Yet, no sooner had Freg carried out his instructions, than he felt his throat grow tight.

'No, turn again,' Mann managed to gasp, and Freg once again did as instructed.

Only turning toward the Hvite Lands, did Mann feel his throat loosen.

'It's something about this place,' Mann complained, rubbing his throat, as though hands had tried to strangle him.

'What, you think the passes are trying to kill you?' Freg laughed as she spoke, but the sound quickly fell away in the silence. 'Bizarre,' she said but didn't disagree with him again.

Mann coughed, his mouth and throat too dry for comfort.

'Do it again,' he instructed. 'Just to be sure.'

'Really? Haven't you nearly died enough times now?'

But Mann reached for the reins, only for Freg to snatch them back and issue the instruction to her reindeer.

'Bloody fool,' she muttered, as Mann again began to gasp and his throat tightened unbearably as the sled headed south.

'What the hell?' Mann complained, when they were once more facing the Hvite Lands. 'I've no idea,' Mann muttered to himself. He'd felt something similar when he'd been pretending to be Jemp, but he'd ascribed that to nerves and worry, and of course, he'd tumbled from the sled when only a short distance from Bosetting.

'Well, it's a good job you like the Hvite Lands,' Freg tried to make light of the situation. 'It seems to me you might be stuck here.'

'But you took me through the passes,' Mann argued, not wishing to contemplate what was becoming apparent.

'Yes, and you didn't speak or move for two bloody days. I wouldn't recommend trying it again.'

Mann grunted.

'It was like you'd frozen,' Freg complained. Mann heard the worry in her voice, as he reached for her hand.

'I don't think we'll attempt that again,' Mann confirmed, sitting back and trying not to over think what had happened to him.

There was so much he didn't know about himself. Much he didn't want to know, and yet, if he couldn't go south through the Passen, that meant he must be from the Hvite Lands. In that case, where had he come from, and why did he have his strange ability and yet couldn't go south?

And where had Jemp gone?

'I suggest you never think of going south again. Think of it as a sure sign you should claim your half of the inn and send Grans away.'

Mann nodded distractedly. Freg was right, and yet, if he secreted himself away in Slutet, how would he ever find out about himself?

ELEVEN

MONTHS LATER

Chapter 11

FREG HELD HERSELF ABOVE HIM, her hands pressing into his chest, as she writhed on top of him. Her eyes were half closed in anticipation of the coming pleasure, and he watched her with a smirk on his face. He never tired of pleasuring her, or of watching it happen.

They'd been together for a while now, and Mann thought it must surely be a year since he'd stumbled through the snow to Slutet.

While little more had happened since his disastrous trip through the Passen in terms of finding out who he was, or why he was, amounted to nothing. Mann was far too comfortable with his life, and his coins, to overly concern himself now with whatever secrets he might once have had. Only Jemp had seemed to know anything that might debase him of his ignorance. Jemp was long gone. Who knew where?

'What's that?' Freg said abruptly, her fingers tracing his skin close to his left nipple.

'What?' Mann asked, he couldn't see what entranced her, although he could feel her fingers pressing into his skin.

'This. Here. Did you get a tattoo?'

'What?' Mann said again, not prepared to deny anything until he knew what she spoke about.

'Will you just bloody look,' she said with frustration, sliding from above him, and slipping from the bed naked, to come back with a small mirror.

She held it over his chest, and he gasped in surprise.

She was right, his skin was marked, with a strange twisting shape, which he was sure he'd seen before, but had no idea where.

'When did you get this?' she asked, but Mann was shaking his head. He just couldn't think of an excuse like that, so he opted for the truth.

'I don't know what it is,' he replied. 'Did you put it there while I slept?'

'What, and then point it out to you later? What would be the reason for that?'

'Well, I don't know what it is. Won't it rub off?' Soft fingers pressed into his flesh once more, as he lay back on the bed, watching Freg's expression. Her lips were compressed, her intent wholly on the mark. He tried to remember where he'd seen the twisting shape before.

Not that he had a great deal of experience to go on. He'd done little since his arrival, other than meet up with Freg and get rid of Jemp. Ah, listing his meagre accomplishments had immediately reminded him. Not that it was Jemp who'd shown him the shape, but rather Helbe. Mann wondered where he'd put the damn thing, and if he still even had it.

But why had it appeared on his flesh?

Abruptly, the door of their room opened. Onna stepped inside without even asking if she could enter. She eyed Freg with mild interest, perplexed by what she was doing, and then she stepped ever closer.

Onna and Mann had reached an agreement regarding the inn. Grans was long gone, clutching the solitary coin that had meant so much to him because Mann wasn't heartless. Now Onna ran the inn, and Mann shared the profits and was wholly responsible for bringing supplies with Freg. The whole thing had been working reasonably well. Onna could, at last, be in the room with him without sighing loudly and generally disapproving of all he did.

'Have you seen anything like this before?' Freg asked Onna, uncaring of her nakedness and that Onna had apparently come for something entirely different.

Onna gingerly stepped closer, her apron tight against her body, as though shielding her from interrupting the naked inhabitants of the room.

Onna peered at Mann's chest, her breath a little fast. Mann smiled without showing it on his face. He'd wondered if Onna had been attracted to him when they'd first met. Only now a look of fury swept over her face. Mann was sure she'd tell Freg precisely what was on his chest.

Her denial surprised him.

'No, I've never seen that before,' Onna stated, 'and you're needed, Mann, trouble with some of the patrons.'

Mann raised an eyebrow in surprise at Onna. She merely arched her back at him and strode from the room. Yet she left the door open and called over her shoulder.

'I suggest you hurry if you want any of your bar left standing.'

The shouts of a drunken individual could be clearly heard through the open door, and with a grimace Mann leapt from his bed, reaching for his trousers and a shirt.

'I knew he'd be bloody trouble,' Mann complained, while Freg settled in the bed.

'He paid good coin to come here,' Freg offered, their argument not new.

'And we should have let him keep it, or left him in the Hvite Lands.'

Closing the door softly, and stepping into his boots at the same time, Mann pulled his shirt closed and began to button it. He could hear more and more of his bottles tinkling and feared he'd have to completely restock his fine selection from Helbe if he didn't hurry.

Helbe, that was who'd given him the small golden, or copper, rendering of the mark on his chest. Perhaps he could ask her about it when he next visited her shop.

'Bloody fool,' Mann muttered under his breath, as he finally arrived at the bottom of the stairs. The inn was filled to capacity; Freg having arrived that day, without plans to leave until the following one. Those keen to go were still there, and so were those who'd just come. There wasn't a spare room in the inn. Business was thriving under the custodianship of Onna and himself.

The scene that greeted him wasn't unexpected, but it still angered him. One of the whores was standing there, Tolly, her dress ripped, and a sharp pink mark showing on her face. The drunken fool, ranting at the bar, and merrily trying to smash anything breakable he could get his hands on, had his trousers undone. There was too much on display even for Mann who appreciated a fine physique and had no qualms about nakedness, until now.

Mann strode to him, forcing his hands behind his back, and giving a sharp nod to Tolly that she should pull his trousers up and cover his indecency.

'What happened?'

'Bloody idiot couldn't… manage, if you know what I mean. He got angry and left the room, refusing to pay.'

'And blaming you, no doubt.'

'Of course, it's always the whore's fault,' she whined.

'Go back to your room, put some ointment on that,' Mann said, a nod for her pulsing pink slap mark, his voice far from unkind.

'What you going to do with him?' Tolly asked although it seemed she didn't really care, her worry more for her looks as she winced when touching the vibrant mark.

'Stables, or lock him in his room. Depends whether he behaves or not?'

'Better the stables for an animal like him,' she spat, walking close enough to the apprehended man she could glare at him and still stay out of reach of his slapping hands.

The captive shook under Mann's arms at her incendiary action. Mann was of a mind to agree to agree and began to manoeuvre himself and his captive toward the door. Onna was stood to the side of it, waiting to open it for him.

'Wait, wait,' the captive man said. Ratet, Mann suddenly remembered his name. 'Let's just have a drink and consider this,' he was gabbling. Mann thought he'd had more than enough to drink already, but decided he could do with one himself.

Settling Ratet on a bar stool, his hands stretched out over the wood, so Mann could grab them if he started acting up again, he walked to the other side of the bar.

It was a sticky mess there. Ale, mead, wine and all sorts of spirits and concoctions were in need of tidying away, and also of restocking. Helbe would be pleased.

'This will need paying for,' Mann muttered, his eyes on Ratet. He seemed a wealthy enough individual, even if trouble seemed to follow him wherever he went.

'Why? You can bloody afford it,' Ratet growled, his eyes following Mann's hands as he wavered over which bottle to try first.

'So what if I can. You smashed everything up. Here, have this,' Mann had settled on a jug that smelled sweet enough. He thought it was probably one of Onna's warm wines, spiced to add even more heat to it, which she handed to people chilled through and through from being outside.

Hefting the jug in his hand, he gave it an appraising glance, a strange thought entering his mind, as he reached for a still whole mug. As he did so, his back to those in the inn, he felt a strange sensation pass over him, a peculiar ringing noise, reminiscent of the same time last year. Mann froze as the jug in his hand simply disappeared, his hands clutching nothing.

'What the?' he muttered, half-turning to see if he hadn't held the jug after all, but it wasn't on the bar top either. Mann swallowed thickly, before reaching for another bottle, this one filled with a stronger spirit. He needed it, to find calm after the shock of what had just happened.

'Here, drink this,' Mann said, his tone brusque. He wanted to be rid of Ratet. He had things to consider.

'It's just a business expense to be born,' Ratet was still complaining about the smashed up bottles and jugs, glasses and beakers. Mann was hardly listening. Instead, his eyes scanned all of the items remaining on the shelf or those that had been knocked over and sloshed their contents over the dark stained wood.

He was looking for something, anything, which might assure him of his sudden suspicions.

When the time had allowed it, and he'd permitted himself to consider it, Mann had felt a worry he was somehow stealing items from unfortunates who would need them, when he made his requests. When his coins had arrived, Mann had thought it a great fortune. Now, well now he had a more profound fear. Bad enough to steal from someone else, if that was what he was doing. But now, well now, and he nodded his head at finally seeing what had been before him after all, he realised something else. He wasn't stealing from someone else.

No, as he reached for yet another old friend, a green bottle of vinegar used to clean the bar tops, and to send any staggering drunk home with a sick feeling in their stomach when they called for yet another drink he didn't want to serve, Mann knew whatever had appeared to him in the past, when he'd 'asked' for it, had merely been his own possessions.

As the thought entered his mind, the green bottle disappeared before his eyes, his cry of outrage only just repressed, as he considered the implications of what he'd realised.

He turned back to the bar, to his inn. He owned half of the inn, through his gambling with Grans, but all that money and the rare coin he'd given to Grans had been his own in the first place.

The logic of the argument almost dumbfounded him. He thought back over his time out in the blizzard. What else had he asked for and been given? What else might disappear before his very eyes?

At the thought, his gaze settled on a small red glass, one he knew only too well. Indeed, he'd placed it there, from his purloined bag of supplies, when he and Freg had taken up a room in the inn to help Onna with the demands of running the inn alone, when they were in Slutet.

That glass had come to him when he'd been out in the blizzard, when he'd just appeared, from nowhere, and he'd now put it in the bar stock. But had it disappeared from the bar, or had it disappeared from somewhere else? Creasing his forehead, Mann peered closer at it, as though it would relinquish its secrets and tell him all he needed to know.

Distractedly, his hand brushed over a pile of coins, just waiting to be placed inside the storage box he and Onna had set up in the cellar of the inn for all coins of high value. They only kept small denominations where their customers could see them, and to trade with. It was for the best.

Pleased to find a chance to escape, Mann with a glance for Ratet, who was sitting sulkily at the bar, but behaving himself, at least, grabbed the coins and bent to lift the cellar door open.

A line of stairs appeared before him, the smell of old earth and spilt ale reaching his nostrils. Grabbing a lamp from the side of the bar and taking it with him, he hardly noticed the smell. No, in a room filled with too-interested people, he needed a moment to himself and took this opportunity as presented.

On the bottom step, he sagged forward, his feet on the floor, his arse perched precariously on the step. He ran his hand through his hair.

All those mysteries he'd been so happy to forget about were suddenly staring him in the face. Just where had he come from? Just how could he summon objects to him, even if they were his own? And where on earth had Jemp been dispatched?

Feeling nauseous with the circling thoughts, Mann stood and meandered over to the small shelf where he and Onna had secured the coin box. They both had small keys for it, as no others did. He lifted his own from around his neck and inserted it into the hold. A soft 'snick' noise and the shimmering of coins greeted his jaundiced eyes.

How long would these stay here? Would they just disappear one day? And if they did, how would he explain that to Onna?

But then his eyes settled on something else, a small object, valuable, no doubt, but until that moment, of no interest to him at all.

Now, as he held the lamp close to it, and lifted it into his large hands, turning the piece from side to side, he had another question that needed answering.

How had Helbe known to give him this?

What did it even mean?

The forever-twisting piece of copper was intricately and delicately made, no hint of a beginning or an end, no sign of a join from the craftsperson that had made it.

No, it was a piece of copper that never ended.

And it was a depiction of that now marking his chest, and it had appeared from nowhere.

TWELVE

THE INN – 999 YEARS LATER

MANN LAPSED INTO SILENCE. The swirl of memories was suddenly just too overwhelming for him to continue.

'You never told me about Freg.' The accusation was harsh in his ear, wrenching him to the here and now. Blinking frantically, as though just waking from a slumber that had lasted far longer than the usual night, he looked to Branwen in surprise.

'What?' the words were out of his mouth before he could stop them.

Branwen eyed him, fury on the face he'd loved for so brief a time.

'Freg. You never mentioned her to me.' There was something underlying the demand, but Mann, too wrapped up in where he'd been, and not where he was, was too muddled to determine what it was.

'I could hardly tell you, could I? And you never asked.' If Mann thought such a response was suitable, he was quickly disabused of the illusion.

Branwen rounded on him, her face a hectic shade of red.

'The greatest love of your entire existence and you didn't tell me.'

Faltering, unsure what to say in his defence, Mann felt his mouth drop fully open in surprise.

What had he done that was so wrong? Only then his anger surfaced. Sod the haughty bitch. What was all this about?

'And of course, you've taken no lover in the last five hundred years, or indeed before that?'

Mann's angry retort elicited a flurry of emotions over the furious molten face of Branwen.

'Well,' she began, as though the answer was ready and available to her. 'Well,' she repeated, and Mann nodded in satisfaction when that was all she could offer.

'Did you tell me about your previous lovers? Will you tell me about the ones you've taken since leaving me? Will you allow me to berate you for daring to take another to your bed, for loving someone when you didn't even know you were in love with someone else, until you met them, five hundred bloody years later.' Mann's hand impacted with the top of the bar as he spoke.

'I did not love them,' Branwen almost shrieked, all eyes in the bar suddenly on them, even those too drunk to know that something was happening between the innkeeper and the golden woman as they barked harsh words one to another.

'I,' Mann faltered again. Had he loved Freg? He'd always assumed he had. But had it been love or something else. Wisely, he held his tongue, his anger draining away with the wounded expression on her face.

'I had no memory of anyone,' Mann reiterated, trying to ease the sting of his past relationship. It seemed that Branwen was having none of it.

'All those damn bloody years Mann, all of them, and never, ever, have we shared what you had with Freg. Never. You damn bastard.'

Hot tears had formed in the corner of Branwen's eyes.

Mann wanted nothing more than to crush her in his arms, but he hesitated, unsure of his reception.

'I waited for bloody five hundred years for you to come back,' Mann whispered, changing tack, horrified by the outpouring of emotion, and yet understanding it all the same. 'Five hundred bloody years. Think about that while you berate me for spending a small fraction of my life with a woman who brought me pleasure and joy. It seems to me we've never managed that.'

But Branwen's face had settled into a rigour of fury, tears cascading over gentle cheeks. Mann wished the eyes of all the others would return to their own business. He didn't like to feel so out of control. Mann even found his eyes straying toward Blane as though he could intercede. But Blane was looking frankly bored with the long story, as he played with his tankard, occasionally slugging from its contents.

Indeed, when Blane showed any interest in anything, his eyes were fixed almost exclusively on the sand timer, as though desperate for the millennium to run out and put an end to this charade.

'Branwen,' Mann tried once more, but she shook her hair, golden locks splayed so she resembled a furious sun about to incinerate itself.

'Tell me more,' Branwen delicately sniffed, her hand dashing at her nose and eyes. 'Tell me how you managed to stay here all these years without being discovered by any of the Nine, or without anyone realising those marks meant more than they thought.' As she spoke, she lifted her chin proudly, indicating the scatter of tattoos marring his chest and which had been revealed by the top of his tunic shifting as he spoke.

Hastily, Mann reached down to reposition his tunic, to flip the top catch closed, but Branwen's hand enveloped his own.

'Don't,' was all she said. 'There's no need to hide any more.'

Reluctantly Mann allowed his hand to drop back onto the surface of the old and scared bar top, his hand reaching for, and then rejecting the drink waiting for him there.

The next part of his story was long and complicated, but he'd tell it all the same.

If only so Branwen would forget her fascination with Freg, the woman who'd kept Mann in Slutet all those years ago, and who he still mourned each year, although her bones were long ashes, and none even knew her name, other than him. And now Branwen.

PART THREE

THIRTEEN

SLUTET INN

Chapter 13

MANN SIGHED DEEPLY. It was a conundrum and one he needed to solve. Much sooner than later.

His patrons were his friends, his allies, and also his enemies. But his long life had become a source of concern. His renown had spread far beyond the little inn he called his home. Now not only was their small settlement, balanced precariously on the edge of an ice sheet as far north as it was possible to go, a strange source of wonder for people to see, now he was as well.

And Mann always knew when the men and women stumbling through the door were there to see him. He could just tell. The women still eyed him appraisingly, whereas the men looked at him as though unconvinced by what they'd been told.

He'd always feared it would be his strange ability that brought unwanted attention to his door. He'd never considered it would be his incredibly long life.

And it showed no sign of ending soon. He was as healthy, and just as youthful looking as when he'd first appeared at the doorway of the inn, nigh on sixty years ago now. Even when his lover, Freg, had aged and died he'd not thought his age would be an unduly tricky problem. Now he knew differently.

As Mann absent-mindedly polished his bar top once more, his eyes fixed on the twin burning fires at the middle of the inn's main room, as he considered his options.

This was his inn, half of it won by gambling, the other half left to him by Onna on her death. Not that he'd been at the inn when Onna had died. Rather, her death had come as a shock to him, her leaving the inn to him an even bigger surprise. One day she'd been there, glaring at him with her vivid jade eyes, that always seemed to know him better than he knew himself, and the next, she'd been dead. Her body already been burned before he'd returned to the inn to mourn her, if that was what he'd actually done.

Mann had no desire to lose his inn, but neither could he risk having it taken from him by the increasingly suspicious people he'd shared so much of his life with.

He needed a plan to ensure he could retain his inn. He couldn't help thinking it meant he'd have to fake his death and resurrect himself, or someone who looked like him. He'd been toying with the idea of a trip somewhere, and an accident and some distant relative, who looked shockingly like him, coming to take over the inn. But could he risk it?

So many of his secrets were locked inside his inn. If he went away, there was no one he could trust to look after his inn if he disappeared for a few weeks or even months.

In the time he was away, it was highly likely something would be discovered that Mann didn't want anyone to see or know about. That something might compromise his return as a 'nephew' or distant relative of some sort. The conundrum had badgered him for nearly a month now. Every day he delayed, another strange face showed up to see the 'old man' of the inn. He needed to do something, but he was buggered if he was going to give up his livelihood and his inn just to divert suspicion from himself.

'Mann,' the sound of his name dragged him from his reverie as he met the eyes of a stranger he'd never met before.

They were curious eyes, almost copper in tone. They lacked the interest he'd come to expect from tourists coming to visit both his inn and himself, and to say they'd been to the end of the known world.

'Yes?' Mann snapped, surprised to have been caught so off guard.

'Mann, good to meet you. My name's Brag. I had hoped there'd be a room for a few nights, seven at the most. I'm just passing through, but wanted to visit Slutet and its renowned inn.' His tone was friendly, almost too open and honest. Mann immediately worried this man was someone to fear, despite his seeming disinterest.

'Of course, we've a few rooms left for the night. A luxury room is ten copper coins and includes all your meals, the more basic is just three, and meals are one coin each. Drink is extra for both rooms, but you can set up a tab and pay when you leave, provided you pay up front for everything else.'

With his worries pressing on his mind, it felt good to focus on something as ordinary as renting one of his rooms out for the night or even a week.

'Good,' Brag commented, 'I'll take the luxury please,' riffling in his waistcoat pockets for his coins. Brag pulled out a pouch and shuffled coins into his hand. They hit each other with a reassuring heaviness. Mann knew they'd be good coins, all of them, as he moved them to his coin box under the bar.

'A drink for you?' Mann thought to ask, and the man nodded again, his cloak falling free from his head to reveal short hair the same colour as his eyes. Mann thought he looked most arresting, impossible to forget after meeting. Mann had a vague idea he'd met him before and yet he couldn't place him.

Shaking his head in annoyance, Mann knew he'd remember someone like Brag clearly and dismissed his thoughts.

Indeed, Brag's whole appearance would prove difficult to forget. His waistcoat was a deep maroon, his shirt beneath a startling shade of white, while his cloak was a flamboyant copper, heavily decorated with swirling patterns. Brag wasn't a short man, and although Mann was still taller than him, he doubted there was any occasion when Brag wouldn't draw every eye to him.

'Just your normal ale, or mead, or wine, or spirit, whatever you have to take the thirst and the chill from a man.'

'As you wish,' Mann muttered, while Brag continued to count yet more coins into neat stacks of ten. It wasn't that Mann wasn't used to seeing so much coin, rather he wasn't used to seeing it so openly displayed. His friends, and patrons, and enemies all, were a suspicious lot, and none liked the others to know how much wealth they possessed, although it was no secret how they accumulated it all.

Not that there was a great deal to spend it on, not so far north. But then, there were huge costs involved in having anything shipped to the north during the short growing season, when the land almost, but never quite, thawed.

Mann selected a warming spirit for Brag and poured it into one of the better-made glasses. He had all sorts of containers for his patrons, it all depended on how much he could trust them not to break them. This man, he decided, could be trusted with the glass, or at least would be convinced to pay for its replacement should he break it.

As Mann poured, he indicated to the woman who helped him run the inn that the room needed to be made suitable for their guest. She nodded, eyes downcast. She was one of those who was beginning to question his long life and young looking face. Not that he could blame her. She was close to fifty, and although working for him was an easier task to many, she looked far older than he did. And she knew it. And that had caused ill-will to fester between them.

Yet for all that, they were friends, but never lovers. He'd sworn off a lover when Freg had died in his arms, her eyes still perplexed he continued to live so hale and hearty.

'There you go, good man,' Mann offered the glass and Brag took a delighted sniff.

'Redcurrant?' he quizzed. 'How did it find its way here?' Brag indicated the inn and Mann felt himself stiffen at the implied slight.

'We have vintages from far and wide. I pay well for any who bring me something a little … unusual.' The trading relationship with Helbe had continued for many years, eventually being replaced by her son, and then her granddaughter, who still maintained their links with the south.

Brag lifted the glass before his lips, as though toasting him, and swallowed down the contents in one gulp.

'I'd like some food, and when my room is ready, a sleep. And then later, well quite a bit later, I've something in my saddlebags you're going to like. A great deal.' Brag spoke with a smile on his unusual face, but behind his façade Mann sensed he was testing him, although for what he had no idea.

'I look forward to it,' Mann replied, as expected, and went about his business, steering himself out from the safety of his bar and out into the open room and toward the twin hearths. Over the one fire, a great cauldron bubbled and burped its way through the cooking process. It was only fully emptied once a month. Other than that it was routinely topped up with different meats and occasional grains and vegetables. It was this the one-coin patrons ate from.

Mann felt they did a lot better out of it than patrons in other inns. The meat was always tender and well-cooked, the grains of the highest quality and if the vegetables were root vegetables, wrinkled and well past their best, it was only to be expected when every supply journey north was subject to the weather conditions.

Instead, Mann went to the other fireplace, where the carcass of a winter fox had been slowly roasting over the burning brands, along with a tray of hearth cakes. He reached for two hearth cakes from their baking tray, placing them on the chunky wooden board in his hand, and then set it on the side to carve thick slices of meat from the roast. The meat was well-cooked, and he swung it away from the central heat of the fire. If he left it much longer, it would be tough and only good for being added to the one-coin cauldron where the juices would soften the meat once more.

Wiping his knife clean on his apron, Mann deposited it back into the soft sheath he wore around his waist and walked to the other fire. The heat was causing sweat to bead down his face. He swatted at it, reaching for the giant ladle resting on the side. He swung it into the cauldron and added juices to the meat and hearth cakes. Happy, he turned to deliver the meal to the man, only to find himself under intense scrutiny.

Mann's steps faltered. He caught himself on the edge of the bar before he could tumble. He growled low in his chest. He didn't like this man. Not at all.

It felt suspiciously as though Brag knew precisely what he was thinking, long before he thought it. And with his mind in such turmoil about the future, the last thing he needed was someone to guess about his past.

Mann indicated a free seat and table, and the patron followed him, cupping his drink and looking around the large and well-appointed room.

'I see why people rave about this place,' Brag tried making small talk as Mann attempted to deposit the meal and leave as quickly as possible. Mann turned to walk away, a noncommittal grunt on his lips, only for a warm hand to rest on his arm.

'I'd like to speak with you, at length, about this place and how it's run. I have an idea to set up a similar place, but in the slightly more hospitable Bosetting. It would give your patrons somewhere to visit along the way here.' Brag sounded hopeful when he spoke, but there was just something about him Mann didn't trust. A feeling reinforced when the man smirked as though he'd heard his thoughts.

Mann shrugged away from the touch.

'When the inn's quiet, I'll let you know, but for now, I'm afraid, I've duties elsewhere.'

Brag grinned, as though he'd been expecting the answer, and turned his attention to his meal, allowing Mann to escape. He did so, deciding the time was ripe for a visit to his cellar. The inn was reasonably quiet. It was a little past midday, far too early for his regular patrons.

Mann wasn't convinced Brag was who he said he was, and wanted some time away from his penetrating gaze.

Cocooned in the safety of his cellar, Mann tried to drive his concerns about the man from his mind. He had far more important things to worry about. Or did he?

Angrily, he resolved to speak to Brag sooner rather than later. He'd much rather know all he could before making any future plans, and one thing was sure, he needed to make arrangements.

———

Three days later, Mann finally managed to catch Brag alone. The inn had been filled to capacity for those three days as an unexpected blizzard had blown in, trapping everyone who was visiting Slutet and ensuring Mann benefited from some excellent, and unexpected, custom.

'Good sir,' he began as Brag indicated he should sit and join him as he drank a warm spirit and contemplated his breakfast of hearth cakes and preserve.

'You've been a very busy innkeeper,' Brag began, trying for cheery although Mann had watched him intently when he'd had a spare moment and knew he'd been mostly sullen, stuck in an enclosed space with so many people he didn't know, and the eyes of all them watching his every movement. Mann could have advised him to cover his bright clothes, but the copper cloak would have caused just as much interest.

'When the weather turns most people turn to drink, gaming and eating. There's little enough else to do.'

'Is that the secret of your success then? You literally trap people here and line your pockets?'

Mann felt he should have been offended by the jibe, but he'd heard it too many times before and just shook his head.

'The previous innkeeper used to raise all his prices just to stop people from drinking and gambling. I leave them the same. It's their own damn fault if they spend too much while they're trapped.'

Brag laughed. 'Ah, I see it works both ways. I would think you'd raise your prices to capitalise on the increased trade, but clearly not. I'll bear that in mind. Watching you work, with only you and your woman to keep everyone happy, I'm beginning to think that keeping an inn is far more work than I'd anticipated.'

'It keeps us busy, and thereby keeps us warm. As you must know by now, there's little more to do here but our jobs.'

'Yet you seem content, happy even?' Mann thought it a strange observation to make to a stranger, but he supposed Brag was right.

'I'm content with my inn and the choices I've made in my life. Why do you ask?'

'Idle interest, nothing more. I've travelled a great deal in my life. I'm always a little surprised by those who choose to remain in one place for a long time.'

'Some of us don't have the coins to travel far and wide or the inclination.' A decision made, Mann decided to begin setting his path to escaping the inn. 'I've distant family not far from here. I plan on travelling to see them soon. I've not met them before.'

Brag nodded, as though that solved his problem with Mann's lack of desire to travel. Then he began to quiz him on the more mundane tasks of running the inn. Quickly Mann fell a little under his spell. A quick question, and an even faster answer.

Brag was filled with questions, on all aspects of running the inn, from the costs of transporting ale and wine, to the problems of keeping food fresh through the incredibly long winter. Mann began to relax. Perhaps Brag really was who he said he was?

Content, Mann returned to his business and his plots, and just about forgot all about Brag. He had more important matters on his mind than a possible competitor in Bosetting. After all, there were a number of inns there already.

Mann had laid some opening gambits with both Brag and his 'normal' patrons, talking about going to visit some family, and asking for advice on the best way to travel and what supplies to take. A plan began to form of how he could leave his inn, fake an accident that would lead to his fake death, allowing him to return to it at a later date, reinvented as his own nephew, or some such.

Mann summoned the local scribe to him two days later, and had him write down, and then witness his wishes, should some accident befall him. The scribe, a young man with a mass of red curls cascading down his back, was both revered by his community for his knowledge and skills, and also a little ridiculed. He could too often be heard speaking about events and people no one else had ever heard of and trying to argue philosophy or logic with the local population, who had no interest, or skills in either discipline. Mann had often turned a blind eye to the patrons who allowed the poor scribe to become too drunk to make his way home again.

The scribe was good for a bit of amusement when the isolation became overwhelming.

As few of the inhabitants of Slutet read, or wrote, or had any desire to learn anything that didn't come by word of mouth from the warmer south, the scribe was often left to argue along with himself, and Mann, when he took pity on him. Or just felt filled with the desire to have a good argument.

As such, and as isolated as he often was, the scribe was the perfect person to help Mann with his plotting and planning. There was little or no chance anyone would listen to a single word the scribe said should he ever raise any concern with the ownership of the inn in Slutet.

Mann's scheming was temporarily delayed when Brag stayed for not one week, but three long weeks. At the end of each week, he laboriously counting out his seventy coins for the coming week. But now he'd made his decision to leave, Mann found it easier to accept the scrutiny and his presence.

And then, Mann had an idea.

Mann had thought long and hard about whose hands to leave his business in when he went away. He had many friends, allies and enemies within Slutet, but could trust no one with something as precious as his inn.

He'd come to have a whole new appreciation for Brag. He'd been deeply suspicious at the beginning of their acquaintance but had quickly come to realise something important. Brag had as many secrets to hide as he did.

Not that he knew what all those secrets were yet, but Mann had caught glimpses here and there of a man who was furtive, desperate not to be exposed, and that fit far too well with Mann's own quandary for him to ignore.

And after all, Brag said he intended to set up an inn similar to his own. Would it not be in his best interests to have some experience with running an inn beforehand?

The more Mann considered his options, the more he convinced himself Brag was the unlooked-for answer to his problem. Eventually, after a long day considering his options and watching the furtive actions of Brag with some casual interest, Mann decided to approach him with the suggestion.

As always Brag sat at the table just close enough to the great double fireplace to feel the heat without being too hot. He was eating his meal, this one, the meat of a white-coated hare and three hearth cakes, with some root vegetables that had been cooked and then allowed to crisp in the juices of the hare.

It was one of Mann's favourite meals. He was looking forward to getting the chance to eat, but first, well first he wanted to approach Brag.

'Could I speak with you,' Mann asked Brag, happy he'd finished eating his meal. Brag looked at him with surprise, his copper eyes clear and bright.

Expansively Brag indicated Mann should sit and pushed his wooden board to one side, a small pool of cooling meat juices starting to form an unsightly skin. Mann wished he'd thought to move it first but now he'd been welcomed to sit, he didn't want to be distracted.

'Of course. What can I help you with?'

Mann wasn't surprised Brag had guessed he wanted something. The man was often more than one step in front of him. Mann wouldn't be surprised if he'd purposefully extended his visit to enable him to build the desire to ask him to run the inn in his absence, seeing the opportunity before Mann had realised it existed.

'As you know I'm hoping to leave the inn for a long trip to

visit family. I've never done so before and need someone to run the place in my absence. With your keen interest in all the intricacies of inn management, I was hoping you might be interested in doing so. I would pay you, of course,' Mann hastened to add, somewhat surprised to see a sour expression on Brag's face. He'd not been expecting that.

'You'd rather a stranger ran your inn than one of your intimates?' Brag probed, and Mann suddenly realised how strange his request must sound.

'I ..' Mann began and then faltered, unsure what to say. 'I.. well, to be honest, everyone here already has a profession to keep them busy most of the time. I don't want to inconvenience anyone and, well, as you've already extended your visit a few times, I hoped you'd be able to again.' Mann tried to keep the apology from his voice, while not sounding too desperate. Mann knew it was this or leaving his home in the hands of men and women he'd rather not allow to explore it too closely, those who already had their suspicions about Mann.

Somehow he thought Brag would keep his secrets far better, and, the fact he wasn't a resident would mean that anything he did discover would be diluted with distance when he returned to the south, or even just to Bosetting.

Brag's face softened a little at his explanation.

'It must be a fine predicament for you,' Brag conceded, looking around the inn. 'Do you think you'll be gone for long?'

Mann considered what to say. He didn't plan on being long, but if he was going to fake his own death and then return as someone else, it might be the work of months rather than weeks.

'A few months, perhaps three at the most.'

Brag looked at him thoughtfully. 'And you'd trust me for so long with your coin and all your wealth?'

'I would,' Mann acknowledged. 'I think it would be better to have someone my friends will keep a close eye on, and yet who's independent. I don't want there to be arguments in my absence.'

'I'll think about it,' Brag announced grandly, he'd leaned back in his chair and was looking around the inn. It wasn't busy, and yet seven of the tables were occupied with a selection of regular patrons and a few travellers.

When the snowstorm that had initially caused Brag to stay longer, had cleared, many of the travellers had hastened to leave, taking their horses, reindeer and sledges back to the less inhospitable south. Some of the locals who'd also travelled south with them had returned a week later with tales of snowdrifts and blockages, some vowing not to leave again. As such, it was no surprise to Mann his inn was a bit quieter than usual.

It was no longer necessary to rely just on the sled service Freg had once facilitated. More and more people now had access to horses and reindeer, and they used them with higher frequency, apart from during the winter.

'You're right. It would be a good experience for me, and I'd like to help you out when you've shared your knowledge with me so openly. I'll let you know my decision come the morning.'

'Excellent, and thank you for considering it. I'd feel more … comfortable if I could travel knowing you were in charge in my absence.'

A small smile touched Brag's copper-hued cheeks as Mann stood and retrieved his wooden board to discard the scraps and clean it for the next patron.

'When do you plan to leave?' Brag thought to ask as he stood and Mann considered.

'As soon as possible. I'd rather be gone before the next snow storm strikes.'

'There will be more storms then?' Brag questioned.

'Oh yes. There are many during this time of the year. They're not easy to predict, either.' With that he walked away, content he'd done what he could. One way or another Mann needed to make his move, and he needed to do it sooner rather than later.

FOURTEEN

TEN DAYS LATER, Mann was busy making his final preparations for his journey to the south. He'd ensured his sled and reindeer were well fed and ready for a journey. Now he was simply worried about all of his secrets and whether they'd be safe in his absence, or whether he should risk taking them with him.

His sled had once belonged to Freg, all of the reindeer distant relations to those who'd first introduced him to the enjoyment and freedom of sledding.

Brag had agreed to his request to stay on in his absence and had spent the intervening period seeing to his own affairs, and shadowing Mann's movements around the inn.

Mann was reassured Brag would cope, and his patrons had become used to the idea. But still Mann worried, and his worry forced him to the back of the deep cellar where he stored his mead and ale. And other things besides.

He'd come to the inn with little but the clothes on his back, purloined from 'somewhere,' and his small red goblet, skis and the strange torch, which he'd never used since.

He'd come to understand the limitations of his ability, and

to become frugal in its use. Even now, Mann knew there were some of his initial requests waiting to be fulfilled. He endeavoured to keep track of all those so he'd be prepared if and when that object should appear in his life, and for however long or short a period.

His coin, accumulated throughout his long life, and those remaining items in his possession were his biggest worry. And Mann felt he was right to worry.

Mann couldn't take those items with him. They'd be bulky or heavy, and he didn't want to have to use them for fear they might disappear to help his younger self. So, he needed to make sure his old hiding place was secure from the keen eyes of Brag and Shel.

Shel was most displeased with him. Whether it was because he was leaving, or because Brag was taking the role she thought should have been hers, Mann wasn't too sure and lacked the patience to find out.

Taking a smoky candle into the dark recesses of the slightly damp smelling space, he counted out the barrels before him.

Mann was always well stocked, ensuring whenever he got a new delivery he moved all of the old barrels to the front, to make sure nothing ever went to waste. That was apart from one of the barrels.

He looked at it now, trying to see it with the eyes of someone who'd never seen it before. Was it starting to show its age? Would anyone who look at it notice the worn braces encircling it, the slight traces of rust and the dust pooling in strange places, no matter how often he cleaned it to make sure it looked like all the others?

Mann wasn't convinced the barrel was safe from such close inspection, but he doubted anyone would think it contained such secrets within its vastness. After all, why would anyone suspect its fake bottom, or understand it guarded an even greater secret buried far beneath it, under the trap door and deep into the layers of permafrost covering the settlement all year round?

Mann kicked the barrel, pleased to hear it sounded naturally wet and full. He'd padded out the false bottom long ago, with his old clothes and even older coins from his manifestation. He'd also taken the time to weigh it down with even more coins so it weighed as much as any barrel. If not more. After all, he didn't want anyone to be able to move it and then discover the trapdoor concealed beneath.

The lamp in his hand sputtered, a gust of wind from somewhere within the inn rushing to find him in the cellar. He looked up without surprise to find Brag watching him, a pensive expression on his face.

'We all have secrets,' Brag commented, his eyes looking anywhere but at Mann. Mann wondered if he spoke in general or if he understood his own secret was here, buried underground and also in the huge barrel.

'We do,' Mann said, forcing a smile to suddenly strained lips.

'Not everyone intends to uncover them,' Brag offered. If he meant to reassure, Mann found it strangely devoid of any real warmth. For a moment he considered he'd made a terrible choice.

Brag's next words and actions were somewhat reassuring.

'Tell me, where do you keep the spirits,' he asked, looking around the cellar as though he'd find them himself. Mann quickly walked away from his secrets, hopeful Brag would forget everything he'd seen.

'Over here, in this box,' Mann stamped his way toward the near end of the cellar, closer to the steps.

There were an assortment of barrels, showing the brands of the maker, but amongst them all stood a large metal container. 'I keep them in here. There's a lock for it. I'll have to give you the key. It ensures no one can help themselves.

Some of them are very expensive to transport all the way here.'

'Ah. A wise decision. Now, and not to be too inelegant about it, we should discuss funds for the inn in your absence. You've made more than adequate provision for myself, and of course you've ensured Shel will be reimbursed for her labour as well. But what about the woman who cleans the sheets, and the man who brings the wood and charcoal, and the hunter who brings you his catches and so on and so on. I almost feel as though this one inn supports all of the inhabitants of Slutet. What would happen if your business faltered? Do you have the funds to keep paying everyone?'

Mann approved of Brag's detailed questioning. It assured him he genuinely was the correct person with whom he left his inn. He had a slight concern that with the amount of time he'd be away, Brag may become too comfortable with his new life-style and want to remain in control of the inn after Mann's 'death.' The only assurance he had this wouldn't happen were the written words of the scribe. The scribe assured Mann his death wishes would be enforced when he 'died.'

'I'll leave you a chest of coins. Come, I'll show you where I keep it.'

Mann led the way even further away from his secrets and up the short flight of wooden steps leading behind the bar itself. There were few people in the inn. Mann felt no concern as he reached behind the three barrels currently open and available for selection lined along the wall to his back, and shared another of his hideaways with Brag.

Mann twirled a piece of the wood paneling to one side and revealed a large wooden chest, so full with dull coins its lid no longer shut.

'This is where I place my takings each day, and from where I pay everyone. It's rare I have to take anything out of here, each day tends to pay for itself, but sometimes there's a need. I calculate if you had no customers at all for six months, there'd still be enough coin in here to ensure all my suppliers were compensated as they should be.'

Mann turned to look at Brag's face, unsure what to expect, perhaps a hint of greed. Instead, the copper-coloured man nodded smartly, his eyes devoid of greed.

'I believe that should ensure everything will run smoothly in your absence.'

Brag straightened from his bent position and nodded at Mann.

'You do me a great honour in trusting me with your livelihood. I assure you nothing will go awry during your ....' And here he paused, as though searching for the right word. 'Absence,' was the one he settled on. Mann allowed a tight smile to touch his face.

Once more he wondered if Brag knew more than he was letting on, but then, why should it concern him even if Brag did. He had his wishes, and he had his plans and nothing Brag could attempt would stop him accomplishing what needed to be done. And then, well then he hoped to be able to continue his life much as before, without facing the same problem for another fifty, or even sixty years.

After all, it was simply impossible his long life would last forever. At some point, he would age, just as others he knew had done, and then he really would need to decide to whom he'd leave his wealth and worldly goods.

———

The night before he chose to depart, Mann had lain awake long into the night considering everything that could go wrong with his scheme. Coming to the realisation, eventually, that everything could go wrong with his half-cooked plans, he finally slept.

Mann was a wealthy man, with a strange longevity to his life. He'd made provision for the inn after his death. Even if Brag did manage to steal the inn from under his nose when he returned, pretending to be his own 'nephew,' he knew he'd be able to get rid of him, even if he had to use the trick he'd first employed on Jemp. And, Mann knew Brag had secrets of his own that could always be exploited, once he determined what they were.

With his sled ready, and the sky clear of possible further blizzards, Mann settled into it and gave the order to his reindeer they should move on. As he did so, Mann waved a farewell to Brag, who'd donned a thick cloak to stand on the wooden steps leading to the inn doorway and wished him a safe journey.

His copper skin tone looked sallow in the stark white of the early morning winter's day. Mann forced himself to swallow down his resurfacing unease.

This needed to be done. He needed to be brave enough to do it.

At Brag's side, Shel whimpered and sobbed, distraught at being left alone with Brag. Mann felt only a small thread of sympathy for her sobbing and whining. He'd not miss her while he was gone.

With delight, his animals began to walk and then trot, leading the sled away from the inn, and in no time at all, Mann was through the black gates and out onto the open land surrounding Slutet. In no time, the entire settlement faded to nothing more than an occasional twinkling light from the lamps that were always lit to guide patrons to his door.

His sled was stuffed with all sorts of supplies, from food to pretend presents for his pretend family, to a sneaky supply of warming spirits to ward away the cold and to ensure that wherever he went on his journey, he always had something with which to barter.

But as his reindeer streaked their way across the snow-shrouded landscape, unease settled in his stomach, and he recognised the problem.

Rarely in his long life had he left Slutet, and certainly, he couldn't travel to the Passen, not again.

No, he was headed to Bosetting, and then on to another, newer settlement closer to the Passen but far enough away Mann knew he'd not succumb to whatever tied him physically to the north.

So used to having exotic visitors from all over, no one had ever taken the opportunity to quiz Mann as to why he never left Slutet, apart from Brag. That had made it easier for him to stay in the one place for so long, and while he didn't fear to leave, he also knew he wouldn't enjoy it.

Mann was a simple man, content with his life. He had enough secrets to conceal without adding more to it. Now, well now he'd have to create and conceal many, many more, as well as dealing with his unhappiness at leaving his longtime home.

Mann tried to relax and enjoy the thrill of scurrying through the harsh white landscape, but he couldn't. His worries from the night before had returned in full flood and combined with his disquiet at leaving Brag in charge, he felt foolish. Why had he chosen to do this? He should simply have stayed in Slutet. Eventually, the questions would have petered out, as more and more of his friends and patrons died out. Then he could have simply reinvented himself and hoped no one noticed how long he'd been alive.

Finally, and only as the day progressed past its peak, and the first shadows of night began to cross his path, did he relax even a little.

In the distance, Mann could smell the smoke of wood fires and knew he had to be within easy reach of Bosetting. Once there he planned on visiting an inn for the night and then exploring the following day. He needed a way of faking his own death, and then he needed a bolt hole to hide away in until he could pretend to be his nephew, fetched by a letter to claim his inheritance.

His reindeer had trotted and cantered all day long, without pause for more than the occasional drink of water from their water bag and a quick sniff of oats. He imagined they were looking forward to stopping as much as he was.

Bosetting was a much larger settlement than Slutet, and had long spilled outside the original black gates and walls he'd first encountered with Freg.

Mann knew, because he paid the tolls on all goods passing through, that entry now depended on being able to pay. Yet when Mann arrived before the high wooden gates that had replaced the original ones, clear glass lanterns lighting the path in the gathering gloom, he was greeted not with a demand for payment, but rather a look of incredulity on the faces of the gate wardens.

'You've come from Slutet?' the larger of the men squeaked. Mann nodded, unsure why it was such a shock for the man.

'Then be welcomed, and enter.' As Mann turned to encourage his reindeer into the sparsely populated street, a hand snaked out. Mann shook his head, but placed the required payment of five bronze coins into the open hand without argument.

'If you have need of an inn, I can recommend one to you,' the remaining guard offered, a hopeful look on his face.

'My thanks, but I've a destination in mind.' Mann turned away, smirking to himself. No doubt the gate warden didn't get the chance to entice many to the innkeeper who was prepared to pay for every referral. Mann knew about the inns of Bosetting. His patrons came to Slutet either filled with remorse for their poor choice, or filled with delight at finding such delightful accommodation.

Mann knew exactly where he was headed.

The interior of Bosetting was a surprise to him, even though he'd prepared himself for it to be different to his memories. It was almost as though no snow fell here. All of the streets had been cleared of the stuff, whereby he'd been expecting muddy tracks through it. Outside every building a large brazier flamed, he suspected to keep the immediate area clear of any new snowfall that might come before the street could be cleared again. There were also two lanterns to either side of the gate, casting a welcoming light into the gloom and lighting the way so everyone could see.

Unceremoniously his sled ground to a near halt on the hard surface, frozen, if not covered in snow. For a moment he worried he might never make it to the inn. Only then his reindeer became aware of the change in surface and began to pull differently, using their weight and combined power to force the sled over the ground, as opposed to gliding. Mann could have changed the sled runners for the wheels, but thought it not worth the effort. Not when he'd be going beyond the walls again so soon and back into the snow covered landscape.

It wasn't a very comfortable ride, but Mann tried not to notice as he travelled through the lit street. There were few people around as darkness consumed the land. Those he did see barely looked at him. It seemed they too were used to an assortment of strangers in their midst, just as everyone in Slutet was.

But Mann was fascinated. Brightly coloured signs hung from above almost every doorway, advertising the business. Some of them even had small display areas where he could see all sorts of bread, meats, fabrics, drinks, leathers, weapons and jewels on display.

The area was vastly more extensive than when he'd first visited Bosetting on that long ago day with Freg.

As he continued his journey into Slutet, the street layout became instantly more familiar to him. A faint memory reminded him of the inn he'd visited when Jemp had disappeared, but it wasn't to that inn that he travelled.

The street before him had been fully cleared of snow and all of the braziers were merrily spitting flames into the sky. The tang of burnt coals mixed with the rest of the smells of the settlement and Mann grimaced. He was used to the clean tang of frozen air, all year round. Being in Bosetting would be an uncomfortable experience on his nose if nothing else.

The shop fronts nearer the hub of the settlement were larger, and the houses had bigger gaps between them. Yet the desire to sell was the same. He admired the elaborate displays of fabrics, fine foods and cheeses and a goldsmith, with a man on constant guard so no one could dare approach the considerable collection of rings and broaches without being spotted.

Mann turned a corner and inhaled sharply. Before him was the inn he'd been looking for. It was a huge building, with smoke billowing cheerfully from its many smoke holes, and eight braziers outside, lighting the path and emitting tantalising tendrils of warmth.

Resolutely, he rode toward the welcoming sight, momentarily tying his reindeer to a handy wooden pole. He bounded up the four steps to glance at the door, decorated with a swirl of seasonal flowers worked through the locking mechanism before pushing it open.

The smell of real, good food being cooked, and the aroma of expensive mead, ale and spirits assaulted his nostrils, as he took in the sight of the well-stocked bar, the convivial looking innkeeper and the neat and tidy tables.

The Fir, for that was the name of the inn, and indicated by the foliage on the door, looked to be every bit as decent an inn as his. Confidently Mann strode toward the welcoming face of the innkeeper where she stood behind the bar, absently polishing bottles. She turned to meet him, her eyes open and honest. He smiled in delight at the attractive woman.

'Good day, gent,' she spoke with a polite, if guarded tone. Just as he did, she chose to make a decision about what she thought of people after she'd spoken to them, rather than by sight.

'Good day, madam,' Mann retorted, a hint of amusement in his voice as he dipped his head low. 'Your inn is very well provided for,' he added, unable to take his eyes from her mobile face. She laughed now, delight in her bright eyes at the compliment.

'It is, yes. Are you looking for a room or just a meal?'

'A room, please, and board for my reindeer and sled, for the week.'

'My name's Haune, and yes, I've a room available,' she answered, not in the least put off by the mention of his animals. 'It's not the best room, would you prefer to see it before you commit?' Haune asked but he shook his head. He'd heard enough to know The Firs was the place to be in Bosetting.

'I'm Mann, from Slutet, I run the inn there, but have to travel south to visit family.'

Knowledge of who he was swept across her face. For a moment concern warred with intrigue on her open and honest face, only then she recalled her business and returned to the matter at hand.

'We'll settle on a price for your room, and you can relieve yourself of your pack, and Sand and Rad can help you with the animals.' As she spoke, her eyes took in his appearance. He suppressed a grin of amusement. Always best to decide on the wealth of a patron before deciding on a price for services to be supplied.

Efficiently they bartered, the sum of seventy copper coins being agreed upon and he was soon ensconced in a room, his pocket lighter the seventy coins, with a brazier happily burning away in the corner. It was more than adequate to warm the pleasantly sized room. He allowed himself only a little while to recover, before he strode outside to check on his reindeer.

The stables were to the rear of the inn, and a large double door yawned open. Stepping closer, he could hear two high voices in a bickering argument. Mann coughed as he walked inside, and was met by not six pairs of eyes, but rather nine. Mann smiled with welcome.

'Good day, gents,' he called. 'These are my reindeer. My thanks for seeing to them so efficiently.' Already the six animals had been divided between two separate stables, and an old dog nosed around them. The reindeer tolerated the old dog, who Mann quickly realised was white-eyed and blind, better than they did the ministrations of the stable hands.

'I'm Sand,' the older man complained. 'Damn big beasties,' he paused in the act of filling the water trough, eyeing the animals with dismay.

'Well trained though,' Mann offered. 'They wouldn't hurt anyone.'

The younger man stuck his hand out to shake it.

'I'm Rad. Pleased to meet you. You're from Slutet. Is that right?' The younger man had messy brown hair, and hay and straw stuck to his coat. It was clear who did most of the work in the stables, but for all that, Rad seemed pleasant enough.

Mann shook his hand, managing not to grimace at the roughness of it.

'This is Good Boy,' Rad said, introducing the dog, now come to sniff around Mann's boots.

'And is he?' Mann asked, keen to make an ally of the stablemen.

'What?' Rad asked, his forehead furrowed in confusion.

'A good boy? Is Good Boy a good boy?' At the question, Rad's mouth opened in shock, while Sand shook his head.

'Bloody idiot,' Sand complained. 'Always was and always will be.'

Mann bent to make his acquaintance with the dog, pleased to have an excuse to do something while he wiped the smirk from his face.

When he stood, Rad was glaring at Sand with outrage.

'There's food in the sled for the reindeer,' Mann interjected. 'Root vegetables and moss. They prefer those to anything else.' As he spoke, Mann was glancing around. There were at least five horses, and other stables were vacant, but prepared, as though they waited for more patrons to arrive. He decided, despite Rad's dubious intelligence, the two men provided good stabling for the guests of The Firs and his precious reindeer would be safe.

With the sky menacing above his head, Mann gratefully staggered into the main room of The Firs, removing his coat as he did so.

Warmth washed over him, setting his fingers to tingling. He looked for the innkeeper, but Haune was busy with other patrons. He settled before one of the fires and allowed the snaking heat to filter up his back.

At some point, he must have nodded off and was woken by a bowl and a mug being placed on the table before him. Haune smirked at him.

'It's been a bloody cold day,' she acknowledged, 'but your room is ready and warm, and this is just the beginning of your dinner.' She indicated the broth as she spoke, placing a well-made metal spoon on the table beside it. He was delighted to see she also had a bread roll nestled on the side of the bowl. He rarely ate bread, it being so much easier and more convenient to just make hearth cakes.

'The pastry maker,' she informed him when he reached for the bread first.

'It's bloody good,' Mann complimented as Haune walked away to serve others.

By now the inn was filling quickly. Mann could tell the patrons here were all wealthy. Thick cloth and even thicker fur edgings covered most of the clothing and shoes, and it lacked the whiff of the poorer traveller.

The broth was excellent, thick and meaty. His bread roll, made from fine flour, was delicious either on its own or when dipped in the broth. Perhaps he should stay here for the duration of his trip away from his own inn? It would be nice to be waited on and have such good food and warm surroundings.

Quickly Mann was served with a trencher filled with succulent meat and ground roots. This he ate quickly too. Whatever the mug contained, it burned his throat on the way down but left his belly feeling the warmest it had all day.

Mann grumbled with contentment and then turned his mind to his plans. He had much to set in motion the following day, but much of what he still needed to do was reliant only on him. He realised he could get to it as soon, or as late, as he wished. If it all went wrong, the only person he could blame was himself.

Haune came to his side, taking away the trencher and leaving behind a goblet of deep maroon liquid. He inhaled its aroma and was delighted to discover it was a rare fruity spirit from the south. It was expensive, he knew from experience, and he sipped gingerly.

Mann was warm and full now as he looked carefully around the inn. The patrons had settled to quiet conversations or games of board and chance with cards. He had nothing to fear here, and so he relaxed, watching the flames in the fireplaces and considering what he still needed to accomplish.

His eyelids grew heavy, and at one point he nodded off

once more, with his head on his hand, only to be woken by a nudge on his shoulder, and the clunk of a mug hitting the wooden table. Bleary eyed he looked up and met the gaze of the innkeeper who winked at him. Haune smiled. 'This will wake you or send you to your bed, but not here. It brings down the tone of the inn.'

Mann reached for the mug and inhaled swiftly. The spirit inside was so strong it made his eyes water. All the same, he took a small swig of the sharp liquid, allowing the unfamiliar spices to tickle his nose. Then he coughed, or rather choked.

He heard a cackle of laughter and met the amused expression of the innkeeper. Her eyes were alight with laughter, and so raising the mug to his lips, he took one long swallow. His eyes burned and his throat flamed, but triumphantly he placed the mug back onto the table. Haune was clearly impressed with his ability to consume it.

'Now, we wait,' she muttered, her tone still amused. Mann thought she was teasing him, but suddenly he could feel sparks flickering through his body. For him, at least, this spirit would work to keep him awake.

Mann grinned with delight, only for it to immediately fade from his face. The sparks had been momentary. Now he felt great weights on his eyelids. Haune was at his side, a hand threaded through his arm as he attempted to stand.

'Sleep for you then,' she muttered, 'I thought it would be the other. But never mind.'

With exaggerated care, she escorted him through the inn, past the watchful eyes of all the other patrons, and back to his room.

Once there, she released him and turned to go.

'My thanks,' Mann managed to slur, as Haune merely rolled her eyes in exasperation.

'Take your damn boots off,' Haune called, and with that, he sank to his bed, as she pulled the door shut behind her. He thought of ignoring her instructions but somehow knew better. With stinging eyes and a thudding head, he lifted his right foot and removed his boot, and then did the same with his left foot. Only then did he let himself fall back onto his bed, and allow his eyes to close.

FIFTEEN

MANN WOKE with a growl of pain and immediately reached for the jug of cold water at his bedside. His hand first missed the jug but then grabbed it and greedily he drank the contents.

His throat was dry, his head sore, and his eyes didn't want to open. Whatever he'd drunk the night before hadn't agreed with him. Not at all.

He must remember not to try any of Haune's concoctions again.

Mann groaned. He needed to accomplish a great deal that day, but all he wanted to do was stay in his bed and feel sorry for himself.

An aroma of food cooking for breakfast reached his nostrils, and his stomach growled just as loudly as he had. There was nothing for it. He'd have to get up and eat and then see how he felt afterwards.

Grumbling, Mann pulled himself from his comfortable bed. He didn't truly remember getting into it, and certainly knew he hadn't undressed. But his naked legs greeted him as he swung them to the side of the bed, the twirling shape etched in a few places in deepest grey.

Mann shrugged. At some point in the night, he must have undressed himself. It wouldn't be the first time. Or, at least he hoped he'd undressed himself. He wouldn't want Haune to have seen the marks covering his body, rarely in the same place two years in a row.

Mann hated to be too warm, something he blamed on his manifestation in the middle of a blizzard in the Hvite Lands. Not that he liked being too cold either. He grinned. He wasn't the easiest man to please.

Hastily Mann dressed, pulling on clothes cold from the floor, and then he descended the creaking stairs to the main room of the inn.

There were fewer people around than he thought there would be. He unconsciously looked through the one window in the inn. It was still black outside, and he wondered just how early it was. He got his answer almost straight away when Haune stopped abruptly as she noticed him, two wooden trenchers swaying unsteadily in her hands.

'Bugger me,' Haune muttered, surprise all over her mobile face. 'I thought you'd sleep all day.'

Mann grinned at her shock, pleased to have proved her wrong. He winced as well. The smile had made his head hurt.

'It hurt you but not quite as much as I expected,' Haune chuckled in delight and then leaned toward him. 'I've been doing that for over a decade. No one's yet managed to wake the next day looking like you. I have to say, I'm impressed. Come, I'm going to give you double breakfast.'

Haune, wearing almost the same clothes as the day before of a dull coloured pair of trousers and tunic, but with a fresh white apron tied around her waist and neck, was as good as her word. As Mann slid onto a chair close to the double hearth, but not too close the heat overwhelmed him, she brought him a huge bowl filled with porridge, and two large pastries. They oozed with a cheery red filling. He smiled, as his stomach grumbled once more.

'Some boiled water and herb,' he asked as she attempted to bring him mead, and she grinned and turned to do as he bid.

'I added a piece of ingefara to the mix. It should help with your headache,' she added, turning away and still chuckling. Mann watched her go with a grimace. He'd impressed her with his stamina, but she was still able to see through his bravado.

Hungrily he dug into his food and considered the coming day as the inn slowly woke around him. The food settled his angry belly, and the steeped herb eased his vengeful head. All in all, he felt much better.

Eventually, as the other patrons exited or returned to their beds, depending on how they felt, he roused himself enough to return to his room, claim his coat and venture outside. Mann had much to do that day, not least of which was deciding how to go about faking his own death.

It was this that taxed him the most as he considered the future. He couldn't allow himself to be wounded or badly hurt for fear he'd truly die. Neither could he vanish. If he just disappeared, no one would believe he was truly dead, and he wouldn't be able to masquerade as his own nephew and return to reclaim the inn.

No, he needed a good death, only without a body.

The settlement was groggily coming awake as he made his way outside. Everyone he encountered on the street raised sleepy eyes to meet his, offering grunts as opposed to mouthing pleasantries. Once more, this suited his purpose.

There was a gang of five strong men clearing away the light snowfall from during the night. Mann watched them filling barrow after barrow of the stuff before wheeling it away. He thought it was a great deal of work when the snow would only fall again later that day, but he supposed it made it easier for people to visit the shops and storefronts along the way.

The shutters had been removed from some of the shops, and Mann appreciated that those offering food were the ones already open. He allowed his nose to direct him and soon came to a small stall offering pastries stuffed with fruits or meats. The stall was operated by a petite, rotund lady, her eyes continually flickering as she arranged her wares to her liking. Eventually, Mann had to cough to gain her attention as she continued to ignore him.

Instantly her watery eyes flashed to his. She attempted a welcoming smile that seemed out of place on her red and rosy face, visible beneath the fur hat she wore.

'Good lady,' he bowed slightly. She dipped her head in reply. 'Might I trouble you for one of your pastries?' he asked, pointing to the one he fancied. Her eyes followed his hand as she picked it up and placed it in a clean piece of linen. He hadn't bothered to barter with her and expected to pay over the odds for it. He was surprised when she only asked for one copper coin in exchange. So, as he reached inside his pocket for it, his fingers found one of the heavier coins, and it was this he placed into her waiting hand.

It was old and heavier than the current copper coins in circulation, which meant she'd be able to exchange more for it when she used it to settle her own transactions.

She felt the weight and looked at him in surprise, but he merely dipped his head and moved on. If he just squinted right, he was sure she had the look of the old baker about her. He hoped the food tasted as good as that he'd sampled long ago.

Mann needed to make a positive impression on a number of people within Bosetting so they'd remember him and speak about him when he failed to return from his journey to visit family. She'd have something pleasant to say about him.

Mann walked along the street, eating the pastry as he went. It was delicious. He was pleased he'd overpaid for the treat. He doubted the woman appreciated her own skills. Perhaps, when he returned as his nephew, he'd invite her to come and cook for him in his inn. It would be good to have something a little bit extra to offer his patrons when the inn was under 'new management.' Mann chuckled at the thought, the future a bright prospect.

The street woke with every step he took, shutters being thrown open, the smell of cooking and metal work reaching his nostrils, as he allowed himself to breathe a little deeper. He was used to the sharp scent of the Hvite Lands and near-constant winter. This hive of activity was new to him and only a little unpleasant.

He passed a goldsmith, a blacksmith, a butcher, and further along, another pastry seller, only here, the pastries were either undercooked or burnt, and yet still there was a huge queue. Mann considered that as he strolled past, his face turned down in displeasure as he realised all the seller had in their favour was the location close to the northern gate, and lower prices.

The gate remained closed, and he paused to admire its structure. It was built of a huge number of tree trunks. He'd have thought it cost a great deal, only Bosetting was surrounded by deep woods on two sides. All it would have cost was the labour of the people who'd felled the trees and transported them the short distance to the settlement itself.

At the base of the gate, there was a small structure. Mann watched as the wardens he'd met the night before spilled from it, and called farewells to each other, and others inside. Their work was over, and now they'd sleep all day before patrolling throughout the night. He heard the screech of complaining wood and saw the black gate being hauled open to allow people outside to enter, and inside to exit, not that any seemed to wait on either side.

Mann hurried in the opposite direction. Bosetting, despite its expansion in recent years, remained circular in nature. As he walked toward the outer ring of houses and shops, he tried to orientate himself to the landscape he knew existed beyond the walls. Yet it was hard to do. The walls reached far above the tops of houses, far taller than he remembered them being, and because the buildings were so tightly crammed together, it was impossible to stand far enough away from the wall to angle his eyesight to see outside without another building getting in the way.

Eventually, Mann gave up trying, and that was when he came across what he'd been searching for. As he turned his head away from another futile attempt to see over the walls, he happened to see a small and tidy sign for the local scribe. Mann smiled when he saw it. He should have realised all along. No scribe was likely to advertise his skills too openly.

Knocking on the door, with the thin quill etched into the gleaming black wood, Mann listened intently but heard no movement from within.

'Good day,' Mann called, knocking once more.

The door shot open, almost knocking him in the face as it opened outward. Hastily he stepped back and looked into the face of a young woman, no more than twenty years to her name. This wasn't quite what he'd been expecting. She had neatly cropped blonde hair, sculpted over her ears. She wore a warm, if serviceable, pair of trousers with a tunic covering her slight chest. Both were a vibrant orange, which clashed magnificently with the purple leather boots enclosing her feet.

She stood, one hand on her hip, the other on the door handle, and she glared at him. Hardly a friendly welcome.

'Good day, madam,' Mann offered, a dip of his head to accompany the words. 'I'm searching for the local scribe. Have I found her?'

His friendly tone and conciliatory words worked wonders on her angry face, and something like relief swept over her.

'You have, good gent. Apologies for our introduction. I'm unused to being disturbed, and even more unused to people expecting the scribe to be, well, someone like me.'

'I'm sure,' Mann consoled, pleased he'd taken the option of identifying her as the scribe as opposed to asking after 'him.' 'I'm after some local knowledge, and perhaps a cartographer, would you be able to help me?'

'Of course,' she retorted, her pleasure at being recognised for what she was, evident in her tone and more relaxed actions. 'Please, enter, but watch your head. The doorway's stupidly low.' She spoke the final sentence with derision, as her finger pointed at the low wooden beam above. Mann only just stopped himself asking for the story. He was sure it would be entertaining, but he had other matters to resolve first.

Mann followed her, having ducked his head low, into a typical home and workshop combined. He could smell fragranced wood smoke and inhaled sharply of it. She noticed his appreciation as she turned to face him from where she must have been working, at a muddled desk, piled high with rolled scripts and a large flat book, open on a page displaying a detailed plan of Bosetting, or so he suspected it to be from where he stood.

'I like to flavour the wood, to detract from the stench of the ink. My favourite is citrus, but I've run out.' She sounded morose as she spoke. 'Apologies, my name's Marnit.'

'And I'm Mann, the innkeeper from Slutet.' She looked at him blankly, and he merely shrugged. He supposed she was probably too young to appreciate a fine spirit or mead. No doubt, as the scribe in Bosetting, she preferred to keep her head clear from all stimulations that might distract her from her work. Had she, indeed, even ever been to one of the inns in Bosetting?

'What specifically can I help you with?' Marnit asked a smile on her lips despite not knowing who he was.

'I've some letters to be sent. I also need a detailed map of the area. I have one,' and here he pulled his dated map from his pack, 'but it seems filled with gaps.' As he spoke Mann passed it to her. Her quick grey eyes darted to the spaces he indicated with his finger. She nodded smartly, biting her lower lip as she concentrated.

'Little is known of the land there, or rather, of the frozen terrain. I understand it shifts each thaw, and that's why few but the most local of fishermen and hunters bother to update the maps. I think they do it because they don't want anyone encroaching on their hunting grounds.' Her voice held a trace of annoyance, as he imagined any good scribe's would. They tended to be outraged by anyone who withheld knowledge they wanted to commit to their pen's nib for posterity.

'I can update what I do know,' Marnit offered, turning the page in her large book to one she was looking for, and showing him where she did have information on the gaps in his map. Mann tried not to look too interested, but immediately he noticed the place he'd tentatively chosen for his 'death' looked even less inhabitable than he'd first thought.

Mann looked back at his own map, as Marnit watched him, waiting to see if he would accept her offer for the work. Quickly, he decided he needed the information she had available copied onto his map.

'Yes, I'd welcome the additions,' he agreed. 'I'd offer you ten silver coins for the map work, and a further five for the two letters I need sending.'

Marnit's jaw dropped open at the generous offer. He nodded to confirm it. His life would depend on what she drew for him. He had no intention of skimping on this part of his plan.

'Agreed,' Marnit stated, stepping forward to shake his hand and confirm the deal.

'What letters do you need?' she asked, and now he paused for a beat. This was actually the more complicated part of the transaction. Could he trust her to keep her silence on what he asked her to write, as all scribes must do? Could he?

Mann glanced around her home and made his decision. She might be young, but she was definitely trained as a scribe and had all the correct accoutrements of the trade, as displayed on her desk and the bowing shelves behind it. Her face was open and honest, and he knew she considered his request, just as much as he weighed up the request he must make.

Mann smiled, to take the sting from his words, and reached into his pack. He pulled from it the copy of his death wishes as written for him by the scribe in Slutet.

'I need a full copy of this, and also, to ask you to read it to me, to make sure he did as I asked.'

'Of course,' Marnit sighed with relief. The demand was reasonably commonplace in an age when so few could read and write. Neither did it matter that Mann had long ago taught himself to do both. He needed the formality of the action. He handed her the rolled vellum quite readily.

But she didn't immediately open it, instead examining the wax seal and turning back to face him.

'You're from Slutet, just as you said,' she acknowledged with a smile, her trust in him growing by this simple proof he spoke the truth.

'I told you I was,' Mann retorted, his mind turning to the final task.

'The other letter will be something I need to dictate to you, and it need not be done today, but the sooner, the better.'

Amused, Marnit looked along her table, where a tray should have held on-going projects but was currently empty.

'No time like now,' she ordered, already reaching for a fresh sheet of vellum and readying her quill and inks as she went, her slight hands holding the long quill expertly, revealing thin, rough hands. The work of the scribe was not easy on hands that came into contact with the noxious inks all the time.

'Will it need to be sealed?' she asked. He nodded to confirm that it would. With her tongue sticking out between her thin lips she reached for a solid lump of black wax and positioned it over the heat of her desk brazier to warm enough to melt. Only then would she be able to seal it.

'Are you ready?' Marnit asked, indicating he should settle himself beside the brazier to keep warm. The room wasn't exactly cold, but neither was it warm. He welcomed the immediate warmth provided by the burning coals. There was also a healthy fire, over which a small cauldron was emitting pleasant smells.

While Marnit might have little work for that day, she must be being paid for something for the room was well stocked, and she had many provisions to keep on doing so.

'Just speak what you want me to write,' she nudged. He stopped to consider his words for the final time. He'd thought about this moment for a long time. It would be a pleasant release to finally speak the words out loud and have them committed to paper.

'Greetings,' he said, and he heard the scratch of the quill over the parchment.

'I write to thank you for your letter to me, advising me of our family connection.' He paused. He wasn't sure how quickly Marnit would mirror his words. He watched her as she formed the letters, her short hair pulled back from her face in a loose circle of yellow ribbon, her face much further from the parchment than the scribe Mann had employed first time around. Evidently, her eyesight was keen.

Although Mann sat in front of her so she wrote upside

down to him, he could still determine when she'd come to the end of the line.

'I plan on visiting with you in the next few days. I've travelled to Bosetting to be closer to you, and will set out as soon as I have a map and enough provisions for the journey.' His words were very formal, but then, he had no face to match to his words, having invented his family. He was finding it hard to infuse any warmth into them.

Mann was vaguely amused to see the effortless grace with which Marnit wrote his words down.

'Best wishes and I look forward to meeting you.'

Mann finished. She turned to look at him when he'd finished.

'Can you end it with Mann, the innkeeper of Slutet?' he asked. She grunted in agreement. All in all, it had been a very short letter for the coin he'd paid, and she looked a little deflated.

'Can you seal it for me, and I'll have it sent on via messenger, and then, perhaps hunters and fishermen. I don't know how many hands it went through to reach me,' Mann shrugged but Marnit was absorbed by her work and with sealing the now rolled vellum. She was paying no attention to his feeble efforts at pretending he had a family hidden away in some snow-bound settlement this side of the Passen. He stopped, pleased he had no need to continue the charade.

Marnit worked swiftly and in no time at all he held the rolled letter in his hands, had handed over his fifteen coins and was being shown to the door.

'I'll have your map and your other document ready for tomorrow,' Marnit announced.

'So soon?' he was surprised. The scribe in Slutet had taken three days just to write out his death wishes.

'Yes, I work quickly but accurately,' she announced,

escorting him to the door and moving to shut it in his face. Mann grinned. She was keen to have him out of the way.

'First light or last light?' he asked, just to delay his departure, and she thought about it.

'I'll complete the work tonight, so first light. Just come, and knock firmly four times. I don't always answer the door.' With that, the door was closed decisively in his face. He was left looking at the etched quill in the wooden door.

Mann grinned. He thought he might quite like Marnit, if only he had the time to get to know her.

Mann detected the hint of a coming storm in the sharp smell of the wind and huddled into his coat. It would be a cold night, when darkness fell, but first he needed to visit the southern gate and see if the gate wardens would send his letter onwards.

He passed people filling the outside braziers as he walked through Bosetting, and others ensuring the lanterns were well lit. Purposefully, he avoided going anywhere near the home he'd once shared with Freg.

The two pairs of eyes that greeted him from inside the small wooden building when he reached the southern gate were filled with suspicion, that didn't fade as he explained his needs. The men were tightly wrapped up against the biting wind, yet they still huddled around a smoky brazier inside the building. Mann sniffed and smelt damp, ale and more unpleasant body odours. The two could do with a good bath.

'It'll cost you,' small, beady eyes explained, a thin tongue snaking out to lick blue lips as the one man considered what he could gain from the transaction.

'But there will be someone heading south?' Mann asked, just to be sure.

'Aye, a sledder will be along come the morning. They'll be going through the Passen. I'm sure they'll take your message for you.'

Mann felt uneasy at the vagueness of it all, but really, what was he worried about? The letter was going nowhere important. It was the act of sending the letter that was important.

'Excellent. Will five silver coins be adequate?' Mann asked, unsurprised when both men perked up at the exorbitant sum.

'Oh yes. More than enough. Now, where is it to go?'

'Litt Passen, for the family of the innkeeper there.' Mann knew the letter would arouse confusion, if it even made it that far, but Litt Passen was not on the usual route through the Passen and he hoped none would ever question where the message genuinely came from. He also hoped who ever received it, simply burned it in confusion.

'Then good gent, consider the message sent.' Mann handed over the five silver coins gingerly, trying not to touch the outstretched hand.

When the fist closed tight around the coins, but hesitated to take the message, Mann grunted in annoyance. Bloody gate wardens. They were all small men trying to make themselves feel better by being difficult and obstreperous.

'My thanks,' Mann offered, keen to be removed from their presence. Bowing himself out of the building, Mann huddled into his coat, and hastened back to The Fir.

Chapter 16

IT HAD SNOWED all night again, and as before, the snow clearers were busy about their work. Already a narrow pathway had been cleared, and all the braziers along the street front were being restocked so they too could drive the snow from the ground.

Would he have to change his name, he mused, as he walked back to Marnit's door, or could he just continue as he had for so long? He wasn't sure he'd given himself enough time to learn a new name and react to it as if it were the name he'd always been known by.

Mann knocked on the door four times, as requested, and Marnit quickly opened it, ushering him inside impatiently. She shivered, turning to lock the door behind them, and Mann immediately surmised she'd not slept since he'd left the day before, as she still wore the same mismatched outfit. Had the work he'd asked her to do truly taken so long?

As soon as he walked into the workroom, Mann realised not. It looked as though a whirlwind had swept through the previously ordered room. He bent to poke some life into the fire that was dangerously close to going out.

Marnit didn't notice his actions as he leaned to take a few small pieces of wood from the neatly stacked pile. When they'd caught from the glowing embers, he added larger and larger pieces until warmth begin to filter back into the frigid room.

Marnit was working as he rebuilt her fire, her quill slowly scratching over a dirty piece of vellum. She made no effort to speak to him, or even to acknowledge he was there. He took advantage of her distraction to take the small kettle to the water barrel and fill it. Then he hung it over the fire and hoped it would boil quickly. He was sure there'd be herbs to steep somewhere.

Out of the corner of his eye, Mann saw Marnit do a double take and then glare at him. It was clear she'd managed to forget he was even there, even though she'd let him in. He turned away, preparing two wooden mugs from the boiling kettle, ensuring the steaming water splashed over the herbs. Immediately his nose filled with a warming aroma. He turned to hand her the mug.

She accepted it, her chill hands touching his as they exchanged mugs. He shivered and looked at the red-tipped nails. He tutted and shook his head. She followed his gaze and shrugged non-committedly.

'When I have work to do I forget to rest, sometimes. It's nothing. In a few days, I'll have nothing to do but sit on my hands and make sure they're in good condition to hold the quill.' She sounded defensive.

'What are you working on, if I can ask?' Mann questioned, and she sucked her lower lip, the mug held between her two hands as though it were a hot coal she wanted to touch, and likewise put down.

'Another paid scribing job, for the owner of The Firs. It's an illustrated copy of her deed,' Marnit turned the heavily illustrated parchment toward him. He noted that not only was her hand neat and tidy, she was also an excellent illustrator.

'She gave me three weeks to complete it. I agreed, but the drawing and preparation of the coloured inks have taken far longer than I thought it would. I don't want to disappoint her.'

'Would she mind if you asked for some extra time? Surely it would be better to maintain the high standards you've set.'

She nodded, but then shook her head.

'The word of a scribe is just that. I must complete it on time. Surely you know that.'

He nodded. Mann did know that, but he genuinely couldn't imagine Haune objecting to Marnit finishing tomorrow rather than today.

'Should I come back tomorrow?' Mann asked. 'I've remembered I need another letter writing. It's no problem for me whether it gets done today, tomorrow or the day after.'

Raising her mug to her lips, she gulped greedily and considered.

'No, it's not a problem, provided it's as short as the one you asked me to write yesterday. I've completed the map and the scribing already.' She searched her desk frantically and then squealed with delight, handing over the items.

'Take your time and inspect them,' she offered, squinting with one eye as she looked at the area of Haune's illustration she still needed to colour.

Mann opened his old map and eased out the wrinkles. Marnit had been as good as her word. The areas she could fill in from her own information were neatly coloured with blues and blacks and even greens, to differentiate between the different land types.

Mann nodded and closed the map. He was more than happy with the quality of the work.

Next, he opened the unsealed rolled copy of his death

wishes. He still needed her to read the contents to him before she sealed it, to pretend he didn't know how to read himself, but he could already tell it was a perfect copy.

'These are excellent,' Mann spoke approvingly. Marnit nodded, as though expecting the reply. He doubted he'd be able to offer her a compliment that made her flush with delight. She was too confident in her writing skills.

'Yes, they are,' she agreed. 'Now tell me, who's the other letter for?'

'Ah, yes, I must send it, along with the copy of this,' and he held up his death wishes, 'to the man in charge of my inn while I'm away.'

'Is he a family member or a trusted friend?' Marnit asked, her eyes wide with surprise. It was a rare and strange thing to abandon a thriving business in the hands of either of those. He paused before answering.

'Neither, just a man I met a month ago, his name's Brag.'

Her reaction was immediate and unhappy.

'Brag. About this high,' and she raised her hand above her shoulders. 'An odd tinge to his skin, like the morning sun.'

'Yes, do you know him?' Mann asked, intrigued. Marnit nodded sharply.

'Did, and I wish I didn't. He's not the most ….reliable of friends,' she offered, her unease at his choice evident in her guarded tone.

'A better choice than the locals of Slutet,' Mann offered with a wry grin. But she was looking at him in a whole new light now. Her opinion of him had changed. Substantially.

He had no idea why.

'Here, give me back that copying,' Mann handed it over to her. She shook her head slightly. 'I need to look at this again as well. If you've left Brag in charge, whatever your reasons for doing so,' and she raised her hands as if to ward off any angry words he might have. 'I need to ensure the original and the copy are much better worded. He has his ways. He always has. Your local scribe, as good as he is, is no match for Brag and his quick thinking.'

As she spoke, Marnit unrolled the vellum and shook her head from side to side, her lips pursed with annoyance. Mann watched her carefully. She seemed much wiser than her appearance suggested. In fact, she spoke with the rich authority.

'Did you meet him when he came through here, on his way north?' Mann asked, all his plans suddenly in disarray.

Her eyes swiveled to meet his, and something flashed in them that made Mann know he wasn't going to like her answer.

'No, I met him years ago, when I was training in the south. He's a tricky character,' Marnit announced, turning back to her work and effectively dismissing him. Mann stood for a moment, hoping she'd say more and trying not to let his worry show, but she neither looked at him nor ceased her work. Neither did she ask him to dictate his letter and eventually, Mann nodded smartly to her bent head and made his way to the doorway. He would have to get it written the next day.

The day hadn't started well, and now it seemed Marnit had filled it with unspecified worries to concern him.

Should he, after all, abandon his project and return to Slutet? If Marnit didn't trust Brag, and it was more than evident that she didn't, why should he?

Mann stood on the cleared walkway and considered his options.'

'Bollocks,' he muttered under his breath. He was loath to begin afresh. It had taken him the best part of the last year to force himself to act. He had no idea how long it might take him to do so again if he merely returned home now and kicked Brag out.

'Bollocks,' Mann shouted, the sound so loud it distorted his word, thankfully, but earned him some strange looks from the few people up and about and walking along the street.

In his hand Mann still held his folded map. Quickly, he unfolded it and gazed at the area he was hoping would help him to pretend to die.

In the bright winter daylight, he could see the skill and precision with which Marnit had completed her task.

The delineation of the rivers, and ice glaciers were all cleverly marked, the colour of the surrounding deep fir forests a stark contrast with their black trunks.

There was life out there, on the cusp of the landscape where the ice met the sea, or the land met the sea, or the river met the ice and the sea, there were any number of combinations. But the area that interested him most, and always had since he'd considered the future, was close to twin forests, similar to the one outside Slutet, but closer to the Passen.

He squinted now. Mann was sure he'd seen what he needed to know the day before when he'd caught a fleeting glance at Marnit's map. Now he looked far more closely.

Yes, Mann could see what he needed.

Mann snapped the map shut, convinced he could feel eyes watching him, but when he turned he was alone. Pensively he gave a final glance at the door to the scribe's home and workshop, but there were no furtive eyes there. He was entirely alone in the street.

Mann needed to visit his reindeer. He should give them a run out on the snow, or they'd be difficult when he placed them back in their running leathers. He also needed to try something. Resigned, Mann headed back to the Firs, worry hurrying his steps. Marnit's cautionary words about Brag had reawakened his suspicions in the other man's motives.

Once more, the sheer scale of The Firs impressed Mann as it loomed before him. It occupied a prime position in the middle of the settlement. Provided you arrived while it was light, it was impossible to miss the imposing roof and its litany of smoke holes, smoke billowing from them all and away into the cloudless winter sky.

The blues of winter had almost given way to the white of ice as he watched the few clouds above his head. It was always this way in the height of winter. It was as though the sheer cold drained all colour from the sky, as it did heat from the body. Reflexively he shivered, reaching the stables.

Mann knocked on the flung open doorway, where it nestled under a low overhanging roof, thick with grass but covered now in snow and a perpetual skein of ice, festooned with long, vicious looking icicles.

'Hello,' Mann called. He received no response but could make out the two voices of Rad and Sand bickering, only the blind dog seeming to hear him as the beast wound its way toward him. The animal might well be blind, but it was a better guard than either of the stablemen. Mann reached down to allow the dog to sniff his head in re-acquaintance, before he meandered back into the warmth of the stables, content there was no threat. Mann smiled wryly, the sound of the on-going argument rich in his ears.

Mann's six reindeer eyeing him hopefully. He strode over to them, a hand outstretched to rub inquisitive noses. There was kicking at the wooden half door separating them, and he laughed.

'Eager are we lads?'

Sand had a downcast expression on his face, as he sidled up to Mann. He was also wearing the least amount of clothes Mann thought he'd ever seen a man wear in the height of winter. Still, sweat gleamed on his muscles and down his neck, his tunic sleeves rolled high, and trousers so short they almost reached his knees, on his strong legs.

'What you doin', gent?' Sand grumbled, as though forgetting they'd spoken the day before.

'I was hoping to take them out for a run outside the settlement,' at Mann's words, the six animals stopped their kicking, happy to wait quietly now they knew they were going to be released from the stables.

'Get the sled, you useless bugger,' at that the small face of Rad appeared, a cheeky grin on a young, flushed face.

'Aye, aye gent,' Rad called, a lilt to his voice. Mann didn't think the two were related in any way, but it was also evident they'd known each other for a long time and were used to each other's ways, no matter Rad's lack of years.

'And enough of your damn cheek,' Sand growled, reaching out to open the stable door and step in with the reindeer.

'Temperamental bastards,' Sand muttered. Mann grinned at the tirade of complaints.

'Yes, they're not the most placid, but they work well together and have helped me out of a few tricky situations.'

'I don't doubt it, living all the way out in Slutet. Why would you do that? It's the arse-end of beyond here. At least we have some amenities.'

Sand carried the warmer skin tone of the southern states, just a shade shy of the deep black Mann only saw rarely in Slutet. Mann was half wondering if he should ask him why he happened to be in Bosetting when Sand answered the question anyway.

'I came north to find a cure for a sweating sickness many years ago. But I found I liked it a bit cooler than where I was born. It's nice not to feel the burn of the sun on my skin. But bugger me, it doesn't half get cold here. Is Slutet colder?

'It doesn't have such high walls,' Mann said, gesturing haphazardly to where he thought the big wooden walls were. 'So it's more exposed, and we don't take the time to clear the walkways of snow each day. Sometimes blizzards will rage for days, if not weeks. It's not for everyone,' Mann admitted with a smirk.

'Only fit for the winter beasts,' Sand muttered, and then he thought of something. 'Have you seen one?'

Mann knew he spoke of the rumoured Hvite Land bears. Few people had ever seen one. They weren't stupid enough to venture into Slutet, but every so often a nasty story would spread of a man or a woman, a child even, lost in the Hvite Lands, ravaged to death by the great beasts, only a hand or foot surviving the encounter.

'Oh yes, but only once or twice. They're quite content to hunt in the extreme Hvite Lands where no one can go. They live on seals and fish and anything else they can find.'

'Are they truly the size of three people?' Sand asked, his eyes wide with amazement. Mann nodded slowly, enjoying himself as he tricked the man, just a little.

'The ones I've seen were massive. And I've seen tracks left behind before now. They were this big,' here Mann held his two hands together, thumb-to-thumb and little finger to little finger, making a huge circle. 'This big, if not bigger.'

Sand nodded, as though expecting the answer. Throughout their conversation he'd been busy harnessing the reindeer, compliant as the leathers were threaded behind antlers and below bellies. Only then Rad appeared with the sled, and chaos ruled until the animals were correctly harnessed to it. They were then content to paw at the ground, and send baleful looks toward Mann in frustration for the continued delay.

'Head toward the north,' Sand offered as he handed the leathers over. 'There are fewer people and the snow less disturbed if you just want a run out that is.'

'My thanks,' Mann muttered, taking a copper coin from inside his coat pocket and pressing it into Sand's hand, and then doing the same for Rad. Neither was uncouth enough to examine the coin there and then, but by the time Mann returned, he knew they'd be even keener to look after his beasts. Rewards such as this, just for performing tasks they were already being paid for, could buy a reindeer a lot of care and attention from the stable men.

'Enjoy,' Sand called. Mann encouraged his six reindeer to pick their way over the cleared streetway, a hard pull, until he dipped his head at the two northern gate wardens, different from the night he'd arrived. Still, they released him quickly enough, so it appeared Mann's reputation was spreading. Abruptly, Mann was outside the high black walls once more, the wind howling in his ears.

His animals pulled easily now over the packed snow. He turned them north. Toward his home, and he thought how straightforward it would be to just head back to Slutet now, deal with Brag and resume his life as though nothing had happened.

Only he couldn't. Not yet.

Instead, Mann did the next best thing and allowed himself to inhale deeply of the frigid air, as his reindeers flew over the untouched snow, their breath clouding in front of them, but happy, all the same. Mann knew how they felt.

Mann allowed the solitude to wash over him and absorb him before he turned his reindeer back toward Bosetting. While he'd wanted to give the animals a run-out, there was also important work to be getting on with. Only, he'd never attempted what he wanted to try before, and temporarily, fear made him push it to one side.

Mann kept thinking, 'just a few moments more', or 'when we've crested this rise', but in his heart, he knew he'd never do it unless he took a deep breath and allowed the words to form.

Annoyed with himself, Mann pulled on the leathers. The reindeer came to a slow stop. Their breath billowed before them, and he appreciated that they wouldn't like being forced to stop their run quite so soon. Gingerly, with his feet already wearing his old, heavy black wooden skis, Mann stood to one side of the sled and the six reindeer.

The lead reindeers watched him with mild interest while the others merely pawed at the ground, keen to be on their way, and ever hopeful of a stray find of lichen. He could understand their wishes.

In the distance, Mann could just about make out the haze indicating a storm was close. That decided his actions for him. From here he could make it back to Bosetting relatively quickly if his plan worked but left him stranded.

Mann worried now he was expecting too much of his strange abilities.

'Bugger it,' he complained to no one but himself, setting his shoulders and allowing the words to form in his mind before he spoke them aloud.

'I would like my reindeer and my sled to return to the Firs Inn stables in Bosetting, at this time, without me,' saying the words in the silence of winter made him feel stupid, but then, he heard the strange noise, and this time a shriek of surprise. Then, somehow, his reindeer and his sled disappeared before his eyes.

Mann waited a moment, breathing heavily. He sincerely hoped he'd not damaged the reindeer. But there was only one way to find out.

'I would like my reindeer and my sled to appear before me, now, from their place within the Firs Inn stables in Bosetting.'

Again there was the strange sound. This time he also heard the usual odd screeching sound. With closed eyes he feared to open, Mann had to count to three before forcing the open. Then, it was to find six sets of eyes watching him in consternation, brown eyes whirling in confusion. The previously bored looking reindeer were making the strangest sound Mann had ever heard. But for all that, his plan had worked. He allowed a bark of delight to leave his mouth before he skied over to them.

'Well done,' Mann commented, stroking them all on their heads, more to calm down than anything else. He offered them a small treat of a root vegetable from his pocket. They ate the food hungrily as he continued to stroke and offer reassurances.

He looked toward Bosetting. Mann was impressed. He'd never moved so many items all in one go before. It made him think that despite his hasty words all those years ago, Jemp might well be alive and well. Somewhere. Although, Mann had no idea where. His words that day had been spoken without thought. He'd never made the same mistake again.

Dismissively Mann wondered what sort of fun he could have had with his strange abilities in the past sixty years if he hadn't been so worried about moving multiple items. Mann was sure he could have brought all of his supplies to Slutet without the need for sleds and reindeer.

Content the animals had been returned to their normal nature, Mann skied back to the sled, running his hands along the wooden frame to reassure himself all was well. He removed first his right ski and hopped into the sled, and then the left and did the same. He picked his skis up and stowed them in the back of his sled.

Then Mann clicked his tongue and away went his reindeer, back toward Bosetting, the mode of transport the one they preferred evident in the smart steps they took.

When he arrived back at The Firs, the day was almost over. Mann was starting to feel the penetrating cold even through his layers of suitable clothing, and fur-lined coat. Coaxing the reindeer and his sled into the stables at The Firs was all too much effort over the snow-cleared street, but eventually, they arrived, and Sand and Rad greeted them cordially as he handed over the leathers and dashed to hover near their brazier.

The blind old dog didn't even bother to investigate this time, staying tightly curled close to one of the other braziers. The old dog could clearly scent the coming storm as clearly as Mann could.

Mann listened to the two men arguing good-naturedly as they went about their business. He was happy his animals would return to these two men when he temporarily disappeared. They'd see to their needs, especially as he had every intention of rewarding them well, both now and in the future.

As Mann started to warm up, he listened to the conversation between the two men, shocked when Sand began to bellow at Rad that he 'knew he'd seen the damn buggers earlier' in the stables, and 'no, he wasn't starting to lose his mind.'

'Bollocks,' Mann muttered softly to himself. He should have thought of that and sent the reindeer elsewhere first, only, well, he'd wanted to know that if something untoward had happened, they'd be well cared for no matter what state they'd arrived in. He had no idea how to diffuse the developing argument and worried it might upset his plans. Perhaps he would have to return the reindeer under cover of night when the time came? He wanted his disappearance to be discovered, not the circumstances behind it.

Perhaps forgetting Mann stood in the stables, the argument quickly escalated, louder and louder, until Mann knew he'd have to intervene, even the blind dog lifting his head to gaze toward where he believed the source of the argument emanated.

'Good gents,' Mann called, walking to where they could see him. Sand, his face almost purple with rage was glaring at Rad, whereas Rad, was openly laughing at the older man. Sand looked only moments away from taking a swipe at Rad.

This was no way to leave the pair of them. Mann needed them as allies to each other, not enemies.

Both turned to stare at him, Rad's mouth falling open in shock. They'd honestly forgotten he was there.

'Don't argue. I'm sure it's something that can be resolved quickly enough,' Mann commented, hoping if he didn't ask about the cause of the argument, he wouldn't be forced to lie or offer vague answers.

For a moment time seemed to stop. Then Sand tried a smile out on his lined face, the expression strained, as one side of his face smiled, while the other still held an angry tint.

'We're just jesting,' Sand stumbled. Mann nodded, content they wouldn't actually ask him about what Sand thought he'd seen.

'Does it normally get so heated?' Mann probed. The two shook their heads, so similar to naughty children that Mann tried not to smile.

'Apologies, good gent,' Rad said, really quite loudly. 'I was teasing Sand. I know I shouldn't. Apologies Sand,' Rad offered, turning to the older man, the hint of regret in his voice.

Sand fixed him with a stern stare, but caught as they had been, and with Sand evidently unwilling to discuss the subject of their argument, he was left with little more than the opportunity to agree with Rad.

'S'okay Rad. I know there was no harm to it. I think I'm just a bit cold and restless.'

Mann felt uneasy at seeing the two men trying to cover up for him, but he too had no choice in the matter.

'I'd like to stump up for a meal and wine for you both,' Mann finally spluttered. He'd already rewarded them with coins, but he needed to win their approval once more, he could see it in their slightly uneasy stances.

'No, good gent. Wouldn't hear of it,' Sand muttered, but Rad looked half tempted.

'I tell you what. I won't make you share it with me, but I'll ask Haune to take the cost from you next time you're in the inn, and you're not working. How's that?' Mann spoke with authority, knowing it was the best way to get the men to agree. No one liked to argue with a patron.

'Then our thanks,' Sand offered, almost, but not quite bowing his head. Mann sighed as the two returned to their tasks. They still whispered harshly to each other, but Mann hoped it was about other things than the sudden apparition and disappearance of his reindeer and sled.

SEVENTEEN

COMING into the main hall of the inn, Mann shivered in delight at the wall of heat that engulfed him and quickly discarded his thick coat.

Surprised the inn was so quiet for what he'd thought was late afternoon, he turned and caught the interested face of Haune.

'You were quick,' she commented. He looked at her in surprise. He wasn't aware

he'd told her of his plans.

'The men told me,' she offered by way of an explanation. She reached for a mug, found a spoonful of herbs and added them to it, before moving toward the fires and swinging the kettle hanging over them towards her. 'Here, I imagine you might need this.'

Mann reached for the mug, but she snatched it back from him before he could get his hand around it. He eyed her quizzically.

'What did you and Marnit talk about today?' Haune questioned, the threat clear he'd only get his drink when he told her the truth.

'Marnit?' Mann asked, and then remembered that she'd been working on something for Haune.

'Not much. I don't think she approved of my choice of inn-sitter in my absence.'

'Is that all?' Haune probed. 'The girl was most distressed when she came here with my illustration. I had to calm her down with more than just this,' she shook the mug with the ingefara in it.

Rapidly, Mann replayed the conversation he'd shared with Marnit. She'd evidently not been happy, but he didn't think it had been more than that.

'Yes,' he said, calmly reaching for the mug, which Haune relinquished slowly, returning to her bar with a pensive expression on her face.

'I think you should ask her for more details tomorrow, when you go back for your scribing. I get the impression she knows a lot more about this Brag than you probably want to know. But, if you want your inn in one piece when you return, you probably need to know what she's concealing.'

'She's young to be in her position,' Mann stated, raising the warm mug to his lips and swallowing the rich liquid gratefully, covering his unease Marnit had spoken so openly with Haune about her concerns. Now Haune glared at him all the more, but he didn't know what he'd said now that was so wrong.

'She's older than she looks,' Haune retorted. 'You should be careful about making assumptions about people, especially with everything I've heard about you since you came here. It seems she's not the only person blessed with the countenance of youth.'

Mann swallowed deeply, using his mug to hide the dismayed expression on his face. Haune was altogether too observant. Haune abruptly laughed at his discomfort and started to prepare another warm brew.

'I hear things, you know, in here about everyone. Marnit

inherited her position from a distant relative. She was forced to come here and leave her studies at the Collegium. She doesn't ever complain about it, but well, I think she'd have been more content to sell the business on and return to her studying.'

Mann inhaled sharply at the words. It was unheard of for the position of Scribe to be sold. In fact, it was one of those rules all scribes agreed upon. Each generation must succeed the previous one. The skill of reading and writing wasn't open to everyone. The intricacies were said to take years to understand, a fact Mann disagreed with, having taught himself years ago. While others could learn to read and write, it was frowned upon. And what was the point? No one who went to the effort would ever benefit financially from the endeavour, because no one was allowed into the select circle of the scribes. They were also the only members of society allowed to charge for their services.

'Does she have a lover or a husband?' Mann asked not for his own reasons, but because he was thinking of the future. Haune misinterpreted him and laughed. A cruel sound.

'I don't think she goes for men such as you. Rather a man with a quill than one such as yourself.' For a moment Mann felt insulted, but then he laughed. It was rare he was criticised for being unattractive. Strangely, it felt quite nice for someone not to comment on his stature, slightly strange colouring, the hue of his hair, and penetrating iron eyes.

'I suggest you watch yourself with her,' Haune offered, and then her face turned sour. 'There have been two people looking for you today. Your reputation precedes you.'

Mann's brow furrowed at her words, instantly distracted from considering his fine physique.

'No one knows I'm here, and I know no one,' Mann muttered, but she was nodding again.

'Well, they knew you. They'll be coming back later. I'd rather they didn't stay long in my inn. Not my sort of patrons at all,' Haune spoke with a wrinkled nose. Mann watched her mobile face with interest.

'Who were they?' Mann quizzed, but she shrugged.

'They gave no names. But I couldn't deny you were here. They said they'd seen you around Bosetting, and others had directed them to my establishment.'

'They came together?'

'No, apart, quite some time apart, in fact.'

'Well, what did they look like?' again the shrug but then she stopped and gave it some genuine thought.

'The man was ridiculously short. I thought him a child and spoke to him soothingly. He snapped at me. I was happy to see the back of him.'

Mann wracked his memory but could think of no one he'd ever met who matched the description.

'The woman? Well, she was prettier on the eye, but all the same, she wore enough weapons to have killed everyone in here single-handedly. I'd rather, she, particularly, didn't stay too long. Not with the hot-heads who sometimes drink in here. Anyone could help themselves to one of her blades, and my inn has only just been redecorated.'

Haune sounded disapproving, and her lips was turned down at the edges but Mann's ears pricked up at the mention of this strange women. He knew he'd never met her either, but maybe he wanted to.

Still, that brought back the question of how they knew him and what they wanted with him.

'I don't know them, either of them,' Mann commented as Haune raised her eyebrows at him in disbelief.

'That's as may be, but they know you. I know they'll be back. Perhaps you could take them outside when they come. Especially the woman. I'd rather not have her in here at all.'

'Did Marnit finish your illustration?' Mann asked, keen to change the conversation to something more palatable.

'Yes, she did. It's beautiful. Look,' and Haune produced the parchment from behind her bar. Mann didn't touch the heavily decorated deed, but he whistled softly between his teeth. Marnit had chosen, or been asked, to produce an exact replica of The Firs, and she'd gone to great trouble to ensure it looked as it did. From the braziers at the front of the building to the huge barrels containing the aforementioned firs, to tiny depictions of Haune, Sand and Rad as they went about their business.

Around the building, Marnit hadn't depicted the rest of the settlement but instead had chosen to decorate it with a veritable forest of fir trees. So much so it looked as though The Firs was situated in a vast forest of firs, with no one around it. It was as though Bosetting didn't exist, just the inn.

'She's very talented,' Mann nodded, reading the words Marnit had written and which confirmed Haune owned The Firs and her deed was valid for a thousand years.

'A long-lasting deed,' Mann commented dryly. Haune allowed a bark of laughter.

'No choice. They either get you with a lifetime one, or one for twenty lifetimes. I opted for the longer of the two. A good business like this takes time to build up, and very little to crumble away to nothing. I'd have thought you'd knew that.'

Mann nodded. He was only too aware. After all, he'd inherited the other half of his inn when Onna died. Her foresight in holding a long deed had ensured it had remained his home ever since, and a home he was keen to keep.

Wherever their conversation might have been about to go it was interrupted by a commotion at the door, and the sight of Sand and Rad, still clearly arguing, stamping their way inside. On seeing both Mann and Haune, they stopped quarrelling immediately and tried to look less angry at each other. Mann might have been worried by the argument but in their wake, waddled someone who could only be the small man who'd been looking for Mann earlier.

A strange roar filled Mann's ears, drowning out the hard words from Haune at seeing her workers arguing. All of his focus was on the smaller man.

For a moment, Mann was able to watch him intently without the other man's notice, for he was too busy watching where he stepped and avoiding being knocked over by the jostling taking place between Sand and Rad. But then the man looked up and fixed him with an intent glare.

Mann was struck by the colour of the smaller man's eyes. They blazed with the light of the brief summer flowers rarely seen near Slutet, the delicate violet contrasting strangely with the black of his pupil. He reminded Mann vividly of the coppery coloured Brag. He considered whether the pair might somehow be related.

'Mann,' the stranger announced, coming forward with his hand outstretched to make his acquaintance. 'My name's Bothal. I believe we've met before.'

In the background Mann was aware of Haune turning to watch their exchange, her hand gestures indicating she wanted Bothal outside, and not in her inn. However the inn remained strangely quiet. Mann was convinced Bothal was confused and not really looking for him at all.

'Good day, Bothal,' Mann replied. 'You are, unfortunately mistaken, I know I've never met you before.'

Bothal's eyes crossed with confusion as he came close enough to have to tip his head backwards to meet Mann's eyes.

'You're sure?' Bothal asked, pressing him, but Mann merely shook his head.

'I'm sure, good gent.' Mann retorted. 'I've an excellent memory for faces and names.' He would have liked to add and violet eyes, but he kept his own counsel on that.

'Then my apologies for disturbing you,' Bothal commented,

already backing away from Mann. 'Please thank the innkeeper for her assistance.'

Mann watched Bothal leave disinterestedly. He hadn't lied to the stranger when he'd said he didn't know him, but neither had he resolved the issue of Bothal's likeness to Brag. That, Mann decided, was going to infuriate him. Especially after Marnit's caution about Brag.

Quickly Mann made the decision to follow Bothal and ask him for more details.

Mann pulled open the heavy door and looked down the four steps. He fully expected Bothal to be standing there, trying to orientate his way down the stairs. But Bothal was gone. Amused more than anything, Mann took the four steps down and looked both left and right but could see no trace of the small character on the street.

Instead, his eyes fastened on someone who could only be the woman looking for him. Hastily he retraced his steps into the inn and grabbed his coat, shivering against the harsh wind. Coming to the door once more, Mann pulled his coat around himself and jumped the four wooden steps to meet whoever this other stranger was.

As Haune had commented, this new outsider glittered with weapons. In the reflected glow of the blazing lamps and braziers, she looked more like walking fire than a person. In fact, he was forced to squint at the glare from her weapons, so when she finally reached him, he found his eyes were tearing from such vivid brightness.

'You are him?' she announced, without preamble, her voice lacking all intonation. He was beginning to wonder who these people thought he was. He had a worry it was something to do with his strange ability but was unprepared to mention it. It had been his secret to keep for far too many years for him to share with anyone on the spur of the moment. His hand strayed to the top of his coat to ensure it was done up tightly, and no hint of his strange marks could be broadcast.

'I'm Mann,' he replied, 'from Slutet.' Whatever she'd been expecting him to say, it wasn't that.

'No,' she countered. 'You are he?' Her voice was abruptly rich with conviction.

Mann studied her face. It was as sharp as the blades on the knives glittering around her waist and down the side of her long boots, which encased even longer legs. The woman was taller than him, and in a strange mirror of his previous encounter, Mann had to angle his head backwards to meet her eyes.

Mann knew with absolute certainty, as with Bothal, he'd never met this woman before. There was no such uncertainty in her resolve.

'I think not. I'm Mann, from Slutet. Who are you looking for? And who are you?'

Briefly, his words permeated her façade. He could see in her pale auburn eyes she was trying to reconcile what he was telling her with the facts she was convinced were true.

'Shlat,' she said, and then. 'So,' she spoke slowly, allowing her mind to decipher his words. 'You're not 'him' then?' she sought clarity. Mann shook his head.

'No, I'm Mann.'

'Ah,' was her only response. Then she turned abruptly, and walked away with just as much resolve as she'd employed when walking toward him. He watched her go with consternation. Who were these people looking for? And more importantly, why did they think he was whoever they were looking for? It reminded him of the brief conversations he'd had with Jemp before his abrupt disappearance sixty odd years ago.

Shaking his head, Mann peered into the shadowy areas where the braziers and the lanterns failed to reach.

He was still hoping to spot Bothal but quickly realised it

would be impossible, as night claimed the place of the day, the shadows lengthening. He was almost resolved to visit the other inns in Bosetting, where he was sure the two strangers would be stopping for the night, only then he caught sight of a rushing Marnit, gliding through the snow cleared streets.

Marnit moved furtively, from shadowed recess to shadowed recess and her stealthy moves piqued his interest. It was her he set about following instead, only for Marnit to stop and round on him less than a hundred paces further on.

'What do you think you're doing?' she hissed, her sudden appearance before him making him catch his breath in surprise. Mann thought she'd moved on already, and anyway, he'd made no noise as he'd tracked her. How had she even known he was there?

Mann was also surprised by her appearance. He'd known she was childlike in build, but now she appeared almost sylph-like. Without her voluminous cloak covering her entire body, she'd have been virtually impossible to see in the full dark of a winter's night.

'I was looking for someone, well two someone's, and then I saw you, so I don't know. I just thought I'd follow you.'

'Oh did you now.' Marnit's voice was hard, cold, like ice at the height of winter. 'Then you can just bloody well unfollow me. I'm about legitimate business, and have no need of you messing it all up.'

As she hissed at him, Marnit's head kept darting from side to side, as though she too searched for someone. Berated, Mann stepped back from her, his hands out to either side, in a submissive pose.

'My apologies,' he bowed, but by the time he looked up once more, Marnit was gone, covered once more by the cloak of night.

Mann sighed, his breath clouding in front of him and further fogging his vision.

'Bugger it,' he mumbled to himself. He'd had enough of his strange afternoon and stepped from the shadows only to catch sight of a fleeting image of shimmering firelight.

Shlat. This time he moved to follow her, unsurprised when she flittered in and out of shadows and light, and eventually stopped at The Three Barrels, another inn within Bosetting. He expected her to walk inside, after all, it was time for evening meals in the shelter of a warm inn. Instead, Shlat skirted the inn and made her way to where Mann assumed the stables were located.

Although the front of the inn was well illuminated, around the back there were but two lanterns, bravely flickering against the wind gusting and pooling in the space behind the inn. Once more Mann pulled his coat tight against the frigid air and peered into the gloom. He could make out little in the dark, although the smell of animals assured him Shlat was heading for the stables.

Mann wanted to follow her, to find out what the clandestine meet was all about, only then he saw Marnit as well. She was heading towards the last place he'd seen Shlat. Mann considered why the two of them would be meeting, and more importantly, why they were doing it in the stables. But he was loath if he was about to endure Marnit's anger once more. So he hung back, hoping no one would see him from either direction as he considered what best to do.

None of this was his business, none of it, and yet it intrigued him. Shlat had come looking for him, or rather 'for him.' Bothal had done the same, although he'd been much keener to accept he'd been misled and that Mann wasn't actually who he was looking for.

And then there was Marnit. He'd thought her no more than a scribe, but her insistence that she knew Brag, and that his death wishes had to be better written than by the scribe in Slutet, implied she perhaps knew more than she was letting on.

All he needed now was for the miniature Bothal to join the two women, and he'd know they must be discussing him or discussing something he needed to know, or should know, or that they thought he knew.

Behind him Mann heard scampering feet and retreated further into the gloom, his back pressed so tightly against the back wall of the inn, he could feel the heat of the building even through his great coat.

Mann held his breath. He was a big man. Hiding so much was difficult.

Yet the figure that appeared around the corner of the inn was intent only on his business. As Bothal looped and skipped, trying to speed his slow progress, Mann's eyes further narrowed. What was all this about?

Unable to help himself, Mann crept ever closer to where he could just discern the heated whispers of three people vehemently disagreeing with each other in the open doors of the stable. Mann strained his ears, trying to pick out the words, but they remained out of hearing distance.

Mann placed each step carefully in front of him, mindful there could be any stray object for him to disturb to alert the co-conspirators to his presence, but he was lucky. Closer and closer he skulked until at last, he heard a word, a word he didn't want to hear. His own name.

Mann gasped out loud. It was one thing to think he was the object of their meeting, it was quite another to have his worries confirmed.

Mann inched ever closer, as their voices died down once more. Only then did he hear the unmistakable sound of a sled over the rough, snow-free ground, coming to the stables. He knew he needed to cover his head with his coat. He couldn't be seen. Not skulking around the backyard of the inn.

Cursing, he swung away from the swaying lantern on the sled, and dodged in and out of the murk as he made his way back to the main thoroughfare. Undetected, Mann gave himself a moment to think, only to catch sight of Bothal following his path.

'Bollocks,' Mann muttered, and hunched his back, trying to look as small as possible. As unlike himself as he could.

Hastily Mann retraced his steps back to The Firs as soon as Bothal had slipped past him. Stomping inside the inn, to the surprise of Haune, he tried to regain some sense of inner calm.

What the hell was going on? And why was Marnit involved with the two characters who thought he was someone he wasn't?

Mann had to assume it was all to do with his strange abilities, and that worried him more than anything. All this time he'd kept them hidden, ensuring no one could even guess at what he could do. But it seemed he hadn't kept his secret well enough. Were the two strangers looking for him because they knew about his skills?

Mann swung his coat from his shoulder, stamping warmth into his feet, heading for a table and chair close to the hearth. Haune watched him the whole time, as did Sand and Rad who seemed to have finally stopped arguing about the reindeer, although both wore sour expressions on their ruddy faces.

Yet no one spoke.

And then the door to the inn opened. Mann found his eyes following the figure that entered with interest. They had a cloak swirled around their shoulders, and for a moment he feared it was Marnit or Shlat, or perhaps someone else who knew him.

Only as they lifted down their hood did Mann understand this was another stranger. He braced himself, for what he feared would be an inevitable deluge of questions.

Only the stranger turned to Haune instead.

'A room?' a reedy voice emerged from the lined face. 'For four days, if possible.' As the man swept his cloak from his shoulders, Mann caught a glimpse of vibrant clothes, festooned with jewels and gold reminiscent of those from the south. He doubted this could be anyone looking for him.

Dismissing the stranger, Mann turned instead to catch sight of Sand and Rad eyeing him with unease. He tried a smile but it made them turn away from him, and then begin a heated whispered conversation once more.

Mann watched them, and then Haune, settling her new patron, and he resolved there and then that he needed to move on. Tomorrow he'd finish his business with Marnit and then the day after, he could leave and begin his perilous journey.

Hopefully, by the time he returned to The Firs, perhaps in half a year, the suspicion he was currently held under would have been forgotten in the wake of his 'death.'

EIGHTEEN

Chapter 18

MANN SLEPT TOO WELL that night, waking much later than he wanted to.

'Bollocks,' he muttered, sliding his feet to the floor and hastily dressing. He'd eaten quickly last night, not wanting to be disturbed by anyone, keen to shut the door and retreat to his own space.

He felt as though Haune, Sand and Rad watched him constantly. Their suspicions weren't unwarranted.

Yet in the quiet of his room, he'd been assaulted with worries and fears about the coming days and had finally forced himself to sleep only by asking Haune for another mug of her strange and potent spirit. It had allowed him to rest without dreaming, and for that he was grateful.

Once dressed, Mann descended to the main room and found it filled with people all enjoying their breakfast. Unlike the previous morning, Haune didn't have time to do more than give him his food and then return to serving all her other guests.

Relieved, Mann allowed himself to examine the rest of the

patrons, convinced he knew none of them. They paid him no attention. That was as it should be.

His meal eaten, he hastened out of the door, ignoring Haune's cry of 'good day' and was assaulted by a vicious snowstorm he'd not even realised was blowing.

Hastily Mann covered his exposed head with his hood and hunched deeper into his coat. He peered before him. The view had turned white and alien overnight. He seriously considered remaining inside, but had tasks to accomplish. The weather was a poor excuse for delaying his intended departure tomorrow. Holding his coat in place against the wind, Mann tilted his head to look at the sky above his head.

Heavy pink clouds hung in the sky, visible whenever the blizzard temporarily cleared. He realised the storm would last at least all day long, if not all night as well.

It was no time to be planning a trip, but he had no choice. Not now he'd come so far.

Re-orientating himself by using the outlines of the buildings he could detect through the swirling snow, Mann set off toward Marnit's dwelling. Even with the exterior braziers batting against the storm, the lanterns trying to stay lit, and the snow movers in the street, it took him a long time to make it as far as the quill etched onto Marnit's door.

Yet his preoccupation with getting there meant he had no time to worry about her reaction when she saw him. Hastily banging on the door, four times, it was opened abruptly, as though she'd been expecting him for some time.

'You're late,' Marnit growled. He kicked the snow from his boots, and swirled his coat away from her as soon as he was inside. She swung the door shut on the storm, with a forcefulness mirroring his feelings.

Mann considered apologising for allowing the cold in, but Marnit was already striding away from him.

'Here,' she said, handing him two rolled vellums, already sealed.

'I checked the language of the death wishes. It's as specific as I can make it. You should tell your scribe to be more precise, a lot more precise. Now, what do you want in your letter for Brag.'

Mann considered, as he watched Marnit readying herself.

'Brag, greetings from Mann in Bosetting. Please find enclosed a copy of my death wishes, in the event of misfortune striking me. I will leave Bosetting tomorrow, and will return as soon as I can. Yours, Mann.'

The words were simple really, but Mann felt it necessary to continue his façade of going on a short trip.

Hastily, Marnit sealed the fresh letter, her expression difficult to make out.

Mann nodded as he took the three rolled parchments, and placed them inside his deep pockets. He dared not open them when she'd gone to all the effort of sealing them with wax and her stamp. No, he'd do that later.

'My thanks for your labours,' Mann said, formally concluding their agreement with a shake of his hand. She returned the pressure on his hand, a fleeting thing, the briefest of touches to ensure the agreement was ended as it should be. Mann didn't dare mention she'd not read the contents of the death wishes to him.

Hastily, Mann swept his coat back over his shoulders and pulled the door open. Without speaking again, he stepped into the faint stirrings of the coming blizzard, hearing the door slam behind him as he went.

Only then did he stop, turn around and peer back at the quill on the door. The small window was covered over. There was nothing but a thin lantern light to illuminate the entrance. He felt reassured that Marnit didn't watch him walk away.

Hunched once more, he made his way to the main thoroughfare. He needed some food supplies, and also to spend some coin so he'd be remembered when he left the next day.

Mann was the only person walking the street, as the snow began to fall with greater and greater speed, and as such, he obtained bargains in all of the shops he visited, the shop-keepers keen to make something on what was sure to be a terrible day of trading. At the pastry shop, he was able to secure an order of ten pastries for early the next morning, the woman charging him twelve copper coins for the trouble of having them ready so early. She had greeted him with a warm smile of welcome. Mann thought once more just how much good will a heavy copper coin could earn you.

In the storefront selling thick winter coats with matching hats and gloves, Mann availed himself of an all-white set, rimmed with the fur of the white foxes, all of which cost him just shy of fifty silver coins. A bargain, he thought, and so too, did the shopkeeper, who offered the price, and then seemed to regret it immediately.

In the joiners shop, he asked after a new pair of skis, and the women smiled and dug around in the rear of the shop until she found a matching set, made from the black wood of the only trees that could survive the terribly long winters.

'I never thought I'd sell these,' she muttered, as Mann tried them on for size, and asked for a few adjustments to the leathers, which she hastily carried out. He smirked at her words. He was a tall man. He'd never met anyone as tall as him in all his long years, apart from the enigmatic Shlat yester-day. He doubted there was much call for skis quite so damn long and heavy.

'They're just what I'm looking for,' Mann announced and held back the grin as she considered a cost for them. He knew they should be expensive, but she'd admitted she'd had them a long time so couldn't inflate the cost. And Mann knew he had to have them. After all, he had them in his sled already. He'd often considered where they'd actually come from.

'I don't even think I made them,' she finally announced. 'Thirty silver coins should cover it.'

Mann nodded. It seemed a fair cost. He counted the coins from inside his coat and laid them on the half counter she clearly used for such transactions. It was cold in the joiners shop, and yet she wore only thin clothes. She noticed his glance and smiled.

'It gets mighty hot when I use my axe or hammer. I prefer to keep it below a comfortable level.'

With the purchase complete, he left the joiners and set out for his final destination. He had much of what he needed to ensure his survival. He'd brought food with him for himself, but it had been difficult to source the right requirements for his reindeer. He was sure much of what they needed would be widely available, but wanted to source as many ground vegetables as he could in case the lichen they craved in the wild was hard to come by.

Mann was convinced he'd seen a general supplier on one of his journeys through Bosetting. He set out once more into the now howling blizzard. He clutched his new black skis to his side while holding a tightly bound bundle containing his brand new coat, hat and gloves as he fought his way along the streetway. The snow clearers had long given up on their fruitless task. Mann was forced to lift his legs high to clear the rapidly deepening snow.

Mann almost gave up, merely returning to The Firs, but this was his final task, and so he pressed on. Resigned, he hunched further into his coat, pulling his hood as low as it would go, while pulling up the collar of his tunic. In the end, there was little of his face visible to any others shopping, apart from his piercing iron eyes.

Mann blinked snow from his eyes, navigating by the faint

glow of the lit lanterns, only to come across the general store and find the storefront bolted shut.

'Bollocks,' he shouted into the wailing blizzard, so reminiscent of when he'd first appeared in the Hvite Lands. Annoyed, Mann turned and began to trudge back to The Firs. His reindeer would simply have to survive with what they had. Not that he feared they'd starve. Far from it in fact.

Initially, Mann was able to use his previous path to retrace his steps, juggling his purchases while considering whether or not he should make use of his new skis, and whether or not he should add his new coat over the one he already wore.

As Mann considered, he argued with himself, first the reasons why he should, and then the reasons why he shouldn't. He simply couldn't decide whether to spare the time, or hurry back. The small area of his exposed face was already festooned with icy particles. He knew he should be inside, not out in the blizzard.

Mann cursed once more and redoubled his efforts to return to The Firs. Better to struggle now, staying warm with the exertions, than attempt the delicate fastenings of his skis or unwrapping his new coat.

So he laboured on. Voices occasionally reached him, calling to each other through the blizzard, or at least trying to but the wind was screeching. He imagined he wasn't the only person to have been caught out by how quickly the storm had set it. Or maybe he was, and they were calling for him. It was impossible to tell.

Mann looked upwards, seeking the shop signs that would tell him where he was in Bosetting, only for his eyes to fill with snow. He convinced himself he could see the welcoming glow of the inn ahead of him, and so pressed on. The sooner he was back, the sooner he could get warm and plan his departure for the following day, when he hoped the storm would have passed.

Eventually, Mann stamped his way up the four short steps of The Firs and knocked heavily on the door barred shut from the inside. He could hear Haune inside, complaining about 'idiots at the door,' and he shouted his name into a rare lull into the storm. Even above the roar of the wind, and through the thickness of the wooden door, he could hear her huff of annoyance at realising who was there.

Mann grimaced. His welcome wouldn't be warm, but neither would she leave him outside to freeze to death.

The blast of heat as Haune opened the door inwards was almost enough to thaw him there and then. He tried to grin, only finding his face too frozen in place to do so.

'Get inside, you daft bastard,' Haune admonished him. He tried to, as quickly as he could, only for his skis to jam in the doorway. Annoyed, she pulled him inside, where he heard a visible sizzle as his ice-cold coat was assaulted by the heat of the fires. Haune reached out to grasp his skis, roughly thrusting them at him, so she could close the door, and bar it once more.

Mann could feel the eyes of everyone in the room on him. He cursed under his breath.

'My thanks, Haune,' he mumbled, as she grunted at him.

'Don't leave a bloody puddle on the floor,' was her admonishment, returning to whatever task she'd been completing before his hammering on the door.

'Apologies,' Mann muttered, feeling even more foolish. He'd failed to stomp the snow from his boots, and now he dripped where he stood. Hastily, he dumped his purchases onto the nearest table, which happened to be empty as it was closest to the door shaking under the windy onslaught.

Then Mann bent to remove his boots, hopping clear of them, so his feet stayed dry. He then swirled his coat from his shoulders and hastily picking up his wet boots, went to place them before the fire to dry. People moaned as he walked past them, bringing with him the cold of outdoors, and he apologised to all and sundry, even Marnit, before he recognised her.

She offered him an annoyed glare. He turned away. He was in no mood to argue with her again.

The inn was only moderately busy. The weather had forced even those locals who might have come in to stay at home. So he sat alone in his cold clothes, just about as far from the fire as it was possible to be. He didn't want to warm himself too quickly.

Haune brought him food, and a warm drink, her expression still sour. Her strong arms were folded in front of her. Je thought she was merely going to walk away, only then she began to speak.

'Rumour has it that you're leaving tomorrow.'

Mann nodded, unsurprised that she seemed to know so much about him that he'd not told her. 'Yes, I think I've stayed too long, and I'm keen to be on my way. I've a family to visit and want to return before the winter begins in full.'

She grunted at that, turning to look back the way he'd come as though she couldn't quite believe what he'd said. She shook her head in amazement.

Mann shrugged.

'This is just a foretaste of things to come. You know that, and so do I.' He opened his mouth to argue with her, but she was already walking away.

'I think you've been stuck in Slutet too long, too comfortable and never forced to leave your inn. In Bosetting, where people still need to make a living during the long winter, we've long understood the futility of trying to travel when a winter blizzard strikes. If you go, you'll be risking your life.'

Her words brought small comfort to him. If he went, well, if he went tomorrow, everyone would be half expecting his death anyway. They wouldn't be surprised when they actually heard about it, and that would play into his hands.

As Mann tucked into his meal, ravenous from the cold, he saw a shadow cross his table and looked up to see Marnit glaring at him.

Mann indicated she should sit, and she did, ungraciously pulling the spare wooden seat back from the table so it scratched over the wooden floorboards, making a screeching noise audible even over the crash of the wind outside.

'You don't make friends easily do you?' Marnit glared. He spluttered around the mouthful of meat he was eating. He was incredulous she'd say that to him.

She nodded, as though he was confirming her words, and not denying them, and looked away from him.

'I came here because of the weather, but also to speak to you. I can't let you leave without knowing what I know.'

Her tone was ominous. Fear pooled in his stomach. What had she guessed about him? What was it that she knew?

'I know Brag. I've known him all my life.' She surprised him by saying. And he returned to his eating. Perhaps this wasn't about him at all.

'I know he's rarely a man of his word, and never to be trusted. He and I are not friends.' She spoke with a wry smile, alluding to her opening line.

'When he came through here, on his way north, I suspected some trouble. But I now know three things that worry me. I'm forced to share them with you even though I don't want to. Firstly, Brag has no trade and only the money he steals from others. Whatever he's told you is a lie. Although why he'd lie, I don't know. Unless, well, unless he knew you were going to ask him to run the inn in your place. How he'd know that I don't know, but Brag often struck me as a man blessed with foreknowledge he shouldn't have.'

'Secondly, now I know all that, I know he plans for you to never return to Slutet. He means to take your place. I think he probably spoke to the scribe there, had him make your death wishes easy to exploit to his own ends, maybe even sent someone after you to make sure you met your death.'

The connections she'd made surprised and worried him in equal measure, but it seemed she'd left her final and most explosive, statement for last.

'I know Brag wears a chain similar to yours. I know he has tattoos of it on his body, just as you do.'

Mann felt his jaw drop open at that pronouncement, and was unsurprised when Marnit looked at him with defiance in her grey eyes. She'd been far more observant than he'd imagined, in fact far more than anyone else ever had, apart from Freg.

Instinctively Mann reached for his hidden chain, while simultaneously pulling his tunic closed. He couldn't imagine where she'd seen his strange chain. And then, as he watched her delight in having her words confirmed, he wondered if she'd known or had trapped him into revealing himself.

But Marnit didn't look pleased with his actions.

'Show me the chain,' she demanded. Hastily he removed it over his head. The chain was a slither of gold, just enough to hold the copper sigil in place, and of course, it was the sigil she wanted to see.

Mann sometimes wondered why he'd had the chain made to hold the sigil. It had seemed like a good idea at the time. Now he cursed himself for a fool.

Marnit was furtively examining the emblem, her eyes closed as she ran her index finger over it and then open, as she looked at the decoration on the two concentric and overlapping circles. Finally, she spoke.

'I don't know what it means. I know it means something, and I know Brag hated me for discovering his sigil. It was different from this. More crudely made but it carried the same general design.'

'I was gifted it,' Mann muttered, thinking back to the day

Hempe had given him the strange sigil that had since snaked all over his body, each year a new rendition added to the others already marking him.

'Brag would never answer my questions about it.' Marnit's tone was sour. There was no evident kinship with Brag. Instead, Mann was convinced she y quite hated Brag.

'I asked him what it meant. He refused to tell me.'

'I can't tell you either,' Mann stated, without haste, pleased to be honest. 'I've no idea what it means.' He didn't think Marnit wanted to know what it meant, she merely wanted to tell him a man he'd thought to trust had lied to him. And that man wore the same sigil, although more crudely designed. He had no idea what it meant.

'Take me back to Slutet with you,' Marnit announced, handing him back his chain and sigil, without another look.

'Take me back, send Brag away, and let me run the inn in your place. I've the skills. I promise to give it back to you when you return. I'll swear on my scribal oath.' Marnit sounded sincere, almost a little desperate. Her face was filled with sincerity, and he wavered.

Both Haune and Marnit were right to caution him as they did, even if he didn't want to hear it. The weather was appalling. There was no real need for him to leave the next day, as he'd planned. Instead, he could wait, return to Slutet, and ensure his inn was whole. Maybe he could even delay his eventual departure until after the winter. Perhaps Marnit would make a far better inn-sitter than Brag.

But then he reconsidered again. Brag might well be a devious bastard, but if what Marnit said was right, he also had his own secrets he didn't want exposing. On the other hand, Marnit was extremely inquisitive. She'd discovered things about Mann no one else had ever truly known or understood and if he left her alone in his own inn? Well, he hardly dared consider what else she might find out about him that he wanted to be kept a secret.

And yet?

'I'll think on it,' Mann finally muttered, not a little angrily. All his plans were going awry, and he felt out of control, and worse, as though he was being manipulated. He didn't enjoy the experience.

'Good,' was Marnit's contented answer. And then she reached into her pockets and pulled out, from somewhere Mann couldn't quite see, a quill, ink and even a piece of vellum. She unrolled the vellum, weighing it down with the mugs and trenchers from the table, and began to draw, totally ignoring Mann.

For a moment, his spoon was suspended before his mouth in shock at her total dismissal of him. Then his stomach grumbled hungrily, and he resumed his eating.

Marnit was a strange creature, and he'd thought she'd become his enemy. Her arrival here, her words to him, all pointed to something else.

Could he trust her? Should he trust her?

When he'd finished eating, Haune came to clear away his empty board, and offer him a mildly warmed spirit.

'I assure you that you'll still be awake after it,' she half-apologised, as he first sniffed, and then sipped appreciatively.

'It's delicious,' he complimented, but Haune was watching Marnit carefully, and then she laughed.

'It's Mann,' she crowed, 'it's really very good.'

Mann looked down at what had so engrossed Marnit. Haune was correct. She'd been drawing, a portrait of him painstakingly etched onto the parchment with firm, fair strokes, that brought to mind an image of himself seen in a piece of glass or a highly sheened metal sheet.

With deft strokes, she'd captured his heavy eyebrows,

scowling eyes, and thick nose, not to mention his large lips and firm chin.

Mann rubbed his chin as Marnit ignored Haune and continued to draw.

'She often does this,' Haune offered by way of an explanation, not really including Marnit in the conversation. As Mann watched, Marnit added his six reindeer and a small rendition of his sled behind him.

It was either a pretty attempt at distracting herself from the storm or, and Mann considered this seriously, a threat. 'I know you,' the image cried. 'And I will always know you.'

Before Marnit had finished, Haune was called away to tend to her other customers, and to officiate another argument between Sand and Rad.

Mann watched the people in the inn, not Marnit, as he considered her words.

Had she meant a threat or had she simply wanted a way out of the closed settlement she lived within? Did she want the opportunity to run an inn and to step away from her role as a scribe? Or was she as devious as she implied Brag was?

As Mann considered, there was another loud banging on the inn door and scowling, Haune shouldered her way to the door.

'Who is it?' she cried, pitching her voice to carry over the sound of the blizzard.

Mann didn't detect a reply, but quickly Haune opened the door and grabbed another stray and hauled them into her inn, closing the door roughly behind them. A sharp wind rushed through the inn, flickering the lamps and buffeting the raging fires.

Mann shivered at the remembered cold, and only then looked up to see the eyes of one of yesterday's strangers raking in his appearance.

Bothal. He'd hoped not to see the man again.

'Apologies, good lady,' Mann could hear Bothal saying. 'I was forced to return to Bosetting having lost my way in the blizzard. Would you have a room for the night?' his tone was anything but pleading, but Haune seemed only too keen to welcome him. It was a complete reversal of her attitude the day before. Mann assumed Bothal had proved his wealth to her, with some sleight of hand across the bar.

'Of course, good gent,' Haune commented. 'Take off your boots and coat, and I'll show you to your room. Then you can come and eat when you're ready.'

The small man bowed so low to her Mann feared his nose would brush the floorboards, but somehow it stopped short.

'And my dogs,' Bothal commented. 'I've placed them in the stables. I hope that's acceptable.' Haune looked surprised at the revelation, but merely grunted, neither in agreement or refusal. Hastily, Haune led Bothal away to the upper floor. Mann wasn't the only one who observed him with interested eyes. Marnit watched as well, her quill still for the first time since she'd hauled out parchment and quill. Mann was sure he heard her say 'bollocks' under her gasp of surprise.

Mann leaned back in his chair, all the way, and considered the strangers he'd met in Bosetting. Everyone had their own secrets to keep, and few were prepared to share them, but he honestly doubted that they were all centred on him. Yet neither could he shake the thought that all of them, even Marnit and Haune, knew something about him he didn't. Maybe he could find out what that was as the blizzard raged.

All Mann needed now was for the other stranger, Shlat, to appear and spend the night as well, and then they'd all be trapped in The Firs.

Mann eyed the barred wooden door sourly and then turned to look at Marnit. She was gazing at him, her quill resting before her. As his movement, she bent to make some adjustment on her drawing of him, but he wasn't sure whether she meant to or if it was just her way of covering her observation of him.

'Are you staying here?' Mann asked, finally realising she was inside, with the door barred close, and showed no signs of leaving.

She nodded, and he became distracted by the other patrons in the inn. For half a moment he wondered how many of them knew him.

Mann didn't think he'd been too obvious in his observation of the party of four gentlemen card players, or the family of two adults and three young children who were playing a contained guessing game. Or of the other individual adults within the inn, who numbered six souls travelling alone. Seven if you included him, and eight and nine if you included Marnit and Haune. And of course, not forgetting Sand and Rad and another man Mann hadn't been introduced to but who seemed to help with the cooking and cleaning, and any work that needed doing in the deep cellar beneath their feet.

But Marnit had noted his actions.

'Those travelling alone are all strangers to the inn, the gents playing cards are locals. The family have come to visit relatives in Slutet but have been trapped enroute. Sand and Rad you know, as you do Haune and me. That just really leaves the smaller man who's a total stranger.

Her words brought a smile to his face.

'I hardly think I 'know' anyone here,' Mann commented. 'I know of you and Haune. I've had some interaction with Sand and Rad, but no one else.'

'And that worries you?' Marnit probed, only for him to shrug.

'No, my own inn is often filled with people I don't know. It's just that The Firs isn't my own inn, and therefore I'm not in control. I don't much like having to rearrange my plans either.

And why are you here?' Mann finally asked and she laughed in delight at his contrary tone.

'I prefer to be here during the long storms. I like to live alone, but when the weather is so severe, I appreciate it's better to share the chores and the heat with others I trust. Haune's an old friend of the family.'

Mann nodded, as though expecting her answer, but he couldn't shake the feeling it was all a bit too convenient.

'Ah bugger it,' Mann muttered, too quietly for anyone to hear, as he stretched out on his chair, determined to enjoy the warmth and the company instead of looking for conspiracy everywhere. When had he become so easily spooked?

NINETEEN

AS HAUNE HAD SAID, the blizzard showed no signs of abating the next day, and so Mann allowed himself to lounge in his bed long after he'd normally be awake. The inn was being pounded by the storm. He calculated that as soon as he appeared downstairs, there'd be a job for him, be it clearing the snow from the steps or clearing a path to the stables. He didn't fancy either. Not with the snow bound to be so thick, and the temperature so low.

He'd not seen Bothal again last night after Haune had shown him to his room. Mann presumed he would at some point during the day. The longer Mann stayed in his bed, the longer he could put off meeting with the man. Although Marnit had been pleasant enough company the night before, neither did he fancy sitting beside her once more, as she drew different images of him, while he worried about the purpose behind the drawings.

Instead of any unpleasantness, Mann leapt from his bed, piled more coal on the brazier, and hunkered down back under the furs. The room wasn't cold, but it was a luxury to be so somnolent. He welcomed the additional heat.

The wind roared outside his comfortable room. He almost felt as though he could feel the weight of snow settling on the roof above his head. When the blizzard stopped, Rad would no doubt have the job of clearing away the worst of the snow. Then the men and women who worked as snow clearers would have the unenviable task of wheeling it away, to wherever they took it, but probably just beyond the gates. Mann doubted there'd be any use for it in the settlement itself, unless there was a cold storage dug underground, through the permafrost.

His eyes closed at the thought of such hard work. He drifted back to a contented semi-sleep. Here, his mind was still, free to consider any stray idea that came to him, until disturbed by a knock on the door.

'Mann, I've saved you some breakfast, but you'll need to come quickly before it gets cold.' The voice was Marnit's. He knew he should be grateful, but he really didn't want to leave the bed and the room. Yet he knew he must. He was hungry and thirsty and in need of a piss.

Grumping to himself, Mann roused from his bed, dressed and opened the door to go downstairs. His ears strained, but he could hear almost no noise from the main room and hoped everyone else had eaten and then returned to their rooms.

He was right. Only Haune worked behind her bar, Sand and Rad keeping her silent company from their ingrained position near the twin hearths, the blind dog resting his head on paws beneath the table.

There was one table with a bowl and a spoon, and a steaming mug of herbs, which Haune indicated with her chin was his to enjoy. Marnit was nowhere to be seen.

Mann settled himself at the table, and began to eat, all the time aware Sand and Rad cast furtive looks his way and then argued in whispers between themselves. He really should have taken more care with his experimental transportation of the reindeer.

'You're still here then?' Haune finally asked, a mild censor to her voice.

'Yes, the blizzard's raging. I'm content to wait another day.'

She nodded at the logic of his actions, and then turned away, paying him no further heed as she went about her innkeeper duties.

With nothing else to do, Mann brought out the neatly folded map from his pocket and opened it up to examine as he ate.

The meal of porridge, mixed with berries, was pleasant, as was his hot drink. Just examining the map made him shiver involuntarily. He considered the wisdom of Marnit's offer of delaying his journey south. It made sense, sort of. The only problem was he intended to take advantage of the winter weather to ensure when he faked his death, his 'body' was never found. That would be more difficult to accomplish in the summer months.

He was nudged from his considerations by the appearance of Bothal. Bothal was well wrapped up against the slight chill in the room, scanning everywhere other than where Mann sat.

Out of the corner of his eye, Mann witnessed Sand and Rad talking animatedly about the smaller man. Some part of him took pity. It must be terrible to spend an entire lifetime being ridiculed just for being smaller than the average man.

'Bothal, good day gent,' Mann began, surprised when Bothal didn't immediately turn to offer a reciprocal greeting, but continued to survey the room. Perhaps, after all, he wasn't concerned by the twittering of the two local men.

Mann returned to his map and his breakfast, only for Bothal to seat himself opposite him, where Marnit had drawn the night before.

'Good day Mann, the man I do not seek,' the small man

laughed at his own joke, his violet eyes reflecting violently in the glow from the flaming fires and few lit lanterns.

'You plan on leaving today?' Mann asked for Bothal had a small pack with him, which looked like it might be used for clothes and possessions.

'No, no, well, yes, I had hoped to but the weather is too fierce.'

Bothal sounded forlorn. Despite his better judgement, Mann couldn't help but question him further.

'Why did you journey north at the start of winter?' Mann felt compelled to ask.

Bothal laughed at his perplexed tone and question.

'Good gent, it's still near enough the height of summer where I began this journey. To the south, the summer is the longer season. Not like here,' and Bothal grimaced, a little comically.

'Did no one tell you about the length of our winters? And how harsh they can be?' But Bothal was already shaking his head sadly.

'Almost everyone I met, but for a man who's never even seen snow before, it's hard to visualise what you've never encountered. I had no idea. No idea at all. I thought it all a ruse to keep me in their comfortable inns.'

Mann smiled at the rueful confession.

'A nasty surprise for you, then. These storms can rage for a week or more, and take as long again for the conditions to improve but then you can be fairly assured of as long again until the next storm. It would give you more than enough time to return to the south.'

The thought seemed to brighten Bothal, but then he grimaced.

'Regrettably I must go to Slutet. If you're not the man I seek, then the one I do seek must be there, for I was assured he was in the north. There's no further north than Slutet. Look, I can see so even on your map.'

For a moment Mann felt a wave of panic at the reminder of their conversation yesterday, only then he looked at the map before him, and started to worry more that Bothal might see something on the vellum he didn't want to share with anyone.

'I'm from Slutet,' Mann hesitated as he spoke, not sure how much to say.

'I know, good gent, I know. But you're not the man. You've told me so yourself, and believe me, the man himself would know if he were he. Never fear. I'll stay here as long as I can, and then hopefully make a brief foray even further north and return to the south for the worst of the weather.' Bothal frowned as he spoke, no doubt dismayed by the thought of all that snow.

'I was born in a blizzard,' Mann offered, swept along by the idea of never having seen snow, and forgetting to whom he spoke, or that his 'birth' had been something entirely different. 'I can't imagine never having seen it. But then, I can't imagine the heat people from the south always speak of. Here, it's either winter or near enough.' Mann laughed as he spoke, hoping Bothal wouldn't question him further, relieved when he didn't. And Mann hoped his indiscretion wouldn't arouse too much suspicion from the man who was already filled with questions.

Haune returned to the bar then, an interested expression on her face. Bothal jumped from his chair and waddled his way over to speak with her about extending his stay.

With the blizzard so bad, and likely to last days longer, Haune was now almost too keen to keep Bothal as one of her patrons. Mann would have thought less of her if he could, but he'd done the same too many times in the past to let her abrupt change of heart mean more than that. An innkeeper was as likely to be swayed by an on the spot decision as anyone else, and as likely to have their mind changed, given enough time, and the promise of shiny coins.

Marnit joined him as he watched Bothal and Haune both try and get the best deal from each other. He did enjoy a good bargaining, but in this instance, they were near as desperate as each other for the deal to be struck so they both gained what they wanted. Bothal paid a small premium, quickly nullified by Haune's decision to feed his running dogs as part of the price.

Mann's ears perked up. He'd never had dogs, only ever reindeer, but was always a little envious of those that did. But put simply, he didn't travel enough to warrant keeping ten or twelve dogs all year round as well as his reindeer. His mode of preferred transport was left over from his relationship with Freg, and he'd not change it.

Marnit saw his interest.

'Bothal has six of them,' she offered. 'They were sold to him as being a quicker and cheaper alternative than reindeer. After all, he only needs them for the length of time of his journey and everyone is always keen to take on newly trained dogs. I imagine he might even double his money when he returns to the south.'

'Just the six? I was always told I'd need twice as many as that.'

'Well,' and Marnit laughed, indicating his size with her eyes and outstretched hand toward Bothal's, 'you are twice as tall as him. It makes sense.'

Marnit was still laughing when Haune appeared before them. Bothal was counting his coins carefully onto the bar's wooden surface, but Haune had something on her mind.

'Mann, could you help Sand and Rad. They checked on the animals yesterday before the storm was too fierce but they've not been back out since. The way is covered with snow and treacherous.'

Mann knew this must be what Sand and Rad had been arguing about, as he leaned around Haune to get a good look at them both. If he went it would give them the opportunity to question him further. He wasn't sure he wanted that but suspected he didn't have much choice.

'Of course,' Mann muttered, unhappily. 'Between us, we should be able to get through.'

'My thanks,' Haune nodded, ignoring his doubtful tone. 'I'd ask some of the other patrons, but I doubt they'd be as obliging and I want it done so I can be assured everything is well below the inn.'

As Mann stood, Bothal slid into his place, while Marnit abruptly stood as well.

'I'll help,' she announced. 'I hate being stuck inside, even in a storm.'

Mann wanted to argue with her, but Haune's silence on the matter proved she had no problem with Marnit helping the three men.

A few moments later, the four of them amassed at the front door. The blind dog hadn't moved. Mann was pleased he wouldn't need to consider the animal outside.

Haune was there, holding out three shovels and giving her employees some instructions. They were dressed warmly, furs covering them from head to toe.

Mann had decided to try his new coat and so was swathed in white, whereas Marnit was dressed in the more common browns and blacks. She eyed Mann's new outfit slightly aghast but made no comment. Mann suppressed a smile. No doubt, he looked outrageous.

Mann braced himself for the shock of the door opening, but still, as Haune swung the door open wide enough to allow the four to exit, he sucked in a shocked breath as the cold engulfed him.

They'd need to move fast and quickly.

Mann was pleased he'd heeded Haune's warning, albeit grudgingly, and made no attempt to leave that day. It would not have ended well. Well, it might have done, but he'd have had to rely on his unique abilities, which would have roused questions from those who witnessed his departure.

Sand and Rad looked at him quickly. Mann nodded. He'd go first as the tallest one there. Grabbing a shovel, Mann stepped through the slanted gap and promptly turned to clear away the snow from the top wooden steps. Marnit was straight behind him, attempting to keep a lantern lit so he could see despite the blizzard.

None of the outdoor lanterns blazed, and neither did any of the braziers. The entire scene was a howling mass of snowflakes and debris uprooted by the force of the wind.

With the steps cleared, Mann gestured for Marnit to hurry down. Then Sand and Rad made an appearance as the door was unceremoniously slammed after them.

Mann continued to clear snow to either side, even though it was getting close to over two feet deep, while Sand and Rad quickly joined him. Sand indicated with his arm the easiest way to get to the stables.

Already, sweat beaded Mann's face. He hastily tried to wipe it away with his gloved hand. Better to have damp gloves than ice on his face.

The three of them made quick work of clearing the snow while the wind buffeted them, even sheltered, as they were, by the high walls surrounding the settlement. Mann was aware they needed to rush, or their path would be refilled with snow on their return, and they'd struggle to make it back inside the inn.

Mann couldn't even hear the sound of the others at work over the roar of the wind. It felt as though only the four of them existed in the world.

When they eventually reached the door of the stables, the

three men laboured furiously to ease open one of the large wooden doors. Snow had piled too high in front of the entrance. It took precious time to move it with the three shovels. Only then could Sand slide open the barred door and finally enter the stables. Hastily they all followed, pleased to be out of the biting wind and freezing snow.

They'd been unable to hear the animals outside the stables, but once inside Mann could hear the outraged cry of his reindeer, the howling of Bothal's dogs and also the sound of stamping hooves.

The lanterns in the stables had all gone out because they'd been left untended for so long. Marnit set to work on lighting as many as she could using the lantern she'd held on their journey, while Sand and Rad leapt to the task of feeding and watering the hungry, and terrified animals.

Mann sought a handful of lichen for his reindeer, their preferred food, as well as a few root vegetables, in a waiting bucket, but for most of their food, he needed to find his sled.

The six animals eyed him dolefully. They knew what the blizzard portended. Mann spoke to them soothingly as he offered them the supplies at hand, and then went to find the sled.

It was in the stable next door but one to his reindeer. It looked exactly the same as when he'd returned it after his brief foray over the snow. Climbing into the seat, he turned and looked behind him. He could hear the two men working to feed the howling dogs and other animals, but he was only concerned for his reindeer.

Pulling open the large sack of food he'd bought from Slutet, Mann chose a selection of the ground vegetables and turned to go back to them, only to meet Marnit almost eye to eye. She yelped in surprise, and so did he.

'Apologies,' he gasped, as Marnit giggled with embarrassment, a strange sound and something he never thought he'd hear from her.

'My fault,' she laughed, suddenly looking very young and carefree. 'I was being nosy, as usual.'

Marnit walked away from his sled, while he followed, racking his brain to decide if she might have seen something he'd sooner she hadn't. He could think of nothing that might alert her to his true intentions.

'They're beautiful,' Marnit offered, stroking the noses of two reindeer at the same time, as she leaned over the side of the stables. They were preening under her ministrations. Mann stifled a laugh.

'And they know it,' he said, holding out some of the vegetables for her to feed them. Contentedly, the pair munched on the offered food, the other four waiting patiently for Mann to get to them. Happy they were all feeding, Mann went to see if Sand and Rad needed any help, leaving Marnit to chatter to the reindeer.

They were, once more, arguing with each other, but stopped abruptly on seeing Mann. He tried a smile.

'You done?' he asked. 'We shouldn't linger.'

'Almost,' Rad coughed, looking anywhere but at his face.

Mann left them to their argument and returned to Marnit. She was talking to the reindeer as they ate everything she fed them. He grinned. Nothing like docile beasts to win around a problematic ally.

The dogs howled once more. He turned to look at them. The six of them were split between two of the stables, and they were all busy savaging some meat Bothal must have brought for them, for it was far too good and rich to have been spared by Haune who had to watch her supplies with such a violent storm raging.

The animals were all different varieties of black and white but shared the same build and alert looking ears. Not that they noticed his interest. They were too hungry to do anything but focus on their meal.

'Savage beasts,' Marnit said at his elbow, her face curled down with dismay at their antics.

'I admire them,' Mann said. 'They have their hierarchy, and they rigidly adhere to it. They're just hungry,' he commented, trying not to grimace at the grinding noise coming from them as they worked on the bones having finished all the meat on the carcass.

'Yuck,' was Marnit's response. 'I prefer your beasts. They're far more placid.'

'Well, that's where you're wrong,' Mann laughed. 'They sorted out who was the boss long ago, but that doesn't stop the others from trying it on, all the time. None of them are good-natured. Not when they're racing each other or when there's something they all want.'

Mann was looking around, staring at the animals. Then his eyes fastened on something that could help him with his growing list of questions. Bothal's sled.

It was much smaller than his, propelled by six dogs instead of six great hulking reindeer. Mann was sure it would contain secrets about Bothal's identity and maybe even who he was looking for in Slutet.

While Marnit watched the dogs, her distaste clear to see on her contorted face, he made his way around to the side of Bothal's sled. He didn't get too close, not to start with. Mann needed it to look as though he had a mild interest in it, and then, well if he could, he'd investigate more closely.

His head turned, trying not to look too guilty, but he could see Sand and Rad busy at their labours. Marnit seemed to be paying him no mind at all. Outside the whiteout roared and the thought of returning to the inn caused him to shiver involuntarily.

Mann took a step closer to the sled, and then another, admiring the leathers and the compact nature of its design, apparently made for a taller person, but which Bothal had padded out with thick linen and cloth to enable him to climb in and out of it easily.

The sled itself was made from Hvite Lands wood, gleaming dully black, even in the gloom of the stables.

It was a handsome piece of equipment, but it was the contents of the rear of the sled that held the most appeal for Mann. He stepped closer and closer, as though he merely wanted to examine it from the other side, only for Marnit to squeal. The noise made him both jump and glance at her in alarm.

It was a strange noise, more like a strangled gasp but she was still standing there, unharmed, just as he'd left her.

'What?' Mann called to her. She beckoned him with her outstretched hands, and with a growl of annoyance he abandoned his examination of the dog sled.

'What?' Mann said again when he neared her side. This time she pointed into the stable containing the dogs.

'Look,' she muttered, and he did, not letting his sudden bad temper get the better of him.

Mann saw little to worry him. In each stable, three of the dogs had calmed as they chewed on bones contentedly. They'd spent some time cleaning themselves first, and any traces of blood or gristle were gone from their thick black and white coats.

'What?' Mann muttered again, only then he saw it as one of the dogs, the one with two black ears and a white nose looked at him with interest.

'Bollocks,' he bellowed, entirely shocked by Marnit's observations.

The dogs were just that, Hvite Land dogs, but their eyes. Well, their eyes were rimmed in violet, like Bothal's.

He turned to stare at Marnit, his mouth open in shock, but she giggled.

'The bastard,' she breathed. Already he knew she understood more than he did. He turned to ask for an explanation, but by now Sand and Rad were finished and waiting impatiently for them at the rattling door.

'We need to get back,' Rad called cantankerously, the shovel already in his hand. 'No doubt the snow will have covered our original path. We'll need to step carefully and probably dig some of it afresh.'

Mann considered asking for more time in the stables, or even remaining behind, but knew he'd never make it back to the warmth of the inn unless they all worked together. He growled with frustration. He needed to quiz Marnit on what she knew, and before they had to speak to Bothal once more.

But now wasn't the time. With a final glance back at the dogs, to be sure he hadn't imagined the colour of their eyes, and a last word of consolation with his reindeer, Mann grabbed his shovel and went to stand by the door, ready to face the tempest outside.

The only person missing was Marnit. She appeared soon enough, a contemplative expression on her face. She grabbed the lantern and checked it was well supplied with oil, and then turned to meet the eyes of the men she accompanied.

'I'm ready,' she trilled. Before anyone could speak another word, Sand had grabbed the door and was pushing against it. Although they'd not long cleared the snowdrift from the outside, it was an effort to open the door. With a sinking feeling Mann realised this blizzard might last more than a few days. He could quite easily be trapped in Bosetting for two weeks whether he wanted to be or not.

As soon as Sand had the door opened wide enough for someone to sneak through, Mann pushed through the gap and began to scrape away the rapidly settling snow. In no time at all the door was fully opened and all of them could thread their way outside. But, and Mann knew they needed to consider this, it would be hard going should they need to come back again if the storm continued, and the snow lay even thicker.

'We should bring one of the braziers outside, put it just under the door. Even that small amount of heat could keep the doorway cleared.' He roared over the scream of the wind. Sand seemed to hear him and hastily went back inside, much to the annoyance of Rad who gesticulated angrily at him.

But Sand was quick, and by then Rad had determined what they were doing, and had uncovered one of the heavy braziers and was attempting to roll it in front of the door. Mann leapt to help him. As Sand shut the door on the stables once more, the brazier was pushed into place, and quickly filled with the coals Sand had brought outside with him.

Marnit stepped forward as soon as the brazier was prepared and grabbed a small piece of wood Sand held in his hand. He thrust it inside the lantern. It caught, quickly, flames bouncing to life along its length, but as soon as Marnit removed it from the lantern, the flame-gutted and died in the strong wind.

Stepping forward, Mann and the two other men made a tight circle around Marnit, hoping to block the wind from her second attempt. This time, the flame safely made it inside the brazier and quickly caught on the other pieces of wood inside. Mann knew they should wait to make sure the coals had also caught fire, but Sand simply slammed the lid on top of the brazier, something rarely used apart from when the snowfall was heavy, nodding as though satisfied.

Mann hoped the idea worked but hastily turned back to clearing snow. The pathway they'd forged was just visible. He scooped the snow rapidly to either side, Sand and Rad following on behind him, doing the same.

It was a laborious process, and despite the deep penetrating cold, also a warm one. Mann could once more feel sweat on his face and pooling down his back, but he worked on.

They needed to get back inside the inn.

Only once did he cease his endeavours, to turn back to see if he could see the brazier from in front of the stable doors. He caught just the faintest flicker of smouldering yellow flame and knew the idea would work, for a time anyway.

The braziers were ingenious contraptions. Although they looked like standard barrels from ale-making and storing salted fish all throughout the long winter, they were actually lined with thick metal sheets, bent to the shape of the barrel, and this prevented the wooden barrels from burning away to nothing. Although customarily left open to the elements, to allow heat and light to escape, the barrels did have a lid with a circle of small chiselled holes to allow the smoke to escape.

The heat the braziers produced could be intense. Hopefully, it would be enough to keep the stable doorway clear from the heavy snowfall.

When Mann turned back to his work, content the idea would work, the other three had moved in front of him. He hurried to catch up before losing sight of them.

It seemed to take a long time, but eventually, they made it to the few steps that led to the door of The Firs, and, having cleared them, Rad hammered on the door. It was opened, eventually, by Haune who ushered them inside and quickly resealed the door.

The main room of the inn was impossibly hot in direct contrast to the outside. Mann quickly removed his heavy coat and boots. A giant puddle of water was forming by the door, but Haune didn't seem to mind, not this time.

Instead, she quickly moved to the hearths and poured steaming water into mugs she'd obviously had waiting for them. The smell of heat filled Mann's nostrils and forcing himself to hang his coat so that it would dry before the heat, he gratefully took his mug and held it under his nose.

The other inhabitants of the inn were nowhere to be seen, and that suited Mann, who turned to look for Marnit. Only she wasn't there.

'Where did Marnit go?' he asked, suddenly worried they'd left her outside, but Haune reassured him.

She's getting changed. Her clothes are soaked. She really needs much better winter equipment, or she'll freeze, but I suppose a scribe isn't in the highest demand in a place such as Bosetting.

Mann hadn't considered how affluent or not Marnit might be, although he knew he'd rewarded her well for her scribing and illustrating for him. He wondered but didn't ask, how she could afford to shelter in the best inn in Bosetting during the worst winter storm for some years if she had little coin to her name. Unless of course it was part of an old family arrangement and she didn't have to pay at all. Maybe it was a previously bartered agreement between the two women.

'Our thanks,' Sand said, speaking for the first time since returning from the stables. 'We wouldn't have managed so quickly with just the two of us.' He was reassuring his old blind dog all was well as the animal nosed around him.

Mann nodded in agreement. The two men would have been at it all day. 'If we need to go again later or tomorrow, if the storm is still raging, let me know. Hopefully, it will subside.'

The two men grunted as though they doubted his words and somehow knew the storm would rage for days yet.

'Just once a day is all that's needed, but our thanks for your help,' Rad eventually offered, the first time he'd spoken to Mann since he'd been caught talking about him. Mann grinned at him, deciding it was time to be friendly.

'As you will,' and seated himself before the fire.

Despite his exertions, he felt invigorated, almost desperate to do something, but there was little to be done within the inn. He could have asked Rad and Sand for a game of cards or chance, but he doubted either would be a good player. Alternatively, he could study his map some more. But having seen the devastation the storm was causing outside he was acutely aware no matter how up to date Marnit's knowledge of the area she'd drawn might be, it could have been changed beyond all recognition by this one storm, let alone however many had erupted since Marnit had first drawn her map. Whenever that might have been. He'd not asked her.

Mann grunted, frustrated and annoyed only to hear the sound of raised voices somewhere in the inn.

He imagined it was the family with the children. Children didn't like to be contained, no matter how bad the weather. But then he recognised Marnit's voice and a lower one. Bothal. Had the girl gone and confronted him on her own about his strange dogs? He stood to go and intervene, but he heard footsteps on the stairs and saw Marnit's feet flying down them.

When she reached the bottom her face was set in an angry grimace. She went straight to Haune, either not seeing Mann or purposefully ignoring him. He watched her go with interest and then turned to the stairs where he could hear soft footsteps once more.

Bothal laboured down the stairs. Really, they were too big for him, and each step down was a real struggle. Mann took the time to think how something as simple as your height could hamper everyday tasks.

Haune and Marnit had disappeared, no doubt into the cellar. Bothal looked to where they'd been and then shrugged, as though the argument meant nothing.

With a smile of welcome on his face, he came toward Mann.

'I see you've made it back in one piece,' at that moment a

great thud resounded throughout the inn. Bothal looked concerned. Mann gazed upward, a faint smile on his face.

'The snow,' he explained. 'It's falling off the roof and landing on the ground. It's good. It'll save the job of having to climb up there and remove it ourselves.'

The explanation seemed to suffice, for Bothal continued speaking.

'You met my dogs?' Bothal asked with raised eyebrows.

'Yes, hungry beasts, aren't they?'

At the mention of the dogs, Mann was reminded of the strange glow around their eyes and also around Bothal's. In the deepening dusk within the inn, Mann could hardly make out the peculiar colour. But he knew it was there all the same.

Bothal grinned, clearly taking Mann's tone as a compliment.

'The breeder who sold them to me said all Hvite Lands dogs are like that. They prefer the meat raw, it keeps their killer instincts intact even when they're trained to run on the leathers.'

'You've not had them long?' Mann probed. Mann was keen to know more about the stranger who'd decided to venture from his southern lands to the frozen north at entirely the wrong time of the year.

'No, just for the trip. The breeder will buy them back from me when I complete my task, but the animals only respond to one owner. They can't be lent or leased or hired.' Mann detected a slight warning in the voice and looked at Bothal in surprise.

'The dogs are mine,' Bothal announced, and then walked away from Mann, to settle himself at another table, one further away from the heat of the hearths.

With his body temperature returned to normal, Mann too was feeling the excess heat from sitting so close to the fire, yet he didn't want to move away because he didn't want to have to make Bothal think he was hounding him. Much better to sit and sweat than interrogate the strange little man.

After all, if the blizzard continued, as seemed highly likely, Mann would get to see the dogs again. Then he could make his mind up about what the strange eye colour meant.

Haune returned to the main room then, alone, her step faltering as she spied Bothal on her way to seeking out Mann. She ploughed on all the same, using her body to block Bothal from seeing and hopefully hearing what she wanted to say.

'Marnit needs to speak with you. She's in the cellar, waiting, but I didn't realise Bothal was here.' Mann understood the problem straight away. He could hardly go to the cellar now. Bothal would know they spoke about him, especially as it seemed it had been he who Marnit had been arguing with.

'Send her to my room, when you can. I'll go and wait for her.' Haune accepted the revised arrangement. Mann was pleased to be away from the fire, and from Bothal. The man seemed so content and placid Mann found it a little off-putting.

Once in his room, Mann sat himself next to the brazier. It was far less warm than in the main room, but he welcomed the lower temperature. He closed his eyes and thought about the terrible storm, and how unexpected its arrival had been. He could usually tell days in advance when the weather was about to change, but then, that was in Slutet.

He waited so long for Marnit to appear that eventually, he fell asleep, only to be woken by the creaking of his door opening.

Dusk had fallen. He had no lantern lit in his room. So he squinted, watching the shadow enter his room, the only light coming from behind whoever it was.

He sat quietly, not convinced it was Marnit. The figure seemed too short and was also moving stealthily. He held his breath and tried not to move, only his eyes tracking the figure and not his body.

Mann couldn't help thinking if it had been Marnit, she'd have brought a lantern with her and would have announced her presence.

The figure, cast around from side to side, as though checking they were alone, and that was when Mann knew it wasn't Marnit. He squinted into the gloom, determined to see who it was, but they simply appeared shapeless as they came further and further into his room, heading for where most people would store their possessions, at the foot of the bed.

Mann watched. He thought it was Bothal, only the shape appeared taller than he recalled him being. And anyway, why would Bothal sneak around his room? He was already convinced beyond all doubt Mann wasn't the person he was looking for. He said that person would know who they were and because Mann didn't, he wasn't that person. So who then was in his room?

A slant of lantern light lit the room as someone walked past his half-open doorway and the shadow froze, but not before it illuminated his entire face.

Rad. Mann choked in surprise. What was he doing in his room?

As though sharing the same thought, Rad started to retreat, thinking better of whatever had brought him sneaking into the room. Mann let him go. There seemed no point in making an issue of it when nothing had happened.

As the shadow slid out of his door, another entered, this time carrying a lantern, but in all honesty, looking just as furtive.

'Sorry I took so long,' Marnit whispered hoarsely. 'He wouldn't leave the damn room, and so I've been stuck in the freezing cellar all this time.'

Mann looked at the blue tint to her cheeks and realised she was telling the truth. She was chilled through and through.

'Come, sit by the brazier and warm yourself up.' He stood as he spoke, and took the lantern from her shaking hand.

She nodded, too cold to argue, and he also picked up the fur from his bed and wrapped it around her shoulders, before moving to light his own lantern with a purloined flame from her own, flooding the room with light.

'Who was just in here?' she asked, her shivering starting to stop as she warmed through.

'In here? No one. I was asleep.' He didn't want to involve Marnit in whatever was happening with Rad.

'Oh, perhaps they came out of the room next door. But even so. Your door was open. You should be more careful.'

Mann nodded, accepting her chastisement.

'I needed to speak to you about Bothal,' she began. Mann nodded encouragingly as he closed the door, doing as she cautioned.

'Were you arguing with him earlier?' he asked.

She grunted and looked resentful.

'I asked him about his dogs, amongst other things. He didn't like being questioned.'

Mann found this intriguing, considering what he knew about their secret meeting the other night. Perhaps they were conspirators but not allies.

'What did Bothal say about them?'

'Just that he purchased them from a dealer and couldn't excuse their nature or their appearance. But I know it means something. It has to.'

Mann considered the irony she was now confiding in him whereas before she'd been less than forthcoming with him.

'Why does it have to?' he probed, as she fixed him with a hard glare.

'Because, well because dogs don't have violet eyes, not

even Hvite Land dogs.' She hissed the words angrily. He wondered what she expected him to do about it.

'He's going to Slutet, to where you live. You should be worried,' she pressed. 'You should want to stop him. He shouldn't go there. He shouldn't find the man he's looking for. I know … I know it's dangerous.' She ended in exasperation and Mann understood the feeling only too well. It was difficult to know something but have no way of explaining how you knew it.

This was Marnit's position now. He had no intention of agreeing to whatever it was she wanted him to do without a full explanation.

She evidently understood this, and it accounted for their clandestine meeting.

'I can only tell you what I know, and it's little enough and makes for a poor retelling,' she growled. He waited for her to say more.

'It's something I learned while I was studying in the south. About a group of people or a gathering of them, or something like that. I don't know if they're born into it, or they have to enter it, but I know Bothal is one of them. They have some creed about bringing about a new age or something. They can only do it by killing certain people. As I said, it's little or nothing, but Bothal has all the marks of it, as did the woman, whatever her name was. They both came to me, looking for whoever this person is, and they thought it was you.'

'But now they don't,' Mann nudged when she stopped speaking, as though a thought had only just presented itself to her.

'No, they don't. Well, Bothal doesn't. But he says he must go north, to Slutet, to your home. I fear he means to kill Brag. Not that I much like Brag, but I can't let Bothal go north. Not now I've the opportunity to stop him. Before the storm struck, I felt hopeless, knowing he was headed to Slutet. Now he's come back, I can stop him. Or go with him, or you, you could stop him.' She spoke hopefully, as though Mann being there solved all of her concerns.

'It all seems a little far-fetched,' he began. She nodded enthusiastically, wholeheartedly agreeing with him.

'I thought so too, but well, I'm more than half convinced now. I'm sorry if I seemed compliant in what they were trying to do. I thought. Well, I saw your sigil, so like Brag's, and I thought it made sense. Somehow. Oh, I don't know,' Marnit answered on a whine and Mann laughed at her.

'Why does this concern you so much? You owe nothing to Brag, or to Slutet. Men and women will always argue and injure each other. It's all part of life.'

'Can you really speak so callously about someone else? No, forget that,' she muttered,' I don't want to know the answer. After all, I've already proved I do. It's just, well, it's one of those strange tales that's gained in popularity in the south, especially at the Collegium. They talk about it as though it's fact. I guess I allowed myself to be swept up in it all. But, well, when I asked Bothal, he laughed. He neither denied nor confirmed what I said, but I saw the savagery of those dogs. I think he has control of them.'

'Of course he does. A deal sealed with coins makes the dogs his. Surely you know that?'

'Well, yes, but I think it's something else. I have this strange feeling he's not who he says he is, that he's one of these people in this strange group. But I know he means harm to this person he seeks. He has blades hidden in his cloak, I've seen them flashing in the light from the fires and lanterns. And his sled is packed too light for a man going north. He doesn't have half the supplies he needs. Yet he's made it this far. None of it makes any sense.'

'Why did you meet him and Shlat behind The Three Bells?'

Mann spoke as though it were acceptable for him to be spying on them. Marnit shot him a furious glance.

'I bloody knew it,' she cried, her voice rising before she could lower it again, fearful Bothal might overhear them, should he be hovering at the door, aware of their meeting.

'You all seemed to know each other quite well,' Mann castigated. She sighed dramatically.

'There's a scribal code. They both knew it and summoned me to meet them. I'm not allowed to ignore it. It's part of being a scribe.'

'And why did they need you?'

She looked at him, of all things, a smile playing around her lips.

'Scribes know everyone in a settlement. They write peoples letters and death wishes. They answer all official documentation from the Collegium and the tax collectors and anyone else with official responsibilities. Scribes know things that other people don't know. We might be underpaid and little regarded by some, but we're a source of great power and information really.' She spoke with pride. Mann tried to reconcile this bright creature with the dour scribe living in Slutet. It simply didn't appear he felt the same way.

Marnit noticed his look and shook her head angrily.

'That fool you have in Slutet is a slur on the profession. But then, no one wants to come to Bosetting let alone to Slutet. If you will live somewhere where the snow falls for more than half of each year, I'm not sure what you expect.'

Mann accepted that with a shrug of his shoulders.

'So what did they want to know? About me?'

'No, not really. Well, okay yes, they did, initially, but then, you'd already met them and assured them that you weren't who they were looking for. Though why you would be, I don't know. If they intended to kill you, why would you own up to being whoever it is they're looking for?'

'So what did they want to know?'

'Well, I might have mentioned Brag to them, that he was in Slutet. I don't know really. It was a confusing conversation, one I wish I'd never had.'

'Ah, so now I understand it. You directed Bothal toward Brag. Now you feel remorse for your actions and want me to do something about it?'

'No,' Marnit answered too quickly. Mann knew he'd interpreted her actions correctly.

'I can't go back to Slutet, not yet,' he commented. Marnit's face fell. 'But you could go, as you said. If you go with Bothal, you can make sure he doesn't harm Brag, and at the same time you can relieve Brag of his role as innkeeper until I return.' Mann tried to sound cajoling, but she was already shaking her head.

'You'd send me there with him? Alone!' she gasped. He nodded.

'Has he come to harm you, or imperil you in any way? No,' Mann answered the question himself. 'Are you of any interest to him except as someone he can garner information from, because of some secret code? No.' He answered the question again, but she was looking at him with rising horror, not acceptance.

'Why won't you go back?' she hissed angrily, her tongue snaking out of her mouth as her brow furrowed in a fury.

'I have somewhere I have to be,' Mann answered. She was nodding along with him.

'I know where you 'have' to go,' she spoke with fire. 'I've written your letters. There's no urgency to what you must accomplish, but there's an urgency in this. A life might be at stake.' Her forehead knit in confusion.

'You've no idea what Bothal means to do. All you know are half-formed truths and a lot of inference. I admit he unnerves me, but I think that's his way. It has nothing to do with murdering people or anything like that.' Once more, Mann tried to be as convincing as possible.

Mann honestly had no explanation for Bothal's motivation, but he would like it if he could persuade Marnit to go north for him, as she had initially wanted, but now seemed unwilling to do. He had a feeling she'd ensure that when 'he' returned as his nephew, the inn would be given to him quickly and in good order, in accordance with 'Mann's' death wishes, she'd written for him.

Marnit watched him with incredulous eyes, and then stormed from the room. He watched her go. He thought she'd be back. Perhaps, but really, provided Bothal wasn't after him, he had no real interest in her worries and fears regarding Brag.

TWENTY

BUT MANN DID NEED to find out what Rad had been up to in his room. Although the wind screeched and wailed outside the inn, Mann felt refreshed from his nap, and so once more descended the stairs.

The main room of the inn was rapidly filling with patrons keen to be fed their evening meal as Mann scanned the place nonchalantly seeking out Rad. As usual, the two men who worked in the inn sat apart from the regular patrons, on a table that still benefitted from the duplicate fires but which others might eschew because it was so close to the bar, where Haune worked without cease.

It suited Haune because from there she could speak with them, and occasionally they rose to carry out her myriad wishes. The blind dog sporadically followed them but mostly stayed hidden beneath the table, and away from the children and people he didn't know.

Mann sighed. He needed Rad alone, and he wanted to avoid Marnit who was pacing angrily and gesticulating as she spoke to Haune, both of them behind the bar.

Bothal had left his earlier place. It had been filled by some of the random strangers who'd clearly bonded during the storm. They were playing a well-intentioned game of chance, using nothing but whatever they could find. No coins were involved, but a veritable selection of odd items had been brought into play. Mann was reminded of his game of cards with Grans all those years ago. He could say, honestly, he'd never managed a Reign since. No one had.

Whatever had been at work that day, and Mann hadn't 'asked' for the cards, it seemed it had been his destiny to win the inn in Slutet for himself.

As Mann circled the table, he spied buttons, semi-precious stones, pieces of wizened fruit and even a few seashells. He imagined at least one of the patrons was a trader, but what the other three people were doing so far north evaded him for the time being. Unless they'd come to hunt? He considered that. He didn't approve of hunting for the fun of it, as these visitors might do, but he had no issues with those who hunted for food.

The Hvite Lands weren't a forgiving environment. The skills to hunt were well honed, they had to be, taking years of practice. Not just silly men and women who 'thought' they could just turn up and hunt the fabled white bear – a legendary creature, as Mann knew from long experience.

Or, Mann considered, they might be visitors, drawn to the region by the tall tales often told about life in the bitter landscape.

Mann eventually chose a table middle distance between the bar and the twin fires and settled down to wait until an opportune moment presented itself. Haune was fleeing around the room, serving meat or pottage to all and sundry, depending on the cost they'd negotiated for their rooms and board. Although Mann ate hungrily, when she dropped a full bowl before him, topped with ample meat, his eyes kept a careful watch on Sand and Rad.

The skinny man seemed comfortable in his surroundings, clearly content his actions hadn't been discovered. Mann knew his complacency wouldn't last long once he was able to confront him.

Eventually, after Mann had eaten his fill, and the room had thinned out with the family of five retiring to their room, where no doubt they shared one bed, Haune asked Sand to help her in the cellar, leaving Rad alone.

Rad had a large mug of ale in front of him, but his eyes were almost closed as he rested his head on the back of the high backed chair. Mann took some pleasure in sneaking up on him unseen.

'Rad, a word,' he began. Rad's eyes shot open. A guilty look crossed his face.

'Mann, good gent, how can I help you?' Rad asked, his voice shaky, his eyes looking frantically behind Mann as though trying to summon Haune or Sand to his side.

'I think you know,' Mann muttered. 'All I want is an explanation,' he continued. 'And it better be a good one.'

'What?' Rad tried, attempting to look innocent and unaware of what Mann spoke about but his resolve quickly crumbled away. He invited Mann to lean in close to him.

'For goodness sake, don't tell Haune. She'll kick me out, and I'm desperate. I'm sorry. I am truly. I didn't take anything.'

'Why not? A change of heart, a stab of conscience or worry that you'd be discovered?'

'A, a change of heart,' Rad tried, but then he shook his head. 'I don't know. I'll be honest. It felt like there were eyes in that room, someone watching me. Anyway, how did you know?'

Mann smirked. 'They were my eyes watching you. You woke me from my nap.'

'You were in the room?' Rad squawked only for Mann to shush him.

'If you tell me everything you know about Bothal, and any other strangers of late, I'll reward you handsomely,' Mann offered, a silver coin appearing before Rad's eyes, and then disappearing again just as quickly. 'I'll forget all about it, and not a word of what happened will leak from my lips.'

'Bothal, the man with the dogs?' Rad whispered, his eyes transfixed by the passing coin. 'Why do you need to know about him?'

'I didn't say I'd answer your questions. I said you could tell me all you knew, in exchange for this.' Mann pulled the shiny coin from his pocket again and slid it across the table. It was an excellent quality coin. Rad's eyes light up. 'There'll be more of those as well. You can earn instead of taking.' Mann tried to ignore the hypocrisy of his words, wincing as he spoke. He remembered an earlier time when his morals had been far more …hazy.

'Okay,' Rad agreed. 'I will. But I don't know much. Not yet. He keeps himself locked in his room. In fact, Haune told him he had to the first night, although she's relented now. She doesn't like him, not at all, and I don't know why.'

As he spoke, Rad was keeping an eye on events behind his back, and when he abruptly shut up, Mann knew Sand had returned. He stood up, obliging the look of panic on Rad's face.

'So, we'll go to the stables earlier tomorrow then?' Mann stated, as though they were midway through the conversation. Rad swallowed quickly and nodded his head vigorously.

'Yes, if the snowstorm continues all night we should go earlier, especially as the snow fall from the roof might have further blocked the path.'

Mann was impressed and appalled by Rad's ability to think on his feet, and he walked away. Haune watched him go. He smiled at her and then went to return to his room.

The boredom of the day was settling on him. He'd decided that more sleep was the only answer. After all, he'd laboured that day. His back and arms were aching from displacing so much snow.

Yet, once back in his room, he felt restless as he tried to settle to sleep and eventually pulled back the furs and went to sit in his chair again.

Mann was thinking. He didn't much like where his thoughts were taking him. It seemed like too much of a risk, even for him. But he couldn't banish the thought from his mind, and now, when all he could do was sleep to the pass the time, he was utterly focused on his stray thought.

Was it even possible? He'd never done anything like it before, but mainly because he'd never considered it before. Not after what had happened with Jemp. But this was different, not at all the same thing.

This time he had a genuine need. It would aid him if it did work.

Then he had a further thought, and a smile spread across his face. It would be much safer to try his second thought first.

And so Mann did. Flinging his coat around his shoulders, and wrestling his feet back into his boots, retrieved from the main hall, he considered the words he'd say at length. It was imperative, as always, he used the correct phrase to avoid disaster. He steeled himself and took a steadying breath.

'I would like to go to the stables in The Firs in Bosetting, at this time?' Mann almost whispered the words as he felt himself vibrate violently. He closed his eyes as whatever happened, overcame him. He only opened them again when he felt the rush of frigid air over his face and smelt the aromatic odour of stabled animals. He grimaced. The experience hadn't been pleasant. He felt colder than he had when he'd first manifested on that night long ago, naked and alone in the middle of a blizzard

Mann shivered as he looked around the stables. Nothing had changed in the time he'd been gone, other than the lanterns had all burnt low. Quickly, he found the supplies and added a well of oil to each of the four lamps that cast warm glows into the large space.

Then Mann hurried to the door and listened. He daren't risk opening the door to check if the brazier still burnt, but he did place his hand on the stout wooden door and felt some slight warmth. Good. It would be challenging to tend to the animals if the snow covered the door once more.

Mann was completely alone. All of the animals slept in their individual stables as he made his way quietly to the sled he'd been trying to examine earlier.

He was hoping to find something about Bothal that could convince him the diminutive man was either a threat or not. He didn't know what it would be but all the same, now he'd made it here undetected, Mann vowed to search thoroughly.

The sled glowed faintly black in the gloom of the stables, and Mann scrutinised it. If the sled belonged to him, where would he hide his secrets? He laughed softly at the thought, and looked over to his own sled, waiting patiently to be used once more. He'd stored his own secrets deep in one of his travel sacks. Would Bothal have done the same?

Being so much smaller than his sled, Bothal's sled had room only for three sacks, and they all bulged with the promise of secrets. Mann wanted to search them, but he didn't want to leave any trace of his search. Although. Well, Bothal would have no idea that anyone would have been able to get to the stables undetected. Did it really matter? Would Bothal not just think he'd misremembered the way he'd stored everything?

Deciding caution was the way forward, Mann found the tie on the first sack and peered inside. It was impossible to see anything.

'Bollocks,' he muttered and walked back to retrieve one of the lamps and bring it over to the sled. He swung the lamp high about his head and then looked into the sack again. It was stuffed with the usual requirements of a traveller. There were furs and spare clothes, and also a set of boots and, and here Mann chuckled, a lot of very warm socks. The smaller man must really struggle to stay warm.

But Mann didn't take everything as seen and sneaked his hand inside the mostly soft bundle, checking nothing was concealed inside. He was disappointed with his diligence. There truly was nothing apart from the items visible to his eye.

Carefully Mann resealed the bag with the rope ties and examined the remaining two sacks. He was tempted to rifle through the bottom one now, but no, he should apply his own reasoning. That told him to go for the second sack. So he did.

As Mann opened the sack, he knew he'd made the correct decision. This sack didn't smell of cloth and clothing but rather of secrets and things long hidden. Mann stifled a smile and reached his hand inside. It caught on any number of enticing things, but as Mann pulled them from the sack his smile faded. It seemed to be filled with a random selection of fairly useless items. There was a single glove, a wooden box filled with spice, three different flints for lighting fires, a container of lamp oil and even some candles, broken and only held together by their wick.

'Why the hell would you take this with you?' Mann muttered to himself, as he shook the sack just to be sure he'd checked everything. It was only then he heard a strange rustling noise and just about upended himself into the sack, searching for the source of the sound.

Eventually, his hand closed around a package of parchment, held together with two frayed pieces of hemp. He pulled it into the light given off the lantern and looked at the top piece of parchment.

It was ancient and water stained. Mann scratched his chin as he decided what he should do next. Should he untie the bundle or would Bothal notice that? Deciding he no doubt would, Mann used his nail to flick through the corners of the parchments, his head canted to one side.

The top one, almost entirely visible beneath the hemp, contained a drawing of a woman, and not one he recognised. She had a strong chin and challenging eyes. He imagined she'd be headstrong and argumentative.

A name had been scratched below the image, but it had rubbed away because it had been stored on top of all the other pieces of parchment. Other than that, there was no indication as to who she was. The portrait was excellent though. Mann thought that if he ever did meet the woman, he'd recognise her straight away.

Flicking through the pile, Mann quickly realised many of the parchments contained portraits of other people, men and women, but never children. He tried to count them, just to see how many there were, but the parchment varied in thickness. Some of the pieces also stuck together, making it an impossible proposition unless he undid the hemp and he didn't want to risk that.

Down at the bottom of the pile, he finally caught sight of someone he recognised. Brag.

'Bollocks,' he growled, rubbing his hand over the portrait, as though he might obliterate it. It was evident whatever conspiracy Marnit feared, there might unfortunately, be some truth to it. Why else would Bothal have a parchment with Brag's image ingrained on it?

Once more, Mann could see where the name had been rubbed away. Perhaps the obliteration on the top parchment was intentional and not through wear?

But why would Bothal have these parchments and why would he travel with them? Perhaps Marnit's half-held beliefs of some strange collection of individuals killing others to bring about a 'new age' had some validity after all. He snorted. It was all too far- fetched for credibility.

Once more Mann fanned through the parchments, this time on the reverse side of the hempen tie. This revealed the other half of the etched drawings and also more words. Mann squinted to make out the cramped writing. Certainly, it was nowhere as neat and tidy as Marnit's writing, and he struggled to decipher it.

He pulled the lantern close to his nose, the vellum bundle in his other hand, held precariously in place between his thumb and smallest finger, and only then realised that the letters were like nothing he'd ever seen before.

'A southern hand,' Mann muttered to himself, annoyed his meddling was proving so fruitless. He couldn't make out any of the words and chucked the bundle back into the sack in frustration. There was nothing for him here.

As the bundle tumbled into the sack, falling over and over, something caught his eye. Mann grabbed it back once more. There was something on the bottom of the final sheet, something he recognised.

With the lantern still in his hand, Mann turned the bundle over and gazed in surprise at what he saw. His sigil. His sigil was depicted on the bottom of the bundle. He ran his thumb over the shape, noting the twisting tails. He swallowed heavily. Mann had never thought to question what the sigil meant. It just appeared on his skin, every year, at the turning of the seasons. But clearly it had a meaning and one Bothal knew, and if Marnit was to be believed, so too did Brag.

Mann was quickly beginning to change his mind about Bothal. It seemed he was a threat after all, and not only for Brag but also for himself. And maybe even Marnit as she'd revealed the extent of her knowledge to him.

Growling, Mann returned the bundle to the sack, and hastily restored the other items before sealing the sack.

He was unsure how much time had elapsed in the stables. The screech of the blizzard had become such a huge part of his consciousness, it appeared normal now, as it howled and screeched.

Really Mann knew he should return to his room, consider what he'd just found out, but he found himself inspecting the sack he'd not yet explored. He was sure it would contain something invaluable to him, something that he needed to know. But to open it he would need to move the other two sacks. He was already worried Bothal would discover his searching. Bothal didn't look like the sort of man who wouldn't have paid close attention to his sled before he left it in the stables.

'Bugger it,' Mann muttered, delving for the final sack. He needed to know more about the short man and what he had planned for Brag and anyone else he travelled all the way from the south to meet. He needed to know more than he was concerned about arousing suspicions Brag's possessions had been meddled with.

Mann picked up and placed the first two sacks on the floor. It was then he heard a metallic sound on the wooden floorboards and looked down.

From somewhere, and he had no idea which sack it had come from, something had thudded onto the floor.

'Bollocks,' he muttered, placing the sack back on the sled, and swinging his lamp so it illuminated the floor. He scavenged around on the floor with his free hand and was forced to his knees as he continued to search.

Under his breath, he kept muttering, 'bollocks, bollocks, bollocks,' some sort of mantra against what he was doing. Mann thought he'd have to give up his search, leave the item lost, only for his lamp to flash onto the object. He picked it up with an exclamation of delight.

'Bollocks,' he all but shouted, lifting the object up to examine it in the lantern light. In his hand, he held a sigil, very similar to his own, in fact almost identical. So much so, he immediately dropped it in shock and then had to find it once more, his chest hammering heavily.

It was beginning to look as though Bothal and Brag both had versions of his sigil and that could mean only one thing. Somehow they knew a lot more about him than he did. It seemed ridiculous to think that if they shared his sigil, they also didn't share his secret abilities. Yet he'd seen no sign of it from either of them.

'Bollocks, bollocks, bloody bollocks,' Mann growled as he restacked the three sacks in some semblance of the order they'd been in and made ready to leave the stables. He wanted to get back to his room, urgently, and decide on what he should do next.

'I would like to be back in my room at The Firs, in Bosetting, at this time, on this day,' Mann spoke clearly and concisely into the quiet of the sleeping stables. He immediately felt the same strange experience as last time, clenching his eyes shut as he went.

Mann opened them when a blast of warm air enveloped him, before immediately collapsing onto the bed. His hand unconsciously sought out his own sigil around his neck while the other rubbed over his chest, where the sigils cascaded down his body.

He shivered again.

'Bollocks,' he muttered softly. What did this all mean?

Mann had a sudden inkling he should leave, now. As he couldn't do so with the blizzard still raging outside, he could use his strange ability. But where could he go? Mann didn't want to risk going somewhere he'd never been before, and that would mean he'd have to return to Slutet. And that would mean explaining his presence and dealing with Brag, who was not at all what he seemed and might be an enemy, not an ally. Or he might be both.

'Bollocks,' Mann couldn't think clearly. This journey had begun as one thing and had abruptly turned into something else, something he had no control over and he didn't like it.

Mann had no idea how to escape from it all. He could take himself back to Slutet using his strange ability, and hide in his room until the blizzard lifted. He could then bring his reindeer and sled to him there, and start all over again, without visiting Bosetting. The idea had a great deal going for it, not the least of which was he could go now. But what would he then do if Marnit and Bothal did come north? He might even meet them on the tracks as they went to Slutet and he tried to escape from it.

Mann strode to his shutters, peeling them open just a little so he could see outside. It was dark out there, but it didn't matter. The window was covered in ice and snow. The storm hadn't blown itself out yet, and might not do for another day at least.

Gently he closed the shutters again and sat in his chair, beside the brazier, shrugging his coat onto the bed as he skirted it.

Mann was tired by what he'd done but was too concerned with the future to sleep.

The only option he had was to give up on his plans to return to Slutet and start a new life somewhere else. The thought chilled him more quickly than his trip to the stables.

Slutet was his home. It always had been. And his options were limited. Mann knew he was somehow restricted to the Hvite Lands. He'd tried to go south before, but something had physically stopped him, forcing him to return to Bosetting and then Slutet.

'Bollocks,' Mann growled. He hated to have his options so curtailed.

He thought of his sigil, of his strange abilities, and then he realised something he'd forgotten about in his panic.

Bothal had no image of him in his stack of parchments. Bothal didn't know that Mann had a sigil, and Bothal didn't know Mann even knew about the secret sigil.

Bothal had already made it clear he was going north to find someone else. It was Marnit who'd decided that person had to be Brag. Provided Mann could keep all of his knowledge to himself, and somehow distract Marnit, then he could still go south, and attempt what he'd been planning all along. Just because all these random occurrences seemed to be connected, it didn't mean that they were. Or that he had to be the one to show the others he was at the centre of those incidents.

The thought calmed him, and slowly his panicked breathing came under control, and he felt his eyes close. He would sleep, and wake the next morning, and he'd pretend he knew nothing as he ate breakfast, went to the stables and then returned for another meal. He'd avoid all spirits, mead and ale to keep his wits about him. Then when the storm cleared, he'd follow his plan, and bugger whatever it was Marnit, Brag and Bothal were up to.

It was none of his concern. He had no intention of revealing himself, even to people who might, or might not, share his sigil and his strange talents.

Mann had been alone for sixty odd years. Why couldn't he just continue as before? All he needed to do was ensure Marnit's silence on the matter. She was already so intrigued by all that was happening, he doubted she'd whisper any hint of her suspicions to those she suspected the most, Bothal and Brag.

TWENTY-ONE

Chapter 21

THE MORNING CAME as it must, and as he descended the stairs to the main room of the inn, he could feel many eyes on him. Mann ignored all of them apart from Haune's. She watched him as an innkeeper would any patron, and he returned her interested face with a nod of satisfaction. The inn was comfortable, despite the raging blizzard. The hearths had never burnt low, and food was in copious supply, although he could detect it was being carefully managed. The inn was well stocked, despite its current isolation.

Mann chose a table alone and far from the others, making his intentions clear, and Haune brought him his food, as she had for the last few days.

'Good day,' he greeted her cordially. She nodded.

'You'll help Sand and Rad again today,' she confirmed for him, and he nodded, even though it wasn't really a question.

'Of course. I must check on my reindeer. Do you think the blizzard will cease today?' he thought to ask. He'd almost become so used to the constant howling he had to strain to actually hear the wailing storm. It had become so 'normal' to him, as so often happened during the winter, that the return to quiet would be just as unsettling as the first few days of the storm had been.

'The storm defies my expectations,' Haune muttered, slipping a warmed mug of herbs onto the table. 'I hope it ends soon, but really, I've no way of knowing. I thought it would have blown itself out long before now.'

Mann nodded at the honesty of her answer. He quite agreed with it. He'd been snowbound before, many times, but this whiteout was refusing to follow any of the usual rules.

'I must ask when you go to the stables, that you and the men bring back some supplies – they'll be heavy, and I regret the necessity.'

Mann quirked a smile in consideration of his thoughts only moments ago.

'It shouldn't be a problem. If we clear the path quickly, we can bring anything you want. Just let Rad and Sand know.'

She grunted in agreement and turned away. Mann watched her go and considered what Marnit might have said to her. Haune didn't seem distressed or worried, rather only concerned with the continual success of her inn.

Mann realised Marnit had told Haune almost nothing about the concerns she'd shared with him. After all, Haune knew Marnit well. Maybe that was why Marnit had confided in him about Bothal rather than Haune.

He looked for Marnit. She was sat alone, staring broodingly into the fires. He imagined her thoughts were consumed with Bothal, but maybe they weren't, for as he watched, her face transformed into a smile. He followed her line of sight to see she was smiling at the family with the children. The three youngsters were engaged in a boisterous game of chance as they sat with their parents.

Mann considered the children. They were close in age, and

he could barely differentiate one from the other. He was impressed with how quiet they'd been during their confinement, although even he could deduce the parents looked worn out.

The children could probably do with being allowed outside to vent some of their pent up playfulness. He doubted the weather would permit it, not yet.

Marnit met his eyes as he watched her, and he didn't look away. He was no coward, after all. What he observed there amused him. He saw defiance and stubbornness. She wouldn't let the matter rest. He admired her for that.

For some reason, everyone lingered within the main room so that when Mann went upstairs to get his warm coat, he felt as though they once more watched him. As he turned to make his way back down the stairs, his coat and boots in one hand, Bothal emerged along the walkway.

'Good day, gent,' Bothal called, his light voice reaching Mann before he turned to descend.

'Good day, Bothal,' Mann replied, turning to be about his business.

'You're going to the stables again?' the small man asked. Mann nodded. 'Might I ask a favour of you?'

'If I can, I will,' was Mann's quick reply. He was feeling more conciliatory toward everyone after his considerations of the night before.

'I'd like an assurance my dogs are all well. I've not seen them for a few days, and feel I should make an effort, but know I'll struggle to remain upright in these conditions.' Bothal nodded toward the outside world. Mann understood only too well his fear.

'They were well yesterday. I'll take the time to ensure they remain so today. Do they need anything special providing for them? Do you have any supplies I should give to them?'

Bothal smiled. 'You're kind to ask, but no, they have all they need. The men know what to give them. But I'd ask another favour of you. A small item, from my possessions.' Mann startled at the words but kept his face straight. Was it some sort of test?

'Of course. What is it that you need?'

'A small trifle, nothing else. I brought a few travel sacks with me. Two of them are heavy and filled with travelling equipment. In the third one, there's a small sigil I have need of. It's about so big,' Bothal went on to describe the very item Mann had seen the night before.

Mann nodded and swallowed. He knew precisely what Bothal was talking about, but couldn't say as much.

'I'll do my best,' he offered with a shrug. Bothal nodded.

'Yes, don't delay your return on my account. It's only if you have the time, and can find it. I need to study it. I may as well do so now rather than delay any longer.'

While Bothal returned to his room, Mann made his way carefully down the stairs once more. All this coming and going was making his legs ache. He wasn't used to so much enforced captivity. If he were home in his own inn, he'd have chores and tasks to complete all day long, whether there was a blizzard or not. Here, he had little to occupy his body. His thoughts were far too active, his body not at all, although he was about to put that to rights.

As the day before, the four explorers met at the doorway, with Haune ready to release them into the snowy day. They didn't really speak, although Marnit was muttering away to herself. Haune quickly announced them ready and with Marnit holding the lantern, and Mann one of the shovels, the two of them erupted from the open door as soon as they could squeeze through it.

Snow and ice obscured Mann's view. He winced his eyes

shut against the blast of frozen air seemingly directed into his eyeballs and nostrils, and further, straight into his head.

He grimaced, and then slipped his way down the stairs. They were somewhat clear of snow, and he almost forget about the shovel in his hand, and the three people who had yet to make their way down to him. Abruptly Mann turned and worked his way back up the stairs clearing each one entirely as he went. By the time the four of them were assembled on the ground once more, only the top step was still covered in snow.

The three men turned a small circle with their shovels and cleared a space for them to stand within almost free from snow. Mann sighed heavily. The snow was lying so thickly on the ground he doubted Bosetting would be snow-free even in the weeks after the howling storm ended. For now, and with the help of Marnit and the lantern, shielded against the fierce blasts, he was able to detect the path they'd cleared the day before.

It had long filled in, but as the path was so much lower than the rest of the fallen snow, it was clear what it was.

Using hand signals and nods, instead of speech, which was impossible above the roar of the storm, Mann, Sand and Rad took up different positions along the semi-cleared way and began their work.

It was heavy going. The snow had fallen thickly since their last trip out, so although the path could be seen, it needed clearing to an even greater depth than the day before.

Still, it was early, and Mann had only just been complaining about his lack of physical exertion, so he tried to enjoy himself.

He could hear no one else about. Neither was there any evidence of footprints in the snow. He doubted anyone else had left their home since the blizzard began. Instead, Mann could smell the mingling of wood smoke in the stiff wind. He spared a thought for everyone as they tried to keep warm and fed behind their closed and barred doors.

Storms such as these often had tragic consequences, especially for those who lived alone. He hoped there were no fatalities as they slowly wound their way back to the stables.

Marnit stayed close by his side. She might not approve of his attitude toward Brag and Bothal, but it was clear she was more confident with him than with the other two men. Not that Mann minded. Sand was far from a physically comforting presence, and Rad was really more skin than muscle.

It took what felt like a long time, but eventually, the doors of the stables came into view. Mann could see where the barrel they'd left yesterday stood partially uncovered. The flames had only lasted for some of their absence, but he was impressed they'd managed to hold out for any length of time. It meant the door was less difficult to reach than it might otherwise have been. They quickly moved the snow aside and crept inside the safety of the building.

It was surprisingly warm in the stables. Sand exclaimed at the heat but didn't think to ask how the brazier had lasted as long as it had. As Marnit moved around, refilling the lanterns and ensuring they were all lit, the animals woke from lazy slumbers and began grumbling for food and water.

Mann sidled up to his reindeer offering them assurances and generally speaking nonsense to them as he rubbed their noses and checked their bodies for any injuries or complications from being stabled for so long. Back in Slutet the animals rarely rested. While he didn't often use them, the residents of Slutet borrowed them and took them wherever there was work that needed doing, be it transporting fish catches, hauling ice from the glaciers or simply taking people out for a ride in the frozen landscape of the Hvite Lands.

Mann found them safe and well and quickly left them to hunt around in his sled for some of their favoured food. Quickly he placed the ground vegetables into their feeder and then stopped to see what everyone else was doing.

Sand was busy feeding Bothal's dogs from supplies Bothal must have transported to Bosetting. Rad was happily feeding the other horses, whereas Marnit continued to be engaged with the lanterns and with restocking the brazier.

Mann knew he'd never have another opportunity quite as good as this one, and so he went straight to the dog sled. He immediately found the sigil Bothal had asked for. When he turned back to the others, he half expected them all to be watching him, with accusing eyes, but it seemed not one of them had observed him, too engaged in their own tasks.

Mann placed the sigil inside his inner pocket and went to chat with Marnit. She sang under her breath as she worked. He wasn't sure he knew the tune, but then stray words penetrated his consciousness, and he smiled. It was a traditional song, one mothers taught their children, and so on and on.

Marnit turned as he approached and gave a half smile.

'I'm sorry I was angry with you,' she shrugged, and he nodded.

'I'm sorry we fell out,' he agreed, and she nodded.

'The storm does strange things to people,' she explained.

'No one likes to be caged in, even when they're used to it.'

'Did you get what he wanted?'

Now he laughed. 'Do you miss nothing?'

'I try not to.'

'How did you know?'

'I don't trust him, and so I'm watching him. It seems I should be watching you as well,' she growled low in her throat. He chuckled.

'He asked me, I could hardly refuse. Anyway, it means I can look at it.'

'Well go on then,' she murmured. He reached back into his pocket and pulled it out.

It was a weighty piece of jewelry but still delicately made from a finely hued piece of copper. It had a beautiful pink glow to it that seemed to pulse with life when it was held in front of the lantern Marnit gripped tightly.

'What does it mean?' she asked.

'I don't know. The shape repeats itself, but I don't know what it signifies. I don't believe Bothal does either.'

Marnit leaned back, her brow furrowed in surprise. He explained without her asking the question.

'He says he needs to study it, that's why he wants it.'

'So where did he get it from?'

'How would I know that? But you know the sigil?' Mann pressed her. She grimaced.

'I've seen it before, as I said. Brag had it, on his forearm. He tried to cover it up, but I'd seen it already.'

'And I suppose you've looked through all your vellums and have found no mention of it.'

She fixed him with a strained smile but was prevented from answering by the arrival of Sand.

'Are you nearly ready? I don't want to linger.'

Marnit shook her head, indicating she had no explanation for the sigil, and turned to Sand.

'Are we restocking the barrel outside, and the brazier in here?'

'Yes, yes. Both of those.'

'Then we'll be ready when we've completed those tasks.'

'Good,' Sand grunted and went to chivvy Rad along. The pair of them were in the far reaches of the stables, heaving and grunting. Mann almost feared to see what they hoped to take back inside the inn.

Marnit carried on talking as she bent to restock the brazier Mann had filled last night.

'I can't believe this lasted all night long,' she muttered. Mann made some sort of grunting agreement. He didn't want to be caught out in a lie. Not when he and Marnit seemed to be on good terms again.

Rad approached him with a sack stuffed with food items, which he handed to Mann without speaking. He couldn't meet Mann's eyes, still riddled with guilt at being caught out as he tried to thieve.

Mann tried the weight of the sack, satisfied it would be easy to carry into the inn. Marnit still stocked the brazier and leaving the sack stacked against the side of the stable, Mann added oil to the lanterns from a plain jug left out for such a purpose. The smell was acrid as it hit the already burning oil. Mann wrinkled his nose in displeasure. It wasn't even cheap oil, but rather a finely fragranced one and still it stank of fish.

Sand approached him next, and another sack of foodstuffs was handed to him. This one was heavier. Mann suddenly realised something. He couldn't carry everything and ensure the pathway stayed clear.

He looked at Sand as the man waddled back toward the rear of the stable. What would he bring next?

Marnit straightened from her task and noticed his puzzled face and raised her eyebrows in question.

He held the sack up and mimed shoveling and her face quickly cleared.

'Ah,' was all she said. 'I'll have to shovel,' she shrugged, but Mann shook his head. They'd not long since cleared the pathway, but the snow was damn heavy. She wouldn't be able to do it.

'Can you carry this?' he asked, holding out the sack with one hand. She smirked a look of contempt at his worry. Yet, as she grasped the sack, and he slowly released his hold on it, she staggered. It would have landed on the floor in a jangle of broken contents if he'd not caught it first.

'That's a no then,' he clarified as she glared at him.

'You make it look light,' she argued. It was his turn to shrug. He was a tall, muscular man. He could carry almost anything.

Mann looked around the room, concerned. Haune had made it clear she needed these supplies, but Sand and Rad were still gathering more sacks. How would they get them back to the main room of the inn?

'We could use this?' a voice called from one of the empty stables. Mann ambled along to see Marnit upending a wooden barrow that had a big wheel on the front of it, and could be lifted at the back to clear the ground.

It looked about four hundred years old. Mann was debating whether it would stay together or not, as Marnit, not particularly carefully, tossed the current contents aside.

He bent to help her. It was then that something caught his eye. Nestled amongst them, in a sack about four hundred years old, was something substantial and intriguingly, labelled with a small, embroidered shape of the sigil Mann had found amongst Bothal's possessions in the other sack.

He suppressed a wry smirk. Bothal had clearly hidden this where no one would think to look, should they have suspicions about him. Mann was sure it would contain the answer to all his questions.

Carefully he stacked it on the floor, amongst the other contents from the barrow, determined to return to scrutinise it later. He then stood behind the barrow and tried to push it. It was stuck firm, and instead of the wheel moving, his stomach hit the ancient wooden handles painfully.

He grunted. 'Bloody wheel,' Mann groaned, but Marnit had already leapt back to the jug of oil. She upended some of its contents onto some dried grass lying on the floor and began to work it into the mechanics of the seized wheel.

By now their actions had caught the eye of Sand. He sauntered over to ask them what they were doing, a sack in each hand, causing him to sweat with the strain.

Quickly, understanding flashed in his eyes. Sand dumped

his sacks on the floor and walked away, muttering under his breath.

When Marnit was content she'd done the necessary she stood back, dropping the dried grasses onto the floor and wiping her slick hands on her trousers.

Mann took the weight of the barrow in his hands and tried to push it, one leg in front of the other. The wheel moved a tiny amount and then groaned.

'Bollocks,' Mann moaned, giving the wheel a kick for good measure, as he returned the weight to the floor.

'It was a good idea,' he offered, but she shook her head angrily, as Sand returned to them. In his hand, he held another jug containing something that smelt disgusting and also a long thin blade with a burnished wooden handle.

'Not been used for bloody years,' Sand muttered as he discarded his gloves, and rubbed some of the black oil onto his hands. The smell quickly warmed the space and once more Mann wrinkled his nose.

'Pure fish oil,' he groaned. Sand laughed.

'Stinks like shit but works every time,' the other man confirmed as he greased the mechanism and wangled the metal blade around inside it for a few moments.

'Try it now,' Sand said, standing and turning around to find something to wipe his hands on that wasn't his clothes. Marnit bent to the floor and picked up yet more dried grasses. Sand gratefully accepted them and rubbed his hands.

Mann lifted the weight of the barrow by the handle and gave it a tentative shove. A shriek like that of a winter cat in heat filled the stables and they all winced. But whatever Sand had done had worked. The barrow moved forward, and Mann rocked it back just to check it went both ways.

'Perfect,' he announced. Marnit smiled with delight.

Sand muttered, 'Good idea, I was concerned about getting everything back.'

Marnit turned to lead the way out of the stable, Sand having added the weight of the two sacks to the one already within the barrow.

Mann grunted and huffed his way out of the stable door they held open for him. It was clear they expected him to shoulder the job of pushing the unwieldy contraption. He struggled to turn it around the quite tight bend of the only partially open door. Marnit leapt forward to add her weight to his endeavours. Between them, they made it back to where Rad was standing, a look of surprise on his face.

'We meant to fix that?' he said, perplexed. 'Must have forgotten about the damn thing.'

Rad had two sacks at his feet. There was also a further one near the brazier. Mann didn't even take the time to consider how they'd have managed without the barrow, as he heaped the sacks onto it and tested it for balance.

As all the top sacks wobbled to the floor, Marnit and Sand scrambled to catch them.

'Bollocks,' Mann muttered. He set about testing each sack and deciding where to best place it in the shallow depth of the barrow.

'Do we really need all this?' Mann moaned when the sacks once more toppled to the ground despite his careful positioning.

'Haune said we did,' Sand growled, his own frustration at the delay making his temper short as he once more tried to shove a sack into a non-existent gap.

'Fine,' Mann growled, managing to balance the barrow leaving only one huge lumpy sack on the floor. It was lightweight but too bulky.

'You'll have to carry this one,' he announced. 'One of you can shovel, Marnit can light the way, one of you can carry this,' he said, holding out the sack expectantly in front of the faces of the two men. 'And I'll push the damn barrow.'

Sand and Rad looked at each other, as though weighing up which job they wanted. When they both grabbed for the sack, Mann was unsurprised.

'Unless one of you wants to push and I'll shovel?'

With an annoyed shrug of his thin shoulders, Rad released his hold on the sack and grabbed the shovel instead. Then Rad looked perplexed, at the pile of three shovels stacked against the side of the stable.

'We shouldn't leave the unused ones here,' Rad said, tentatively. Mann groaned.

'No, we shouldn't. Otherwise, we might get stuck inside again. Bollocks,' he muttered, striding over to pick up the two spare shovels. Mann managed to work the one down the side of the barrow, but there was just no room for the second one.

'I'll carry it,' Marnit said, holding her hand out for it. 'Then, if we get stuck, we can use it to dig our way out.'

'Fine,' Mann mumbled, grumpily. He'd just about had enough of this trip to the stables. The cold was starting to be felt through his layers of clothing, and he was keen to eat and drink something warm.

With a final look at his reindeer, who watched him without interest, he nodded to show he was ready.

At that Marnit flung the door open letting a bite of cold into the stables, and then stepped out herself. Rad went next with the shovel, Mann behind him, leaving Sand and his sack to close the door and trail behind them..

Immediately Mann choked on a mouthful of bitter air. The storm showed no signs of lessening.

'Bollocks,' he muttered once more, as the wheels of the ancient barrow ground through the snow. He could hear little but could see where Rad was ensuring the integrity of the pathway as Marnit illuminated the doorway for Sand to bolt it shut.

In the time they'd been in the stables, snow had built up

once more on their corridor through the heaped stuff. Mann realised he wouldn't be getting to eat and drink anything warm anytime soon. It was going to take ages to get back to Haune and the promise of the fire.

Mann groaned again, the wheel of the barrow seizing for a long moment before it gave and jerked him forward.

'Bollocks, bollocks, bollocks,' he muttered, a mantra under his breath as he squinted through the icy blast and focused on what Rad was doing, and where Marnit was indicating he should go.

Behind him Sand shouted incoherently, his voice lost in the swirl and screech of the storm. Mann pushed and shoved, struggling to turn the barrow when their path twisted or turned, and all the time he muttered under his breath. 'Bollocks, bollocks, bollocks.'

Quickly, sweat beaded down his shoulder blades, pooling in the well of his back and he distracted himself by dreaming of a hot bath.

Eventually, the door of the inn came into view, a beacon of light in the gloom of the day, as Haune had left a covered lamp out for them. Rad stomped up the few steps and hammered on the door. While they waited for it to open, they emptied the barrow, passing as many sacks as Rad could hold up to him. Sand stood behind him on the third step and Marnit hovered to the side, making sure they could all see what they were doing.

When the door opened, the sacks were roughly thrown in. Mann, retrieving the last sack, looked at the barrow in consternation, before upending it, and leaving it where it was. It blocked the doorway, but the snow was too tightly packed to either side of the pathway to push it anywhere else. Anyway, they might have need of it.

Quickly he indicated Marnit should rush up the stairs, and he followed closely behind.

The door banged shut as soon as he was inside, and heat overwhelmed him. His nose prickled with the sudden rise in temperature. Messily, he tried to remove his boots, coat and hat and gloves all at the same time, as Haune watched him, catching the items in her waiting hands.

Sand, Rad and Marnit were all doing the same. The sacks were forgotten about on the floor as they staggered to the welcome tray of hot drinks Bothal, of all people, had left on the side of the bar. Cupping the mug, Mann blew on it and greedily gulped the hot mixture, feeling his inner body slowly thaw. The feeling of a raw throat and mouth quickly faded. Then his stomach rumbled. A sound so loud no one could ignore it.

Haune was busily sorting through her provision sacks, but even she heard it and laughed.

'I'll feed you in a moment. I promise.'

She had made two piles of the sacks and turned to walk away with one of the smaller ones.

'I need this,' she muttered as she walked past him and behind the bar. She was gone for long moments. In that time, Mann made his way over to the fire and settled himself before it.

He was too hot, as sweat beaded down his face, but was content to enjoy the warmth. It was far better than being too damn cold.

The main room was sparsely populated. Only Bothal was there, a wry smile on his face as he watched the four explorers.

'It's not stopping, is it?' he asked Sand. The older man shook his head.

'Doesn't look like. Damn thing,' he grumbled. 'But the animals are all well,' Sand hastened to reassure. Only then did Bothal glance at Mann, but all he did was offer a smile of confirmation he'd completed the task. He returned to considering the fire, and what it was Haune had secreted away from the pile of indistinguishable sacks. Mann was rapidly coming to the conclusion everyone had just as many secrets as he did.

Once more his stomach rumbled. He inhaled deeply of the aroma from the cooking pot and looked at the hearth with the meat roasting slowly over it. It wasn't entirely cooked yet. He'd have to content himself with a bowl of pottage when Haune finally returned.

Marnit was busying herself with the lamp, twiddling with the catch on it, a look of concentration on her face. Idly he wondered what ailed her, as she squealed in rage and shook her hand.

'It's hot you know?' he called to her. She rounded on him.

'Oh really? Who bloody knew a lantern, burning oil, could get damn hot.'

Her fury added to his warmth. He smiled, internally.

'What are you doing with it?' he quizzed.

'It won't bloody blow out,' she complained. 'I've tried to remove the well of oil, but it won't budge. Something's jamming it.'

'You should ask Sand instead of burning yourself. He seems to have a knack for these things.'

But at that moment she let out a cry of triumph and fixed him with a self-satisfied smile as the flame slowly died.

Mann was just about to speak further when Haune arrived, a strained look on her face, as she brought four bowls with her, and quickly filled them and handed out the hot food to her staff and patrons.

'Is everything alright?' Mann queried. Either she didn't hear him, or she pretended not to for he got no reply as he settled to his meal and thought about what he'd discovered in the stable.

Mann already knew he needed to go back, to unearth exactly what he'd seen, but he needed to wait until his absence wouldn't be noticed.

In his pocket, he fingered the object he'd found for Bothal. It felt warm from being nestled against his body as he'd worked to return to the inn, but he doubted the intricate device was usually so well handled. Or perhaps it was. The delicate piece of metal, twisting and turning so it flowed in and then out of itself was enough to exercise his fingers as they probed and wound their way through the spaces and along the length of metal. It felt, to his fingers at least, as though there should be an end to the shape, but there wasn't.

Only when he caught Sand watching him quizzically did he stop his constant fiddling and ensure the object was safely stowed inside his pocket. He'd need to find an opportunity to return it to Bothal, and sooner rather than later. While Mann held it, he felt weighed down by the secrets it contained, and he had more pressing puzzles to uncover.

Marnit joined him, her eyes focused on her food and not on him. When Sand and Rad started to argue softly about some small matter to do with the stables, he made his excuses and ascended the stairs, to all intents and purposes heading for his room.

But at the top, he spied Bothal and quickly made his way over to him, and handed him the small object. Neither of them spoke, not wishing to draw attention to their clandestine meeting. Bothal met his eyes, a hint of thanks in them. Mann swallowed deeply as he turned away. There was much more to the violet-eyed man than Mann could ever hope to understand. It made him uneasy.

Abruptly he opened and then closed the door to his room, and stood, unaccountably out of breath, pleased to be out of the eye-line of anyone else. He'd spent more than enough time being watched for one day.

Mann slumped into his chair, appreciating the warmth of the brazier and shuddered to himself. He rubbed his hand across his forehead. He felt his head slump forward, and rested his arm on the side of the chair. He considered the disarray his plans were currently in.

Perhaps, as Marnit had suggested, he should just return to his home, live his life for another five or ten years, and then make an attempt again. Only he found himself utterly exhausted from thinking about it all the time. The thought of starting all over again was just too much to contemplate. He'd set his plans in place. He'd need to go through with them, as he'd decided the night before. All this time stuck in Bosetting was making him doubt himself in a way he never had before.

And that meant he needed to know what it was that Bothal was hiding.

Or did it? Did it really matter? There might be similarities between them in the knowledge of the never-ending shape, etched all over his chest, each and every year of his long life, but did that mean that Bothal had the same affliction. Should it even concern Mann if he did?

Mann had realised, when Freg died, his life would be long and solitary. The questions and yearning for knowledge that had once riddled him with anxiety no longer tormented him. He merely wanted to live his life in his inn and tell what lies he needed to, to do so. If it meant manifesting every sixty or so years as his own 'nephew' then so be it. He had no desire to meet others who might share his strange talents. They'd surely only add to the burden of keeping his elongated existence a secret.

No. Bothal presented him with an interesting problem, but one he could, and probably should completely ignore.

Content with his decision, Mann allowed his eyes to close, and sleep to take him. He was exhausted, by more than just the physicality of his trip to the stables. He needed sleep and the oblivion it presented him with.

He slept and woke in the same position, his neck screaming in agony and a grimace on his face. The brazier had burnt low.

He shivered violently, which only made his neck hurt even more.

'Ow,' he moaned, leaning forward to add more fuel, and to open the door on the brazier so the flame quickly leapt and caught hold, filling the darkened room with warmth and light at the same time.

He stretched out his legs, trying to ease his aching back. His boot connected with something hard. Looking down he caught the glint of something glittering and bent down to retrieve it.

Confused, he held in his hand the object he'd given to Bothal before falling sleep. Or at least, that was what it looked like. Mann peered into the gloomy shadows of his room. Was there someone in there with him, as Rad had been before, or was he truly alone?

Instantly his hand went to his neck, ferreting between his skin and his tunic, questing for his own sigil. His bewilderment only increased when he felt it, under his hand, safe and hidden.

'Hello,' Mann said, deciding it was best to make the first move. Then he stood, abruptly, and dashed to the door, flinging it open and allowing the light from outside to flood the darkened space.

But there was no one there. He felt foolish, as well as perplexed. What was going on? Why was he now aware of three small renditions of the never-ending sigil?

Stepping from his room, Mann reached for one of the lamps and used it to light his own. Light quickly flooded his room. All the same, he flashed it into the darkened recesses, wondering if maybe someone was hiding there.

But he was entirely alone. Mann thought it should have comforted him, only it didn't.

Aggrieved he settled in his chair, turning the object he'd kicked in his hand. It was not Bothal's, that much was immediately evident. Bothal's sigil was heavier, made perhaps from a purer copper than his own. This one, as Mann eyed it critically, flashed silver instead, a colder metal.

Who did it belong to?

Mann had no idea and thoughtfully threaded it onto his chain so the two sat side by side, the tattoos on his chest appearing to compliment them.

It was then he remembered the strange sack he'd found in the stables. Standing, Mann opened the door once more, listening to the sounds of the main inn. Much was quiet. It was apparently not a meal time. Most residents were in their rooms, perhaps hoping to sleep away the tediously drawn out afternoon, as the storm howled and whined, if possible, at a higher pitch than before.

Wave after wave of snow crashed against his window-panes. Mann shrugged. Now was as good a time as any to investigate further.

Closing the door, and wedging his chair behind it, and beneath the handle, Mann reached for his coat.

'I would like to visit the stables in The Firs, in Bosetting, at this time.' Mann closed his eyes against the screech of his words. When he opened them once more, he was standing precariously close to the brazier that still retained its heat, shaking and sweating at the same time. For the first time, Mann considered there might be a physical cost to these strange journeys he made, and as quickly dismissed it. He would have to think about it at another time.

The animals in the stable didn't even seem to notice his arrival, and that was good.

Reaching for a lamp, Mann made his way back to the stable where Marnit had found the barrow, and dumped the contents on the ground.

His eyes quickly found the sigil on the sack. He pulled it clear, feeling the weight in his tired arms as he did so. He'd used muscles that were rarely used in his active if confined life in Slutet. Wincing, he dropped to one knee, the lamp on one side, and the sack on the other.

The sack had no tie on it. He was able to reach inside eagerly.

His hand closed on something hard, with sharp edges, too heavy to take out one handed. Instead, he pulled his hand out, and rolled down the sides of the sack, revealing a beautifully crafted wooden box filling the entire bottom of the large sack.

The wood had the sheen of something exotic from the south, not the black of the nearby firs. It held the promise of warmth as an enticing spice engulfed him. But Mann's hands were already running over the box, for it wasn't plain wood, but rather decorated with many renditions of his sigil, in all shades, from copper to silver to gold, and many colours in-between, even somehow managing to make one or two appear to be violet.

Mann gasped at the beauty of the box and tongue between his lips, he lifted the lid, carefully.

It squeaked a little, on hinges perhaps not used to being opened, and revealed its secrets.

Mann gasped at the contents, his hand touching before he truly understood what he was looking at.

Inside the box, laid out on a padded shelf, lined with velvet, were eight small characters. They might have been pieces from a board game, perhaps something played in the far south, but Mann wasn't convinced. Picking up the first piece, he twirled it between his large fingers. The piece was about the length of his middle finger, large enough for a considerable quantity of detail to be added to the carving. Although from what it was carved, Mann wasn't sure, because it certainly wasn't any wood he'd ever seen.

He almost dropped the piece when a shaft of warmth laced through his fingers, as the figure seemed to come alive. Hastily, he returned it to its place, but then picked up another of the characters, and then another. Then, as he reached the sixth character, cold recognition washed through him, for surely he was looking at a small rendition of Bothal.

Even the size of the piece was smaller compared to the rest. Hastily, Mann picked up another of the characters. This one, he was convinced, was a rendition of Brag.

Mann whistled softly between his teeth, as he carefully turned all of the pieces so they faced him.

It was apparent he looked at Brag, Bothal and even Shlat, right down to the long knives she wore around her waist, carefully picked out on the carved piece.

What was it Bothal had? And why did he have it?

Only then did Mann realise the shelf he looked at was just the topmost part of the box's treasure. Carefully, he lifted it clear and was greeted by nine perfect copies of other people, most of whom he'd never met either. Although, and here he inhaled sharply, one did have a striking similarity to Jemp.

What did Jemp have to do with all this?

Carefully, Mann replaced all of the pieces on the bottom layer. His forehead wrinkled in thought. He stood once more and made his way back to Bothal's sled. With less care than he should perhaps have shown, Mann reached for the sack holding the vellums and took them back to the wooden box.

Flicking through the sheets, he quickly confirmed what he thought. The drawings Bothal carried with him were of the carvings, or rather, of the real people the carvings had been based on.

Mann, realising he'd lingered a long time, hastened to return the vellums, and restore the sacks to their correct positions in the dog sled. Yet he hesitated over the small carvings.

There were nine on the bottom, but only eight on the top. What would cause the discrepancy? Was it truly a game or was it something more invidious?

A noise in one of the stalls made him jump. Laughing softly

to himself for being so easily spooked, Mann returned the top layer of the box to its correct position and closed the lid on the wooden box. Only then did he cover it with the sack, and stuff it back amongst the other discarded sacks from the barrow. His mind was ablaze with possibilities and fears.

'I would like to return to my room, in the inn, The Firs, in Bosetting, at this time.' Mann spoke the words carefully, for all that he was so distracted. He was relieved when he returned to where he wanted to be, the chair still wedged under the door, the room warm from the brazier.

Removing his coat, he set it to one side and moved the chair from the door. As he did so, it swung inwards, the shocked face of Marnit's meeting his gaze.

'I've been banging for bloody ages,' she complained.

'Apologies,' Mann offered, saying nothing more. She canted her head to one side, biting her lip, as though she wanted to say something but now wasn't sure she truly wanted to do so.

'It's time to eat,' she eventually said. Mann nodded, walking through the doorway, and turning to close it behind him. As he did so, Marnit's nose wrinkled.

'What's that smell?' she asked.

'Dinner,' Mann announced, as casually as he could, sniffing as he followed her down the stairs, aware he carried the smell of the wooden box on his hands.

He'd need to avoid Bothal at all costs, for Bothal would instantly know Mann had been ferreting in his secret wooden box, if the box did indeed belong to Bothal. Although, how Mann might have accomplished such would perhaps perplex him greatly, and make him dismiss the possibility. He hoped.

Mann's mind was awash with the repercussions of what he'd discovered, but before he reached the final step, a colossal realisation came to him.

Whatever strange events were trying to happen around

him, one thing was sure, Brag, Bothal and Shalt were repre-
sented by the carvings and the drawings. But Mann was not.
Was he, after all, a part of their puzzle, or had he merely
discovered something he had no right knowing?

Either way, his identity was a secret. If he could keep it
that way.

TWENTY-TWO

Chapter 22

THROUGHOUT HIS MEAL, Mann's mind worked frantically.

He'd learned a great deal, in a short space of time, and now had to decide what to do with his knowledge.

Marnit spoke to him, asking him questions as they ate, side by side, before the fires, but he knew his answers were unsatisfactory, his mind elsewhere. Eventually, she fell to silence. He was grateful for it.

Bothal, thankfully, made no appearance, and so he sat, in contemplative silence, as Marnit again reached for her vellums and began to draw.

While the wind moaned and whined around every outer corner of the inn, Mann could still hear the scratch of the nib over the vellum. Unexpectedly, it soothed him.

For a long time, he considered asking Marnit to copy the images Bothal carried, or if not the images, then the small carvings. But, and this was important to him, he didn't want to involve her in anything that might prove dangerous. With the amount of knives Shlat carried, Mann couldn't see how it couldn't prove to be dangerous.

Neither, and this was selfish he knew, did he want to encourage her to believe in the strange theory she had. Even if, ultimately, it proved to be correct.

No, he needed to solve this himself, involving as few people as possible.

His thoughts turned to the second sigil he wore around his neck.

Where had it come from? Was there a way he could find out?

Who did he suspect could have one of the sigils? Mann knew Bothal had one, and Marnit had told him Brag also had one. But who else?

Shlat. The thought of re-encountering the knife-wielding woman wasn't a comforting one. But, Mann thought it impossible she'd made her departure before the storm had hit, and he had an inkling she was still somewhere within Bosetting. But where?

It was highly likely she was in one of the other two inns. He could, as he'd discovered, use his skills to go there, and search for her. But his sudden appearance would spark questions he didn't want to answer if he was discovered prowling through the inns at night. No, he needed to be more circumspect in solving this part of the mystery.

'Fine company this evening,' Marnit huffed at his side. Mann, shocked from his thoughts, turned to stare at her. Only then did he notice how few remained in the main room of the inn, and that Haune sat with them as well.

She was counting out coins into neat piles, dependent on what colour or metal they were made from. Mann watched with mild amusement. He was used to doing the same and felt a sudden pang for his home in the inn. He'd not been gone many days, and already he was unhappy at being away.

'The storms are both good and bad for business,' Haune grumbled, carefully examining one of the coins she held up.

'Bloody hell,' she muttered, standing to take the coin closer to one of the few lamps that still burned. 'This is a 'bastard'.' She said the name with awe. Mann leaned closer. He'd not heard the name, and yet he recognised it all the same.

'This is worth a thousand times the value of a silver coin. I've never seen one before. Who could have given me such and been wealthy enough not to even notice?'

For a moment, Haune's eyes sought out his own, but he'd not had one of those coins since he'd handed one over to Grans on settling the matter of Slutet inn nearly sixty years ago. And he hadn't known then it was called a bastard.

Mann imagined he knew who'd paid with the coin. Bothal.

'What should I do with it?' Haune asked, worry sheeting her face. 'I can't accept this as payment for lodgings and food, but how can I find out who gave it to me?'

It was a conundrum and yet Mann shrugged.

'Keep it. If the person misses it, I'm sure they'll ask you about it. Certainly, I would.'

Marnit was nodding as well, her hand out because she wanted to look at the rare coin.

Haune handed it over without a second thought. Marnit ran it between her fingers, and then held it on its side between her thumb and finger.

'It's made of pure gold,' Marnit said, half in awe and half in amusement. 'Not the most sensible metal for such a purpose. It's likely to bend and twist out of shape.'

Yet even Mann could tell that the coin was in fantastic condition, as though freshly minted.

Amused, Marnit handed the coin back to Haune, whose expression remained worried.

'Keep it,' Mann advocated again. 'It was handed over in honest exchange for your labours. That's all there is to it.'

'Fine,' Haune eventually said, in aggravation, placing it to one side of her other neat piles. 'It's mine. I'll keep it.' Yet,

Mann could hear the hesitation in her voice and chuckled softly.

The production of the coin had made Mann's thoughts turn again to Bothal. How wealthy was the small man? Where had he come from, other than some vague idea of the south. And why, oh why, did he carry drawings of Brag and Shlat, and himself, and even a small carving of Jemp?

Shlat. He was convinced she held the answer to many of his questions. And if not her, then whoever was the owner of the sigil he wore. He was determined to find out.

In his room, hours later, tired of pacing and thinking, Mann finally muttered the words he'd been focused on for so long.

He held the sigil in his hand.

'I would like to go to the person who owns this sigil, at this time, on this day.'

Mann closed his eyes, hunkered into his coat and boots, his door wedged shut, as on the previous occasions he'd done the same.

When he opened them again, Mann stumbled and landed on his arse.

Wherever he was, Mann couldn't tell, but he was, at least, stooped in the dark and out of the direct sight of any peering eyes.

Mann was relieved to hear the storm raging outside, the howling and screeching strangely comforting.

Wherever he was, it was still somewhere within the Hvite Lands.

Slowly his eyes adjusted to the dark. Shapes made themselves visible. Mann was in a bedchamber. That he was sure about. Staying still, he listened for the telltale exhalation of someone in sleep but heard nothing. Hesitantly, Mann took three steps toward the bed, hand out to see if anyone lay within it.

He touched nothing but the soft furs and quickly walked to

where he could see the door outlined against a light beyond it. Reaching out, Mann gripped the door handle and listened carefully. There was a hum of conversation beyond, but it sounded far away. Taking a deep breath, Mann pulled the door open a little, and then gasped in dismay.

He was in his inn, in Slutet. Quickly, he glanced at the door he hid behind, his heart thumping loudly, and then seeming to stop as what he feared was confirmed.

Mann was in his inn, in Slutet, in the room Brag was staying in.

Mann wanted nothing more than to slam the door and return to Bosetting. But he had to see, and assure himself all was well, despite what he now knew.

Again, he peered out of the door, his ears straining to block out the screech of the storm, and then he walked to the banister. Below, he caught a brief glimpse of a few people in the inn, most hovering around a table where four people played at cards, Brag amongst them.

With a critical eye, Mann eyed his inn. All seemed well. The twin hearths warmed the room, the bar was neat and tidy, and he knew it was time to go.

However, he also wanted to check his own room. On silent steps, Mann walked to his room, out of sight of the main room, pleased to find the door intact, the handle unmoving under his hand because only he had the key but it was in Bosetting and not here, with hi,. All was as he'd left it.

Hastily, Mann spoke the words under his breath,

'I would like to be in my bedchamber, at this time, in Slutet Inn.'

When he opened his eyes, his belongings greeted him, even though there was no light inside the room. Mann reached out, touching his bed, and his chair, and avoiding all of the strange and bewildering objects he'd placed in his room. For a moment he considered simply staying, sitting in his chair and waiting for the storm to stop before reappearing, but he shook his head, dismissing the idea. He needed to be in Bosetting, ready for when the storm ended.

Before he stood to leave, Mann's eyes swept over his room one final time, catching sight of something that was out of place.

On hands and knees, he went to the flat object on the floor, feeling vellum under his fingers. He lifted it up, but it was too dark to see anything. At the movement, he felt boards moving under his hands, and he froze.

The wooden floorboards from his room extended out onto the hallway. There was someone out there. Yet he could hear nothing. Clutching the vellum in his hand, Mann thought the words he needed to leave the inn.

'I would like to return to my room in The Firs, in Bosetting, at this time.' With eyes closed, he felt himself settle. A wave of warmth cover him. Only then did he open his eyes and look at what he held in the weak light from the brazier. There were words, but it was too dark to see them.

Mann strode to the door, moving the chair from under the handle, where it was wedged, and opening it wide.

Outside the door, a lamp blazed. In the light it cast Mann glanced at the vellum he held, gasping in surprise, for the vellum contained none other than a portrait of himself, on the same rough vellum all of Bothal's drawings were etched onto.

With a stifled cry of outrage, Mann returned to his room, flinging open the brazier and feeding the vellum to the smol-dering flames.

Only then did he breathe more easily.

Why was there a drawing of him on his bedchamber floor in Slutet?

What was happening in Bosetting and Slutet and why did it all seem to involve him?

Not that any answers were forthcoming that evening. Far

from it, and when Mann woke the next morning, the first thing that struck him was the complete and utter silence.

The storm had finally ended.

'Bollocks,' he jumped from his bed, fear flooding his body so that no sooner had he stood, than he had to stumble back to rest on the bed, light headed.

The blizzard, which had disrupted his plans to begin with, had, for the last few days, been a source of some comfort. While the winds raged, and the snow grew only thicker, no one could make a move in the strange game Mann had found himself involved in. Now he worried his hand would be forced before due consideration had been given to all the possibilities.

A knock on his door had Mann trying to compose himself.

'Hello,' he called, unsure who it was.

'Mann, its finally ended,' Marnit's excited voice reached through the wood. 'But the bloody doors welded shut, and Haune hopes you'll aid Rad and Sand to dig us out.'

The request was simple enough. Mann found himself agreeing without thought.

'I'll come,' he called. 'Just a few moments longer.'

'There's no rush.' Marnit trilled. 'It's not like the snow will be cleared in a day, but Haune wants to ensure the animals are well.'

Her light footsteps could be heard moving away from the door. Mann failed to rise, even though he knew he should.

His head throbbed, and kept circling back to one fundamental fact, one he hoped could give him some advantage.

While Bothal, Brag and he assumed Shlat should also be included in his list, were well aware of what they thought was happening, Mann was oblivious. Mann hoped to use his ignorance to great effect.

With that in mind, he dressed and strode down the stairs. There was a palpable excitement in the air as everyone clustered in the main room of the inn. Marnit waved him to a table where she'd saved him a bowl of pottage and some hearth cakes. He eagerly ate. It would be a long day. He needed to ensure his body could cope with all of the demands.

Only when he'd taken his fill, did Mann rise, and join Haune, Sand and Rad, where they were making themselves ready to go outside. Mann strained to hear the sound of others about their business outside, but all was silent.

Haune glanced at Mann, a ghost of a smile on her face.

'Freedom, but only if we can open the damn door. Otherwise, we'll be stuck until everyone else can dig out, and come to our aid.'

'And if we dig ourselves out, we'll have to go to everyone else's aid,' he spoke with cutting humour, but knew it was the truth. 'Come on then,' Mann said, turning to greet Sand and Rad. The two, not arguing for once, were watching him hopefully. It was evident they expected him to be the determining factor.

Haune had already unbarred the door. Now she stepped aside, returning to her place beside the bar. For a moment, Mann gazed at the door perplexed, unsure whether it opened inwards or outwards, but then shook his head. Of course, it opened inwards. Why else bar it against the wind?

'Right,' Mann said, turning to the two others, wishing everyone else wasn't watching his every movement in the inn.

He walked up to the door and pulled on the handle. It was, as he'd expected, unmoving. Haune had set a brazier close to the door, in the hope the heat would work its way into the wood, but it was having little impact.

Mann held the handle, thoughtfully. How could they open the door? The only option seemed to be to hang on the door with all their weight.

'Grab the handle, Rad,' Mann instructed the youth, 'and when I say turn, turn. Sand, you take the other side.' They all shuffled into position, even though there was little room.

'Be ready to jump aside should the door yield. The snow will cascade inside.'

Sand nodded his head, while a look of worry crossed Rad's. Mann was busy trying to work out how to best use his weight to force the door open.

Mann placed one hand on either side of the reinforced door bar, while Sand mirrored his actions.

'Pull out and down,' Mann instructed, hoping his idea would work. 'Turn,' he called, swinging his weight through his hands. Rad did as instructed, holding onto the door handle so it was clear of the locking mechanism.

Mann felt the door give. If only a little.

'Keep it up,' he instructed through gritted teeth, he was swinging down so much he almost sat on his heels.

Mann heard an ominous creak, followed by a crack. Then he was scrambling on his backside to get away from the slowly opening door, Sand doing the same, opposite him. Rad had already dashed back toward the bar.

However, not a single snowflake sneaked its way inside the door. Rather, as Mann lumbered to his feet, he appreciated the snow outside had frozen, solid.

Where they'd cleared the steps the day before, the snow was only about a foot deep, but it was crisp, frozen, hard, and he knew it would be slippery. How they'd clear the rest of the icy crust, he had no idea. If they were lucky, they'd be able to slide their way to the stables, but he couldn't see anyone would be going anywhere for some time to come, as he was finally able to see the true extent of the storm.

Little of the settlement could be seen. The streetway was completely blocked. The occasional glimpse of black wood was all that could be seen of the other buildings close to the inn. While the snow wasn't deep enough to obscure every building, the low hanging roofs, thick with snow, dragged so low they almost met the depth of snow.

Shivering, Mann was joined at the door by Haune.

'Bloody hell,' Haune whistled, Marnit also shouldering her way to peer outside.

'Bloody hell,' she mirrored, while Mann worked the brazier, on its three legs as close to the door as he could.

'Shall we risk it?' he asked, eyeing the brazier, and the top step covered with snow, with a calculating look.

'If we don't it might never thaw,' Haune said, peering into the street as though there might be other people out there, which of course, there weren't.

'I agree,' Mann concluded, hoping the brazier stayed where they could get to it, and didn't slip and slide its way down the four steps to ground level.

Carefully Mann positioned the brazier, and then, counting to three under his breath, let go. For a long moment, it looked as though the brazier would slide away, but then it settled in place, as Mann let out his held breath.

Like Haune, he then had a good look outside. The compacted snow was so frozen it shone with the tinge of the blue of death. It was Mann's turn to whistle.

'This could take days to thaw,' he announced. 'Days and days.'

The wind had dropped away to nothing, but the temperature, already well below freezing, had fallen even further. His breath plumed before him, freezing as soon as it impacted the air, and tinkling to the ground like glass.

'Can you hear that?' Haune asked, turning her head to one side.

'No, I can't hear anything,' Mann confirmed.

'Exactly,' Haune said. 'There's no one about, and there won't be for days.'

Mann thought there was no point in agreeing with her, it was obvious.

'We should shut the door,' he said instead. 'Give the brazier some time to work, and then see if we can make it to the stables.' Mann didn't really want to wait, but he thought it only happenstance the brazier stayed where it was. The thought of a fall on the ice had him wincing. It would be too easy to slip and case severe injury. Far too easy.

Haune nodded her agreement. All of them stepped back inside. Mann removed his coat, while Rad and Sand looked on, as put out as he was to have to delay their journey to the stables.

A hum of conversation welled within the inn as the door closed, but Mann, Rad and Sand remained inside.

'We have to wait,' Haune announced, striding to stand amongst everyone. 'The ground's frozen, all of the snow has frozen. No one is yet about their business.'

A loud groan of dismay greeted those words. All who were dressing as though to leave, stopped mid-action, disbelieving what they were being told.

'You're just saying that,' an angry man shouted, but Haune was shaking her head.

'You're welcome to try. But where you'd go, I don't know, even if you made it down the damn steps.'

'Show me,' the man demanded, a heavy cloak around his shoulders, his voice expecting to be obeyed.

'See for yourself. The door isn't barred. But watch the brazier.'

Haune spoke with contempt in her voice that Mann respected.

The man, the father of the three children, seemed confused by the words, only then he stomped his way toward the door, and wrenched it open.

Others followed suit. Mann rolled his eyes when all of them meekly shut the door, and returned to their families or friends, shaking their heads only moments later.

It was clear they agreed, now, with Haune's assessment of the situation.

'Apologies,' the father said. 'I thought it a ploy to keep us here, paying for our bed and board. I should have thanked you for keeping us safe.'

Haune grunted and said no more.

'The day will continue as all the others we've endured together. Any questions, or anyone who needs to negotiate another night's board, can do so when they're able. I'll cast no one out should funds be low, but I have many small jobs that can be done in exchange for meals and beds. Don't be afraid to ask.'

A few nodded at Haune's more than generous offer, and Mann smirked. More than a few looked relieved by her suggestion, the father amongst them.

Travelling was a precarious business. Mann had known many to simply run out of coin far from home and with little chance of adding to the depleted store. Mann had been known, on occasion to waive people's bills, but never so they knew. They might simply arrive in Bosetting and find themselves with more coin than they started the journey from Slutet with. Had they simply miscounted? It was always possible.

Bothal was amongst the number in the main room. He looked neither pleased nor relieved. Mann found that strange. Bothal was heading to Slutet, to some sort of showdown, perhaps with Brag, but also possibly with someone else, someone who might, or might not be Mann. Bothal's reserve made it difficult to tell whether he looked forward to his task or not.

Haune pulled Mann to her side.

'Do you think it'll be possible to clear the way to the stables?' Her voice was rich with concern.

'Today, I don't know. Tomorrow is more than likely.'

Haune sighed heavily.

'This bloody weather,' she complained, turning to work her way behind the bar once more.

'It's not been like this for many a year,' Mann agreed vaguely, careful not to reference exactly when a blizzard had blown for so long, and left behind so much snow, that had turned to ice. It was rare but had happened on at least six occasions throughout his long life. Not that he was going to share the knowledge.

'I would consult the records,' Marnit said, at his shoulder. 'But they're in my shop.' Her tone was rueful, her fingers itching to be doing something with ink and vellum.

'You should write a record of this one, all the same,' Haune consoled, watching Marnit carefully.

Mann felt a touch on his shoulder and turned, expecting to see Sand or Rad. Instead, Bothal watched him.

'Could I trouble you for a word?'

Mann nodded, although he'd sooner not have done, and walked to the table Bothal had taken command of as his own, while all around him the other inhabitants slowly slunk back to their own activities for the day. These had become routine throughout the last few days of being contained inside the inn.

Mann sat, Bothal opposite him, and he waited.

Mann was expecting Bothal to speak to him of the strange sigil. His words somewhat surprised him.

'I fear there's a thief in the inn.'

'A thief?' Mann whispered the word, looking around him as he did so, his eyes wide with shock and relief. 'Are you sure?'

'Regrettably, yes. Some items have been taken. Well, one item in particular, and a few others I suspect as well.'

Mann suddenly viewed all around him in a different light. Bad enough to travel and run out of coin, but two times worse to steal to make up for the lack.

'Why tell me, and not Haune?'

Here Bothal looked concerned, and also guilty.

'You helped me, before, and I hoped you could help me again. I appreciate you're a man of discretion, and more, you aren't from Bosetting.'

The same could be said for other members of their party, but Mann held his tongue.

'What do you want to do, catch the thief? What did they take, anyway?'

'An item of only sentimental value,' Bothal shrugged, as though it meant nothing, but Mann was immediately intrigued. He tried to contain it, suddenly unsure if Bothal wasn't trying to entrap him into revealing more than he wanted. 'It means everything to me, but is of little or no value to anyone else. I'd simply like it returned.'

Mann fell to silence, considering the options available to them. In his own inn, Mann would have had it be known that any stolen item could be returned, under cover of darkness, or left out on the bar, with no repercussions. It seemed Bothal didn't want to take such an opportunity.

'I believe the girl has it, Marnit.' As Bothal named who he thought was responsible, Mann understood why Haune had not been the preferred option. Marnit and Haune were firm friends, possibly related. Certainly, they shared a close tie.

'I know you're friendly with Marnit.'

'I employed her to do some copying, before the storm.' Mann said the words and then regretted them. There was no need for him to say so much. He needed to be more careful.

'I could ask her if you want. But I'd need to know what it was that she took.'

'No, no,' Bothal was shaking his head. 'I wouldn't want you to put yourself in such a position. Perhaps, instead, you could arrange for her to accompany you to the stables when you go.'

Mann was instantly conflicted. He had no love for Bothal

and didn't want him ferreting amongst Marnit's possessions. It was impossible to know what he might discover.

'I'll think about it,' Mann eventually said, trying to think his way out of this new predicament. If only the snow hadn't frozen, then he'd be on his way by now, instead of still stuck in Bosetting trying to work out what the best thing to do was.

'You have my thanks,' Bothal said, as Mann made to stand and walk away.

Eyes trailed him back to the bar, Haune pausing in her duties, as Mann slumped onto a stool.

'He'll be gone soon enough,' she tried to console, but Mann was shaking his head.

'It could be days yet, a week even. This ice will take its own sweet time, if it thaws at all.'

As Haune had suggested, Marnit had found a seat for herself, close to the fires, and was busily scratching away, no doubt writing a record of what had happened here, how long the storm had lasted, and how many had been marooned in the inn. Mann knew such tasks were an essential element of each settlement's scribe. That was why they received a share of the taxes as payment.

For a moment Man's thoughts returned to his own scribe, in Slutet, and Marnit's unhappiness with his less than precise wording of official documents.

Marnit and his own scribe received little in exchange for their responsibilities, and much was expected of them. Mann wondered if he might have a way of making both of their lives a little easier. After he 'died.'

He pondered the idea, to distract himself from Bothal's request. Moodily, he swigged at the pot of ale Haune had poured for him, while he hoped the brazier would falter and make it impossible to visit the stables at all that day.

If it had been closer to night, he could have risked his own search of Marnit's room. But, he realised, he didn't even know which room was hers, and of course, Bothal hadn't actually told him what had been 'stolen'.

Time dragged. Mann watched Haune turn and re-turn her timekeeper, on every occasion, he opened the door, checked on the brazier, restocked it, and returned to his seat.

The temperature outside didn't rise, and before long he appreciated if they did make it to the stables, they'd be returning in the dark. Mann knew he should share the worry of the others, Sand and Rad especially, but if they didn't make it through to the animals via the door, he knew all wasn't lost. Another night time trip wouldn't be unduly difficult for him, and of course, it would allow him time to try and infiltrate Marnit's room and seek out whatever it was Bothal thought she had, if anything.

In all honesty, Mann couldn't envisage Marnit stealing. She had no need to, and if it was something to do with Bothal, he was convinced she'd have shared that knowledge.

In which case, what was it Bothal wanted from Marnit?

Only then a cold dread settled over Mann, for he suddenly realised exactly what it was Bothal wanted. Whether he believed Man's assertion he wasn't who he was looking for, Bothal evidently still wanted a drawing of Mann, to add to the ones he already had. Or, if it wasn't Mann's portrait, it was someone else's. Marnit often sketched, probably not even aware she had so many drawings of people and strangers.

Mann glared around at those in the inn. There was no one else he'd even considered as potentially involved in what was happening, but perhaps Bothal knew differently, or maybe, Marnit had other portraits with her, that Bothal had caught sight of, and which he'd recognised as being somehow involved in all this.

Perhaps Marnit had a drawing of Shlat that Bothal coveted?

Perhaps, perhaps.

Mann found his mind endlessly turning over possibility over possibility.

He was sure of one thing, he didn't want Bothal getting his hands on any of the portraits. He'd have to speak to Marnit about it, or, and this option appealed to him more, he'd have to remove the portraits himself.

Only, he wouldn't burn them, as he had the one he'd found last night in Slutet. No, Mann would take them to Marnit's workshop where she'd be able to discover them when she returned home, and Bothal had disappeared to Slutet, or better, back to the Passen, never to travel north again.

'Mann,' Sand called to him. Mann realised Haune had once more turned the timekeeper. 'I think we can go,' Sand advised, although Mann groaned at the knowledge. It was getting late, and yet if they didn't take advantage of the small thaw the brazier had produced on the steps, they'd only have to do the same tomorrow, for the snow would freeze again during the night, Mann was sure of it.

'Okay,' Mann grouched. 'Let's try this.'

Sand and Rad looked about as pleased as he did, as they made their way to the door, and peered outside.

A soft pink glow lit the sky, the promise of plummeting temperatures in the lack of cloud cover.

'Let's try this,' Mann confirmed, as he stepped gingerly from the door. The step, while not devoid of ice, could at least be walked on without fear of slipping. From there, Mann placed his foot very carefully on the second step, and then on the third below that, before turning and gesturing for the shovel.

With it in his hand, and the brazier returned inside, Mann chopped at the ice and snow. The top step was uncovered remarkably quickly, but the second step was more difficult.

Sand liberally sprinkled the clear step with salt, to stop it from refreezing, while Mann chopped and chopped at the second. It had only benefitted a small amount from the warmth of the brazier, but Mann was able to hack away a good deal of the frozen snow so he could then place a foot on the ground, and try and do the same with the fourth step.

Again, Sand doused the cleared patch with salt.

The third step was more difficult. Mann managed to only cut away enough frozen snow to allow two carefully placed feet on to it.

Once they were doused with salt, Mann tried the fourth step, but it was impossible. By now his arms were aching. The shovel felt as though it weighed the equivalent of four beer barrels. He gestured Sand to his side.

'That's all I can do.'

'Is our pathway passable?' Sand was trying to look behind Mann. Mann turned and tested the frozen snow with his boot, seeing how slippery it was. His foot shot out from beneath him. He only managed to stay on his feet because Sand grabbed him roughly.

'No,' Mann's smile was rueful with thanks.

'Then we'll throw salt as far as we can, and hope that come the morning, we can follow the path further along. It's a shame, and I pity the animals, but they'll survive another night. They have water aplenty.'

Mann agreed, contenting himself with the knowledge he'd go to the stables later anyway.

'I still can't hear anyone else about their business,' Mann said, as Sand stopped and listened.

'No, they'll wait. The inns are always the first to clear after storms. The houses and other businesses will wait to see if it's worth their while making an effort.'

Nodding, Mann made to return to the inn door, where Rad hovered. It was clear he didn't much want to come down the tricky steps.

'Go back in,' Mann called to him. 'We're coming now anyway.'

Even under his layers of coat and furs, and with his face covered so only his mouth, nose and eyes showed, Mann could see the relief in Rad's demeanour. It poured from him. Mann could only wish it could be used to melt the frozen snow.

'Come on, let's get back inside and tell everyone the news.'

But before he could turn, Sand grabbed his arm, forcing Mann to look at him.

'I've been watching you,' Sand said, a judgement in his hooded eyes. 'Don't think everyone is as blind to you as you want them to be.'

Mann was startled by the words, but was unable to retort for Sand was already halfway back inside.

Mann watched him go, biting his lip.

He could end all this, now, if he chose to. Go back to Slutet by speaking the command. Only he couldn't. That option, as attractive as it was, would result in far too many questions being asked, and Mann would be forced to leave his inn forever.

No, he'd have to endure in Bosetting and hope not to catch the eye of anyone else who suspected him.

Mann grumbled under his breath and hurried back inside.

He'd never wished more that he'd stayed in Slutet away from this shit storm.

TWENTY-THREE

Chapter 23

THERE WAS a palpable sense of disappointment from the main room of the inn when Mann stepped back inside.

It was apparent they'd not been gone long enough to make it to the stables, as Mann shrugged his coat, gloves and hat from his body. Yet, it was only disappointment. No one complained or accused Haune of trying to line her pockets again.

Indeed, the father of the small family was busily chopping root vegetables, and what remained of the meat, so he could make a pottage for the evening meal, one of his young daughters assisting him. Upstairs, Mann could hear footsteps going from room to room, as the mother helped with refilling the braziers. Others were dotted around the inn as well. All in all, it seemed a much happier place now that those who needed work had it.

Mann grimaced though. His plans to visit the stables and Marnit's room would have to wait until the hive of activity had settled down. Otherwise, he was too likely to be missed.

'Mann,' Haune called to him, where her head stuck out of

the cellar door. 'Could you help me?' she asked with a scowl. Mann jumped to do just that. He wasn't entirely convinced Haune needed his assistance. She probably wanted to speak in confidence.

The cellar was accessed via a short flight of steps, almost a ladder, but with just enough angle to them to allow people to carry goods freely up and down without having to hold on to prevent a fall.

It was as similar to his cellar as it was possible to be.

He was met with fierce eyes when his feet hit the wooden floorboards, and he turned to greet Haune.

'What is it?' Mann asked, suddenly very concerned.

'There's a thief in the inn,' Mann groaned at the news. Not once had he been called upon to help with the matter of a thief, but twice.

'Why, what's missing?' but he thought he probably already knew.

'The 'bastard' is gone,' Haune whined, her ill-humour clear to hear.

'Are you sure the original owner hasn't simply claimed it back?' Mann asked, hoping that might be the simple explanation, although he doubted it.

'No,' Haune hissed. 'I hid it. Away from all the other coins. No one could have known where it was unless they'd been hunting through my possessions for something else.'

This then was disturbing news, and Mann's eyebrows furrowed on his forehead.

'Someone has been through your room?' Mann asked, to be sure. 'And taken nothing but the 'bastard'?'

'Yes,' Haune complained, cold fury on her face. 'I don't know how. I keep it locked, all the time.'

'Do you suspect anyone?' Mann was thinking frantically. He didn't like where those thoughts took him.

'Bothal,' Haune announced. 'He's been taking far too much interest in everyone else's activities, and room allocations. Of everyone here, only he would know where my room even was. For instance, do you?' Haune demanded to know. Mann shook his head, admitting he didn't. In fact, apart from his own room, and Bothal's he'd paid no attention to who slept where, more concerned with keeping his own secrets.

'What do you want to do?' Mann asked, sure Haune had already devised a way of getting to the truth of the matter.

'I want you to search Bothal's room for me. I'd ask Marnit, but she's no good at searching for anything.' Haune's voice was filled with vexation. Mann hesitated to agree to her demands.

'How will you keep him from his room so I can look?' he didn't quite manage to keep the incredulity from his voice, and her sharp glance told him as much.

'He doesn't seem to sleep,' Haune shared with him. 'At night I come down here, and he's sitting at one of the fireside tables, consulting some vellums or something, by the light of two lanterns. It happens every night. He must find it easier to do whatever it is he's doing when everyone else is asleep.'

The knowledge disturbed Mann more than he thought it should, but he nodded all the same. He'd like to rummage through the rest of Bothal's possessions. Haune had just given him permission to do so.

'I'll do what I can,' Mann eventually agreed, trying to keep everything clear in his mind as to what he needed to accomplish that night. One thing was sure. He'd be exhausted come the morning.

Haune grinned suddenly, as though she'd not been sure he would agree.

'My thanks,' she said, and then turned about her business. Mann lingered for a moment longer, enjoying the smell of the cellar, slightly earthy, a little exotic, and certainly, reminding him of home. Whatever he needed to do in Bosetting that night, he couldn't wait for the thaw to come so he could get on with his own plans, and return to Slutet.

That night, people didn't linger in the main room, but rather ate, shared some pleasantries, which were growing stale by now, and departed to their rooms amongst much yawning and complaining about how tired they were. Mann followed suit, pleased he'd have longer for his nighttime excursions.

It was always the same for those unused to the raging blizzards that routinely rattled the north. Most visitors found their sleep disturbed while the storms blew, and then struggled to go about their day to day business when it had ended because they were so sleep deprived. Hopefully, everyone would sleep deeply that night.

In his room, Mann set everything as he needed it, with the chair under the door handle, and the handle locked. He also, just to be sure, moved the wooden chest sitting below his bed to the door as well. He didn't want to take any chances of his absence being discovered when he had so much to do.

Then he sat to wait, before his brazier, enjoying the gentle heat and trying not to doze, as the inn settled to sleep. The inn building moaned and groaned, the roof protesting against the snow, the windows against the icy tendrils that would be snaking across their pitied surface. From cold, to ever colder, the Hvite Lands wood was being truly tested.

Mann waited until silence ran through the inn. Then he waited even longer, just to be sure. It was then he heard footsteps outside his door, as though someone hovered there, unsure of their next steps, only to descend the stairs to the main room. Bothal, Mann suspected, based on Haune's observations earlier.

Mann had intended to go to the stables first, but now he reconsidered. Perhaps he should go to Bothal's chamber first, and see if he could find Haune's lost 'bastard.'

Standing, Mann looked at his waiting coat, but then discarded the thought. He was right. He should go to Bothal's room first, only he'd barred the door, and didn't want to risk the noise of moving everything.

Huffing, he reconsidered again.

'I would like to stand outside my chamber, in The Firs, in Bosetting, at this time.'

Mann closed his eyed, but then opened them again, just as quickly. It had taken no time at all, and he was stood peering at his room number. Quickly, he glanced over the railing, content to see Bothal settling himself at one of the hearth tables. The inn was cast in darkness, apart from the dancing flames of the fire before it gutted to embers and few lamps that Haune kept burning each night.

'I would like to go to Bothal's chamber, in The Firs, in Bosetting, at this time.' Mann kept his eyes open, knowing the action would take but a moment. Then he laughed at himself. He was in a stranger's room, one he suspected of being Bothal's, but the door was open a little. Clearly, Bothal was adopting the policy of appearing as though he had no secrets with such a ploy. Mann knew it was often the best way of keeping those secrets, for people saw what they wanted to believe, and not what was actually under their noses.

Using the slant of light, Mann surveyed the room. It was a little larger than his, but overall, it was precisely the same. Everything was positioned in the same place. Only Bothal seemed to have more luggage than Mann. While Mann carried just a backpack with him, Bothal had two wooden chests, neither of which were secured with a lock.

Quickly, Mann turned to the smaller of the two, opening the lid, and running his hand through the contents, unsurprised when he felt only clothing and furs under his hands. This then, was where Bothal stored all of his rich clothing and travelling furs. Yet, near the bottom Mann's hand encountered something hard. He chuckled. A smaller wooden chest. He tried to lift it, but it was heavy, no doubt stuffed with coins.

All the same, Mann pulled it clear with some effort and opened the small wooden chest.

In the slant of light he could see little, but running his hands into the chest revealed it contained no coins, but rather something fitting tightly into the box. Mann replaced it quickly. He had no time to be distracted by something he wasn't looking for.

The second wooden box was more difficult, as he opened the lid quietly. It was stuffed with all sorts of strange objects. It was impossible to determine what they all were in the muted light. Mann thought the objects were vellums or rolled scripts, or some such, and only when his hand closed on a money pouch did he lift anything clear. Without opening it, he felt the weight of the coins, and gasped, for it felt as though Bothal carried only 'bastards' in his money pouch. Mann could tell because the coins weren't oversized, but rather over-heavy, made as they were with a heavy weight of gold.

Well, at least he knew who'd probably given Haune the coin. It also seemed unlikely that someone who had so many of the bloody things would steal someone else's coin, which he had, in all likelihood, meant to give to Haune.

Rising to his feet, Mann swept the room with another glance, but he could feel time passing pressing on him.

'I would like to go to my chamber, in The Firs, in Bosetting, at this time.' Mann arrived with a soft thud and reached quickly for his coat, hat and gloves. He would at least be able to assure Haune that Bothal wasn't the culprit.

Hastily Mann spoke again, just under his breath.

'I would like to be in the stables, in The Firs, in Bosetting, at this time.' This time he did close his eyes and shivered violently when he arrived in the frozen stables.

The smell of excrement hit his nose, as did the sound of

animals in distress. Quickly, he reached for a lamp, and lit it with the small implement next to it. Mann had considered bringing a lamp with him but hadn't. He wasn't sure what would happen to a flame when he travelled.

At the small light, the animals stilled. Mann hastily set about restocking the depleted lamps, refilling the braziers, and sorting water and feed for all the animals. He had root vegetables and lichen for his reindeer. He found raw meat for the dogs in the back of one of the stables where Rad and Sand kept their equipment, it was a little frozen, but he was sure they'd be able to chew it and thaw it. He also took the time to check every animal seemed well.

Mann didn't want to do too much that others might suspect something strange had happened, but neither could he let the animals endure when it was within his power to help them.

As a final act, Mann took one of the braziers and placed it as close to the stable door as possible. Like the front steps, he hoped the heat would go some way into melting the ice on the other side of the wooden door for when they were able to reach the stables from the outside. Hopefully that would be on the following day.

Satisfied, Mann stopped and listened. Other than the rustle of bedding, and the occasional nip or low from the dogs or the reindeer, there was utter silence. Even from outside. Mann shook his head. This might not be the only time he had to do this. Not if the temperature didn't rise quickly enough to melt the ice.

Before he went back to his bedchamber, Mann also followed his nose to where he suspected Haune kept some of her supplies. There were sacks, and also barrels filled with fluid and Mann suspected, meat that had been salted and left there, in the chill of the stables.

Hastily, Mann surveyed what he saw with his eyes. It seemed Haune was well provisioned, once she again had access to everything he saw. He left everything where it was and muttered the words.

'I would like to be in my bedchamber, in The Firs, in Bosetting, at this time.' Mann opened his eyes to see his room exactly as he'd left it, although he carried the scent of the stables with him. Quickly, he removed his coat, hat and gloves, and moved them away from the brazier, where the smell might intensify, and to the shutters, where he hoped the utter cold from outside might diffuse the aroma.

Once more he listened to make sure the inn was silent. He might well be pleased the wind had died, but it was making it difficult for him to mask his movements. Each step he took, seemed to force an outraged shriek from a wooden floorboard struggling to know whether it expanded or contracted in the aftermath of the terrible storm.

Now Mann needed to determine what to do about Marnit and her drawings of him. This was more difficult, as she'd be in her bedchamber, and Mann didn't want to wake her and answer any of her questions as to why he was in there.

Mann had an inkling of an idea but wasn't sure if it would work or not. Still, it seemed he should try it, rather than risk discovery.

'I would like the drawings done by Marnit, which are at this time stored in her leather folio, in her room at The Firs, in Bosetting, in my hands.' As he said the words, he winced. Mann was trying to be as specific as possible, sure if he wasn't, something awful would happen. He was pleasantly surprised when he felt vellums in his hand and looked down to discover a small selection of about ten drawings.

They weren't all of him, that much he could tell when he flicked through them, but there were three of him. He was sure Bothal would be pleased to get his hands on them. Mann listened, waiting for an outraged screech when Marnit discovered the theft, but there was nothing above the complaints of the building.

Now, should he take the drawings to Marnit's workshop, or should he send them there? This had tormented him for some time because he was keen to look around the workshop when Marnit wasn't there. But could he risk it?

Annoyed with himself, Mann said the words.

'I would like to be in Marnit's workshop in Bosetting, at this time,' he clamped his eyes shut, his hands on her drawings, and shivered violently when he opened them once more.

Marnit's workshop was doused in gloom, the only light coming from a slight gap in the shutters, from where the icy exterior was illuminated by the pink of the winter sky.

Yet, Mann could see very well the workshop was in total disarray. He couldn't imagine Marnit would have left it in such a state.

Turning in a circle, he slowly took in all he could see, and then pounced on a lamp, lighting it quickly. The warm glow filled the workshop, and Mann held the lamp up high.

No, he was sure Marnit hadn't carried out the ransacking of the workshop. More, he had the feeling it had been done by either Bothal or Shlat, for he was convinced few others would have been interested in Marnit's collection of vellums, which now spilled from their storage place, in an untidy heap, sliding onto the floor.

What was it that they searched for?

Cold dread filled Mann as he rifled through the disturbed vellums, until he came across an ancient journal, beneath them all, the pages crisp under his probing fingers.

He turned the journal so he could see what it was, holding the page in place with his finger, while he looked at the cover. It gave little away, made of fine leather smelling of age and longevity.

Turning to the first page, his heart skipped a beat. The

journal was a record of the people of Bosetting, its purpose described in flowing letters. 'An account of the people of Bosetting, including births, deaths, marriages and financial records of importance.' With growing worry, Mann opened the page his finger had been marking, fearing to see what he knew would be there.

Whoever had ransacked Marnit's scriptorium, they'd been searching through the archive for Bosetting, and the name they'd happened upon was none other than Freg's.

He'd forgotten the scribe recorded such things. Indeed, Mann had only the faintest of recollections of the scribe who'd been in Bosetting at the time. Mann was sure he'd been a youngish man, with floppy, long hair and a continually running nose. Mann had no memory of what had happened to the scribe, but his heart sank even further when next to Freg's name, he saw his own, Mann of Slutet, listed as the person who'd inherited all of Freg's property. Over twenty years ago.

'Bloody hell,' Mann whined, flicking through further pages of the journal to see if his name appeared again, pleased when it didn't.

The scribe's hand had stayed relatively constant throughout the last twenty odd years. Only in the last few years had the writing changed, no doubt when Marnit had arrived in Bosetting.

Freg had left Mann her business and her homes in Slutet and Bosetting. Mann had little use for them, and had shied away from doing anything about them. They reminded him too much of Freg. Now he wished he'd thought to act sooner to dispense with the two buildings tying him to her. The reindeer were much easier to explain away than the buildings.

He'd need to rectify that.

But, and this perplexed him, how would Bothal or Shlat, or whoever it was, even know about him and Freg? She'd been dead for well over two decades now, and few remembered her but him. How could Bothal or Shlat know she was anything to do with him? Unless, well, unless Jemp had someone managed to send word to whoever it was to inform Bothal or Shlat. Mann was convinced Jemp was involved in the strange conspiracy as well.

But, would that make them as old as he was, or had they simply been given the ancient information?

Mann shook his head, fury and confusion making him feel belligerent.

He needed to get out of Bosetting as soon as he could, and 'disappear' for some time.

Unsure now whether Marnit's workshop was the best place to hide the drawings of himself, Mann turned around in a slow circle once more, seeking out a suitable hiding place, if one even existed.

He started at Marnit's worktop. It was liberally covered with various sizes of vellum, some in the process of being cut, and also jars of ink, and tied together nibs and quills. It was then he recalled Bothal's approach of leaving his secrets in plain sight. Smiling at his idea, Mann slipped the vellums he clutched under the unused ones, unsurprised when he couldn't detect the additional bulk no matter how he canted his head from side to side, or forward and backwards.

Mann went to the front door then, expecting it to show the signs of forcible entry, and relieved when it didn't. All the same, he checked the lock and the door bar, wondering how Marnit had made her way from the workshop to the inn, as it wasn't through the door he'd used when conducting his business with her.

Mann moved through the workshop, looking for another door, unsurprised when he found it, and the bar lock had been snapped on it.

Whistling between his teeth, Mann stared at the obliterated

lock. It would have taken someone powerful, and skilled, to cause so much damage.

Yet, even with the bar lock broken, the door remained shut, and so, happy he'd done all he could, Mann left the workshop.

Back in his room, he shivered and bent to the brazier with his hands outstretched. He'd forgotten to wear his coat to Marnit's workshop. He felt intolerably cold. He swirled the fur from on top of the bed, and settled in his chair, before the feeble brazier.

His room was undisturbed. He was pleased about that, but his mind was not.

Who'd been into Marnit's workshop, and were they genuinely hunting him down? Had it been Shlat or even Bothal, perhaps accounting for Bothal's late arrival at the inn? Mann could only guess. He worried the new problems would keep him awake, but in only moments his eyes closed, and he slept, in his chair, before the brazier, in The Firs, in Bosetting.

———

Loud banging woke him what felt like a moment later.

'Bloody hell, Mann,' an outraged voice reached him from the other side of the door, and Mann struggled to his feet.

'Just a moment,' he complained, his voice ragged and dry. He coughed. 'Just a moment,' he reiterated, although he could clearly hear the huff of annoyance from the other side of the door. Marnit. Just who he didn't want to see first thing in the morning.

Hastily, he moved the wooden chest back to its original place and then removed the other chair from beneath the lock, before forcing the door open and meeting her angry face. Marnit pushed past him, without asking for permission, as Mann rubbed his forehead.

'What's the matter?' He had a fair idea but asked all the

same, as he took in her outfit. Today she wore her usual collection of mismatched colours, blue trousers, a vivid violet tunic, and on her feet, white boots. How impractical, he thought, before listening to her complaints.

'Someone's been in my room,' outrage coloured her voice, although she tried to whisper. 'They stole some things, and Haune says it's not the first incident!' Whether Marnit was angrier that he knew, or more furious with Haune for not telling her, Mann wasn't sure.

'What did they take?' he whispered back, trying to encourage her to more secrecy, but she shook her head, refusing to tell him.

'It's not what they took, it's that they took it at all,' she growled. 'And it's not the first time.'

'Did Haune tell you what was stolen from her?'

'Yes,' Marnit's voice was getting louder and louder. 'You need to find out who did it,' she complained, standing before him, her eyes peering into his. Mann held still. If she was this angry about a few drawings, what would she be like when she saw her workshop had been ransacked?

'And are your lost items of similar value?' he asked, just to be on the safe side.

'All of my money,' she just about shrieked, while Mann's confusion grew.

'So someone is stealing money?' Mann had an idea of who it might be, and now it was his turn to grow angry. Rad had assured him he wouldn't do it again.

'Nothing else?' Mann asked, just to be sure.

'Some drawings, nothing important,' Marnit complained. Mann suddenly wished he'd burnt the vellums as he took in her dejected stance. It seemed it was all about the coin with these people.

'You know who did it,' Marnit accused, but Mann shook his head.

'I bloody don't.'

'Haune said,' and here she paused, looking around as though someone might pop out from any stray corner of the room, 'that you were going to search Bothal's room last night. Did you?' At least she dropped her voice to a harsh whisper as she asked the damning question.

Mann's anger only grew.

'Did she tell you anything else?' he demanded to know, refusing to answer her, and cursing Haune at the same time.

'No,' Marnit said, her hands bunched into fists at her side. 'No, why, what didn't she tell me?' Now Marnit was growing angrier and angrier.

'Right, downstairs. We three need to talk.'

Without pausing, Mann thrust the door open, shocking the mother who was walking along the hallway, a load of linens in her hand. She squealed as Mann held up his hand in apology. The woman looked about to argue, but then noticed Marnit's equally furious departure from his room, and held her tongue.

Downstairs, the main room was quiet. Mann looked about in confusion.

'Is it even morning?' he asked no one in particular. Was it possible he'd only slept for a few moments?

Haune's head popped up from the cellar as he spoke. Mann made his way toward her. Marnit in his wake.

'Yes, it's morning,' Haune confirmed. 'But everyone yet sleeps. Apart from Marnit, and the mother of the children. She's pleased to have some time to think her own thoughts.'

'Marnit woke me,' Mann growled, when they all faced each other in the small cellar, the door above their heads pulled tightly closed. 'What did you tell her for?' Mann demanded of Haune.

'She was upset about her own coin. I said you were already handling it.'

'Great,' Mann complained, his hands high in the air in frustration. 'It isn't who you think it is,' he hissed, 'and it would be better if you asked me about sharing our secrets.'

'How do you know it isn't him?' Haune asked. Mann beckoned them both closer and whispered.

'He has lots, and lots, and lots of those 'bastards.' He's got no reason to steal them.'

'Then who the bloody bollocks is it?' Marnit complained, her voice too high.

'Shush,' Mann and Haune turned to her at the same time. She looked rebellious, her face flushed and hectic with fury, and with being reprimanded by the two people she seemed to trust the most.

'I don't know,' Haune whined, wringing her hands together. She looked genuinely horrified at having to consider someone else in her inn as a thief. Mann was trying to determine whether to name Rad, or keep it to himself. After all, he might be wrong.

Was it possible the stolen coins were something to do with him? But he dismissed the thought. He had his own coins, ready and waiting, for when they were needed. He only ever took from himself in such circumstances, never another, or so it had always proved.

'How's the weather?' he asked, changing the subject. He was almost desperate to be gone from Bosetting.

'Warmer,' Haune said, indicating he should listen, and indeed, he could hear the trickle of running water from outside.

'Right, I'm going to the stables,' he muttered. 'Get Sand and Rad. When I get back, we should all have thought about what we want to do about this thief before they get to leave, perhaps even today, but probably tomorrow.'

The two nodded as he spoke. Mann turned to stomp back up the cellar stairs, but then stopped.

'Anything else weird been going on?' he thought to ask, to be on the safe side.

'Some food has either gone missing or been miscounted. A few mugs of ale as well. Nothing to worry about,' yet the news stopped Mann in his tracks.

'Are all the bedchambers in use?' Mann asked, a slow realisation dawning on him.

'No,' Haune said, slowly, her thoughts suddenly mirroring his own. 'We'll check,' Haune announced, 'while you're in the stables, and the inn is reasonably quiet.'

'Good. It might be that you have an unexpected visitor somewhere, one who likes coins, and ale.'

Marnit's mouth dropped open in surprise, her hand stifling her surprised shriek this time.

'Shush,' Mann and Haune again commanded. She nodded, fear replacing her anger.

'But who?' Marnit whispered. Mann was too busy thinking the same to answer, as he returned to his room in search of his coat, hat and gloves. This whole situation was becoming altogether too bizarre.

At the top of the stairs, he realised he'd left his chamber door opened, or rather, Marnit had, and he cursed. How could he keep secrets, if anyone could see into his chamber? Yet, as he gave it an appraising glance, Mann could see nothing that gave him away.

Content, he grabbed his belongings, and turned to leave, carefully closing the door as he went, and ensuring it was locked. He wasn't as assured of himself as Bothal and all his secrets.

Down the stairs once more, and Rad and Sand were waiting for him. Mann eyed Rad speculatively, but then dismissed him as the thief. He still looked terrified whenever Mann looked at him, there was no chance he'd try his luck again while Mann remained in the inn.

'Come on then,' Mann instructed, the three shovels waiting for them. Haune hovered by the door, apparently desperate for Mann to be gone, so she could get on with her own searching.

'Be careful,' she cautioned as he walked to the door. As it opened easily under his hand, Mann was assaulted by a blast of ice-cold air that had him wishing he'd put his other coat on. Yet, the steps had remained relatively clear of snow and ice. Mann quickly made his way to ground level. From there, he slowly turned around, listening. It still appeared they were utterly alone.

Rad and Sand swiftly joined him, and in a trail, they began following their visible track to the stables. It was filled with snow, but at a lower level than the snow lying all around.

The snow had reverted to its normal structure, thawing at some point in the night. Mann tried an experimental dig into it. His shovel entered the snow easily enough, although it came away heavy and cumbersome.

'It's starting to melt,' Mann complained, turning to move the snow he had out of the way. 'We can clear the path, but it'll be heavy, wet work.' Mann didn't relish what must be done, but until it was, he couldn't leave Bosetting, and the strange situations he'd become embroiled in.

Without complaint, Sand and Rad joined him, and between them, they set about clearing the path again. Not that they could go all the way to the flat ground beneath the snow, instead they could dig down until they reached the still frozen level. Mann thought it would be enough. After all, his sled would need something to run over to leave the stables. The reindeer didn't particularly enjoy it when the ground under hoof was devoid of all snow and ice.

They worked in silence, apart from their breathing and the thud of the shovels. Mann felt his back and arms start to ache long before they rounded the side of the inn, and could make out the stables in the distance.

The sun rose, higher and higher, in the watery sky, and still, Mann heard no sound of others trying to do the same. Eventually, he was forced to pause, while Rad continued. The younger man was small and wiry, and yet he had the strength to carry on, whereas Mann and Sand were about done in.

'Bothal told me of the south,' Sand said into the silence. 'He said there's never any snow. Can you imagine it? No snow, ever.'

Mann shook his head, rubbing some warmth into his chill face.

'In all honesty, I can't imagine it, no.'

'Me neither,' Rad joined in. They were within about ten steps of the stables now. Mann was trying to summon the enthusiasm to complete the task they'd set themselves. 'Nearly there boys, nearly there,' Rad joked. Mann chuckled at his attempts to galvanise them.

'How will Haune reward us?' Rad continued. 'Fine ale, a glass of fruity wine from the south, or perhaps, a fine meat broth.'

Mann laughed again, while Sand shook his head.

'She'll give you a clouting and tell you to stop talking about bloody food and ale. I'm starving. No breakfast this morning, and the greedy buggers will have eaten everything by the time we get back.'

Mann listened to the older man's stomach gurgle and felt some sympathy. He too was tired, hungry and terribly thirsty.

Hefting his shovel once more, he laid it into the snow. With every movement, his arms twinged, his back as well.

'A hot bath,' Mann chuckled at Rad. The youth nodded, a delighted smile on his lips.

'A hot bath, warm wine and a rich, meaty broth. Cor,' Rad continued, 'she doesn't appreciate how cheap we are!'

With the three of them laughing, they finally made it to the door of the stables. Mann eyed it with interest. It seemed the indoor brazier had been at work, helped no doubt by the noticeable rise in temperature. The door looked like it would open easily.

'Poor beasties,' Sand complained, resting on the handle of his shovel, his breath harsh between his lips. 'I bet they're hungrier than we are.'

Rad reached the doors first, reaching out to see if the mechanism that barred entry would. With a cry of delight, he hoisted the lock, and it slipped loose, the door thrusting outward.

Rad skipped inside. Mann waited for some sort of complaint about the state of the stables, but Rad said nothing. When Mann reached the door, Rad was busily refilling the brazier, so he could move it outside the doors, keeping the way clear.

Mann sniffed the air. It smelt of excrement, and he winced at the thought of having to muck the animals out after all their work already that day. Sand too looked exhausted, but Rad was filled with renewed energy. He dashed from one task to another, without noticing he was the only one to feed the braziers, the water troughs and find food for all the animals.

Bothal's dogs put up a long mournful cry, while Mann's reindeer kicked at the doors on their stalls. He could well understand they were fed up of being locked up inside.

Looking around him, Mann made a quick decision and went to open the door on the stall for his reindeer. He was content for them to wander around while he mucked them out. After all, where could they go but to the inn door? Even with their powerful back legs, he doubted they'd be able to vault above the snow reaching almost to his chest.

'Watch out,' Sand called, but quickly realised what Mann was about, and subsided, busying himself to help Rad. Neither of the men commented that the animals seemed less distressed than they might have thought.

Quickly, Mann cleared the muck from the first stall of his reindeer, moving it along to the far stall where the manure was piled, so it could freeze, and be put to whatever use Haune, Rad or Sand concocted. Mann also found dried roots for them, and filled their water high, and also their food trough.

Only then did he look up, amused to see his reindeer were stood in the doorway, and had gone no further. It was as though they discussed the terrible conditions between themselves, j as he did with Rad and Sand, one head moving between the other two.

Taking an object from his pocket, he blew into it, and the three returned to him. As they did so, he ran his hands over their noses and foreheads, making sure they were well. Warm brown eyes met his.

With the first three locked up once more, Mann turned to his remaining three reindeer. These were the most placid of the six, the ones who ran behind the leaders. As such, even though he opened the stable door wide for them, they hovered inside, getting in his way as he worked to clean them out. In the end, he shooed them out, content they'd not even make it to the main stable door, and certainly not risk a hoof outside.

As tired as he was, Mann found the work rewarding. It was good to do something physical, even if he wished it didn't involve a shovel.

When the other reindeer were tended to as well as Mann could, considering the circumstances, he followed the noise of Rad and Sand's endeavours and found them forking fresh bedding out for the few horses in the stables. The horses seemed as angered by their incarceration, but it was the dogs causing the most problems.

They were running at the door of their stables, trying to work out a way of jumping free. Mann winced more than once as he heard them land heavily and awkwardly, the stables too high for them to escape.

'Daft buggers,' Sand complained. 'I'd let them free if I thought they'd come back.'

Mann was nodding, the dogs were very distressed, but they weren't his, and he had no command over them.

'Is there more meat?' Mann asked instead. 'Maybe some bones for them to chew on? If not, I think we might need to get Bothal down here, after all, they belong to him.'

'Rad, see if there are any bones for these damn foolish dogs,' Sand bellowed, as a small face appeared around a corner. Rad still seemed filled with joy and rushed off to do Sand's bidding.

'I wish I had his energy,' Sand complained, making Mann laugh because he thought the same.

'Do we need to take anything in for Haune?' Mann queried. 'I could get one of the reindeer to carry anything that's heavy.'

Sand considered the words, thinking carefully.

'There's some oats she wants. I'd normally take a small sack through, but, if the animal can take the lot?' Sand left the sentence hanging hopefully. Mann chuckled.

'Yes, yes. The problem will be the steps, but I'll deal with that when I get there.'

Quickly, Mann pulled his lead reindeer free and spoke to the animal.

Only then did Mann make his way to the far corner where Sand was rifling through the sacks.

'Damn thing should be here,' Sand muttered, working his way through the stacked sacks at the front, his frustration clear to hear. Mann took himself to the back of the stable, surprised by how many sacks Haune had in storage. As he prodded and kicked, he felt something he knew shouldn't be there. Bending, his curiosity once more aroused, Mann worked his hands beneath the sack and the wooden floor.

He felt hard metal, sharp blades, and he gasped as his finger encountered a sharp edge and began bleeding.

'Bollocks,' Mann complained, sucking his finger. Hastily he moved a few sacks, in the end, unsurprised with what he found. Shlat's knives flashed dangerously from their place of hiding amongst the food sacks, while Mann ran his hands over their edges, more carefully this time.

His suspicions regarding the thief in the inn intensified, but he quickly covered the items again. There was no need for others to know what was stored here.

'Here it is,' Sand abruptly exclaimed. Mann shot up, keen not to be seen covering something else up. Sand was already suspicious enough about him.

Mann joined Sand, and between them, they staggered back to the waiting reindeer and settled the sack containing the oats onto the animal's back. The reindeer's eyes bulged at the load, but then calmed.

'Come on then, boy,' Mann said to his beast, and together they left the stables.

The day was turning fast. Mann wanted to hurry but knew better. If he needed a lamp on the way back then, he'd have to bring one.

The reindeer didn't slip, even once, sure-footed as ever over the slippery surface, and in little time, they arrived at the door to the inn. Mann stepped carefully up the stairs, to hammer on the door.

It was Haune who opened it, a surprised expression on her face when she saw the reindeer behind Mann's shoulder.

'Sand said this would be useful?' Mann offered, indicating the sack of oats on his reindeer's back.

'Well, yes, yes, it would,' Haune confirmed, still surprised to see the reindeer, although it seemed she had something else to tell him as well.

'I'll hand it up to you,' Mann confirmed, turning away, keen to complete one task before another problem presented itself. But Haune followed him down the stairs.

'Marnit and I searched the inn. We found someone.'

Mann had expected to hear as much. 'Who is it?' he asked any way.

'A woman, the one who was looking for you.'

Mann nodded.

'Why didn't she ask for a room, like everyone else?' Mann questioned.

'I didn't think to ask her.' Haune was clearly perplexed by his question. 'Logic dictates she had no money, which is why she's stealing now.'

'Well, possibly,' Mann agreed. 'But I'd like to speak to her, see if that's truly what happened.'

'Why?'

'Well, it might just be a bloody coincidence,' Mann complained, busying himself with the sack of oats, to distract himself from marching into the inn and asking the questions himself.

Haune huffed softly, considering his words.

'Fine, well, I'll ask,' she conceded, helping him lift the sack, taking the steps carefully. The sack was almost too much for Mann, but he managed to get it so that it dangled over the top step. That would have to do.

'We'll be back soon,' Mann said, turning to try and turn the reindeer around. The space was tight, but he managed it the beast only complaining a little.

He didn't look back at Haune, sure she'd be asking his question even as he walked.

Back in the stables, Sand and Rad were waiting expectantly, while Mann hastily returned his reindeer, and ensured the stable door was closed tightly to prevent them escaping.

Only then did they leave. The doors closed easily, and in no time at all, they were all back in the inn.

Mann peered around the main room, expecting to see Shlat, but she wasn't there. Neither were Marnit or

Haune. Once more his stomach grumbled, appreciating the smell of the meal cooking over the glowing coals of the fire.

Sand and Rad made their way straight to the fire, helping themselves to bowls and then food. Mann wanted to do the same, but first, he wanted to see Shlat for himself.

Making his way upstairs, Mann searched for Haune and Marnit, hoping to find them quickly. He listened at doors, and eventually knocked on one, about as far from his own as it was possible to be.

'Go away,' Marnit called. Mann shook his head at her irritated tone.

'It's me,' he spoke, and the door flung open. Inside, over Marnit's shoulder, he could see Shlat and Haune. Shlat sat on the bed, which had evidently been much used, while Haune watched her from a chair. Shlat wore the same clothes she'd had on when he'd first met her. They were wrinkled and no doubt, stinking.

'Here's our thief,' Marnit crowed, but Mann cautioned her to silence, stepping into the room and closing the door behind him carefully.

He eyed Shlat with curiosity. Without her shimmering coat of knives, she seemed far less dangerous, and also, far more. What could she accomplish without her weapons?

'Why didn't you book bed and board?' Mann demanded, standing at the foot of the bed Shlat sat on.

Shlat refused to answer, her mouth tightly closed, fury turning her features ever darker. Her eyes almost glowed in the gloom. Shlat looked feral, and about as wild as the animals living in the Hvite Lands.

She looked even gaunter than last time he'd seen her, and she'd been thin then.

'Have you been eating?' Mann asked, a gentler question.

'When I could,' was the sulky reply.

'Could we have a bowl of pottage for her now. I'm sure she must be starving.'

Marnit looked mutinous at the request, but Haune stood and left the room without complaint.

Mann waited, silence filling the room. He could wait for his answers. He'd waited this long.

Shlat watched him, her eyes filled with fury and loathing.

Haune returned and handed over the bowl, and spoon, which Shlat looked like refusing until Mann's stomach rumbled, and a smirk lit her eyes.

Then she dug into the food, eating neatly, but quickly, while Mann watched hungrily.

'Why didn't you book bed and board?' Mann asked again, hoping her tongue might have been loosened.

'I couldn't risk being discovered,' Shlat said moodily.

'So you hid, and you stole?' Marnit complained, jabbing her finger at Shlat.

'I hid, and I stole food,' Shlat confirmed.

'What about other items?' Marnit asked, her forehead furrowed, her tone outraged.

'Just food, and of course, bed and board. I did place a 'bastard' in the wooden box, to cover my costs,' Shlat added quite testily. It seemed, other than hiding, she'd done all she could, to be honest with Haune.

'Who were you hiding from?' Mann questioned, knowing this was the crux of the problem. Would she say Bothal? He really wasn't sure.

'An enemy. There's no need for you to know who they are. Provided you keep my secret until I can leave. Will it be soon?' She pleaded, apparently desperate to be gone.

'Someone in the inn though?' Mann queried, already realising Shlat wouldn't share her secret with him.

'Yes, someone in the inn.'

'A day more, at most. I would hope,' Mann said, and he indicated to Marnit and Haune they should leave the room.

'We'll keep your secret,' he promised. 'We'll also bring fresh water, fuel for the brazier and anything else you might need.' Mann spoke without asking Haune for permission, but she was nodding all the same. At that Shlat relaxed a little, and reached into her pocket.

'Here, it's not your fault someone stole your payment. I would settle the bill again.'

Haune looked about to argue, but Mann shook his head, indicating she should take it.

'Your possessions are safe, in the stables. But how did you get in here?'

'Through the door, when no one was looking. I have some skills with concealment.' Shlat almost smiled with pride in her accomplishments. Mann wasn't sure what he'd expected her to say, but he was disappointed with the mundane answer. He couldn't deny it without raising suspicions about who he was, and what she was.

'We'll let you know when you can leave. Where are you heading?'

'Passen and then the south,' Shlat confirmed, with no trace of guile about her.

'The way south should clear quicker than the way north. So, yes, a day, maybe two, just to be on the safe side. And now, good day.' It was Haune who spoke.

But Mann had one more question yet.

'Why did you come to Bosetting?'

'I was looking for someone called Blair. I understood he lived here. It seems the information was incorrect.'

'And why did you seek this Blair?'

'That's none of your business,' Shlat snapped, and Mann nodded. What had he expected from her? That she'd spill all of her secrets before the three of them?

Together they trailed from the room, and carefully closed the door. No light shone from inside. Mann wasn't surprised that Shlat was desperate to leave such tight confinement.

Moodily, Mann stomped down the stairs, almost shaking with hunger.

Haune quickly served him a huge heaped bowl of pottage and slices of juicy meat, and then sat beside him, Marnit to the other side.

The three children of the father and mother who were busying themselves with chores around the inn occupied the main room; whereas Sand and Rad had seemingly eaten and departed to whatever tasks they wanted to be getting on with. Mann thought Sand would be sleeping, but Rad, well Rad could be doing almost anything. Was he their thief after all?

'So who's the thief?' Marnit hissed, annoyance in her tone.

Mann couldn't tell her he'd stolen her drawings, or rather moved them to a safe place. No, he'd have to maintain that charade.

It was who was stealing the coins that concerned them all.

'I've no idea,' Haune moaned, her hands twisting together on the table before her.

'Do you think we have another secret resident?' Marnit asked, leaning forward. Mann stifled a sigh, she might be annoyed, but she was also very much enjoying the sequence of strange events. If nothing else, Mann supposed, it made their confinement pass more quickly.

'Are there any other rooms unoccupied?'

'Well yes. There are thirteen bedchambers, including mine.'

As she spoke, Haune's forehead creased. She rose and dashed back up the stairs. Mann watched her with annoyance. After all, they were in the middle of a bloody conversation.

But Haune returned moments later, a question on her lips.

'Come with me,' she demanded, trying not to make too

much fuss, but already the eyes of the three bored children were on her.

Mann stood once more, his legs and back aching, causing him to groan. Marnit was more sprightly, dashing up the stairs as though she could have carried on without ceasing for days.

Upstairs, Haune whispered to them both.

'Walk along the hallway, check the room numbers. Tell me what you see.'

Perplexed Marnit and Mann did as requested.

Marnit counted under her breath, Mann in his mind.

Room number one was to the far left, so Mann's room, number six, ended up about level with the top of the stairs, two, three, four and five in between.

On they walked, seven, eight, nine, ten, eleven, and now they were close to Shlat's room, thirteen.

Mann stopped, did a double take and walked back the way he'd come. Marnit too was staring at a space that should, by rights, have held a door for room number twelve, but it didn't.

Marnit turned to Mann, and Mann to Haune. She was shaking her head, her hair slipping from shoulder to shoulder as she did so.

'Not just me then?' Haune commented.

'No, this is most … odd? I take it number twelve is normally there?'

'Yes, it was there before the storm.'

Mann ran his hands along the wooden walls, looking for some sort of join to show where the door once was, but there was nothing.

'It can't just bloody disappear,' Marnit complained, kicking the wood in exasperation.

'No it can't, but it seems that's what's happened.'

'But how?' Haune demanded to know.

'I genuinely have no idea.' Mann was as perplexed as they

were. It was impossible for a room and a door to just disappear.

'An illusion?' Marnit announced, assured of the answer. 'The door is really there, but we can't see it.'

'But why?' Mann asked, turning to meet her wild eyes. Really Marnit fluctuated from rage to amusement to making bold statements without a flicker in-between.

'To hide another thief? One who can do illusions,' Marnit shrugged her slight shoulders, as though that solved everything, and walked away, leaving Mann and Haune to stare at each other in shock.

Just what was going on in the inn?

TWENTY-FOUR

THAT NIGHT MANN, Haune and Marnit agreed to do something they'd never done before. All three would keep a watch for a part of the long night, and see if they could determine the identity of the thief.

Mann wasn't overly keen on the idea. He wanted to sleep and consider his own problems, but it was possible the thief was a part of his problem. It forced him to agree to Haune's heated requests, even though he'd rather not have done.

Mann agreed to take the second watch, perhaps the most difficult, for he'd get to sleep, only to be woken by Haune and would then need to wake Marnit, before sleeping again. The other two would be having either a late night or an early waking.

But Mann thought it most likely their thief would be awake during the middle part of the night. He was keen to determine who it was.

When Haune woke him, with a rough shake on his arm, her eyes were red-rimmed with fatigue, as he groggily pushed himself to full wakefulness.

'Nothing,' she complained in a whisper, clearly disappointed. 'Mind, Bothal hasn't long retired for the night so it might have delayed our thief.'

'Agreed,' Mann whispered. 'Now sleep, and I'll see you in the morning.'

Mann had tried to determine the best place to 'hide' while he tried to stay awake. For him, there were many, many options. Eventually, he decided the best place was to lie behind Haune's bar. From there he'd be able to see all of the main room of the inn, and more importantly, would have access to the sand timer. He wanted to track his time awake, if only so he knew how much longer he had to stay awake. He knew from experience time passed unevenly during the night, especially when he was tired.

When Haune left his room, Mann followed her, checking to ensure there was no one in the main room. He also cast a glance along the hallway to where room number twelve should have been. It was still missing.

Quietly, Mann made his way down the stairs and scurried across the room to reach the bar.

The twin hearths emitted the banked heat for the night, but still, he shivered, pleased he'd thought to bring his coat. Mann had decided, when he was in position, he'd stay alert by considering everything he needed to think about. From the thief to the appearance of Brag's sigil on his floorboards, all the way to who it was Shlat was hiding from. And why she, and Bothal, seemed to be looking for someone called Blair.

The name meant nothing to him. He couldn't shake the belief it probably should.

Lying down, Mann made himself as comfortable as possible, with his head angled so he could see much of the room, and certainly, the area around the fireplaces, where food had been left out for whoever their thief was. A few stray coins had also been left gleaming on the bar. An enticement that might or might not work.

Mann settled to wait. With the end of the storm, it was almost impossible to hide the sound of any movement when the inn was so still, but he tried, all the same. He refused to move position, even when his legs tingled, and he started to feel the cold because the floorboards were old and much worn, likely to creak if he so much as farted.

No, Mann would wait, and he wouldn't alert the thief to his scrutiny, or so he told himself, considering what he'd do in the next few days.

Firstly, he needed to arrange for another legal document to be written, only this one not by Marnit. That meant he'd need to write it himself or have someone else skilled enough to do it. Mann already knew how he'd solve that problem, so he dismissed it as almost done.

Secondly, he needed to convince Marnit to travel north with Bothal, carrying instructions for her to take over the running of the inn. Brag would leave Slutet, or at least, his inn. Mann was hopeful Brag and Bothal would know each other, as seemed possible from the carvings Bothal carried. Then, they'd both realise whatever they were trying to achieve was impossible.

While Marnit went north, he'd go south, have his 'accident,' end up 'dead,' but with his reindeers returned to Bosetting. Then, as per his death wishes, his 'nephew' would inherit the inn. When that was accomplished he could go home when enough time had elapsed for him to grow a heavy beard, moustache and let his hair grow long.

A sound distracted him from his thoughts, the soft touch of a foot on wooden floorboards. Mann tensed, his senses alert. This could be it.

He peered intently into the inn, along the floor, but could see no feet. Still, he held his position. Another soft sound reached his ears.

Every muscle in his body strained to catch a sight of the thief, but he cautioned himself to patience. He didn't want to scare them away before he'd seen them steal something or until he knew who it was.

Eventually, so slowly as to be painful, Mann detected a shadow on the floor near to the faint glow from the hearth. He understood his thief was about to be revealed.

Was it, as he'd thought Rad, or was it someone else? A stranger perhaps?

Still, he waited. He heard the soft clink of coins and knew they'd been pocketed. Now he needed to see a face, and put a name to who it was.

A figure moved into his line of sight, but with their back to him, and their body covered by a large coat, from which only two small legs peered. Mann watched intently, fearing to blink in case they disappeared. He was as convinced as it was possible to be, he didn't know this person.

A stranger then. Perhaps the person in room twelve, who'd managed to somehow conceal the room as well as themselves.

Still, Mann watched, but the figure seemed intent on some purpose he couldn't quite decipher, until, he understood. They were making a bid for freedom, now the storm had stopped, there was a route out of the inn.

'Bollocks,' Mann muttered to himself, struggling to come to his feet as the shape made a turn to head toward the door.

'Bollocks, bollocks, bollocks,' Mann groaned, knowing it was impossible to get to the door before the person managed to raise the door bar and make their way outside.

Coming to his feet so slowly it was painful, Mann tried for a final glance at whoever was in the room, but their back remained facing him. He realised it was impossible. He'd have to catch them outside.

Hastily, he moved around the bar, trying to hurry his feet, as the door bar was lifted and a blast of cold air shot into the room.

'Bollocks,' he shouted, but the person either didn't hear

him or was determined to make their escape. With a loud bang, the door shot back into place. The thief had escaped.

Mann hustled to the door, quickly yanking it open, just in time to catch a fleeting glimpse of legs rounding the corner to head for the stables.

'Bollocks,' Mann swore, pulling the door closed after him, and jumping down the steps, in an unwise move that saw his legs sliding from beneath him as they impacted the icy surface. Landing on his arse, the wind knocked from him, Mann thumped his chest, trying to force his body to fill with air.

Stumbling to his feet, he careered along the path to the stables. After all, there was nowhere to go from there. No other streetway in Bosetting was clear. The thief would be stuck, or so he tried to convince himself.

The door to the stables was open, the animals letting up a cacophony of noise as they were rudely woken from their slumbers.

Dashing inside, Mann pulled the left-hand side of the door closed, and then reached for the right-hand side as well, to trap the thief inside the stables. Only he never made it.

A thump to the side of the head, and Mann sprawled on the floor, half in the stable, and half out.

Coldness enveloped him, and yet he felt someone dragging his legs so he was within the stable before they slammed the door shut behind them. Mann tried to focus on whoever it was, but his eyes were fogged, his head pounding, and the person shot from sight as Mann's eyes closed against his will.

The sound of his name being called brought him around much later, groggy and cold, aching all over.

'Here,' he croaked, his voice sounding as rough as a door in need of greasing.

'Here,' he tried again, trying to recall why he lay on the floor of the stable, the doors closed behind him, the air cold all around.

'Bollocks,' he complained, his hand on the back of his head, as he fought to sit upright.

Rattling on the door alerted him to someone on the other side, but he had no time to shout a warning or let them know where he was before Marnit was falling over him.

'What the?' she said, as she tumbled to the ground beside him, confusion and concern warring on her face.

'He's here,' she called, to whoever was helping her search. Haune shot through the door, a look of anger on her face, that quickly subsided when she saw Mann's predicament.

'What happened?' Haune demanded to know, pulling the door closed behind her, while Marnit struggled to her feet, and bent to help Mann. He wobbled, the lump on his head pulsing, as he winced in the light from the lamp Haune had promptly lit and held too close to his eyes.

'The thief escaped. I gave chase, but they hit me, as you can see. How long have I been lying here?' he shivered as he spoke.

'No idea,' Marnit said, 'but you didn't wake me. When I woke, I looked for you, and then found Haune. We've been hunting for you for a while. It all depends on when you came outside.'

Haune was striding through her stables, peering into every compartment, as though the thief might be lurking there.

'Where have they gone?' she asked with confusion. 'Surely not into Bosetting itself?'

Mann shook his head and winced as pain lanced through his skull. 'It's the only logical conclusion,' he concluded.

'But did you see who it was?' Marnit pressed.

'No, I saw only legs beneath a large coat. It was as though they knew I was watching and kept their back to the bar.'

'Damn bastard,' Haune complained. 'Let's get you inside. It's freezing in here.'

Mann wasn't inclined to argue, but he was annoyed with himself for losing their prey.

'We'll never find them now,' he complained, following Marnit back inside. He could tell the level of snow had shrunk a little overnight, but still not enough to make travel easy.

'No, we won't,' Haune agreed. 'Unless they turn up dead somewhere. Where would they go with the snow so thick?' she thought out loud. 'It's madness.'

Mann agreed but was struggling to take his coat off, and so didn't answer. While Haune continually muttered under her breath, she made Mann a warm drink and then offered him breakfast. Mann accepted it all of it without argument. He was cold, tired, and achy all over.

When Sand and Rad appeared, disheveled from their own sleep, Haune fed them, and ordered them to the stables, without Mann. Whether they were curious as to why Mann was sitting, resting before the fireplaces, as opposed to helping them, they didn't ask.

'If we want to continue the search, or even allow your patrons to leave, we'll have to dig more paths today,' Mann voiced what he'd been considering for some time. A few sets of steps cut into the snow to the side of their path to the stables, and they'd at least be able to calculate what needed to be done to escape, or indeed, where their escaping thief might have run off to.

'Agreed, but you shouldn't do it. Not now. Sand and Rad can.'

'No,' Mann argued hastily. 'If I do it I can search for footprints in the snow. See if we can track the thief.'

'If you wish,' Haune said, her expression far from hopeful. 'And of course, if you think you can.'

Mann's face curdled at her words, but it proved prosaic when he tried to lumber to his feet a short while later.

The main room of the inn had filled with patrons and then emptied once more. He still felt foolish as he struggled to stand under the slightly amused scrutiny of Marnit and Haune.

'Bloody bollocks,' he complained, eventually standing tall. It was a huge effort but done, all the same.

At the door, there was a rumbling knock. Mann looked at Haune in surprise, not expecting visitors.

'It's Rad and Sand. They were going to bring wood for the fire. They were hoping to dig out the barrow first, but I'm not sure if they managed it.'

A biting slice of cold air shot through the inn as Haune opened the door wide, and Mann grimaced, gritting his teeth.

'Be careful,' Haune admonished. Mann cast his eyes over the door, seeing Sand and Rad trying to manoeuvre the barrow inside. It was over-filled with logs and kindling, and he couldn't see how it would even make it through the door, only for it to do so.

Stamping their feet clear of snow, and removing their coats and hats, Sand and Rad shot him reproachful glances, before moving to the hearth. Within moments they were freely sweating as they loaded the wood into the recesses below the firepit, where the fresher wood from the stables could dry out before it was used.

Mann swept out of the only just closed door, reaching for a shovel as he did so.

'If I don't come back before dark, come looking for me,' he called, sliding past Haune before she could argue with him.

Once outside, he finished fastening his coat and tugged his hat and gloves back on. Everything carried the aroma of animal shit, but that was to be expected, given his time lying on the floor of the stable.

Trying to ignore the cold, Mann walked down the steps and

looked at the snow to either side of their hard forged path. At least no new snow had fallen, but it was still impossible to see much of what lay beyond the snow. Certainly, no one else had accomplished what he, Sand and Rad had since the storm had ended.

The smell of woodsmoke was pleasant on the wind. Mann was at least reassured others in Bosetting had made it through the terrible storm and he wouldn't be the only one seeking to find a path to the outside world.

Picking a likely spot, Mann pushed his shovel into the snow, hoping it would come away easily. It almost did, but Mann still winced. This was going to take a great deal of effort, just to satisfy his curiosity.

'Bollocks,' he complained, setting about the unpleasant task he'd set himself.

He sweated and strained, making a neat pile of the snow he cleared, to the side of the path so it wouldn't impede their passage to and from the stables. Testing each step up as he made it, Mann was almost sure the snow would take his weight when he finally made it to the top layer.

Higher and higher he went, and only when five steps had been cut into the snow, did Mann ascend them, and look around.

The wind was deceptively mild at the top, and when he turned, he could, at last, see the shop fronts, and houses lining the street on the opposite side to the inn. Not that he could look at any people, but he could hear the scrape of shovels in the snow.

Before he announced his presence, he looked for any footprints in the snow, finding some heading in a haphazard zigzag down the street. Mann paused to consider but taking a firm grip on the shovel, followed them regardless.

Each step he took, he tested with his front foot, wishing he'd brought his snowshoes with him so he stood less risk of sinking into the deep snow. Swallowing nervously, he considered returning back the way he'd come, but if he did, he was sure Haune and Marnit would insist on coming with him. Mann didn't want that, not yet.

Cautiously he made his way forward, making sure he left tracks so he could follow them back. Although, he reasoned, it was hard to miss the two-story inn, even when it was dusted with snow.

Mann walked for long moments, and then came to a stop, because the footprints abruptly stopped, right in the middle of the street. He looked around, seeing if there was anywhere the thief could have gone. But there was nothing, just nothing. Empty air greeted him and nothing else.

'Bloody bollocks,' he complained loudly, his cry eliciting a response from someone.

'Hello,' the cry went up, a shrill sound in the quiet, and quickly joined by others.

'Hello,' Mann called back, shocked to have a reply to his complaint. 'I'm from The Firs. Are you well?'

'Bloody cold,' one voice shot back, but then a vast swell of conversation sprang up, which Mann tried to follow. There were at least ten voices, some deep, some high, all insistent.

'Will the snow ever clear?' one demanded to know, testily.

'It's lower than yesterday,' Mann offered.

'Well that wouldn't be hard,' another voice called sarcastically.

'Does Haune have food to spare or wood?' another voice called.

'I do.'

'I do.' Another confirmed.

'But how do I get it?'

Mann looked around.

'Are your doorways cleared?' he called. 'I built some steps

up onto the snow. You could try the same, or, if I can work out where you are, I can facilitate exchanges.'

As he finished speaking, a flash of red caught his eye. Carefully, Mann made his way to the colourful cloth.

'Hello,' he said, peering down into a cold, but hopeful face. The doorway of the shop had been cleared back about two or three feet, but no further.

'Who are you?' was the outraged cry because they couldn't recognize him.

'Mann, from The Firs. I'm a patron,' he explained.

'I thought it would be Sand. Here, I can pass this up to you, if you can grab it.'

The woman, swathed in furs, with only curious eyes visible, had a small wooden crate with spare root vegetables and a string of sausages in it.

'Can you take them to whoever asked for food? And see if they have any wood?'

'Keep your linen up,' Mann commanded, bending as low as he could to grab the crate, and then standing carefully so he didn't overbalance when he held it tight in his hands.

'Who was after food?' he called. 'Hold up something bright so I can find you.' A streak of blue caught his eye on what he took to be the opposite side of the roadway. He took the crate to yet another doorway, remembering to test the snow with every step he took. This one had been cleared of more snow, the need of the inhabitants to leave, clear to see. Tired faces greeted his arrival and the rumble of empty bellies, audible in the quiet.

The man he passed the crate to was already licking his thin lips with relish.

'She asked if you had any fuel to spare?'

'Yes, yes, wood aplenty. Food not so much.'

And so it went on. Mann managed to help those ten voices, and made his way, as darkness was falling, back to the inn.

He'd not discovered what he wanted, but there was a consensus amongst the people he'd spoken to, that they'd all try and either dig a path or steps into the snow, to enable them to exchange goods with one another.

———

Four days later Mann stepped from The Firs for what he hoped was the final time. The street, if not yet devoid of snow as when he'd first arrived in Bosetting, was passable. People called to him with a wave of their arm.

Few in Bosetting didn't now know his name. It might help his plan, soon to be enacted, or it might not.

Beside him, Marnit walked with Bothal, neither of them pleased. Haune had already offered him her thanks when they'd said their farewells inside the inn. Life was pretty much restored to normal. Yet, Mann had too many unanswered questions. Now, it seemed, wasn't the time to be finding those answers.

After a great deal of persuasion, Mann had convinced Marnit to travel north for him, and take over the running of his inn. She carried letters thanking Brag for his help, but dismissing him all the same, the excuse being Mann's delay in Bosetting, and not wanting to hold up Brag's return journey.

Whenever Marnit spoke of Brag, Bothal's face curdled. It was clear the short man knew Brag better than Marnit. He wasn't at all keen to know he waited at the end of their journey to Slutet.

Marnit carried other secrets with her, but they were for him, Haune and her to know, and no one else.

Marnit had discovered the destruction of her workshop. Sand and Rad, feeling charitable, had promised to right it all in her absence.

Shlat had disappeared some nights ago, her knives as well.

Mann didn't miss her lurking presence, but was annoyed he didn't know who she'd been hiding from. All in all, the storm had proved too big a distraction for him. His priorities were on leaving, not solving niggling questions, or so he berated himself.

Not that he'd been sleeping easy for the last few nights. Instead, he'd been very busy, collecting what he needed from Slutet in the middle of the night, and leaving behind what needed to be found.

He might have hated the delay and the distractions, but it had clarified his plans, and now he knew it wouldn't fail. He was annoyed by the deceits he'd have to employ, and more, he was sad his unexpected friendships with Haune and Marnit would come to an end.

Together they made their way to the stables. The dog sled was ready to depart, and so too was the reindeer sled, the one going north, the other south.

Sand and Rad watched on hopefully. Mann chuckled, as he offered them each a handful of copper coins. There'd be plenty more where that came from for them, but they weren't to know that, not yet.

'Safe travels,' Sand offered. Mann nodded. 'And my thanks for all your help,' Sand continued. Mann grunted. The older man's warning still hung between them, despite their show of friendship.

'It was no problem. It kept us all busy.'

With nothing else to say, Mann spoke to his reindeer, pawing at the ground and keen to be gone, and then settled himself inside his sled.

'Safe travels,' he called to Marnit and Bothal, before giving the command to move on.

The reindeer jumped at the slap of the reins, keen to be gone. Mann negotiated his way down snowy streets to the main gates. Only the east was accessible to him, much of Bosetting still impassable. It only added a small amount of time to his journey, and now time had become irrelevant to him.

Mann waited at the gates, just to be sure Bothal and Marnit had made it this far and then he raised his hand in farewell, and allowed the reindeer to have their head.

It had been nearly two weeks since he'd arrived in Bosetting. The animals were fractious and keen to be moving.

Mann loosened his hold on the reins and allowed them to have their way as soon as they were clear of the black walls.

The sharp, clean smell of the snow hit his nostrils, and he coughed at the first true inhalation. He'd missed this.

Next time he had to 'die' his plans would be far less complicated, or so he vowed, a contented grin on his face. And he wouldn't be getting caught out in a once-in-a-century fierce bloody snowstorm. Never again.

TWENTY-FIVE

Chapter 25

HALF THE YEAR had elapsed before Mann, or Tate, as he had to get used to being called, once more rode into Bosetting.

It had been remarkably easy to fake his death. All things considered.

The trick had been in having the reindeer returned to the gates of Bosetting without him. From there, much had happened quickly, even down to the enactment of his death wishes. He could perhaps have returned earlier than he had, but Mann had been keen to have his beard and moustache fully covering his face, and his hair, long and snaking down his back. It was hard to mask his tall frame. He'd need to rely on learnt mannerisms and facial hair to do the job.

He had, of course, made some night-time excursions to both Slutet and Bosetting.

As such, he knew much of what had happened in Slutet when Bothal had arrived with Marnit. Even now, he smirked considering the scene he'd observed between the two men, which neither thought had been observed by any other than themselves. Not that it had provided him with any answers as to their true intentions.

'Why don't you have the damn drawing?' Brag had complained testily, his copper eyes shimmering in the lamp light. 'Or the bloody carving? Before you've always had both. Now it's as though we search without being able to see.' True frustration had soured Brag's voice.

'I'm not to blame for that,' Bothal had retorted, his colour high and his disappointment palpable, his violet eyes pulsing with suppressed anger.

'Then who is? No one else has access to those. No one else can do what you can do?'

'All the same, it's not my responsibility. Anyway, you assured me he was found.'

'Well, I bloody thought he was.'

'And you planned on 'stealing' this inn?'

'Teach the bastard a lesson,' Brag whined.

'Only it wasn't the right sodding person. Was it?'

'Well, that's not my fault.' Brag continued to whine.

'You dragged me here,' Bothal complained. 'I've endured a blizzard, a bloody blizzard to get here, and I had an unpleasant encounter with Shlat.'

'Where is she now?' Brag asked, peering around as though she might jump out at any moment, more alert than Mann had ever known him.

'Gone. Goodness knows where. She disappeared. Hiding away in the inn, but not from me.' Bothal's forehead creased at the thought, perhaps realizing he didn't know who Shlat had hidden from. Mann had been unsurprised to discover Bothal had been aware of Shlat's presence all along.

'So what do we do now?'

'Well, I still have an inn to steal.'

'Really, that's all that drives you? What about,' and Mann had held his breath, hopeful all his questions might be answered. 'You know?'

Ah, perhaps not.

'Why should I give a shit? No one else does.'

'One person doesn't.'

'No, many more than one. Do you see anyone else trying to find him? No, I didn't think so.'

'Well, I'm going back to the south.'

'Good, you make the inn look untidy.'

'You do know this is Mann's inn don't you, and he'll be back, soon, to claim it.'

'The weather's severe, he's taking chances, and his scribe is poor at writing death wishes. I have every possibility of inheriting this place.' Brag had sounded sure of himself.

'I think not,' Bothal laughed. 'I think you might need to speak with Marnit first.'

'Marnit isn't important. A scribe, nothing more, just a very nosy scribe.'

'Hah,' Bothal had chuckled, delighting in knowledge Brag didn't yet have.

'She knows far more about you than you know about her. And Mann has sent her here for a purpose.'

'What purpose?' suspicion had bloomed.

'I can't spoil the surprise.'

Mann had felt that there was no love lost between the two, although they undoubtedly knew each other, possibly too well, and both hoped to accomplish the same thing.

'When you realise it's time to leave, you can come with me, for a few very high-value coins.'

'I won't be going anywhere with you.'

'Fine, then the cost has just doubled.'

'What did Marnit tell him?'

'Enough. You really should have been less honest with the girl.'

'She knew it was all a joke.'

'She didn't. Or, if she did, she doesn't any more. Now she thinks it's serious.'

'Damn,' Brag shook his head. 'But, she might still be won over.'

'I doubt it, but good luck.'

Even now Mann shook his head at Brag's ambitions. It was that which bothered him the most, for he hoped Shlat, Brag, Bothal and any other who might have been searching for someone, who might or might not have been him, were long gone, and far to the south.

Now it was time to see if the second half of his ambitious scheme would work.

Stepping from the sled he'd ridden into Bosetting, Mann looked around him. Little had changed in his short time away. The shop fronts were busy announcing the trader's goods, and the streetway was bustling with people. True winter was some distance away. As such, buying and selling was a pleasant occupation, the same couldn't be said once winter hit.

The owner of the sled who'd given him passage turned to him, a sad smile on his face, as the horses were instructed to stop.

'I know you never met your uncle, but if you go into The Firs, the innkeeper there will be able to tell you what little she knows. There, it's down that street.' The woman pointed, for all Mann knew the way far too well.

Mann nodded his thanks. 'I hope to meet you again, soon,' he continued, and the sledder laughed.

'Indeed, perhaps I'll head toward Slutet one day. I've never seen it yet.'

Mann walked to The Firs. This was one of the most significant tests he'd face in the coming days. Haune and Marnit, and also his reindeer. He hoped they weren't too friendly toward him.

With half a smile plastered onto his bearded face, he bounded up the four steps to The Firs and flung the door wide. A gasp of shock reached his ears. He turned to face Haune, who was stood behind her bar, as always. He knew a moment of keen longing to be in the same position.

She looked no different to the last time he'd seen her, short apron tied around her waist, long blonde hair pulled back from her face. If there was a stray crinkle or two to her skin, Mann thought it added to her appeal, rather than detracted from it.

'Good day, innkeeper. I'm Tate. Sledder Wale thought you would help me. I'm Mann's nephew.'

'Nephew?' Haune exclaimed, the ghost of sorrow still in her eyes that had leapt, just for a moment, on seeing him. Mann suppressed his dismay at his subterfuge.

'Yes, he was on his way to visit us, when. When. Well.' And here he stopped. The story was that Mann had somehow tumbled from the sled, perhaps while sleeping, and his body had fallen down a steep slope to disappear under the glacier ice and be swept away. That Mann's reindeer had returned to Bosetting when they found themselves without a master was a happy occurrence, alerting all to Mann's death.

'Right,' Haune said, her eyes still uncertain. He was unsure what she distrusted the most. His assertion of his identity, or the story he told.

'Mann was a good friend,' Haune eventually said, and then grimaced, perhaps finding the words too bland.

'The sledder said I might find answers here.' Mann, or Tate as he must now be called, didn't want to press the point, but had to, all the same, if only to prove his ignorance.

'Answers to what?' Haune asked, suspicious all over again.

'What my uncle was up to, how he seemed, I don't know. Why he left the inn to me?'

'I can't help with anything that didn't happen during the short time he stayed in my inn. It was an odd time, but he made the best of it. I was saddened by his loss. We, we have his reindeer, in the stables, if you're planning on taking them back to Slutet.' She sounded both hopeful and melancholic.

'Marnit, my relative, she's been running the inn in Mann's place. It'll be good to see her again,' Haune continued gamely, clearly trying to make the best out of a bad situation.

'Marnit, the scribe?' Tate/Mann asked brightly. It would seem strange if he were filled with sorrow for a man he'd never met. As such, he'd decided to opt for jolly in his exchanges with the people he'd met only half a year before.

'Yes, her. Why? How do you know her name?'

Now Tate/Mann smiled and stepped forward.

'Here, she wrote this letter to my family, and also produced a copy of his wishes.' He opted not to say 'death wishes' he didn't want to upset Haune further.

'Oh yes, of course. She did. I'd forgotten all about that.'

'She's also named as one of his beneficiaries.'

'What?' this was news to Haune, as it should be. Mann had made use of his scribe in Slutet for this item, visiting in the middle of the night, and leaving his instructions, before collecting them a few days later. This was how he planned on removing himself from association with Freg, whose age was better known by the people of Slutet and Bosetting than it was comfortable for Tate/Mann to have known.

'Yes, yes,' again his voice was high and filled with excitement.

'He left a dwelling to her, here in Bosetting.' As he spoke, Tate/Mann handed over the vellum so Haune could indeed see what he spoke about.

'Well I never,' Haune whistled through her teeth. 'A dwelling such as that would provide a great deal of security for Marnit. A great deal.' Slowly, a sudden and solitary tear slid down her face. Haune dabbed at it irritably.

'Here, a drink,' Haune offered, turning her back on Tate/Mann to cover her grief. 'A fine ale, and then perhaps food. Will you be staying the night, or travelling on?'

'A night's board, if you please. It's too late to embark on a journey I've never made before.'

Haune nodded, as though expecting the answer.

'Then I should warn you Brag, a man once connected with your uncle, still resides in Bosetting. He isn't a resident here, but he might hear of your arrival. He's not a pleasant individual.'

'He and my uncle fell out?'

'Yes, and no. Your uncle replaced Brag with Marnit. I still don't know all the details. Brag has been here, on a few occasions, spreading salacious rumours about the two of them. None will listen to him. Yet Brag refuses to leave, although we'd all like it if he went.'

'Ah,' Tate/Mann hadn't been aware Brag was still there. In fact, he'd rather hoped he wasn't.

'Well, if he comes in tonight, point him out to me. I'd be most obliged.'

Haune nodded and turned away again. Tate/Mann lifted his ale, drinking deeply and savouring the taste.

His time away hadn't exactly been under straitened circumstances, but he would much prefer it when everything was ordered once more.

The door swung open again. Tate/Mann turned to stare at the figures entering the inn. He tensed, only to relax when he discovered Sand and Rad, arguing good-naturedly as they entered the room.

Both stopped abruptly, looking at him with consternation.

He looked the same as Mann, obviously, but was different. It didn't mean they didn't recognise him, rather that they didn't expect to.

'This is Sand and Rad,' Haune quickly made the introductions. 'This is Tate, Mann's nephew.'

They looked him over with interest.

'Have you come for the reindeer?' Relief filled Sand's voice.

'Yes, I have. Are they a handful?'

Rad shook his head. 'No, but they don't like Sand. Not at all.' Rad's voice burbled with laughter, as he stepped close and shook Mann's hand.

'You sure look like him,' Rad offered, 'although you have much more hair, and are much younger than him.' With his words exhausted, Rad helped himself to a drink and settled beside the fires.

Sand lingered, his brow furrowed. Mann knew what worried him, but said nothing. It wasn't his responsibility to ease the man's soul. Any payment Sand had taken in exchange for caring for the reindeer was fine, provided Sand was alright with it.

'You knew my uncle?'

'For a few weeks, nothing more. More by reputation, to be honest. I respected him.' Tate/Mann grinned at the reply, not having expected it at all, considering if the judicious supply of copper and silver coins left in the returned sled had forced Sand to reconsider his opinion of Mann.

'Then I'm pleased you knew him. Can I go visit the reindeer?' Tate/Mann asked, abruptly.

'Yes, they're in the stables, round the back. You can't miss them. Watch them, they bite.' Tate/Mann chuckled at Sand's rueful tone and headed for the door.

Outside, he paused, just long enough to orientate himself and then skipped to the stables. He was eager to see his old friends, and also keen to meet them when no one else was around. It would prevent anyone wondering why they got on so well from the beginning.

Even from the street way, he could hear the lead reindeer, as though they knew he'd returned to them. He grinned again. He felt exhilarated.

The stable doors creaked as he entered. He pulled them

closed behind him. No one could witness what was about to happen.

The reindeer were in the stalls they'd been in when he'd stayed in Bosetting, and he reached out to them.

'Hey there,' Tate/Mann called, stretching out to rub his hand over the snouts of the three lead reindeer. He didn't ask them if they'd missed him, for it was worthless. He'd never wholly abandoned them throughout the last few months, instead visiting them when he could.

'Tomorrow, Slutet,' Tate/Mann promised, moving to the other stall. The three following reindeer watched him with reproachful eyes. He chuckled, pleased to be reunited with them for good. This reminder of Freg he could keep, whereas others he needed to discard.

'Have you been fed?' he asked them, a few hooves connecting with the wooden doors at his words. They couldn't reply, obviously, but Tate/Mann hustled away to look for some root vegetables and lichen, if any remained.

But as he passed one of the stalls, he stopped and doubled back.

'Dogs?' he questioned. Leaning over the stable door. He was sure he recognised them. Weren't they Bothal's dogs? He peered closer. They didn't have the strange violet sheen of Bothal's. Instead they carried a green tinge in their eyes. What had happened here?

He counted them, just to be sure. Six. He was sure Bothal had purchased six dogs for his journey north. Were these the same ones?

Tate/Mann shook his head. It was none of his business. It never had been. He needed to remember that.

Tate/Mann found food for the reindeer and ensured his sled was in good repair. He also looked through what remained in the back of the sled. He chuckled at what hadn't been used, and what had been taken. Tate/Mann had no qualms with any of it. He'd planned for it, after all.

Then he fed the reindeer, enjoying such a routine task. The reindeer appreciated his ministrations and soon calmed down. Perhaps they could smell the scent of Slutet on the air, just as he could.

Haune fed him well that night, and he was unsurprised when she gave him the key to his old room. He'd not asked for that particular room. There'd seemed little point.

Come the morning, and with no meeting with Brag, which pleased him, Tate/Mann bid the inn goodbye, promising to return at some unspecified time in the future. He had little intention of returning, not if it might make him reveal more of himself than he wanted to, but neither did he want to hurt anyone's feelings.

The reindeer were harnessed together. Tate/Mann stepped onto the sled with a rush of joy. This was it. Everything would soon be righted, and Marnit would have been rewarded for her loyalty. That was something he was pleased about.

She'd run the inn well in his absence. It had prospered, despite a decline in visitors who didn't want to get trapped in the far north ever again. Tales of what had happened when Mann had first arrived in Bosetting had travelled far past the Passen. Perhaps fueled by Bothal's complaints, and maybe even Shlat's, as they'd returned to their warm southern climates.

Give it a few years, and everyone would forget, and trade would boom once more. It had happened before, and it would happen again. The north was a hostile place and never to be relied upon.

Nor had the storm that delayed him been the final one of the season. Indeed, he'd barely managed to escape Bosetting when the snow had begun again, whipped into a frenzy. Mann had scratched his head at the abundance of snow. Not at all like normal. For a wild moment, he'd considered whether someone had been directing the weather, making it so bad. He'd dismissed the notion with a laugh. His time in Bosetting had made him suspicious of much he saw and knew. Bothal, Brag and Shlat had been real eye-openers.

Carefully, Mann directed the reindeer to the street, waving farewell to Haune, Sand and Rad as he went, and then along the road until he came to the northern gate and its wardens.

It stood open, enticingly, as though tempting people to explore the vast expanse beyond. Grinning, Tate/Mann waved his farewells and set himself on a path toward Slutet.

It took some time to reach the true snow and ice that never melted, no matter the season, and only then did he let his reindeer fly over the snow and ice.

Tate/Mann was strongly reminded of his journey with Freg all those years ago, and for long moments he allowed himself to mourn her one final time, before banishing her from his thoughts. Freg had been his lover, but she'd been dead for two decades, it was high time to move on, maybe even take a new lover. Perhaps, and he chuckled again, he should have found one in the south and brought her home with him.

Not that he'd actually been south. No, as Tate/Mann sped ever homewards, he considered his tactics of the last few months, and how complicated they'd become. What had started out, to him at least, as something easy to accomplish, had proven to be anything but.

As he'd planned, Mann had left Bosetting having sent Marnit north with Bothal to wrench back the inn from Brag. Marnit had warned him Brag wasn't to be trusted, and Mann had quickly come to realise the truth of her words. Another with the same markings as him, with all of his attendant secrets, was not someone Mann needed to contend with when he returned as Tate.

For himself, he'd aimed toward the area he'd discovered on

Marnit's map of the north. It was vaguely toward the Passen, but via a slightly obscure path he'd known none would want to follow, after his reindeer appeared back in Bosetting, without him. Yet, he'd underestimated how difficult the path had been, and how unforgiving the weather. In the end, he'd had to act sooner than he might have liked, to protect himself and his reindeer. Even now he was unhappy with how events had played out.

Only three days after leaving Bosetting, Mann had returned to it, just not by any conventional route. No, he and his reindeer, their tracks made in the snow so any who wanted to could follow them, had been transported through use of his strange abilities to Freg's home in Bosetting.

It wasn't precisely dilapidated, but Mann knew he hadn't kept it in the best possible condition. Neither had he been able to accomplish any repairs, because he'd not wanted to be observed by anyone. Instead, for that first night, he and his reindeers had all sheltered together, in one of the stables, with only a small brazier for light and warmth.

Come the morning, Mann had spoken the words, and his reindeer had left him, and he'd relinquished all control of the situation. Then, he could only allow events to play out as they must.

He'd moved inside Freg's house then.

The strong gates still stood to prevent anyone from entering the property. Not that anyone had, for two decades. Indeed the building had been mostly abandoned, apart from Mann's belongings he'd carefully catalogued to enable survival inside for as long as necessary.

He couldn't risk smoke rising from the thatch that might excite someone's interest, but he had braziers aplenty and had consoled himself he need only live in the smoky environment for a few months, nothing more.

Mann had food to last his exile and provided he only ever left at night, when darkness had fallen, he was sure he'd remain undetected.

There had been a few heart-stopping moments when he'd nearly been detected, but all that was done now.

Initially, he'd thought he'd stay for four months, but the business of settling his death wishes had taken longer than he'd hoped. Only after five months had he emerged from his self-imposed captivity, and moved himself away to a settlement near the Passen. From there he'd made himself known as Mann's nephew, and eventually taken the sled north.

It hadn't been easy, but it also hadn't been too difficult for him. He'd spent time in his inn at Slutet, watching Marnit at work and ensuring Brag and Bothal both left, and he'd also been in Freg's home in Slutet. There he'd been able to store far more than he'd managed to take to Bosetting because no one paid any mind to the old building in Slutet.

None of it would have been possible without his abilities. Without them, Mann would have had no choice but to disappear, for many years, and risk losing his inn and his livelihood.

But, he considered, his abilities and his long life must be connected, somehow, so he couldn't have had one without the other.

When his reindeer had been found outside Bosetting, in the early morning sunrise, Mann knew there'd been great consternation and some had set off to try and find him. He'd ensured enough of the sled's tracks remained to give an idea of where he'd gone, and when they'd come to a stop, on a high rise, with a steep slope leading to a glacier lake that shimmered beneath the surface of the thick ice, those searching for him had given up.

Mann hadn't been surprised, and it had been his plan all along for that to happen. He'd thought of crashing into a lake, or some such, but Marnit's map had shown him an alternative. No one would expect to find a body for months, if not years, and when one didn't appear at the opposite end of the river that flowed all the way under the Hvite Lands, no one would think anything of it. They wouldn't remember a man had died there many years before.

Within sight of Slutet, Tate/Mann slowed the reindeer, even though they were too keen to be in their stables and wanted to press on. For all the times he'd woken fed up of his monotonous existence, he wanted to savour the sight of his home, and really soak it up.

Sixty years in one place hadn't been easy on him, but he wasn't about to give it up. Not with the difficulties he encountered travelling south through the Passen.

As his reindeer pawed at the snowy ground, trying to dislodge some of the hard frozen surface, Tate/Mann delighted in the view of Slutet. Even after sixty years, it was a small settlement. It took a hardy soul to even consider digging through the layers of snow and permafrost to reach the ground beneath into which staves for new buildings could be thrust. It took an even hardier soul to find a business that could be carried out to support who ever lived within that dwelling when completed, and an even more resolved individual to survive through the bitter and harsh winter storms.

Yet Tate/Mann loved the place. Almost from the first moment he'd seen it, in the daylight, after manifesting in the middle of the Hvite Lands. It was his home, and he was here to claim it back for himself.

With a sharp slap on the reins, the reindeer resumed their journey. He allowed them to race as fast as they wanted, all six of them moving together as one. A rare occurrence.

At the gates, Tate/Mann slowed, forcing the reindeer to come to a stop, yet the gate wardens simply waved him through, no doubt recognising the sled, and not immediately realising what it meant.

With a soft command, the reindeer came to a stop. He bounded up the front steps of his home, keen to see its interior, to announce he'd arrived.

A broad smile on his face, he pulled the door open, expecting to see Marnit behind the bar, as welcoming and guarded as Haune had been. But utter silence greeted him.

'Hello,' he called striding inside, already cataloguing what needed to be done in the next few days to restore the inn to the way he liked it, flicking at the dust marring some of the higher shelves, realising Marnit was too short to reach them.

He tutted softly to himself.

'Hello,' he called once more, his forehead furrowed. Where was Marnit?

'Who are you?' an angry voice called, striding down the stairs.

'My name's Tate, Mann's nephew, come to claim the inn.'

The scribe of Slutet looked him up and down, tilting his head to one side and then the other, looking for a resemblance that he must have found.

'Good, you've arrived, not a moment too soon.'

'Why, where's everyone?' Tate/Mann asked again, a smile on his face, pleased to be home, pleased to be safe, delighted to see Marnit again.

'If you mean Marnit, then I'm afraid I must tell you she's dead.'

Staggering at the words, it was Tate/Mann's turn to examine the scribe as though looking for a semblance of something he could recognise because the words made no sense.

'Dead?' Tate/Mann said, just to be sure, reaching for and finding a chair to slump on to, his shock overpowering.

'Yes, overnight. I believe she was poisoned.'

Marnit, murdered?

That could only mean one thing to Tate/Mann, and as tears leaked from his eyes, he appreciated all of his careful plans had come to nothing.

Marnit was dead, and he knew who the culprit was.

And, it was his bloody fault. All his fault.

TWENTY-SIX

SLUTET INN – THE MILLENNIUM

Chapter 26

MANN FELT tears in his eyes as a warm hand touched his arm.

Branwen's golden eyes, rather than being angry as before, showed a hint of remorse for Mann's experiences, and also a great deal of confusion.

Irritably he stood, and, surveyed the inhabitants of his inn.

It should be relatively easy he thought, to find those he sought. Not Marnit, poor Marnit, but he did expect to find Brag, Bothal and Shlat, perhaps others he'd not even known knew more about him than he did.

Mann could feel eyes on the back of his head. He ignored them, too intent to find an answer, once and for all.

Jenna had spoken of the Nine and the None. He'd once encountered a strange cast of carvings, containing only seventeen pieces. He'd known then the missing piece should have been him, but he'd refused the challenge, slinking from Bosetting instead, too keen to live another life than find out about the one he should have had.

It had been Bothal who'd held the pieces. Bothal who'd wanted to know who he was. And possibly Bothal who'd stolen one of Marnit's drawings of Mann, although how it had ended up in Slutet had never been answered. Perhaps, perhaps, Bothal had managed to move it there, or maybe Brag. Or some such. Mann had never determined if they had gifts such as his, and if they had, what they might have been.

The card players played on, but Mann's eyes had alighted on a figure sat all alone in the far corner of the inn, out of any direct lamplight. Mann might have served him his ale and meal, but he certainly hadn't 'seen' him when he did so. Otherwise, Mann would have realised straight away.

'Bothal, how good to see you again,' Mann spoke low, coming to a stop before the table, upon which Bothal had placed a box, the same wooden box Mann had once discovered, the wood polished so brightly it almost shone brighter than the flames of the fire.

'This could all have been dealt with much sooner if you'd only been less stubborn,' Bothal complained, in his high voice, hands busy on a piece of bleached bone. 'An entire lifetime of searching and I'd found you in the first place I looked, after all. Only neither of us knew it. You're a selfish bastard Mann, you always have been.'

Mann shook his head, reaching out to snatch the carving from Bothal, hardly noticing Bothal called him Mann and not Blair, refusing to be drawn by yet another complaint about him.

'I don't think so,' Mann explained, taking the small likeness and snapping it in two, before turning to cast it on one of the hearths. Instant blue flared in the heart of the fire, a sudden explosion of heat warming the room against the raging storm outside.

'Think what you want,' Bothal's voice was calm, despite the destruction. 'Precautions have now been taken against your stupidity, Blair.' Now the name was said, but derisively. Mann shook his head in anger.

Mann stormed from Bothal, the conversation doing little to ease his mind at the use of the name that wasn't his, and yet felt like it should be. Now he searched for Shlat or Brag. How had he missed so many people converging on his bar at one time?

The answer was of course simple. He'd not been looking for them, so why should he recognise them after all this time?

Once more Mann peered into the darkened corners of his inn, searching, but he found no one else until he turned back toward Branwen. Then he saw Brag, in animated conversation with her, Brag standing beside Branwen as he gesticulated wildly with his arms.

'You bastard,' Mann stepped between Branwen and Brag, pushing the copper man backwards, and only just not reaching for a knife to cut the smug expression from his face.

'You killed her,' Mann moaned, the horrors of that day, nine hundred years ago, coming back to him full force. 'Why did you do that?'

'Who?' Brag said, a cocky expression on his face, that didn't sit quite right. Mann knew Brag was wholly aware they spoke of Marnit.

'Calm down, Mann,' Branwen tried to intervene. 'We aren't allowed to kill. Rules, and all that.' She spoke flippantly but Mann knew he was right, despite her bloody 'rules.'

'Then I suggest you re-educate the bastard because he killed a young woman called Marnit who'd done nothing but watch him too closely and listen too carefully.'

Before Branwen could say more, her usually warm eyes, turned cold with fury, Brag held his hands up in capitulation.

'I confess I did. Annoying bitch. It seemed only fair to give you such a gift, for cocking everything up, as you did.'

Bothal had joined the rest of the supposed Nine, his expression filled with fury to match Mann's.

'He stole from me and killed the girl. I've long known. It was the end of our arrangement to hunt you down.'

'Why shouldn't I kill you now?' Mann menaced, but Brag unexpectedly laughed.

'I know all that you think, sometimes before you even think it. It would be impossible for you to kill me, even if I could be killed.' So furious, Mann didn't even realise Brag had shared his special talent.

Mann growled again, stepping closer to Brag determined to get a fist on his nose, but another body got in the way.

'Bloody bollocks,' Mann bellowed, everyone in the inn watching him curiously, through alcohol dulled eyed, only for Shlat to meet his wrathful gaze levelly.

'If anyone gets to kill him, it is I,' she complained, looking down on Mann and forcing his eyes upwards.

Mann gasped, while Branwen shushed them all.

'Come on, people. Let's not discuss this where everyone can see. Or rather, let's discuss it without the need for violence.'

'Brag killed the girl and meddled with my attempts to track down Mann. When I went to Slutet, he tried to kill me as well.' Shlat's voice was as bland as ever.

'But dearies, we can't die?' Branwen spoke slowly, as though amazed by the stupidity of it all, her eyes wide with misunderstanding.

'Look, Mann's not the only damn fool around here,' Brag exclaimed, his coppery eyes as murderous as Mann's own. 'If he can be a total arse about everything, then I figured we all could be.' The defence, pathetic as it was, had Mann laughing with derision.

'You blame me for all this, and then use me to justify the murder of an innocent woman? I don't bloody think so.'

But Branwen's hand was on his arm, her strength surprising him, as she restrained him.

'Let it go, Mann. There's too much you don't know, or understand.'

Angry, Mann sat heavily on a bar stool, and turned to Branwen, questions forming in his mind. But she shook her head.

'Laws, dearie,' she said, but more softly this time, her eyes filled with compassion none of the others seemed to feel toward him, as they all moved away from the potential altercation.

'You always were a rash man,' Branwen advised, running her finger along his chin, to reach his lips. It was so reminiscent of their first meeting, Mann was forced to shake his head to remind himself of where he was. He had an inn full of people, most of them in need of serving, and a few desperate to convince him nothing was as it appeared. He couldn't just start up with Branwen where they'd left off over half a millennia ago.

'Where have you been?' Mann asked, thinking it his most pressing question, before reconsidering. 'Why did you leave?'

'Questions for another time,' she responded, but Mann didn't think she'd ever tell him the truth. Moodily, he sunk back into his memories, determined to elicit some sort of response from her.

PART FOUR

TWENTY-SEVEN

Chapter 27

MANN PAUSED in the middle of his task, unsure what had disturbed him from his quiet contemplation of the slight tediousness of his life. A tedium he rarely resented, while admitting it was tedium.

He glanced around his well-appointed inn. He was alone, completely alone. Even the twin hearths were simply consuming the wood and charcoal laid on them some time before.

Mann glanced at the tables, one at a time, noting how their dark wood gleamed brightly, cleanly, comforted by the sight of such mundanity.

His inn was deserted apart from him. That was just the way he liked it.

The height of summer. Outside, the weather was as mild as it ever got in the Hvite Lands, and Slutet was busy about its business. Well, everyone was. Apart from Mann.

But something had fractured his quiet enjoyment of the moment.

Still paused in his task, he listened carefully, considering the possibility his stable hands were rowing once more, the sound drifting up through the thick floorboards, curtsey of the open cellar door. But no, whatever it was didn't come from them.

With a shrug of his shoulders, Mann resumed the desultory wiping of his glasses, a red one in his hand, only for the inn door to bang open in a swirl of clothing and long hair. He blinked and then blinked again.

'Dearie, a drink please,' an apparition before him, all golden hair and smiling summer eyes. He found himself doing exactly as instructed without even thinking about it.

'No, not that one. The blue bottle,' she trilled, 'always the blue bottle.' Her long finger pointed. Mann again did as asked, without even considering whether she could afford the expensive drink or not, its taste only appreciated by a very small number of individuals who frequented his remote inn.

'In the red glass,' she trilled, pointing again, delight on her face at the delicate object he'd been cleaning. He did as asked once more, handing her the drink.

She gripped the red glass tightly in her hand and lifted it to lips that pulsed with life. He couldn't move his scrutiny from bright eyes that seemed to reflect all he knew about himself.

'Branwen,' she offered, holding out her free hand, as though testing him.

'Mann,' he muttered, only for her to laugh at the name.

'Not very original, is it dearie?' she said, laughter mingling with the words.

Mann didn't know what to say. No, it wasn't very original. He couldn't deny that, but it was his name, and he was used to it. 'It's a family name,' he tried to explain.

'I imagine it is,' Branwen chuckled again, over the lip of the glass. She had a beguiling voice that made Mann want to reach out and touch her, just to check she truly was as delightful as she sounded and he didn't imagine her.

'Will you require a room for the night?' Mann asked, unsure whether he hoped she would or wouldn't.

'Yes, I've come to Slutet to find an old friend. It might take me a few days.'

The thought entranced Mann.

'Let me know if I can help in any way,' he said, thinking of ways to extend their conversation beyond the normal innkeeper and patron narrative. 'I've lived in Slutet for many years.'

'Yes, I imagine you have,' Branwen offered again, indicating Mann should refill her red glass. As he did so, he shuddered a little, almost snatching the glass from her hand, but she stopped him, a gentle caress on the back of his hand.

'I'll keep the glass, thank you. It's just the right size.' As she spoke, Mann refilled it, almost wincing as he did so. The bloody red glass still haunted him. He should have refused her request for it, but had simply forgotten its twisted legacy at her instructions.

Behind Branwen's back, the door banged open again. One of Mann's stable hands staggered into the room, heavy bags in both hands and a slim box held under his armpit. Mann appreciated the weight of those belongings.

'Ah, thank you,' Branwen said. 'You are too kind to offer to bring my things inside for me. Is there a room they can be taken to?' Turning back to Mann, she eyed him speculatively.

'Yes, yes, Bubs can take them to Room Five. It's the best one,' Mann said, again failing to consider whether the woman could afford the high price or not.

'Thank you ,Bubs,' Branwen purred. Mann watched with wry amusement as Bubs struggled with his load, completely under Branwen's spell so he didn't even consider arguing, as he usually would have done about going up the wooden stairs to the upper level.

Bubs was far from a young man, untried with women. But

Branwen was not at all the usual sort of woman who travelled to Slutet to view the great expanse of the Hvite Lands and then return home to tell everyone she'd been to the end of the world.

'Did you arrive with the sled?' Mann asked, even though he knew it was a stupid question. There were no other means of travelling to Slutet, and there hadn't been for the nearly five hundred and fifty years he'd lived there. Not for strangers who didn't want to risk becoming lost on the way.

'Yes, the woman, what was her name again? Ensured the journey was smooth and almost pleasant, despite the chill winds.'

'Grundy,' Mann interjected. 'Grundy runs the sleds. And the winds are really not that chill. Not for Slutet.'

'Well, they felt cold to me. I'm used to a more temperate climate.'

She'd taken her red glass to the table closest to the twin fires, and settled herself in one of the fine armchairs. From there they could still speak easily, for the inn remained empty.

'Were there many other people on the sled?' Mann asked, considering if there would be more visitors for the night, or if he could devote all of his time to Branwen?

'Two others,' she began. 'But they seemed to know Grundy, so probably locals.'

Mann might have found the news dismaying, a real dent for his profits, but he was simply pleased to have Branwen to himself. Or he was, until Bubs returned, and hovered close to Branwen.

'My thanks, dearie,' she said to the other man, a lazy smile on her lips.

'Can I do anything else for you?' Bubs asked.

'I'm sure you'd like to, but no, I have all I need. Apart from a bowl of the delicious stew the good innkeeper is serving tonight. Is the meal ready?' she directed her question toward

Mann, but Bubs was already rushing to find a wooden bowl and fill it with the slow-cooked meal from the cooking fire.

Mann allowed him to perform the task. Only when Bubs hovered once more, having placed the bowl before Branwen, did Mann felt compelled to speak.

'Bubs, you're needed in the stables, not in the inn.' Mann knew he sounded a little petulant. Yet Bubs, usually quick to jump to the sound of any slight, only bowed his head and withdrew from the main room of the inn. Mann could hear him stomping his way down the steps, and walking around to the rear of the inn where the stables were sheltered, whistling merrily to himself.

Branwen ate. Mann tried to busy himself around the bar, worried about the red glass and hoping today wasn't the day it disappeared.

'Come, sit with me.' Branwen offered, and with barely a thought, Mann did as instructed.

'Bring the blue bottle,' she commanded. Mann collected it, adding another glass as he made his way to the table she occupied.

He didn't much like the syrupy spirit she'd opted for, but he'd drink it all the same. He was mostly immune to the effects of anything alcoholic. It helped in his role as an innkeeper if he could still drink with all of his customers, but never get drunk.

'This inn belongs to you?' Branwen asked.

'Yes, all of it. A family bequest,' Mann offered, just saying enough, his habitual rectitude surrounding the ownership of the inn winning through despite his desire to do whatever he had to in order to please her.

'A fine building. Old?' she asked.

'Yes, it's stood since the turn of the last millennium, or so I was told by my uncle who left the inn to me.'

'A truly ancient building then. I imagine it's seen a great deal of change in its lifetime.'

The phrase made Mann chuckle loudly, earning himself a questioning look from Branwen. He knew how little the inn had changed throughout his tenure. He knew only too well, and yet he couldn't say as much.

'When I became the owner, I carried out a great deal of repair work to the inn, keen to have it stand for many years to come.'

'I imagine you did,' Branwen muttered softly, almost too low for Mann to hear.

'This stew is delightful. Did you make it? Another old recipe perhaps?' There was a strange inflection to her tone Mann didn't understand. All the same, he shook his head.

'No, I have a woman who comes in and sets the stove for me. She can make the most delicious meals from the most sparse of ingredients.'

'Then I should be complimenting her, and not you.' Branwen teased. Mann felt a silly smile touch his cheeks. What was the matter with him?

'Where do you come from?' Mann tried to make reasoned conversation to cover his response.

'Far, far to the south, somewhere I doubt you've heard of from up in the Hvite Lands.'

'And what it is that you do there?' Mann asked, surprised when he detected a slight hesitation in her response, as though she considered best how to answer.

'A lady of wealth,' she eventually said, offering nothing further.

A silence fell between them, Mann frantically thinking of something to say. He usually spoke easily with the travellers to Slutet, keen to inform them of Slutet's charms, while working out how much he could charge them for staying in his inn.

'And where do you come from, if the inn was left to you by your uncle?'

'Ah, not from far. A small settlement close to the Passen. You probably came through it, and didn't even realise.'

The news seemed to come as a surprise to Branwen, as though she'd been expecting another answer.

Abruptly she stood.

'I think I'll get some rest. Could you show me to my room?'

'Of course, I'll light the brazier as well. It can get cold quickly, even at this time of the year.'

Taking a brand from the fire, and holding it over a small iron box, for just such eventualities, Mann made his way up the stairs, turning to the left as he came to the top. He could hear Branwen following on behind.

Room Five was the furthest from the noise of the main room in the inn, and also benefitted from two small windows. Just enough natural light to not rely on candles when the days were bright.

Opening the door, Mann held it for Branwen to enter, and then made his way to the brazier. She stood in the doorway, half in and half out, as though undecided.

Mann quickly set the dry tinder alight and heaped the waiting fuel upon it before closing the small door, knowing full well the brazier would quickly warm the room.

'There you go,' he offered, with what he hoped was a welcoming smile. 'I'll leave you to rest. It'll be a quiet night, I would hope. Not many locals at this time of the year. If you want to eat again later, just come whenever you fancy it, and if not, then I wish you a good night.'

Mann bobbed his head low as he made his way to the door, but Branwen didn't move. Indeed, she stayed half in the room, while Mann tried to shuffle his way past her. Halfway in and halfway out of the room, Mann felt Branwen move against him, effectively stopping his movements.

'I've heard a great deal about the inn and its innkeeper,' she purred, a hand on his chest, her breath hot on his cheek. He shivered at the touch. He'd been without a woman this iteration of his 'nephew.' Somehow it had felt easier.

'Then I hope I please you,' Mann replied softly.

'I will see,' Branwen said softly. Mann felt his body respond to her delicate touch in ways that were too obvious.

'I'll come down again later,' Branwen eventually said, stepping wholly into her room, waiting for Mann to fully leave the space.

'Then I'll speak to you later,' Mann hoped his sudden hunger for her wasn't reflected in his voice, like it was in other places.

Once behind his bar, the red glass back in his hand so he could move it away from Branwen's sight, Mann sighed heavily.

Branwen had a strange effect on him. One he'd not experienced for a very long time, if ever. So much so, he still didn't know if she could actually afford the charge for the room and for staying in his inn. Never, in all his years, had he allowed anyone to even sip a drink without coin changing hands. He'd learnt that from Grans, the man who'd gambled his pub away, much to Mann's advantage.

The thought of Grans turned Mann melancholy. Once he'd understood his strangely long life, he'd become more distant from people. But back then, when he'd had Freg, Onna and even Grans and the three whores, he'd become involved in them and missed them a great deal when they'd all died, one after another, leaving him with the inn and a long life, and no explanation. Even now.

Marnit's death still cut him, as did the knowledge Haune had never again spoken to him for all she'd lived a good, long life in Bosetting. There were even occasions when he'd have welcomed the constant bickering and distrust from Sand and Rad.

Time and again, Mann had tried not to form friendships

and bonds with people, but it was hard, and time and again, he'd failed and mourned lost loved ones.

Not that he'd gone out of his way to find an answer to his longevity, but it was evident to him, festooned as he was with the tattoos of the never-ending symbol once given to him by Helbe, one for each year he'd lived, that there was a purpose to his long life.

Yet, he was marooned in the Hvite Lands. He'd tried to get through the Passen on only one occasion, with Freg, but he'd been unable to make it through conscious. His throat had drawn tight. He'd been forced to return to the Hvite Lands before consciousness returned.

How could he ever learn his life's task, if he even had one, if he was stuck in Slutet?

There had even been occasions when he'd wished his encounters with Brag, Bothal and Shlat hadn't ended as they had. After all, perhaps they'd held answers for him. But no. Brag had killed Marnit, Mann was sure of it, and no matter the times he might have considered hunting him down for answers, it had only ever been revenge on his mind, and not a desire for answers to any of the bewildering events of his first 'death.'

That Mann had never seen any of them again assured him, after all, he'd not been the person they hunted for. Even though he'd come to think he must have been.

Disgruntled with his thoughts, Mann waited for Branwen to appear, becoming even more out of sorts when she failed to do so. She'd promised much but was apparently not going to fulfil those promises. With no one in the inn, Mann barred the door tight and stomped his own way to bed.

His dreams that night were strange and bizarre, so he woke, sweating, irritable and unable to remember where his mind had taken him.

Lying in bed, he heard a thud from somewhere in his inn

and was reminded of Branwen. He hauled himself out of bed, dressing for the day, and stumbled downstairs.

His cook, Tane, was busy at work, a range of foodstuffs around her. She was chatting more animatedly than Mann thought he'd ever heard before. She was, as he was, a person of few words. Slow to anger, slow to please, he and Tane were very much of a muchness.

Surprised, Mann went to investigate, unsurprised Branwen was sitting beside Tane, watching everything she did, her eyes bright with interest.

'Good morning, Tane, Branwen,' he decided on being civil, and pleasantries exchanged, quickly made his way to the bar, and then, when he could feel Branwen's appraising eyes on him, even lower, into his cellar.

The smell of the cellar was always a comfort to him. Here he could hide from everyone in Slutet and also from himself, if he needed to.

Inhaling the comforting scent, he sought for his usual equanimity and when he failed to find it, took himself to another source of comfort, his wooden moneybox. Ancient now, and with only his key remaining, he quickly opened it, and saw everything was as it should be inside.

He used to fear the day he visited the cellar, and all of his reserves had disappeared, back through time to help him in an earlier bind. Yet, one night in a fit of frustration, he'd made sure the coins, all of them, that had appeared to him within the inn so many years ago, were always inside another of his moneyboxes. That one he kept hidden behind the more noticeable one, the lock always open, and the coins always inside it. To either side of the secret stash, he also kept two stacks of coins, again, ones he knew he'd lose when the time came for those items to disappear from him.

Surveying his cellar, Mann saw all he'd so far managed to gather. The clothes that had saved his life were there, as were the hat, sealskin gloves and the pair of boots that both fitted him, and the one that didn't fit him. He still shook his head in amusement when he considered that. The ancient skis he'd bought in Bosetting were also there, and so too was the rucksack that had come to him. Yet there were still items missing. He'd never yet found the torch and had lost the original one, many years ago. Neither was there anything he could do about the cooked meat he'd savoured on that night.

One day his stew pot would be missing a goodly portion of his dinner.

Some of the items had already disappeared from his life, most notably on the night he'd realised the items he'd seemingly summoned from nowhere were actually his own. As to Jemp, he had no idea when the man would reappear, or even if he would.

There was also a large barrel of beer, he replaced routinely, but which he knew would one day disappear.

Sighing heavily, he sought to find his good humour.

'A man with worries,' a light voice asked. Mann turned in shock to find Branwen standing before him.

'How did you get down here?' he asked, hastily closing his moneybox, and turning to check how his cellar might appear to those who couldn't possibly suspect his secret.

'The ladder, dearie,' she purred, and Mann allowed that.

'My,' she said, sweeping her hands along the tightly packed shelves, a low whistle coming from between her lips. 'A very, very well stocked bar,' she muttered, arching an eyebrow as she came across another of the blue bottles she'd drunk from the night before. Only then her hand lingered over another.

'Although, this here has always been my favourite.' She lifted the bottle, delicately removing the stopper to inhale of the too sweet fragrance inside. Mann grimaced as the aroma wafted over to him.

'How does this come to be here? And accompanied by so

many little companions.' She squealed with delight. Mann's ill-humour evaporated as she watched her evident pleasure at his stash of fine wines and spirits.

'I have good contacts,' Mann offered, and then noticing the thick sheen of dust added, 'as did my uncle, and his relatives before him.'

'My, my dearie,' she purred once more, 'you certainly did. A fortune in exquisite delicacies and no one to appreciate them, I would have thought.' She paused, as though waiting for him to disagree with her, but she was right.

There had been a time when he and Freg had delighted in their trading contacts with Helbe. Mann doubted he'd touched any of the bottles since her death, and then, within two decades, that of Marnit's.

'Shall we sample just a smidge,' Branwen smiled. Mann found himself already reaching for two mugs, left in the cellar so he could sample the beer and ale when he needed to do so.

'Why not upstairs?' she trilled, already making her way back up the ladder, the bottle held tightly in one hand, as she wound her way up the small space.

Returning the two mugs to their place, Mann again swept a glance around the cellar. Aside from the dust and the vast quantities of bottles and jugs, containing countless fripperies, he was sure there was little else of interest. Apart from the spare clothes, and the boots. But they, he hoped, were well hidden behind the spare barrel of beer.

Peering through the cellar door, Mann caught a swish of Branwen's beautiful blue dresses, as she made her way to the other side of the bar. A stirring of desire reminded him of the brief time he'd lived only for his own pleasure. Could he do so again? Did he even want to?

Carefully, he followed Branwen up the ladder and then returned the cellar door to its correct position, before standing. Branwen was sitting opposite him, the red glass he'd thought hidden well, in one of her own hands, a smirk on her face no doubt for finding it, against his wishes.

Bemused by her determination, Mann reached for a green glass to match the other, as though it meant nothing to him. She delicately poured him a small quantity.

Immediately, the inn filled with the slightly sickly smell of the drink, but it was heady as well. Lifting her glass high so the mixture seemed to pulse in the light from the lamps, Branwen toasted his glass, and then swallowed the liquid in one greedy gulp. Mann followed suit, for all it was too early for him to be drinking.

At the fireplaces, Tane fussed with her ingredients, a tuneless whistle coming from between her lips. Mann had almost forgotten the older woman was there. She was almost bent double, her black dress more grey than anything else, her bones showing through the fabric, so skinny was she. Mann knew she never ate as much as she needed to, and it wasn't because of a lack of coin.

'Another,' Branwen asked, already pouring into the two glasses, without awaiting his response.

Mann could feel the strong drink having an immediate effect on him, but he smiled and sipped again, trying not to grimace. He wasn't a fan of one of his customers being able to consume more than him.

'Oh dearie, you like?' Branwen giggled, sipping her drink coquettishly.

He hiccupped a laugh. He didn't much, but Mann wasn't about to say so.

Instead, he aligned his glass with hers and poured two more shots. She swayed a little on her stool. He laughed. Hopefully, this little game would be over soon.

Once more she swigged her glass empty. Mann mirrored her movement.

Out of the corner of his eye, Mann could see Tane had

finished her work and was preparing to leave. She only ever stayed as long as she had to inside the inn. She wasn't a drinker, and neither did she like the company of others. Mann reached under the bar, ready to exchange coins with her for the labour. She'd never accept payment upfront, only on the day she actually performed her task.

The transaction was always carried out silently, and today was no different. He watched her walk away, amused when she swayed a little, or he did. It was impossible to tell.

When Tane was gone out the main door, he and Branwen were alone, with nothing but the bar between them and a, by now, half-filled, bottle of spirit.

Mann considered what might happen next, as Branwen again filled their glasses. Was this her attempt to entice him to her bed, or was it something else? He honestly didn't know.

With the next drink consumed, Mann turned to gaze at the door. It was unbarred, and any could come inside if they chose to. But the street outside was quiet, few around in the middle of the day because they had their own professions. Should he bar the door, on the off-chance he wasn't misreading the situation?

Staggering from behind the bar, Mann turned, and Branwen was beside him.

Her breath was sweet with the scent of the drink, as she licked her lips, pressing herself against him.

'You don't know me, do you?' Branwen purred, but he was too drunk to truly comprehend the intention behind her words.

'No, but I'd like to,' he offered. She laughed, throwing her head back so her warm neck stretched out before him, just waiting for lips to caress it.

'Then I suggest we have another drink,' she slurred, reaching again for her glass and the dusty bottle. Mann reached out to intercept her.

'I think maybe we've both had enough,' he murmured, his lips connecting with her neck as a shiver of delight rushed over him. She turned her head, keen to reciprocate.

Mann was unprepared for the explosion of heat that engulfed him, and he stepped back, confused, while Branwen's golden eyes danced. She licked her own lips, perhaps savouring the taste of him, as she had the spirit she'd drunk.

'The drink?' she said, but Mann was far from convinced. He tried to ignore his growing excitement, going so far as to put the bar between them once more, but Branwen reached over and ran her hand over his cheek and then along his lips.

'There's no point in resisting,' she mused. She leaned over the bar, her hand still on his face, holding him still so her lips could connect with his own.

Again, a bolt of surprise shot through Mann, as their lips touched, and he found himself powerless to resist, as Branwen had said.

Only when he leaned so far forward the myriad pieces of the bar stuck into his body, reminding him he even had one, was he able to break away. He was breathing heavily, Branwen doing the same, and both bit lips as though daring the other to deny what was happening.

Gulping, Mann stepped around the bar, this time staying far from Branwen as he went to fix the door bar in place. He and Branwen didn't need interrupting, not when their passion was running so high.

As he turned to return to her side, she stood in front of him, hands reaching for him, her need evident in the high colour on her cheeks.

Without further thought he engulfed her in his arms, their lips reconnecting, and never again coming apart, no matter how long they remained molded to each other.

In his chest, his heart thudded, and his breath came faster and faster. It took all of his resolve to lift her into his arms, make his way up the stairs of the inn, and take her to her room number five, where they finally succumbed to their passionate needs.

———

When he woke, the room was cold and dark, but the bed wasn't, and so he lingered, the aroma of Branwen rich in the air.

When Mann considered their antics together, he was surprised by one thing. There had been real passion there, a genuine need. Yet they'd been soft and gentle with each, their love-making slow and luxurious. He'd only known such care before when he and Freg had spent so many years together.

The thought disturbed him slightly, the feeling that the connection with Branwen was so quick and complete when he hardly knew anything about her, other than her name.

With firm resolve, Mann stood and busied himself with restocking the brazier, by the light of a single lamp.

Only then did he dash from the room, the smell of his dinner wafting up the stairs, to remind him the food would spoil if not tended to.

Naked, apart from his trousers, Mann leapt to swing the cauldron from above the twin hearth. He stirred vigorously with the long metal spoon waiting for such a task, pleased to find the meal hadn't burned. Turning to the side, Mann splashed a jug of water into the cauldron, enough to cool it a little, and swung the entire contraption to the side, where it rested, near the heat but not over the intense heat of the heart of the fire.

A banging at the door reminded him he might have customers, and he hastened to let them inside. Lifting the door bar, he remembered his nakedness, and hurriedly returned the wooden bar, while he sought for something to cover the strange repeating pattern on his chest.

Shrugging a coat over himself, he removed the heavy bar and opened the door. Two people stood on the other side of the door, concern on their faces that dissolved when they saw him.

'Bloody hell. What you been doing?' the smaller of the two said, stomping his way inside, without so much as a hello.

'It's time to eat,' the other said, rubbing his stomach as though he'd never been fed in his entire life.

'Apologies, come in. I was resting,' Mann explained, gesturing to his outfit. 'I'll go and dress. Just give the meal a few moments yet. Help yourself to drinks.' He said the words and then winced. His servants didn't know him for his generosity. It would instantly make them suspicious of what he'd really been up to. But it was too late, the words were said, and so he left them hanging in the air, and bounced back up the stairs in search of his tunic.

He found it discarded on the floor, in room number five. It was warmer in there now, but the figure in the bed snored softly, and so, picking up his shirt and his boots, he quickly closed the door and dressed.

When Branwen woke, he hoped she'd not be too angry with him for abandoning her. After all, he had a business to run. He couldn't spend his time lounging in bed.

Mann laughed at himself. Despite his slight worry, his steps felt light as he skipped down the stairs once more, avoiding the knowing looks from his two men, the stableman and the stableboy.

'What news from the south?' Mann asked. The two were always eager to be told everything and anything when the sled arrived. They'd have spent their time tracking down and chatting with any of the locals who might have arrived the day before.

'Everyone was talking about the woman and some strange

event in the Passen. But it was all a bit vague.' Bubs sounded disappointed the haul of news wasn't better. During the warmer weather, if it could be called as such in the Hvite Lands, he always expected to hear much about the world beyond the Passen.

Mann wasn't fussed about anything from beyond the Passen. He was content with Slutet and little else. After all, if he couldn't go there, why care about events happening to people he'd never meet?

Mann went to join his servants, the closest to friends he currently had, and then, his stomach rumbling, stood again and filled and handed around three wooden bowls stuffed to the top with Tane's creation. With no guests, other than Branwen, they could all enjoy superior portions. It might not make him any coin, but sometimes, he preferred the inn to be quiet, and the food to be plentiful.

They ate and drank, Mann noticing even though he'd offered them whatever they wanted they'd taken only a mug of ale. He appreciated their due diligence. As the evening wore on, Witent produced a deck of cards and began to deal them.

Mann chuckled to see the cards, a reminder of how he'd come to own the inn, but the three played only with broken bits of coins found in the inn. There was a small container filled with them, which Bubs grabbed and divided up.

Mann took away their wooden bowls, all burping and full, and replaced the drinks, with something a little stronger, and more to the men's liking. He was filled with good cheer, keen to share his agreeable humour while Branwen slept. Once she woke, he doubted he'd be sitting around playing cards for any significant length of time.

The fires burned low as they played, Bubs occasionally restocking them with small pieces of wood, more for the light than the heat. Eventually, the conversation fell away, and so did the card playing. It was late, way past time to retire for the night.

It was Witent who made a move first, standing and yawning. The two had rooms within the inn, but they were accessed from an outside door, separated from the rooms of the guests and within easy reach of the stables.

Bubs joined Witent, and together they made their way to the front door. Mann watched them go, laughing and talking with them, before once more barring the entry to all visitors. He moved around the inn slowly, checking everything was in its right place, before thinking to wash the bowls and spoons, glasses and mugs, and to ensure the remaining food, and there was enough for a few portions yet, was well away from the heat of the fire.

Then he sat back in his chair, two glasses in front of him, and the dusty glass bottle, now only half full, before him. He settled to wait, eyes half closed, his mind wondering and considering the events of the day.

A soft hand on his face brought him back to the here and now, as he gazed into Branwen's golden eyes. He'd been sure earlier they had a strange hue to them, and now he was sure of it, not quite yellow, closer to golden sunshine. Almost entirely normal, but not quite.

'Hello dearie,' she breathed, her lips almost on his as she spoke.

'You slept a long time,' Mann offered, his breath already catching in his throat, heartbeat immediately raised as she ran her soft hand over his cheeks before coming to rest on his lips.

'You wore me out,' she laughed, kissing him soundly. 'But now I'm hungry,' she pouted, 'and in need of a drink.' He leapt to fulfil her demands, while she sat and poured herself a drink.

The bowl he handed her was as generously filled as the ones he and his companions had enjoyed, and she sniffed appreciatively.

'The smell of this infected my dreams,' she laughed, dipping her spoon in and carefully moving it to her mouth. 'I think I could eat enough to last three days.' She laughed softly, amused by her joke.

Mann settled to the silence, toying with his drink Branwen had poured, determined not to watch her eat for fear of making her self-conscious. They would either talk, or they wouldn't, but they had all night and no one to interrupt them.

'I didn't expect to find you here,' Branwen whispered, as she pushed her now empty bowl aside. Mann wasn't sure if he should have heard those words or not and chose to let them pass without questioning her. What she said could have had many meanings.

'I don't usually do such things,' she eventually said, her eyes on the logs burning in the fireplace, the flame a gentle yellow and orange because the more combustible material was reserved for the heart of winter.

'Me neither,' Mann replied, hoping they spoke of the same thing.

'But sometimes there's no choice, I suppose,' she wheedled, as though trying to convince herself, not him.

'Apparently not,' he concurred, reaching over the table to twine his fingers through hers. She didn't pull away, but instead leaned closer to him, a smile curling her lips.

'It won't last,' she whispered, 'nothing like this ever could.'

He silenced her worries with a kiss. Not that he didn't agree with her, but for now he was content to allow whatever must happen, to happen without fear of a future that already stretched out too long before him, lonely, and always alone.

———

Mann was woken by soft hands on his chest, and he peeled back his eyes to see Branwen scrutinising him. Swearing, he reached for a shirt, thinking to cover his markings, but she held him steady.

'They're very delicate,' she offered, sliding herself lower down his body, a coy smile on her face. He might have expected her to question the strange decoration on his body more but was quickly distracted by her gyrating against him, reaching out to bring her lips to his.

She chuckled, the sound exciting him even more, and only later, when they lay panting beside each other, did he remember her examination of him. But before he could ask her about it, there was a banging on the door of the inn. Mann once more found himself leaping from the bed. No doubt it was Tane, keen to be about her duties, or even a customer, although that would surprise him.

'Run away, innkeeper, I'll be here when you can spare the time.' For a moment, he took it as a criticism and turned sharply, but Branwen was watching him with a smile in her golden eyes.

'As soon as I can, I'll return,' Mann promised, dressing hastily, and rushing down the stairs.

Tane's toothless grin met his as he yanked open the door. She barely gave him a glance, but shuffled inside, keen to be done. His two servants were also there, slightly embarrassed smiles on their faces.

'She asked us to help wake you,' Witent tried to explain. Mann was in too good a mood to berate them.

'Get back to the stables, and see to whatever needs seeing to,' Mann complained, turning away from them.

'There's little to do,' Bubs whined. Mann knew what was coming next. He could, he supposed, allow the pair of them inside for the day. They were skilled enough at keeping the bar for him, and as they'd shown last night, they didn't always abuse his generosity.

'Then perhaps you could tend the inn for me,' Mann

offered. 'I've other tasks requiring my attention.' He considered the word 'task' carefully before saying it, but even so, the two exchanged knowing looks with each other. Mann allowed it without rebuke.

They weren't bad individuals. They couldn't be. Mann had long ago refused to accept anyone within his inn he couldn't tolerate for extended amounts of time. It was almost impossible to know when you might next be marooned in Slutet by the weather.

This pleased the two, despite their meaningful glances. They leapt to look as though busy about their work. Mann nipped down into his cellar, retrieving a selection of coins, ensuring he had the ones Tane would require for her services.

Other than that, Mann could think of nothing that might cause problems for his servants, and so, pointing out the coins, and leaving Tane's on the bar, he leapt back up the stairs, taking two steps at a time. Yet, room number five was deserted, the bed cold. Turning, Mann peered over the banister just to be sure he'd not missed Branwen. Perplexed, he turned and made his way to his room, shivering as he opened the door, for he'd neglected his brazier, which never usually went out. Quickly, he rebuilt his fire, before realising where Branwen had gone.

His inn, as small as it was, still boasted a hot room, complete with bath, and it was always kept running, for who knew when anyone might need to feel clean. It was a relatively new addition, if you could count two hundred years old as new.

Mann knocked on the wooden door and opened it wide. Inside, steam obscured his view, but he caught a hint of warmed, naked flesh, and quickly stepped fully inside.

A flicker of long, golden hair and he knew he'd found Branwen. She was more than aware of his arrival, yet she didn't speak, continuing her ablutions.

Mann watched her, intrigued, as she combed her long hair, shimmering with dampness, and plaited it.

'Well, you could help,' she complained, unfazed she sat naked before him. Again, he hastened to do her bidding without thought. As he reached for her hair, his finger strayed onto her shoulder, and a shiver of excitement rushed through him.

Mann tried to concentrate on her hair, but it was impossible, as she sat before him, unclothed. All he wanted to do was continue their love-making. Branwen was hardly trying to not entice him. Eventually, his lips slipped to her shoulders, and then her neck, before he kissed her once more, and she returned the intimate gesture.

'I doubt there's room for two,' she moaned, but even that increased his passion, as he slipped from his clothes, and slid into the bath beside her. It was, as Branwen had suggested, almost too small for the pair of them, but all the same, he managed to find room, and then pulled Branwen to him. She came with a smile, perhaps even a smirk for his keenness and ingenuity.

Settling over him, her legs mingling with his, she kissed him again, her tongue lingering inside his mouth. She moved over him and began to gently rock. The sensation was exquisite, apart from the occasional slap of displaced water over the side of the bathing tub.

He moaned and groaned, Branwen enjoying herself as much as he was, and only when they'd finished their pleasure of each other, did she settle herself in the tub, her back to the wood.

'I can't imagine we'll be very clean now,' Branwen complained, her damp hair tangled and knotted. He shrugged gamely.

'There's always warm water,' he offered. 'A woman like

you is much rarer.' As he spoke, his hand caressed her chin. She licked his hand.

'As is a man such as you.' She laughed as she spoke, dunking her head under the water, as she again began the task of washing her hair.

Mann watched her and thought of nothing else.

'Tell me,' Branwen asked, later, when they'd finally removed themselves from the bathing room and back to room number five. 'Why is it your reputation travels far and wide, but never you?'

The question startled Mann, for all it was one he was used to being asked. He somehow felt it would be harder to lie to Branwen, but he tried, all the same.

'I prefer the cold and the winds, the isolation and the loneliness.' He hadn't meant to sound quite so miserable, and even his laugh at the end of the sentence sounded forced.

'Oh really,' she asked. 'And what have you seen of the south?'

'Nothing,' Mann confirmed. 'Nothing, I only know what others tell me. The inn, of course, keeps me busy.'

'Of course,' she confirmed with light laughter. 'Always your precious inn.' Still, she smiled. Yet Mann could hear the complaint in her voice.

'Tell me, why have you never been to Slutet before? A woman such as you, who travels so widely, could have been here more than once, surely?'

'Oh dearie, there's so much more of this world than you could possibly know, stuck here, in the cold and the ice, with the snow and the loneliness. It takes a special sort of person to appreciate this, as it were.'

Again, Mann felt as though he was being mocked, but Branwen quickly made light of it.

'I suppose with the trade routes, you can get anything you want, whenever you want it, anyway. Even if you don't yet know what it is t you want?' Her eyebrows rose as she spoke. Mann chuckled.

'What is it, fine lady, that you believe I'm missing from the south?'

Sharpness snapped in her eyes. Yet she waved her hand as though dismissing her quick show of rage.

'You'll never know what it is to feel truly warm, to have the sun warm your skin, instead of flames.'

'Is that it?' he asked. 'Just heat? I can have as many baths as I like, to keep warm.'

'Well there are foods, and people and places. Buildings you should see, places you could go. Have you ever seen the sea?'

'Why would I wish to see the sea? It's black with cold and good only for hunting seals and fish.'

Again, Branwen laughed.

'Ah, there are many more delicacies of the sea that would delight you, and it's not always black with cold, but often warmed by the sun, and gentle on your skin. The salt can even heal those with afflictions of the flesh.'

'Even so, I'm content in Slutet.'

'But there are only about forty-five houses. How can you live your life knowing so few people?'

Now his forehead creased in thought.

'I don't wish to know more than that. How would I ever remember all their names?' Branwen giggled softly, the conversation dying away.

In the evening, Branwen appeared in the main room of the inn. Her skin glowed with warmth and the sheen of precious metal. Mann blazed to see her. The inn was a little busier than the previous night. Mann had little time to speak with her as he served patrons and refereed games of chance and cards.

She sat with Bubs and Witent, Grundy also joining them.

Mann feared to know what they spoke about. Every time he passed their table they were laughing, although Branwen's eyes never left him, no matter where he was in the inn.

She'd pushed aside her favourite spirit, and now drank a dark wine, fruity with the hint of the south, relishing each and every mouthful. Mann found it difficult to concentrate, relying only on his years of experience, all of them, to ensure he didn't make a fool of himself. He even found it hard to calculate the bar bill of his patrons and was sure he undercharged and would be out of pocket, no matter how many people he served that night.

After the last patron had left, Bubs and Witent ensuring they staggered their way home well enough, Branwen stood beside him.

'You're comfortable here,' she snapped, a strange sentiment to anger her. Yet she didn't pause for his answer, before stamping her way back to room number five, and slamming the door behind her.

Mann was perplexed but held his tongue. They were just casual lovers, nothing else. She had no true hold on him. All the same, he knew the sentiment to be false, even as he thought it.

As he cleared the bar, carrying out a routine that had calmed him most of his long life, his thoughts kept returning to her, and pining for her.

In the end, instead of retiring to his bedchamber for the night, he sat beside the fire, content to listen to the crackle of the banked fire rather than his own thoughts. There was peace to be found in such a simple act. The inn settled to the night around him, the familiar creaks and groans assuring him all was well, even the long distant grunt of his reindeer, restoring his equanimity.

Who was Branwen, after all, to waltz into his inn, into his bed, or rather he into hers, and then question his life choices? If she left the following day, then so be it. He knew Grundy was heading off to Langt, as he'd asked for a variety of items to be brought to him, or if not available, to be ordered from the traders further south. They'd included a bottle or three of Branwen's favourite spirit, but he might cancel that order now.

Or perhaps not. He really wasn't sure.

Eventually, he appreciated Branwen wasn't coming to him, and he doused all but one of the lamps and made his way to his bedchamber. A night of uninterrupted sleep would be good for him.

Only when he arrived in his bedchamber, there was another already asleep in his bed. He smirked. They'd both been waiting for each other, only in the wrong places.

Quickly he undressed and slid into bed beside her, trying not to let the warmth out. It was far from freezing, but all the same, it was a pleasant change to climb into a prewarmed bed. Branwen didn't stir at his movements, or as he rolled over and enclosed her in his arms.

He sighed with happiness.

———

Three months later, Mann watched Branwen affectionately. She was up to her elbows cleaning out one of Tane's cook pots, listening to the older woman talk. Branwen liked to cook. She wasn't very good at it, as Mann often endured, but she was keen, and Tane was happy to instruct her, even when it meant repeating herself every other day.

He and Branwen hadn't ever spoken about the future. There seemed little point. They were devoted to each other, the passion running strong whenever they were alone together.

But he couldn't deny t every so often he was confused by her questions and obvious disapproval of his answers.

Mann remembered when they'd first met she'd said she

didn't expect to find him here. Who then had she come hoping to find? The question confounded him, whenever he thought of it, which admittedly, wasn't that often. Certainly, Branwen had made no attempt to find anyone else in Slutet, even though she'd used the excuse to explain her arrival.

Now, Mann busied himself in his cellar, chuckling, as he restocked the shelves of rare spirits he and Branwen had been slowly making their way through. Branwen's meal that night, when it was cooked, might be edible, or it might not. Either way, he'd still have to eat it. Bubs and Witent wouldn't. They'd taken to keeping stores for themselves in the stables. Small cook pots, which Tane prepared for them when she suspected a Branwen-sized disaster coming.

Yet, as they all sat down to eat that night, the inn deserted apart from the four of them, Mann sniffed in delight. It smelt good, and even Bubs and Witent were managing to look half-excited.

Carefully Branwen, her hair tied back in a long braid to prevent it slipping into their meal, spooned four bowls of deli-cious looking, wild-caught stewed reindeer. Mann watched hungrily, and then he blinked, and then he groaned.

His own bowl, handed to him by a brightly smiling Branwen had contained the most substantial chunk of meat of the four, but in-between Branwen serving it, and Mann receiving it, the damn meat had disappeared with a strange ringing sound in the air.

Bollocks. Of all the bloody times! Mann fumed, and then, ensuring no one could see his bowl, dug hungrily into what remained. Luckily, there were copious amounts of root vegeta-bles for him, as well as some rare mushrooms, grown in the dark of Tane's cellar, and only rarely shared.

He joined in with the praise from Bubs and Witent aimed at Branwen and hoped there might be more for him when his bowl was cleared. Branwen's scrutiny was intense, and at one point he even found himself pretending to chew the lost meat, because she was looking at him oddly.

'More?' she asked, pleasantly. Mann nodded, relieved to be getting more. 'There's just vegetables and mushrooms,' she admitted, returning his bowl to him, refilled, and Mann nodded, ruing his missing dinner.

Still, he had to admit, it could have happened at a far worse time, and at least he now knew what he'd eaten that first night of his manifestation, all those many years ago.

———

Winter coated the land as he shivered in his bed, trying not to consider the necessity of getting out of it.

The night before the inn had been raucous, filled with people he didn't know who'd come to Slutet just for the sake of it so they could say they'd been to the far north in winter. They were lucky. The winter storms had yet to strike in their full ferocity. They'd be able to leave come the morning. Not everyone was as lucky.

Branwen had distanced herself from much of the conversation, and indeed, she'd slipped away to her room during the evening. Mann had chosen not to join her. He'd been tired beyond imagining, and her silent mood had warned him he wasn't required. Not then, and probably not now. All the same, he reached across the bed, hopeful she might have changed her mind. But her side of the bed was cold, abandoned, and that enticed him to risk leaving his bed.

Hastily he dressed, bounding from one foot to another. The night had been bitterly cold. His brazier, while warming the room, was ineffectual against the cold wooden beams of the floor.

Before he left his room, Mann reached for the heavy keychain holding the key for the doors of the inn, all of them, and then squinted in the gloom, unable to find them. Scrunching his face, he ran his hand over the scared wooden surface of his dresser one more time and left the room, confounded. Perhaps, as unlikely as it was, he'd left them behind his bar.

As he passed room number five he thought longingly of Branwen in her warm bed. Yet he forced himself to concentrate on the task at hand. He needed the keys to open the inn.

By the banked light from the hearth fires, and his own memory, Mann walked behind the bar, running his hand along the ledge that normally held the keys during the day. He came up empty-handed. Where had the keys gone?

Bewildered Mann looked up into the eyes of Tane.

'You're up early,' she called, the door already closed behind her.

'Was the door open?' Mann asked, confused. He got no reply but a grunt, which he took for a yes. Hastily he dashed to the door. It wasn't like him to leave it unlocked. The ring of heavy keys rested in the wooden lock. He'd never leave the keys in the locking mechanism. Never.

'What the?' Mann asked himself, yanking them out and peering outside.

It was a bright, clear morning, the grey of night hovering at the distant edges of the open sky, but mostly it was gone.

Mann went to slam the door shut, but then he caught the sound of a voice he knew well and watched in shock as Grundy directed her sled out of Slutet, and toward Langt. Branwen was settled beside her, and Mann recognised her luggage in the back of the sled.

'What the hell?' Mann said again, his heart sinking at the sight. He didn't bother to shout or run after the sled. Branwen had made her mind up.

He'd thought her silence of the night before had been

because the inn was busy, not because she'd decided to end their relationship.

Hurt, tears almost brimming from his eyes, Mann turned back into the inn, Tane watching him with compassion.

'The bitch runs high, and then runs altogether,' she commented, with some sympathy.

'Did you know?' he asked the older woman, unsurprised when she shook her head.

'No, but I suspected. Branwen liked to play the part of your lover. But Slutet was too small for her. What is there here for a woman like her other than you?'

Even those words hurt. Mann clamped his mouth shut, afraid to say anything more for fear of what Tane's reply might be.

'Will she come back?' he finally asked, of no one, although Tane answered all the same.

'One day, when she's bored of everywhere else.'

It wasn't the least bit of comfort.

TWENTY-EIGHT

SLUTET INN – THE MILLENNIUM

Chapter 28

SLOWLY THE INTERIOR of the inn came into focus as Mann wrenched himself back from his memories.

Branwen was watching him with fondness, that hardened as soon as she realised he scrutinised her with his eyes firmly on the present, and not the past.

'Well dearie,' she battered her delicious eyelids at him. 'This could be a most interesting night, all things considered.'

Mann was unsure which part of his story she referred to but was distracted by Blane, who'd sidled close to Branwen and sat beside her now. He was watching Mann with his impenetrable silver eyes, as though he too had found the answer to many of his questions.

Mann glared at him. He hadn't wanted the other man to listen to his reminiscences about Branwen.

'Now, you tell me of your life,' Mann asked softly, keen to hear she'd missed him, or some such, or even where she'd gone after their time together. Or even, and he smiled slightly, that she was back because, as Tane had once offered, she was 'bored.'

But Blane hissed, perhaps a warning, and resolve settled

over Branwen's face. He'd be getting nothing from her. Not tonight. Mann cursed the silver-haired man for interfering. If only he could get Branwen away from here, perhaps to his room, then he could lean on her to tell him more.

Around him, the work of the inn, and of enjoying the turn of the millennia continued apace. He suddenly saw it all with jaundiced eyes. All this was his, but according to Branwen, it would be gone between one blink and the next.

'Ah bollocks,' Mann screeched, winking, and then blinking again as though unable to believe what he was seeing.

At the sound, both Branwen and Blane turned to see what had so shocked Mann, as a low rumble of amusement swept through Branwen's body.

'Ah, the inestimable Jemp, I wondered when you'd make an appearance. Leaving it a little late, aren't you.'

Mann's jaw dropped in disbelief as before him, Jemp finally reappeared. Mann had long considered what had happened to Jemp to be a total mystery. Certainly, he'd never dared utter the same words again, not after his failure with the coins. It was apparent his abilities didn't extend to making people or things disappear. Taking them somewhere was acceptable, but losing them for all time wasn't.

Jemp stood, still in the same clothes as when they'd last met, so many years ago, looking both out of place and yet totally at home. He wore a scowl of annoyance as well as his cloak of thick fur.

'You bloody bastard,' Jemp muttered, face contorted with sudden anger as he spotted Mann. 'I had sodding things to get done,' Jemp complained, and then looked around, noting faces and location, but not recognising either.

'Where the bloody hell am I?' Jemp complained. It was Branwen who answered.

'Slutet, my dear, on the eve of the new millennium.'

'I should have bloody guessed,' Jemp answered bitterly.

'Where have you been?' Mann asked, his curiosity getting the better of him.

'I was in Bosetting, and now I'm in Slutet. I was just there, and now I'm here. You bloody idiot. You can't do that to a person!' There was a screech of outrage in Jemp's voice that turned to disbelief when he spied Jenna, still sleeping.

'What did you do to her?' Jemp gasped, his grievances seemingly forgotten about in the outrage at what had happened to Jenna, as he rushed to her side.

'She was her usual self,' Blane muttered dryly, as though that explained everything that needed to be known.

Behind Branwen's back, Jemp bent low to try and wake Jenna, despite Blane's repeated requests he not. Not that there was any significant threat to Blane's demands, instead he sounded bored, as seemed to be the case about everything in the short time Mann had known Blane.

Branwen fixed Mann with a harsh stare, trying to force Mann back to their conversation,

'What's important now is you remember what you've forgotten, or this will all happen again, with no resolution in sight, and quite frankly, I miss flushing toilets.'

Mann was amused by Branwen's wry tone, even if he didn't understand what she was talking about. What, after all, was a flushing toilet? It sounded different to the latrine he kept, and which had to be scoured clean every so often to prevent the smell permeating the interior of the inn.

'I know nothing, other than what I've told you.'

'Yes, but what you've told me is actually quite a lot. You need to decipher what it is you've missed out of your narrative, and then, well then, things will happen, as they must.' She shrugged as she spoke, her hand encircling the mug before her.

Mann fell to silence, his forehead furrowed, aware, from the sand timer he'd turned on the bar the new millennia was almost upon him. How could he possibly work out what it was he didn't know in the remaining time?

He'd lived a millennium without ever discovering what it was, or who he was. And it seemed many people who did know who he was, and what he was, had come into contact with him, and yet they'd said nothing to him. Mainly because he'd denied being the person they sought. But that hadn't always been the case.

Perhaps that was why Branwen had left him, all that time ago? Was it his failure to make any attempt to understand what he was?

'Was it because I was shackled to Slutet that you left me?' Mann finally asked, trying to decide what it was about his life that had been most restricted because of his strange abilities. His grief from her leaving was still raw, even now. Half a year together and he'd pined for her ever since, in a way he'd never thought of Freg, or he never considered when he thought of Halla or any of the other women who'd graced his bed throughout that time.

'You weren't shackled to anything,' Branwen complained, 'apart from your own ignorance.' She turned her back on him, involving herself in the on-going conversation, now almost an argument, between Blane and Jemp about Jenna's still form.

Mann sulked, just a little, at her dismissal of his questions.

All these mysteries and never any answers. There was a reason he'd stopped thinking about it all when he'd first been forced to 'die' and then return as himself, avoiding the plotting of Brag at the same time, and being forced to live with the knowledge he'd been responsible for Marnit's death.

Thinking of that time reminded him of the strange events he'd witnessed in Bosetting so long ago. The place no longer existed. It had been abandoned after a particularly violent winter, which few had survived, although Slutet had endured the battering without problems.

It had taken a century, maybe even two, before someone had begun the new settlement at Langt, to the south of Slutet, and almost directly north of the Passen. Not that it really mattered to Mann. He'd only ever been able to travel as far as either of those two places. Any further, and he'd been forced back. Something had always bound him to the Hvite Lands, and Slutet had always been his home.

A millennium in one place should perhaps have been tedious, but Mann had never allowed that to concern him, content simply to enjoy what he had.

Mann's forehead furrowed even more. Why was it he'd been bound to a specific location? It didn't seem as though that happened to the others. What was it that was different about him to them? Was that what Branwen was trying to remind him of?

The thought made sense. Yet he kept his mouth closed. There was no point in asking her for answers. She was determined to hold her tongue, her silly argument about 'laws' riling him, Blane's over alertness to their conversation, making it impossible for her to help him, even though it was clear she wanted to do so.

Distracting himself, with the thought of her naked and in his arms, Mann considered what little he'd known about her back when they'd first met.

Branwen had appeared one day, and they'd fallen into a passionate relationship. They'd spoken surprisingly little of either of their pasts. He found that strange now. It was evident Branwen had known him for who he was. Yet, whatever she'd discovered during their encounters, it had clearly not been what she'd been hoping for. Perhaps that was why she'd left?

However, and here he sipped slowly from a glass goblet before him, tasting the sharp texture of the heat of the south, she'd come back to him, now, as had so many of the Nines and the Nones.

It was evident to him she still anticipated him finding a way to solve the riddle of his own making.

But how?

'Why did you never ask me about my markings?' Mann asked, tapping her on the shoulder to get her attention, determined to get an answer to at least one of his questions. After all, Freg had questioned him about them. In fact, and here he wrinkled his forehead in thought, she'd even asked Onna about them.

'I know what they mean. Why would I ask you about them?'

'So you assumed I knew what they were as well?'

'No, I realised you had no idea. I didn't want you to know I knew what they meant. It was easier that way. You'd have been annoyingly inquisitive had you known. Remember, I had to follow the 'laws.'

'So my ignorance didn't upset you then, although it does now?'

'Mann, I can't help we've always been tied to each other. And I can't help you've repeatedly tried to drive a wedge between us. It was nice, for once, to be the one in command.'

Those words stung, and yet Mann couldn't really say why. She'd left him, without explanation, but it seemed he might have done it to her before. If only he could remember anything before his appearance in the blizzard, naked.

'Why was I naked?' Mann demanded to know. Now she laughed, a deep chortle that surprised him.

'You're always naked. I've always put it down to your sexual proclivities, but I don't actually know why.'

'So you're not naked then?' Mann asked, just to be sure. Branwen shook her head, her eyes alive with laughter.

'Bloody bollocks,' Mann complained softly, shivering at the memory of his frozen balls and cock.

Sipping once more from his drink, Mann closed his eyes,

blocking out the noise of the inn and the arguments and drunken advances going on around him. He needed to remember something he didn't know he'd ever known, let alone forgotten about. It was a puzzle Mann needed to solve, but without any starting place, and certainly, no finishing place.

Behind his closed eyes, Mann allowed the last millennia to swirl around him. So many people and lives he'd interacted with, it still saddened him he'd loved and lost so many. Even those he'd not particularly liked had left behind an indelible hold on him that could never be removed. So many memorable dates each year. So many people to remember and honour.

His thoughts turned to the first people he'd encountered, specifically Onna. As the memory of her surfaced in his mind, his head spun, rapidly, and back to one of the darkened tables in a corner, a wry smile on his face.

Onna. How could he have forgotten her inquisitive eyes and disgust at his sexual appetite?

'Is she a Nine or a None?' he asked Branwen's back. Barely raising her eyes to see where Mann pointed, a peal of laughter escaped her mouth.

'What her? A None, of course. And one who never much liked you. Why, have you met her before?'

'Onna, yes. She's the first person I ever saw.'

'Sly bitch,' Branwen complained, almost standing, only for Blane to restrain her.

'Leave her alone, Branwen. It's almost time. No need for the usual cat fight?'

Onna's eyes met his then. The green. How could he have forgotten? The green of the dogs' eyes in The Firs when he'd returned as Mann/Tate, after his first fake death. Had she been there as well, back then, when Marnit had been murdered? Had she, perhaps, been behind the secret doorway in the inn? Had she been the one who'd escaped across the snow when he'd thought to try and capture a thief? He'd not witnessed her first 'death,' or seen her body. Everything was beginning to make sense to him now.

'Focus on what you need to find out. Not the bitch.' Blane's words, perhaps the kindest the silver-haired youth had yet spoken to him, wrenched Mann away from his thoughts of that long ago time.

Onna watched him, even now, as though daring him to act, her jade eyes ablaze with suppressed heat. Why hadn't she told him who he was? What had been in it for her to extend his ignorance? Had she done more to him with her strange concoction than douse his sexual appetite? Had she enjoyed seeing him waste away his life with Freg?

Yet, Mann's thoughts swirled through the memories quickly. Any clue to his past lives could only have occurred in the first moments of his manifestation in the blizzard, he was sure of it. Other than that, and his meeting with Branwen, and those others he now suspected of being Nones or Nines, he had no recollection of his others pasts.

It could only be in the brief moment before he'd become conscious of where he was, that anything could have happened that might allow Mann to solve Branwen's urgent demands.

Somehow, he decided it must be connected with his inability to leave the Hvite Lands, to travel through the Passen and feel the heat of the sun on his skin.

However, nothing came to him. Nothing at all. Other than, and he tried to replay his first sight of the Hvite Lands and the blizzard again in his mind, a strange sound. A heavy sound. A thudding sound.

Branwen met his eyes fully this time when he tapped her on the shoulder. The urge to take her in his arms was over-whelming. It seemed she had other matters on her mind.

'I missed you,' Mann whispered, taking his chance, and

cupping her chin in his hand. Her skin felt as soft and delicate as when they'd last met, and his desire rose. For a moment her eyes softened. He thought she'd kiss him, only for her to slap his hand away.

'We can have a lifetime of that, in fact, millennia of it, if you could just sort your shit out.' Her rage was instantaneous, causing Mann to flinch back in the wake of it.

'Tell me how you know so much?' Mann persisted, all the same.

'Because I'm not a bloody idiot. I don't make stupid requests to whoever it is that commands us. I keep hold of all I need to drive this world from one millennium to another.'

'And what is that?' Mann urged. Her eyes lit with a modicum of respect.

'Laws, dearie,' she breathed, relenting and leaning in closer to him, laying a delicate kiss on his lips that ignited all of his ancient passion.

'Surely we have some time?' Mann whined. He could hardly think straight with her scent enveloping him.

'We can have all the time in the world, you damn fool. Just do the right thing.'

He thought then of Branwen's laws. There seemed to be many of them.

'Blane,' he called to the silver-haired man. Blane raised his disconcertingly uninterested eyes to gaze at him.

'Tell me of your laws,' Mann asked, unsurprised when Blane's hand intentionally reached toward the bag he'd brought with him to the inn, which now rested beneath his feet. It was a great bulging sack, filled with who knew what. Mann had his answer all the same.

Jemp was watching him with an arched eyebrow, his jaw set stubbornly in a scowl, whereas Jenna was struggling to wake from her enforced sleep. Both held their tongues. Mann wondered what it cost them to be silent.

Neither of them looked surprised by his request directed at Blane, or indeed perplexed when Blane's lips tightened and he said nothing.

'And you, Branwen, tell me of your laws?' Mann turned to Branwen. Again, it was all in the eyes, as Branwen flicked a glance toward her luggage. It rested by the door to the inn, two sacks and another bag, made of gently tanned leather, with two handles shimmering in the firelight.

Mann smiled. Such a simple thing. Perhaps it explained his fascination with writing everything down.

Mann leaned toward Branwen once more, as though about to kiss her, but really reaching for something he'd felt before, but only when they were together. Their passion for each other had masked something else, a certain something preordaining they'd always be together, and that they must rely only on each other, or so Branwen had implied. At the end of his instant attraction to her, he could feel something else as well, leading both into Branwen's luggage and also further away.

Mann had never used his abilities in such a way but suddenly felt foolish for ignoring what had been there all along, just waiting for him to give in to the strange urging within him. Too much sex, or so he berated himself.

Mann was tied to the Hvite Lands and had been ever since he'd manifested and failed to catch the sound of something heavy falling onto the snow covered glacier. What a bloody idiot he'd been.

'I would like my book of laws,' Mann whispered, his lips touching Branwen's as he muttered the words, her body finally relaxing against his as he spoke, relenting, and allowing herself to seek comfort from him after all.

A wet thud on the bar before Mann announced the arrival of his long lost book, but he was beyond rational thought, with Branwen in his arms, as she turned to kiss him with more than her previous passing peck. Mann watched her, as she closed her eyes, and threaded her body around his. They were inter-woven, no ending and no beginning, endless, always and never, and so much suddenly made sense to him.

Such a bloody stupid thing, he thought. Such a bloody, bloody, stupid thing and the world around him erupted in a mass of cheering and shouting, before fading away to nothing but darkness and the bone numbing chill of a blizzard.

TWENTY-NINE
A BEGINNING ONCE MORE

Chapter 29

THERE WAS SILENCE.

And then there wasn't.

A swirl of snow and hail, a blizzard of ice and sleet fell on the deserted wintry spot where before there'd been nothing but white. A silence rang out deeper than quiet, as complete as nothingness, the thud of something heavy hitting the ground, seeming to add to the silence, rather than shatter it.

'Bollocks,' the voice boomed preternaturally loud as the revolving snowstorm of ice disappeared as quickly as it had arrived, depositing in its wake the most ridiculous of sights. A naked man, struggling for balance as he sunk thigh deep in the snowy landscape. In his wake, a more natural whiteout continued to blow, making it hard to focus on his quivering shape.

'Bollocks,' echoed once more, the voice strong and thunderous, although there was no one to hear it.

'Bollocks,' sounded again, accompanied by a jiggling from foot to foot that should have been impossible in the thigh-high snow yet which he accomplished easily all the same. His feet, already turning blue in the cold, reached almost to shoulder height as he tried to save them from the perils of frostbite.

'A bloody blizzard,' he managed to shout, his anger and rage causing spittle to fly from his mouth where it immediately froze, landing on his exposed chest with an icy tinkle of broken glass.

'Bollocks, bollocks, bloody bollocks,' he gasped, rage adding an intensity to his voice that he'd never heard before.

'Bollocks, bollocks, bloody bollocks, they were bloody right,' Mann gasped, his breath steaming before him as he continued to jiggle and then, from nowhere, another voice emerged.

'Dearie, I think you might be needing these,' a pile of clothes materialised before him, held out on a thin arm enclosed in what looked like white fur. A thick winter cloak, fur-lined trousers and tunic, even a comfortable looking pair of waterproof boots and matching gloves formed the bundle.

Quickly he shrugged into all the clothes he'd been presented with, as he balanced on the deeply thick snow, trying to stay on top of it all and not sink into it. His body quickly turned from ice blue back to deathly white, and although he couldn't see it once it was covered in clothes, gloves and cloak, to a healthy looking pink as well.

He swept his cloak around his shoulders, making sure the deep fur collar covered his mouth. He'd already had more than enough icy particles entering his open mouth, and freezing before falling down his exposed chest.

His jaw had been clamped shut with cold, but now he was able to open it inside the fur collar. He breathed deeply, allowing the delicious warmth to enter his cold and frigid body.

'Now dearie,' and a similarly clad woman appeared out of the deep gloom and swirling snow, a laden sled behind her, stuffed with supplies, with two lanterns casting a bright yellow light over the immediate area and showing him how well-prepared she was. It was pulled by six sturdy looking reindeer, their coats thick and healthy, deep fur covering all of their bodies, even their hooves. Their antlers glistened with the sheen of forming ice, their breath fogging before them before it too solidified and turned to small pieces of tinkling ice. He considered that. Did the reindeer need to take the same precautions he had? Did they need something to cover their mouth? Before he could speak a light voice commented.

'Shall we begin?' Her voice sounded golden, as gilded as her appearance as she settled herself in the sled, taking control of the reins and making her intentions to lead clear. 'And don't forget your little book,' she trilled, her voice high with excitement. He turned to hunt the area where he'd manifested for the precious item he'd failed to obtain last time around, being careful not to overbalance and lose his footing in the snow. He didn't wish to make a total idiot of himself. Not like last time, when, thankfully, there'd been no one around to watch.

Finding the book, down at the bottom of the hole he'd made with his feet, Mann reached for it with his hand. Touching it for the first time in over a millennium with his fingertips, he managed to grab a firm hold on the item, and bring it up out of the hole. No wonder he'd not seen it last time, it wasn't exactly large. He'd been too busy trying to protect his body from frostbite. All things considered, the book was surprisingly light-weight and unimpressive for the huge impact it had exerted on him.

Mann smirked at the amiable tone in Branwen's voice, amusement suffusing his face, as he called.

'I've found it,' his joy ringing through those few words.

At her next words, his delight drained away. In an outraged tone she shrieked, the sound preternaturally loud in the snow shower.

'Let's do this again! You bloody idiot.'

ABOUT THE AUTHOR

Lissy Porter is a pseudonym for an author who usually writes in a very different genre.

Follow Lissy on Instagram, Amazon or BlueSky.

https://www.throneofash.com

Join Lissy's mailing list to keep up to date with bookish news

instagram.com/lissyporterauthor

bsky.app/profile/lissyporterauthor.bsky.social

ALSO BY LISSY PORTER

It Ends at The Wall

The Throne of Ash

Station 15 (coming soon)